JUBAL SACKETT
A Bantam Hardcover / June 1985
Bantam paperback edition / June 1986

All rights reserved.
Copyright © 1985 by Louis L'Amour Enterprises, Inc.
Cover art copyright © 1986 by Bantam Books, Inc.

This book may not be reproduced in whole or in part, by mimeograph or any other means, without permission.
For information address: Bantam Books, Inc.

ISBN 0-553-25673-4

Published simultaneously in the United States and Canada

Bantam Books are published by Bantam Books, Inc. Its trademark, consisting of the words "Bantam Books" and the portrayal of a rooster, is Registered in U.S. Patent and Trademark Office and in other countries. Marca Registrada. Bantam Books, Inc., 666 Fifth Avenue, New York, New York 10103.

PRINTED IN THE UNITED STATES OF AMERICA

H 0 9 8 7 6 5 4 3 2 1

WILDERNESS BATTLE

"I will take the last man," I suggested.

Keokotah made no reply. He would fight his own battle, as I would. Each of us had his own skills and his own ideas on how to expend them.

The Natchee were a hundred yards off, the last man some fifty yards further, when I selected an arrow and bent my bow, waiting just a little longer. They came on. Keokotah slipped down to a better position. The last man had to round a boulder and to do so must almost face me.

He was at least fifteen feet behind the next man when I let fly. . . .

AMERICA'S #1 BEST-SELLER

LOUIS L'AMOUR'S

JUBAL SACKETT

D1016357

Bantam Books by Louis L'Amour
Ask your bookseller for the books you have missed

BENDIGO SHAFTER
BORDEN CHANTRY
BOWDRIE
BOWDRIE'S LAW
BRIONNE
THE BROKEN GUN
BUCKSKIN RUN
THE BURNING HILLS
THE CALIFORNIOS
CALLAGHEN
CATLOW
CHANCY
THE CHEROKEE TRAIL
COMSTOCK LODE
CONAGHER
CROSSFIRE TRAIL
DARK CANYON
DOWN THE LONG HILLS
THE EMPTY LAND
FAIR BLOWS THE WIND
FALLON
THE FERGUSON RIFLE
THE FIRST FAST DRAW
FLINT
FRONTIER
GUNS OF THE TIMBERLANDS
HANGING WOMAN CREEK
HELLER WITH A GUN
THE HIGH GRADERS
HIGH LONESOME
THE HILLS OF HOMICIDE
HONDO
HOW THE WEST WAS WON
THE IRON MARSHAL
THE KEY-LOCK MAN
KID RODELO
KILKENNY
KILLOE
KILRONE
KIOWA TRAIL
LAW OF THE DESERT BORN
THE LONESOME GODS
THE MAN CALLED NOON
THE MAN FROM SKIBBEREEN
MATAGORDA
MILO TALON
THE MOUNTAIN VALLEY WAR
NORTH TO THE RAILS
OVER ON THE DRY SIDE
PASSIN' THROUGH
THE PROVING TRAIL
THE QUICK AND THE DEAD
RADIGAN
REILLY'S LUCK
THE RIDER OF LOST CREEK
RIVERS WEST
THE SHADOW RIDERS
SHALAKO
SHOWDOWN AT YELLOW BUTTE
SILVER CANYON
SITKA
SON OF A WANTED MAN
THE STRONG SHALL LIVE
TAGGART
TO TAME A LAND
TUCKER
UNDER THE SWEET-WATER RIM
UTAH BLAINE
THE WALKING DRUM
WAR PARTY
WESTWARD THE TIDE
WHERE THE LONG GRASS BLOWS
YONDERING

Sackett Titles by
Louis L'Amour

1. SACKETT'S LAND
2. TO THE FAR BLUE MOUNTAINS
3. THE DAYBREAKERS
4. SACKETT
5. LANDO
6. MOJAVE CROSSING
7. THE SACKETT BRAND
8. THE LONELY MEN
9. TREASURE MOUNTAIN
10. MUSTANG MAN
11. GALLOWAY
12. THE SKY-LINERS
13. THE MAN FROM THE BROKEN HILLS
14. RIDE THE DARK TRAIL
15. THE WARRIOR'S PATH
16. LONELY ON THE MOUNTAIN
17. RIDE THE RIVER
18. JUBAL SACKETT

JUBA[L]
SACKE[TT]

LOUIS L'AM[OUR]

BANTAM BOOKS
TORONTO • NEW YORK • LONDON • SYDNEY • AU[CKLAND]

To Hazel and Charlie Daniels—
His fiddle-playing would bring
The Sacketts right down from the hills

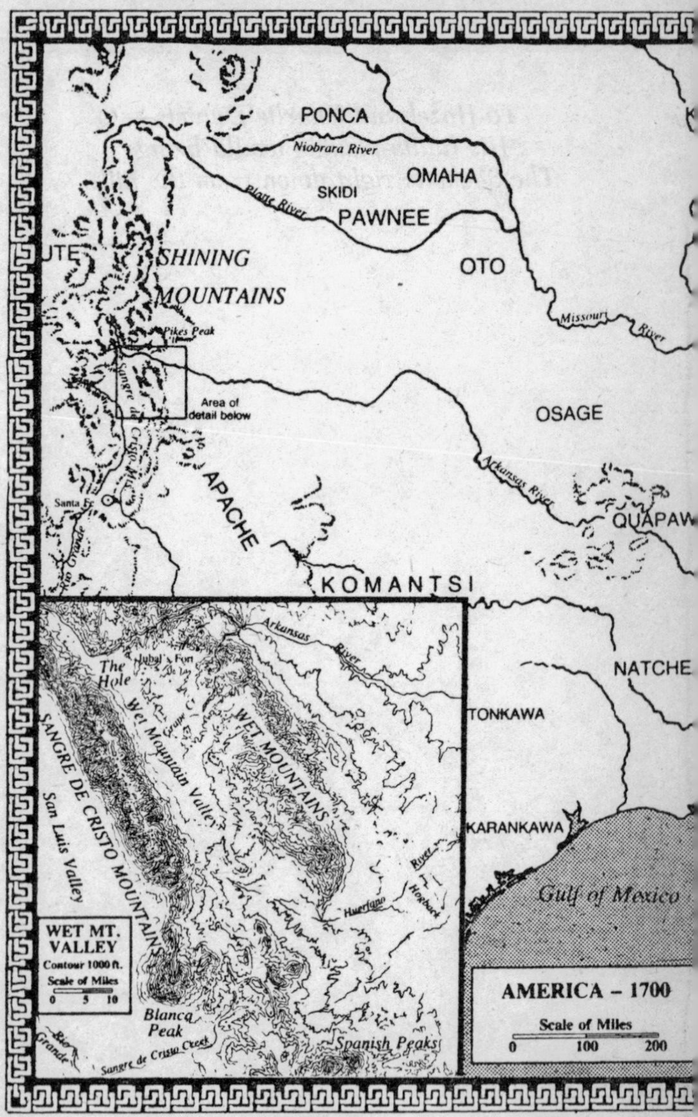
PONCA
Niobrara River
OMAHA
SKIDI
Platte River
PAWNEE
UTE
SHINING
MOUNTAINS
OTO
Missouri
River
Pikes Peak
Sangre de Cristo Mts.
Area of
detail below
OSAGE
Arkansas River
Santa Fe
APACHE
QUAPAW
Rio Grande
KOMANTSI
Arkansas
River
Jubal's Fort
The
Hole
NATCHE
Wet Mountain Valley
WET MOUNTAINS
TONKAWA
SANGRE DE CRISTO MOUNTAINS
San Luis Valley
KARANKAWA
River
Huerfano
Hogback
Gulf of Mexico
WET MT.
VALLEY
Contour 1000 ft.
Scale of Miles
0 5 10
AMERICA – 1700
Scale of Miles
0 100 200
Blanca
Peak
Spanish Peaks
Rio
Grande
Sangre de Cristo Creek

Map by Alan McKnight

1

A cold wind blew off Hanging Dog Mountain and I had no fire, nor dared I strike so much as a spark that might betray my hiding place. Somewhere near, an enemy lurked, waiting.

Yesterday morning, watching my back trail, I saw a deer startle, cross a meadow in great bounds, and disappear into the forest. Later, shortly after high sun, two birds flew up suddenly. Something was following me.

Warm in my blanket, I huddled below a low earthen bank, concealed by brush and a fallen tree. The wind swept by above me, worrying my mind because its sound might cover the approach of an enemy creeping closer. There he could lie waiting to kill me when I arose from my hiding place.

I, Jubal Sackett, was but a day's journey from our home on Shooting Creek in the foothills of the Nantahalas, close upon Chunky Gal Mountain.

All the enemies of whom I knew were far from here, yet any stranger was a potential enemy, and he was a wise traveler who was forever alert.

Our white enemies were beyond the sea, and our only red enemies were the Seneca, living far away to the north beyond Hudson's River. No Seneca was apt to be found alone so far from others of his kind. The Seneca were a fine, fierce lot of fighting men of the Iroquois League who had become our enemies because we were friends of the Catawba, who were their enemies.

Whoever followed me was a good reader of sign, for I left little evidence of my passing. Such an enemy is one to guard against, for skilled tracking is a mark of a great hunter and a great warrior. Nor do I wish to leave my scalp in the lodge of some unknown enemy when my life is scarce begun.

What was this strange urge that drove me westward, ever westward into an empty land?

Behind me were family, home, and all that I might become; before me were nameless rivers, swamps, mountains, and forests, and beyond the great river were the plains, those vast grasslands of which we had only heard, and of which we knew nothing.

About me and before me lay a haunted land whose boundaries we did not know. What little we had heard was from the tales of Indians, and they shied from this land, hunting here but always moving and returning to their homes far away. When the night winds prowled they huddled close to their fires and peered uneasily into the night. There was game here in plenty, and when the need was great they came to hunt. We did not know what mysteries lay here or why the place was shunned, but they spoke of it as a dark and bloody ground.

Why, in such a land of meadows, forests, and streams, were there no habitations? Once it was not so, for there are earth mounds, and friendly Indians had told us of a stone fort built they know not when nor by whom.

Who were those who vanished? Why did they come, build, and then disappear? What happened upon this ground? What dark and shameful deed? What horror so great that generations of Indians feared the land?

There was a legend of white men, bearded men who came to live along the rivers in a time long past. All were killed. Some said it was done by the Cherokee, some by the Shawnee, but it was an old memory, and old memories have a way of escaping their origin, carried by word of mouth or by intermarriage from one tribe to the next.

There are rumors, also, of a dark-skinned people who live in secluded valleys, a people who are neither Indian nor African, but of a different cast of feature who hold themselves aloof and keep strange customs and a different style of living. But we know nothing beyond the rumor, for their valleys lie far from ours.

I do not come to solve mysteries, but to seek out the land.

My father was Barnabas, the first of our name to come to this place beyond the ocean from the England of his birth. Of Barnabas I was the third son, Kin-Ring and Yance born before me. My elder brothers had found homes among the hills. My younger brother, Brian, and my one sister, Noelle, had returned to England with our mother, my brother to read for the law, my sister to be reared in a gentler land than this. I do not believe I shall see them again, nor hear of them unless it be some distant whisper on the wind. Nor shall I again see my father.

I had been called the Strange One, like the others but different. I loved my brothers and they loved me, but my way was a lonely way and I went into a land from which I would not return.

Of them all my father understood me best, for with all his great strength and magnificent fighting ability there was much in him of the poet and the mystic, as there is in me.

Our last evening together I would not forget, for each of us knew it was for the last time. Lila, who prepared our supper, also knew. Lila is Welsh and the wife of my father's old friend, Jeremy Ring, and had been a maid to my mother ere they departed from England.

My father, Lila, and I have the Gift. Some call it second sight, but we three often have pre-visions of what is to be, sometimes with stark clarity, often only fleeting glimpses as through the fog or shadows. All our family have the Gift to some degree, but me most of all. Yet I have never sought to use it, nor wished to see what is to be.

I knew how my father would die and almost when, and he knew also when we talked that last time. He accepted the nearness of death as he accepted life, and he would die as he would have wished, weapon in hand, trying his strength against others.

We parted that night knowing it was for the last time, with a strong handclasp and a look into each other's eyes. It was enough. I would keep his memory always, and he would know that somewhere far to the westward his blood would seek the lonely trails to open the land for those who would follow.

A faint patter of rain awakened me and I eased from under my blanket, preparing a neat pack. Daylight, or as much as I was likely to see, was not far off. It had been snug and dry where I had slept, but with only a few inches of overhang to shelter my bed from the rain. I had shouldered my pack and girded my weapons before the thought came to me.

Smoothing the earth where I had slept, I took up a twig and drew four crosses in the earth.

The red man was forever curious, and to most of whom we call Indians four was a magic number. He who followed would come upon this mark and wonder. He might even worry a little and be wary of seeking me out, for the Indian is ever a believer in medicine, or as some say, magic.

So it was that in the last hour of darkness I went down the mountain through the laurel sticks, crossed a small stream, and skirted a meadow to come to the trace I sought.

Nearly one hundred years before De Soto had come this way, his marchings and his cruelties leaving no more mark than the stirring of leaves as he passed. A few old Indians had vague recollections of De Soto, but they merely shrugged at our questions. We who wandered the land knew this was no "new world." The term was merely a conceit in the minds of those who had not known of it before.

The trace when I came upon it was a track left by the woods buffalo, who were fewer in number but larger in size than the buffalo of the Great Plains. The buffalo was the greatest of all trailmakers. Long ago the buffalo had discovered all the salt licks, mountain passes, and watering holes. We latecomers had only to follow the way they had gone, for there were no better trails anywhere.

When I came upon the track I began to run. We who lived in the forest regularly ran or walked from place to place as did the Indians. It was by far the best way to cover distance where few horses and fewer roads were to be found.

My brothers ran well but were heavier than I and not so agile. Although very strong I was twenty pounds lighter than Kin-Ring and thirty lighter than Yance.

Our strength was born of our daily lives. Our cabins and our palisades were built of logs cut and dragged from the forest. The logs for the palisade stood upright in ditches dug for the purpose. Only in the past few years had we managed to obtain horses from the Spanish in Florida, who broke their own law in selling them to us when they departed for their home across the sea.

Every task demanded strength, for the logs used in building the cabins were from eight to twenty inches thick and twenty to thirty feet in length. There are "slights" and skills known to working men that enable them to handle heavy weights, but in the final event it comes down to sheer muscle. So my brothers and I had grown to uncommon strength, indulging in wrestling, tossing the caber, and lifting large stones in contests one with the other.

Our Catawba friends marveled at our strength, for quick and agile as they were, and very strong, nothing in their lives called for the lifting of heavy weights. Unaccustomed to lifting, their muscles were longer and leaner. They were excellent wrestlers, however.

At an easy trot I moved through the forest, my moccasins making no sound on the damp leaves underfoot.

Emerging upon a hilltop not unlike the balds found in the higher mountains, I drew back against the wall of trees, letting my soiled buckskins merge with the tree trunks and brush, scanning the vast stretch of land that lay before me.

For the moment the rain had ceased, although far off against a mountainside I could see a rainstorm drawing its gray veil across the distant hills. Never had I seen a land so lovely.

Carefully, I studied my back trail or that portion of it visible from where I stood. There was nothing in sight. Had I escaped my unknown pursuer? Not for a moment did I believe that.

Somewhere before me lay the river called Tenasee, and the long, narrow valley of which we had heard. My father had put this task upon me, to find a new land to which we could move if necessary.

My father was a fugitive from England, sought because it was mistakenly believed he had recovered King John's lost treasure from The Wash. Also, we had settled upon our land with no grant from the king or governor, although we had proved useful to the powers that were in Virginia, and they had not been inclined to cause trouble. Yet a new governor might be appointed at any time and my father had warned us that we must seek a new land further west and make our plans if something were to go wrong. We could then, at a moment's notice, pick up and move west beyond the reach of the king or his minions.

"See to it, Jubal," my father had said. "Find us a westward way. The king does not realize the size of this country nor how that size will affect its governing. In the old country, land was held by the king and given to his great lords for their services to him, and it was farmed by serfs. There one must cling to one's place or become a landless man. Here there is land for all, and no man need work for another."

He paused and looked into my eyes. "Do you remember your brothers, Jubal, and all who bear our name. 'Tis a wide and a lonely land, but if we stand together we have naught to fear."

"I shall not forget."

"And pass the word, Jubal. Let your sons remember, and your daughters.

"My envy for you is great, Jubal, for I, too, would see the lands where you will walk. I wish I might feel their rain, accept the shade of the trees, and smell the fragrance of those distant pines." After a moment he added, "I, too, shall go west, Jubal."

"I know."

"Where the chips fall, there let them lie."

"It shall be so."

For too long I stood staring across that vast and lovely land thinking of my father and the long way he had come from his birth in the fens of England to his arrival here, among the first of those who came to this land.

The far-off veil of rain diminished and then faded. A shaft of sunlight falling through a hole in the clouds revealed a long, loaflike mountain.

Chilhowee . . . from there I would turn north. I did so abruptly . . . and it saved my life.

A hard-thrown spear thudded into the tree where I had been standing, its shaft vibrating with the force of the throw.

Dropping to the earth I rolled swiftly over and over, coming up near a fallen tree, bow bent and arrow ready . . . waiting.

2

My position was a good one, and above all, I had his spear before my eyes. It was a very good spear, handsomely crafted, and he would not wish to lose it. Therefore I had only to wait, and when he came for it I should have one enemy less.

It had never been my way to seek trouble, but if one is attacked by a man whose time has come, who would stand in the way of fate?

My back was well covered by a gigantic uprearing of roots and earth from a fallen tree, and scattered near were many pine cones on which nothing could step without making a sound. Nevertheless, I could take nothing for granted. My bow bent slightly, I waited.

For a long time there was no sound. The Indian is a great hunter and as such he has patience, yet my life in the wilderness had taught me patience also. One learns to adapt to the land in which one lives.

My ears were tuned for the slightest sound, my entire body alert to move or adjust. Nothing happened, and the slow minutes plodded by on lagging feet. The low-hanging branches held shadows away from the sun, and the tree trunks were dark columns with only small spaces between. It needed a quick eye to catch any movement among them.

A thrush flitted from one branch to another and then took off down a long lane of the forest toward the trace I had followed. Somewhere a squirrel chattered irritably, but I heard no other sound, and even a moccasin whispers lightly when it moves.

Glancing about I managed to keep a corner of an eye upon the spear. Suddenly, a faint sound. My head turned. Quickly I glanced back. The spear was gone!

Exasperated, I swore softly to myself. I had been a fool! That sound that had diverted me—he had thrown a stick or a chip, and like a child I had taken the bait.

Moreover, now he had his spear in hand once more and it was, perhaps, his favorite weapon. Certainly he had thrown it with skill, and only my unexpected movement had saved my life. Would I be so lucky again?

Undoubtedly on recovering his spear he had moved, but in what direction? He wanted to kill me, so he would be waiting in ambush somewhere. At the same time it was best for me to move, for he would soon discover where I lay, if he had not already done so. A moment longer I waited.

There was, alongside the great fallen tree, a narrow way that was free of the scattered pine cones, and the branches of the dead tree did not begin for at least thirty feet.

Swiftly, silently, I moved, keeping low alongside the tree and then ducking under it among the hanging bark. Waiting, I heard no sound, and I plotted my next move. Again a swift move and I was among the standing trees, flitting away, an impossible target for a spear . . . if he saw me.

Months before I had come this far west, exploring a route to the Great River of which we had heard, and I knew that the trace I planned to follow made a great arc not far ahead, so moving through the thick of the forest I headed for that trace. Hours later, when I reached it, I found no tracks upon the path. Apparently, I was before him. Again I settled down to running.

What manner of man was he who followed me? A

wandering hunter seeking a scalp? Few Indians traveled alone. Usually there were small parties of them when they went either hunting or seeking war. Yet this man was alone. A strong warrior, no doubt, sure of his skills, and a man to be reckoned with.

On and on I ran, running easily, smoothly. Several times I glimpsed the tracks of buffalo and once those of a deer. Later, as the afternoon drew on, I stopped for a drink at a small creek. Near the water's edge there were the tracks of a large bear. They were fresh tracks made within minutes of my arrival.

After a careful look around I made four small crosses inside the bear track.

Now I no longer ran, but walked, alert for means of obscuring my trail. I walked upstream in the water for a short distance, pausing to make sure the swift current was wiping out my tracks in the stream bed. Then I followed a smaller stream for a hundred steps, followed a log from which the bark had fallen away, and then stepped off onto a rocky ledge and followed it to the end, careful to disturb none of the leaves or gravel scattered upon it. Then deliberately I changed direction and went back toward my last night's camp, now far away.

There was a path high among the rocks of which I knew, and when I reached it I found no fresh tracks. This path ran along the way in which I wished to go. As I walked I thought of Pa and how he would have enjoyed this, but so would Kin-Ring and Yance, although Yance would have been inclined to try to ambush my pursuer and have it out with him.

I had no wish to kill the man even though he had tried to kill me. If it became necessary, of course . . .

Night was coming and I was alone. It was time for rest and food underneath three ancient oaks beside a small stream, one leaning far out, on a grassy bank with driftwood scattered along the stream.

A fire, meat broiling over a flame, a time of eating, of listening to the rustle of water and the subdued crackle of flames, and then of sleep. This is what I wished for, but could not quite have, for a man had followed me and might find me again.

He had come shrewdly upon me, and I did not doubt he would work out the trail I had left for him. Many another might have lost it, but not this one, I thought. Yet I would wait, for I had an idea.

My fire was the work of a moment. A handful of crushed bark, a few slivers of pitch pine from an old stump that I had carried with me, then a blow with flint and steel, a spark, then a small tendril of smoke, a puff or two from the lungs, and a flame. It was not always so easy. To light a fire properly one must prepare it well. Fire, man's first and faithful friend, and ever a potential enemy.

He who followed might come to my fire, and something told me he would. He was curious now, as all wild things are inclined to be, and I believed he wished to know what manner of man I was.

Where I was pointed no white man went, although Indians had told me that far to the westward there were men who spoke like those of Florida and who wore iron headdresses. Westward lay the Great River, which some say was discovered by De Soto, but we who know of such things knew it was discovered twenty years earlier by Alvarez de Pineda. Who else might have seen the river we do not know, but there are rumors of others who came, of much fighting and dying.

My fire blazed up, a small, hot blaze but larger than usual. Deliberately I was inviting him in. By now he knew it was not my custom to build large or very bright fires, and he would recognize the invitation. As he was curious about me, so I was curious about him. Who was this stranger who wandered alone where all went in company?

He had tried to kill me, but that was expected where any stranger was a potential enemy. Drawing back into the shadows with a great tree at my back, I waited. My longbow was placed near in plain sight, but a pistol lay in my lap. My visitor would be friendly, I hoped, but if his destiny was to die I would not stand in his way.

Chewing on a bit of dried venison I listened and

waited. Then, suddenly, he was there at the edge of the firelight, a man as tall as I but leaner. He was an Indian of a kind I knew not.

With my left hand I gestured to the earth beside the fire. He came forward on light feet, yet before he seated himself he hung a haunch of venison over the coals.

"Meat!" he said.

"Good! Sit you."

With a small stick I pushed coals under the meat and added a few sticks, which began to sizzle pleasantly.

"You go far?"

"To the Great River, and beyond."

"I have seen the river," he said proudly, "and the Far Seeing Lands beyond."

"You speak my tongue."

"I speak much with Englishman. My village."

An Englishman? So far west?

"Where is your village?"

"Far." He gestured toward the north. "Many days." He looked directly into my eyes and said with great pride, "I am Kickapoo Keokotah."

"A nation of warriors," I acknowledged.

He was pleased. "You know?"

"Every wind carries news of Kickapoo bravery. In every lodge a warrior would wish to have a Kickapoo scalp—if he could."

"It is true." He spoke complacently. "We are great warriors and wanderers."

"What of the Englishman? Where is he now?"

"He is dead. He was a brave man, and took a long time to die."

"You killed him?"

"It was the Seneca. They took us both."

"Yet you escaped?"

Keokotah shrugged. "I am here."

Our fire was dying from neglect. I added sticks as did he. He cut a sliver from the venison. "I would learn from the Kickapoo," I said. "You are old upon this land."

"We come, we go." He glanced at me. "You have a woman?"

"It is too soon. I have rivers to cross."

"My woman is dead. She was a good woman." He paused. "The best."

"I am sorry."

"Do not be. She lived well, she died well."

We sat silent, chewing on the venison sliced from the haunch. "You are from over the mountain?"

"Aye."

"You know of Barn-a-bas?"

Startled, I looked up. "You have heard of him? What do you know of Barnabas?"

"All men speak of Barn-a-bas. He great warrior. Great chief." He paused. "He was great warrior."

"*Was?*"

In that moment my heart seemed to stop, and when again it throbbed it was with slow, heavy beats.

"He is dead now. They sing of him in the villages."

My father . . . *dead*? He was so strong, so invulnerable. No trail had been too long, no stream too swift, no mountain too high.

"He died as a warrior should, destroying those who attacked him. So died he who was beside him."

"Only one died with him? A young man?"

"So old as Barn-a-bas. Older." He looked hard at me. "You know this Barn-a-bas?"

"He was my father."

"A . . . eee!"

Again a long silence. I remembered my father and grief held tight my chest, choking in my throat. I stared at the earth and remembered the few arguments we had had and the unkind words I must have said. I had been a fool. He had been the best of fathers and it was never easy to be a father to strong sons growing up in a strange land, each coming to manhood, each asserting himself, loving the father yet wishing to be free of him, finding fault to make the break easier. So it had been since the world began, for the young do not remain young and the time must come when each must go out on his own grass.

I had known he would die, and almost how, but I had not thought it to be so soon.

In silence by the fire with only a strange Indian for company I thought of Barnabas Sackett, who sailed first to this wild land and then returned for our mother.

Our mother? Did she know by some strange intuition of our father's passing? She had gone home to England to rear our sister, Noelle, in a gentler land. It had been a wise decision we had believed, we had hoped.

My brother Brian had gone with her to read for the law in London.

What of the others now? Of Kin-Ring and Yance? Kin-Ring, my strong, serious older brother, born on a buffalo robe in the heat of an Indian battle, with my father's old friend, Jeremy Ring, standing over my mother to fight off the attackers as the child was born.

What of Yance? Wild, unruly Yance, strong as a bear, quick to anger, quick to forget.

Would I see them again?

Deep within me a knell tolled . . . I would not. I knew I would not see them again even as both my father and I had known his time was near, for we were of the blood of Nial, who had the Gift.

My brothers had their world, I mine. Theirs was in the mountains that lay behind me, and mine was the westward way.

Keokotah looked across the fire at me. "You are son of Barn-a-bas. I am Kickapoo. We will walk together."

And so it was.

3

Stark and black were the tall trees, growing misty green along the branches with the budding leaves of spring. I walked to drink water from a running stream and startled a perch, twenty pounds at the least. It swam away, disturbed by my presence. Downstream a deer lifted its muzzle from the water and crystal drops fell back into the stream. It glanced disdainfully at me and walked away, seemingly unworried by our coming.

With morning our wood smoke mingled with the lifting mists and we heard no sound but the soft crackle of our own fire and the slight hiss of some damp wood we used. A movement in the wild clover made us look up to see something vast and shadowy, some monstrous thing, coming toward us through the meadow grass, emerging slowly from the mist.

It stopped, smelling the fire at last, and seeing us. It faced us, massive and horned, a huge buffalo bull with a great mass of wool over its face, shoulders, and hump, wool that sparkled with morning dew. Wreaths of fog hung about it as it stared from small black eyes almost buried in the wool.

The buffalo was no more than fifteen yards away and behind it there were others.

It stared at us, undecided as to our importance. It dropped its head then, pawing at the grass.

"Meat," Keokotah said, "much meat."

With one of my two pistols I aimed at a spot inside the left foreleg and squeezed the trigger. The pistol leaped with the concussion, and I placed it on the ground beside me and took up the second, but held my fire.

The great buffalo stood stock still, staring at us; then slowly the forelegs gave way and the beast crumpled and went to its knees. Then it rolled over on the ground.

The others simply stood, staring stupidly, unalarmed by the sound because, being unfamiliar with firearms, the sound might have seemed like thunder. One young bull came forward and sniffed at their fallen leader, smelling the blood and not liking it. We stood up then and walked toward them, and the young bull put its head down, but at our continued approach it backed off and they began to walk away across the meadow.

Glancing at Keokotah I noted his features were unmarked by surprise. Had he seen or heard a gun before? Later, I learned he had not, but he was a Kickapoo, not to be astonished by such things.

With our skinning knives we went to work, each in his own way but working well together, cutting away the hide and selecting the best cuts of meat. There was fuel here, so we built up our fire and built drying racks for the meat, cutting it in strips to smoke and dry the better. Then we staked out the hide to be scraped and cured.

Nobody in our time could have been better armed than I. For general purposes I carried an English longbow, with which our father's training had made us expert, and a full quiver of arrows. I also carried a razor-sharp twelve-inch blade. My true strength, and one which I had not intended to reveal except in emergency, lay in two long-barreled firearms my father had taken from a pirate ship. Obviously a part of some booty the pirates had themselves taken, the pistols must have been made for some great lord.

They were matched repeating pistols with carved walnut stocks elaborately dressed with scrollwork, masks, and figures of gold. The operating mechanism was nothing less than a masterpiece, designed—according to the story my father had heard, and which he passed to us—by one Fernando, the bastard son of the Cominazzo family of armorers, of Brescia. When that noted family fell upon evil times and was taken by the Inquisitors, Fernando escaped to Florence, carrying only his tools.

Anxious to obtain a place for himself he labored in secret to create the two pistols. Charges of powder and ball were carried in tubular magazines in the butts, the openings closed by a revolving breechblock into which were cut two chambers. To load, one simply pointed the pistol toward the ground and rotated a lever on the side of the gun. This dropped a ball and a measure of powder into one chamber, sealed off the chamber, primed and closed the flash-pan.

The pistol could be fired twelve times without reloading. Fernando had taken the finished pistols to the Lorenzoni and won a place in their establishment. Much later, other such weapons were made by the Lorenzoni.

Barnabas had never used the weapons, worried by what seemed a too complicated mechanism. When I was allowed to examine the guns it seemed to me that I could handle them. They were both beautiful and deadly, but when traveling I preferred to use the longbow and conserve my ammunition. The two pistols I carried in the scabbards provided for them.

My father had grown up using the bow. In the fens where he had lived it was the most effective way of hunting, whether for birds or for larger game. As we grew up we boys vied with one another in shooting at marks, often at incredible distances for a bow.

Until I killed the buffalo Keokotah had seen only the scabbards. He was aware of firearms, for he had had contact with the French in the Illinois River country, yet I intended him to believe they were single-shot weapons.

Keokotah was not yet my friend. We were two strangers traveling together, but at any moment he might choose to kill me. The rules of conduct Europeans were supposed to apply in their dealings with each other were the product of our culture. The Indian, of whatever tribe, came from another culture with none of our ethical standards. He had standards of his own, and in most Indian languages the words stranger and enemy were the same. To attack by surprise was by far the best way, as he had long since learned, and what to us might seem the basest treachery he might consider simple logic.

My father had gotten along well enough with Indians, but he trusted few of them and few trusted him. It was simply the way it was, and it would need many years, if ever, for the white man and the Indian to come to any understanding. What the white man considered charity the Indian considered weakness, yet if a stranger penetrated an Indian village without being seen he was treated with hospitality as long as he was within the village, for the Indian tried to keep peace in his own village. Once the stranger left he might be killed with impunity. This was the usual practice, yet there were variations.

Keokotah might travel with me for days, and then, no longer amused or curious, he might kill me and travel on without giving it another thought. And he would expect the same from me.

At every moment I must be on guard, for at any moment I might be attacked without warning.

We might become friends, but that lay in the future, if ever. Meanwhile, I would be careful, as would he.

Westward I had hidden a birchbark canoe when on an earlier trip to the Great River, and now we went that way, taking our time, learning the land as we passed over it.

That English friend the Kickapoo had known—I must learn more of him. Where had he come from? A prisoner of the French? Taken at sea? Or somewhere ashore? Who was he? What was he?

Yet I had begun to realize that Keokotah did not respond to direct questions.

Upon the brow of a low hill we paused to study out the land. A deer moved across before us. The Kickapoo looked about, and then he looked over at me. "Somebody come."

I had seen nothing, yet I must not betray my lack of knowledge. My abilities must seem equal to his. To surpass him might be dangerous, and in any case, unwise. He must never know how much I knew.

I gestured westward. "Hiwasee over there," I said, "many Cherokee."

He shrugged. "Who are Cherokee? Nobody. I am Kickapoo."

We remained where we were, studying the country. He might be an enemy, but out there before us there were certainly enemies. The Cherokee we knew, and they knew us. So far we had been friends, but the Indian was often a creature of whim, and the man with whom I traveled was no friend. I might be judged accordingly.

"Somebody come." That was what he had said. How did he know? What had he seen that I had not? And who was coming?

My canoe was less than a day from where we now were, but I said nothing of that. When we came to it would be soon enough. To talk too much is always a fault. Information is power. Also, these paths I knew, and I watched to see if he knew them too, yet in no way did he betray himself.

Watching Keokotah I was puzzled. His attention did not seem to be directed to any particular point, yet he was alert, listening.

His apprehension affected me. What had he sensed? What was he expecting?

A small grove of trees clustered behind us, and before us the hill sloped away toward a meadow lying along a stream. Above us the blue skies were scattered with puffballs of cloud. It was very still. The deer we had seen earlier came out of the brush again and walked to the stream.

I started to move but Keokotah lifted a hand. As he did so an Indian emerged from the forest near the stream and stood still, looking carefully about. That he was an

Indian I was sure, but he was clad in garments unfamiliar to me. His head was wrapped in a turban. As he stood two others followed him, one of them an old man.

The old man looked up the slope at us and said something to them we could not hear. The first Indian then faced us. "Sack-ett?" he asked.

I stepped forward. "I am Jubal Sackett," I replied. We were separated by all of a hundred paces but in the clear air our voices sounded plain.

"Our father wishes to speak with Sack-ett," the young man replied.

Upon the grass he spread a blanket and then another for me. He stood back, waiting. The old man came forward and seated himself cross-legged. I started down, and the Kickapoo said, "It is a trap."

Two more Indians came from the woods and stood silent, waiting. "They are five," I said, "but they do not threaten us. They wish to talk."

"Five? Five is not enough. I am a Kickapoo."

"And I am Sackett," I said, "with whom they wish to speak. Do you come. You can help us speak."

Reluctantly, he followed, and I went down and seated myself opposite the old man.

For a long moment we simply looked at one another. His features were those of an Indian but with a subtle difference. What the difference was I could not have said, but perhaps it was only that he was a kind of Indian I had not seen before.

He was old, so very, very old, and age had softened features that once must have been majestic. Old? Yes, but there was no age in his eyes. They were young, and they were alert. He wore a magnificently tanned white buckskin jacket that was beaded and worked with colored quills in a series of designs unknown to me. On his head was a turban such as the younger man wore, tight fitting, snug. What hair I could see was white and thin.

He spoke in Cherokee, a tongue with which I had long been familiar. "I have come far to see Sack-ett," he said. His eyes were friendly and appealing. "I have come to ask for help, and I am not accustomed to ask."

"If there is anything I can do—"

"There is." He paused again. "The name of Sack-ett is known, but I expected an older man."

"My father, Barnabas. He was our strength and our wisdom, but he is gone from us, killed by the Seneca."

"I have heard. I did not believe it true."

"Nevertheless, I am a Sackett. If there is something my father would have done, it shall be done." I paused a moment. "What is it?"

One of the others had kindled a fire, and now with a coal he lighted a pipe. First he handed it to the old man, who drew deeply on the pipe and then passed it to me. I drew deeply on it also and would have handed it to the Kickapoo, but he drew back.

It seemed to me that the pipe ritual was not a customary one with him, but I did not know. That the old man was a Natchee Indian I was sure, but our contact with them had been slight, for they lived far to the south along the Great River. It seemed to me he was endeavoring to follow a ritual of other Indians and one with which he believed me to be familiar. It was an unusual experience, for the Indians I had known kept to their own ways and rarely borrowed those of others.

"The day is long," I suggested, "and you have far to go."

"I go no further. I am here."

Puzzled, I looked about me, but he only smiled. "It is Sack-ett I have come to see." He paused and laid the pipe aside, perhaps realizing I was as unused to the ceremony as he. "You are known to us. The Sack-etts are great fighting men but wanderers also."

"It is true."

"You are just men."

"We try to be just."

"You have come from afar but you take no more than you need. You do not take scalps. You do not make war until war is made upon you. This we have heard."

"It is so."

"Your people build houses, plant fields, gather in the forest for food. Sometimes you hunt."

"It is so."

"It is told that Ju-bal Sack-ett goes toward the setting sun. You are he?"

"I am."

"Why do you go?"

"I do not know. Perhaps because it is a place I do not know.

"One night I awakened in the darkness. It was very still. I lay wide awake, listening for something, and then it came to me. A voice said, 'Go!'

"One afternoon I was alone upon a mountain and I looked westward and a voice said, 'Come!' It is my destiny, I think."

The old man was silent for several minutes and when the silence grew too long I started to speak but he lifted a hand.

"The Natchee are a strong people. We are Children of the Sun. But one day a woman arose among us and spoke with a strange tongue. She spoke aloud with the voice of a man long dead and she said an enemy would come among us, an enemy who would seem to be a friend. This enemy would bring strange goods and strange presents and he would speak good words to us, but one day one among them would seek to destroy our sacred places and drive us from them to live like dogs, with no worship, with no ritual, with no memory of what we were or what we had been.

"We were to find a new place. We were to prepare to leave all behind and go into a strange, far land and prepare a place against the time of madness. We were to go where the sun goes behind the mountains and there find our place. In her man's voice she described the place and told us where to go."

"But you have not gone?"

"It was but one voice, and none of us wished to go. We love our land. It has been ours forever, I think. We lingered on, but the voice came again, and then a strange boat came and men gave presents and took things from us and went away.

"Now some began to believe, and at last it was said that some should go and find the place that is to be ours. Most did not believe, but finally one was chosen to lead the way."

"And he went?"

"*She* went. Fourteen in all. Ten men and four women went." He paused. "None have returned. We fear them dead."

The tall young man we had first seen, spoke suddenly. "She is not dead. She is mine."

I did not like him.

"They are to be joined together," the old man said.

"This has been decided? I do not know your customs."

"*She* will decide. She is a Sun, a daughter of the Great Sun." The old man paused and I thought I detected a gleam of humor in his eyes. "She is a strong woman. Beautiful, but very strong. She will decide." He paused again. "He believes he will decide. He is a Stinkard."

"I can see that."

The old man explained. "Ours is a different world from yours. First are the Suns, who rule. Second are the Nobles, third are the Respected Men, and fourth are the Stinkards. It is our custom that a Stinkard must always marry a Sun."

"So he will marry this woman?"

"As I said, she will decide."

"*I* will decide," the young man said.

"His mother was of another people than ours. Among her people women spoke when spoken to. He often speaks of this. Yet," the old man added, "he is very handsome. Many women look upon him with favor. He is a great warrior, one the greatest among us."

"And why have you come to me?"

"You go westward. You are a great wanderer. I think you could find this woman. I think you could tell her she is needed."

For a moment I thought of this. "If she is to be his woman," I said, "why does he not go?"

"He is needed. We have trouble."

"How long has she been gone?"

"Four moons. She is great among us."

Four months? There would be no tracks. How to find her? It was impossible. Nothing was known of the land to the west. There were vast plains into which no man ventured unless he could follow a stream, for none knew where the water could be found, and most said the distances between water were too great. Later, when men had horses to ride, they might venture into those plains. Now it was foolhardy and not to be seriously considered.

"Do you know where she went?"

"We know. We *think* we know."

He sat silent for a few minutes, thinking. Then he said, "Tonight, upon a skin, I shall draw a map. I do not know if it is the place, but such a place is in our memory. It was to such a place she went."

"Or planned to go. Who knows what has happened? There are other Indians." I glanced at the old man. "She is beautiful, you said? Such a one would be wanted."

"She is no ordinary woman." The old man's eyes met mine. "She can be dangerous."

"She is a witch?"

"No! No. But we Suns have knowledge—" He shrugged. "Nobody will live who tries to take her without her wish." He gestured at the young man, now across the camp. "Not even he will attempt her."

We talked longer and of many things. I did not want to look for this woman, nor did I wish to find her, but he had come to me for help, believing in the Sacketts. After all, we were going west.

In that I was like my father. From the day he landed upon our shores his one wish was to travel to the far blue mountains, yet once there he wished to see beyond them. So it was with me. All this land about us was unknown and I wished to be among the first to see it. I wanted to drink from those lonely streams, walk the high passes of the mountains, and travel down the valleys by paths I made myself.

Was that all I wanted? Until now, yes. I wished to see, to know, to find a world of my own in an unknown land. I did not know what else remained for the future, but there was in my dreams something haunting, something shadowy, something that would take no shape. Whatever it was, it was a place or a time that I must find.

We slept that night beside the stream. Keokotah was disgruntled, and I thought perhaps he might leave me and go on by himself as he had been before our meeting. Yet he did not.

Before I fell asleep I considered long the problem of the Natchee woman. My father had built a reputation as a trusted man. He was known as a warrior, yet he was also known for wisdom, and that respect and reputation had gone far afield. Such people as the Natchee, whom we did not know, knew of him. When in need they had come to him, or to us, for help. How could I do less than carry on in my father's name?

The land that lay before us was vast and unknown, even to most of the Indians. Anyone traveling west must confine himself to the rivers and streams, and all of those streams must begin in higher ground, probably in the mountains.

Every step of the way was a step into danger. There had been rumors of strange Indians coming down from the north, a fierce lot who destroyed all before them, but warlike Indians were to be expected upon the plains. Long ago an Indian had told my father they could not live without war, and certainly they did not wish to.

Our choice was simple. We would avoid trouble when possible, face it when necessary. We would have to scout the country with care. When we found Indian sign along the stream we would have to swing wide into the plains, holding to low ground. I was still thinking of this when I fell asleep.

Keokotah was irritable when morning came. "I no

like," he spat, and he indicated the tall young man whose name I had not yet heard. "I will kill him, I think."

"Wait," I advised, "his time will come."

"Hah!" Keokotah said contemptuously. "His time has come and passed. He should have been drowned at birth."

Unfortunately, I agreed, and it was not fair of me. What did I know of him, after all? He seemed arrogant, and he wanted the Natchee woman, but since she was beautiful, no doubt many did. I had never seen her but I knew I did not want her. She did not seem like an easy companion.

True, I knew little of women, but I had seen my father and mother together and theirs was an easy, friendly, loving relationship of mutual understanding. Each had a role to fill and each did so, and together they made a team. In another way, Yance and his wife were the same. The examples I had were all of women who were not abrasive, each strong in her way, and each a companion as well as a wife.

Yet I was not looking for a woman. My time would come, but a wide land lay before me and it was to that land that I belonged. I would drink from a hundred streams, make paths where no men had been, and eat the meat of strange animals before I died.

Our campfire was lifting a thin smoke to the sky when the old man came to sit near me. He passed me a roll of hide, but when I made to unroll it he put a hand on mine. "Only when alone," he said. "I trust you."

Well, all right, but did I trust him? I decided that I did and wondered if I was too trusting.

"He"—the old man indicated the young man who was not near the fire—"must not know. He would go to her, and there would be trouble." He paused. "I do not know how it is with your people but in ours there are people opposed to people. He is of one group, I am of another."

"And she?"

The old man hesitated. "If the Great Sun dies it is she who will say yes or no, and the Great Sun is not well.

He"—the old man indicated the young man—"wishes the power. If he marries her he believes he will have it."

"If they are married will he become a Sun?"

"No, he will remain a Stinkard."

I did not wish to become involved in the affairs of a people of whom I knew little and could not know who was right or wrong.

"I am going west," I told him, "and I will look for this woman, and if I find her I will tell her she is needed at home. I can do no more."

The old man stirred the coals. The fire was dying. Soon we would be moving along.

"It is a fair land," the old man said. "I envy you. Never before have I regretted my youth, but now I would be young to walk west beside you.

"I do not know what lies westward, but we have heard strange stories of ghost cities among the mountains, vast cities hidden in the folds of canyons. And we have heard of witches and wolves and of skinny, naked things that run in the night, things not to be seen by day and things that bring fear to the heart.

"I do not know what lies out there, but you will see it all, come to know it. My body is old but my heart is young. It will go west with you."

He arose suddenly from beside me. "Find her, Jubal. Find her for us. It will cause much trouble if you do not."

"What if she does not come back?"

He turned to look at me. "If she is happy, it will be well. You may think I only look to our people, but it is not true. She is not my daughter, but she is like a daughter. I was one of her teachers, and believe me, I wish only happiness for her."

"She will be happy with you?"

"Who can say? She would not be happy with *him*. He is a bitter, ambitious man. She would rule, and not him, although he does not believe that, nor does he want that. She would kill him, or he would kill her. I feel sure of that."

"I will try to find her, and if I do, I shall deliver your message."

"Remember, she is a Sun. Elsewhere she would be less than with us. The beliefs of others are not ours, and their ways are different. She is accustomed to power and the use of power. She is a strange woman."

Why it should come to me then, I could not say, but suddenly I remembered words from the Bible. "For the lips of a strange woman are as honey, and her mouth is smoother than oil."

I shook my head irritably. A vagrant, foolish thought. If I found her I would tell her to go home, although something in my mind said, not to him.

4

Long we sat by the fire, speaking in the Cherokee tongue. The old man was named Ni'kwana, and the fierce young man was Kapata, with an accent on the first syllable. Kapata was also the name for the hawk. The name suited him well enough.

He held himself aloof, disdainful of our conversation, but several times I saw his eyes straying to the buckskin on which Ni'kwana had drawn his map. I moved it closer to me. He saw the move and his eyes flared with anger.

He was taller than I by several inches, a lithe young man of uncommon strength. He could prove a dangerous antagonist.

Ni'kwana spoke of the prophecy. "We have seen no such men since the Warriors of Fire," he explained, "but each wind brings whispers to make us wonder. Is it true, then? Are the Warriors of Fire returning?"

The Natchee Indians were one of the few who had any tradition of De Soto, with his muskets and cannon, and it was his men who were known as the Warriors of Fire.

"He will not come again, but there will be others," I admitted. "You would do well to beware."

"Our neighbors, too, grow in strength," Ni'kwana

said, "and as they grow stronger they become more arrogant. The Creek were once our friends but I fear they are no longer. They look with envy on our fields and our stored grain."

He was silent then, thinking as he stared into the fire. Finally he said, "I fear for our people and our way of life. Strange men come and go and the tribes are restless. Our people are uneasy in the night and the young men are restless, their eyes always looking to the horizon. You come from another world. Tell me . . . what is happening?"

"There is but one thing we know, Ni'kwana, and that is that nothing forever remains the same. Always there is change. Your people have remained long undisturbed by outside influences. This may seem good, but it can be bad also, for growth comes from change. A people grows or it dies.

"Over there"—I gestured toward the east—"are people without land. Others have land but wish for more. Now this land has been discovered by them and they will come seeking."

"Westward there are vast lands and no people. Will they not go there?"

"I wish it might be so, but those who come will not go further than what they can see. They will buy some land but will take more. They do not believe this is wrong, for they, too, believe they are The People, and it has been the way of the world for men, animals, and plants to move in wherever there is opportunity and where they can survive.

"In the land where my father dwelt there were a people called Picts, then Celts moved in, and after them, Romans. When the Romans moved out the Angles, Saxons, and Danes moved in, each new people taking the land and pushing the others out or making slaves of them. Then the Normans came and dispossessed all the others, and their king took all the land for his own, giving it to those who served him best."

"It does not seem just."

"It never does to those whose land is taken." I paused

and then asked, "And your people, Ni'kwana? Did they always live where they now are?"

His eyes met mine and after a moment a faint smile came to his lips. "We, too, came from elsewhere. It is not remembered whence. Some say we came from the south, some from the east."

"It could be both. You may have come from the south, settled for a while, and then moved westward."

"It could be so."

We talked long into the night, and the fire burned low. The others slept. "This woman we are to seek? She has a name?"

"She is called Itchakomi Ishaia. We know her as Itchakomi, or even as Komi."

"Is it not unusual to send a woman on such a quest?"

"She is a Sun, a daughter of the Great Sun. Only he, she, or I could decide our future. Only she is young enough or strong enough to travel so far."

"And you, Ni'kwana? Are you a Sun?"

"I am." He looked into my eyes again. "I am also Ni'kwana, master of mysteries."

What we Sacketts knew of the Natchee Indians had been little enough and that mostly at secondhand, from tales told by the Cherokee, Choctaw, or Creek. These tales might or might not be true. The master of mysteries was akin to a high priest, but something more, also.

Ni'kwana then asked, "You, it is said, are a medicine man?"

This was believed of me by the Cherokee, for twice they had come to me when illnesses among them did not yield to their own practice. My father's friend Sakim had taught me much, and I had learned much from medicine men of the tribes who were friendly to me, yet Sakim had taught me much else besides, and some word had gotten about of my Gift.

"So it is said."

"It is also said that you, among your people, are also a master of mysteries."

"I am no master, Ni'kwana. I am one who lives to

learn. I go west because there are lands there I do not know, and perhaps to find a home for myself."

"Perhaps your home will be ours, also."

"If the Ni'kwana is there, then I could learn from him?"

"Ah . . . The way is long, and my muscles tire. I do not know, Ju-bal, I do not know. But," he added, "you could be one of us. I think your ways are like our ways." He smiled wryly. "At least, the ways of some of us.

"It is wise"—he spoke suddenly, sharply—"not to trust too much. We Natchee do not all believe alike. There are factions."

"Kapata? You said he was not of your blood?"

"His mother was a Karankawa, from the coast far to the south. Kapata has much of her ways and her beliefs, and they were a wild, fierce people. His mother, it is said, was a fierce woman, and the Karankawa were eaters of men."

"This I have heard."

Rising from beside the fire I said, "Tomorrow I must go. And you, Ni'kwana? Do you return to your village now?"

"I have been too long away, and the Great Sun will need me. He grows old, and he is not well. You will find Itchakomi?"

"I will try."

With my blanket I went alone to a place beside a rock, and there I slept. When dawn came Ni'kwana still sat beside the fire as he had when I left him. Whether he had moved or slept I did not know, but Keokotah was ready and waiting, impatient to be away from these people he neither knew nor trusted.

We ate lightly, but as we moved to go, Kapata was waiting. "She is my woman," he said, glaring.

"Convince her, not me," I said, and moved to pass him.

He reached for my shoulder but my knife was drawn. "Touch me," I said, "and they will be calling you Kapata the One Handed."

For a moment I believed he would attack, but my knife was inches from his belly, so he held his hand. It was well he did so, for I am a man of peace and would not have liked to send him crippled into the time after this.

We walked away then and left them staring, some with hope, some with hatred. For myself, although I liked Ni'kwana, I was pleased to be on my way. Keokotah, even more eager to be away, took the lead and soon broke into a trot. I followed, running easily and liking the path as it wound through the greenwood.

When we came to where the path divided, I took the easternmost. Keokotah hesitated. "The other is closer to the Great River," he said.

"I have reason. We will take the right-hand path."

He shrugged and motioned to indicate I should lead, which I did. We were nearing a river now and also the place where my canoe was hidden. The river we would follow also led toward Hiwasee, where there were Cherokees. It had been the home of other Indians before them and was a well-known place. So far as I knew none of these Cherokees had known us, but as I was beginning to learn, my father was known to them, and I myself, in a lesser way.

My canoe remained where it had been hidden, and Keokotah was much pleased. Birchbark canoes were not common. The Iroquois, for example, used only clumsy dugout canoes and were not skilled in working with birchbark. Mine was light and graceful, an easy canoe to be carried across portages by one man, but preferably two.

Beautiful was the morning when we went out upon the river, with the sunlight gathering diamonds from the ripples, and overhead a few idle clouds loitering over the blue meadows of the sky. We simply allowed the current to take us along, using the paddles only to maintain direction.

Once a great cloud of pigeons flew up, darkening the sky for a full two minutes as they swept by, a dusty brown screen between us and the sun. Further along we encountered three buffaloes swimming the river, but we had plenty of buffalo meat and had killed three wild turkeys earlier in the day.

This was my world and I was at ease with it—with the river, its waters still strong from melting snow, and with the dark, mysterious walls of the forest on either hand. I had never known the ease of cities or the trading and haggling of the marketplace. What I now had was what I wanted, to know the wilderness at first hand, to wander its lonely paths, to discover, to see, to feel, to search out the unknown and meet it face to face.

"You have been to the Far Seeing Lands?" I asked Keokotah.

"I have. Others of my people have. We Kickapoo are great wanderers."

This he had said before and I acknowledged it, for so I had been told in the lodges of the Cherokees.

"No people lived there," he said, "until now. A few came, then more, but they are very few even in this day."

"Where do they come from?"

"North, they come from the north, always there are people coming down from the north. And some from the east.

"There are people like you who sell guns to Indians. The Indians who have guns make war against Indians who have none, and the Indians without guns come westward to escape. These Indians push against other Indians until finally some have had to go out into the Far Seeing Lands."

It made sense. We had heard that the Dutch at Hudson's River were trading guns to the Indians. One thing more I had learned: more than any other Indians the Kickapoos, because of their inclination to wander, knew most about other tribes.

The Indian did not own land. A tribe might claim an area for hunting and gathering, but a stronger tribe might push them out, or they themselves might move when game became scarce.

Other things I learned from the casual talk of Keokotah, and one of these was that only those Indians who were present when an agreement was made need abide by its terms. A chief was so by prestige alone, a prestige won by his greatness as a warrior, his success as a leader, or his wisdom in council.

That night we camped on the bank of a creek emptying into the Hiwasee. It was a grassy shore with forest all around, fuel enough, and a good place to hide our fire. We talked much, and as we talked Keokotah's tongue loosened and words forgotten returned to him. His English friend had taught him well, obviously impressed by Keokotah's quick intelligence.

Once during the night I caught a faint sound from the forest, not a sound of wind among the trees, not a sound of an animal moving, but of something else, someone or something. I lay wide-eyed, listening. Keokotah seemed asleep but with him one never knew.

Our fire was down to a few coals, our canoe bottom up on the shore, our weapons at hand.

All was still, and I heard no further sounds, yet I had heard *something*.

Morning came and Keokotah said nothing. Had he heard the sound in the night? Did he not think it important? Or was it a sound he had expected? How could I know there were not other Kickapoos about? So I said nothing of what I had heard.

It was a lazy, easy, sun-filled morning. We watched the river for other Indians but saw none. Hiwasee could not be far away down the river, and many Indians would be there.

"What game is further west?" I asked him.

He shrugged. "Like here." There were deer of several kinds, one his English friend called wapiti. "I do not know what is wapiti. Much buffalo west. More than here. Bears, ver' large bears. A bear with silver hair almost as large as a small buffalo."

"A bear? As large as a buffalo?"

"Not so great. Nearly. He has a hump on his back and he is hard to kill. You see this bear you go away before he sees you. He ver' fierce bear."

He dipped his paddle and the canoe glided around a

rock, and Keokotah added, "There is big animal, big as a bear, maybe much bigger. He is yellow, long hair, very long claws. He dig. Much dig.

"Then there is big animal, much meat. He have long nose, two spears."

"*Spears?* An animal that carries *spears*?"

Keokotah made a sign for a long nose and two curved spears. An elephant? *Here?*

I had never seen an elephant, although Sakim had drawn pictures of them, and my father had, I believed, seen one in England.

"No." I shook my head. "Not here."

"I speak clear." Keokotah was suddenly very dignified. "I see only one time. Long time. I know old man who hunt him many times. He is big, ver' big animal. Much hair."

That was wrong. I knew about elephants and they did not have much hair. Only short, stiff bristles sometimes. "There is such an animal, but he does not live here."

That was a mistake. "He lives." Keokotah spoke stiffly. "I see him."

He did not speak again for many hours and I knew I had seriously offended him.

The idea was preposterous, yet how could he have even known of such an animal? His English friend, perhaps? But why would Keokotah lie?

Twice we sighted Indians on the shore, and once a canoe tried to overtake us, but it was no such canoe as ours and we left them far behind.

Suddenly Keokotah pointed. A land mass seemed to block the river. "Hiwasee!" he said.

As if commanded by the sound of his voice, two canoes shot into the main stream, each propelled by four paddlers. Dipping their paddles deep, they overtook us, one on either side.

"Cherokees." I spoke to Keokotah. "Hold your hand!"

5

They were beside us, weapons ready. To attempt escape was to die. If we fought, the odds were against us, but I had friends among the Cherokees over the mountains. Even here I might find friends.

We had traded with Cherokees at Shooting Creek, and we had carried trade goods to Cherokee towns to the south and east of us.

Of Barnabas they must surely know. His name had become legend. Kin had often gone to their villages and had many friends among them, but of these Over Hill Cherokees we knew too little and that only by hearsay.

Kin and Yance had hunted with the Cherokee, and had been on war parties with them. Yance, I had heard, was especially loved by them, my wild, rowdy, and reckless brother of great strength and an unfailing sense of humor.

How could they know of me, the Quiet One? He who walked in the shadows among the laurel sticks and stood alone on the balds when the sun was rising?

"Hold your hand," I warned the Kickapoo.

"They are enemies! I fear none of them!"

"I know you do not fear and they know it as well, but

if you would live, hold your hand and be guided by me. I am not their enemy and they shall know it."

"Is it that you fear?"

"If you walk beside me you shall see if I fear, but if they will permit I shall be a man of peace. I have no feud with the Cherokee."

"They need no feud. A scalp is a scalp."

My friend the Kickapoo was no fool, but we had no choice. The friendship of the red man was based upon different considerations than with us, although there were places where our trails of belief crossed. It behooves one to be wary when among strangers and not to trust too much.

To the shore we were guided, and when we drew our canoes up on the land one of my captors reached for my bow. Their village was close-by.

Drawing it away from him I stared into his eyes and said, "I am a friend. I am Sackett."

The warrior's hand fell away. "Sack-*ett*!" he exclaimed.

"He is Sack-ett," another said. "He has the face of Sack-ett."

"*I* do not know him," another said. "I do not see him."

"We come as friends, to smoke with the Cherokee. Then we go to the Great River, and beyond."

A Cherokee pointed at Keokotah. "He is Kickapoo. What do you with our enemy?"

"When he is with me he is no enemy to the Cherokee. He is a great wanderer. Together we go beyond the Great River. Perhaps we shall cross the Far Seeing Lands."

"The land is dead. There is no water. The grass is brown and old, and the rivers do not run."

"I shall find water. My medicine is strong. For me the land will not be empty."

The brave who said I had the Sackett face now spoke. "I know him. It is he of the great medicine."

They stood a little away from me. What they knew of me I had no idea, but it was no time for questions. "I would walk in your village. I would smoke with your chiefs. I would sit down with your medicine man. When I am with you my medicine is your medicine."

People had come out from the village and they stood back from us as we were escorted into the gate. The village, surrounded by a strong palisade, was a number of lodges roofed with bark. Outside one of the huts an old man sat cross-legged on a buffalo robe.

He looked up at me and then gestured that we be seated.

We sat opposite him and he took a pipe and smoked and then passed the pipe to me. I puffed and then passed it to the Kickapoo, who hesitated ever so slightly and then smoked and returned the pipe.

It seemed to me there was sly amusement in the old man's eyes. "You are Sack-ett?"

"I am."

The old man studied my clothing and then my long-bow. Then his eyes went to the scabbards at my waist. "What?" he asked.

"The voices of thunder," I said, "the voice that kills at a distance."

The first Cherokee extended a hand. "I will see."

"They are medicine. I give them to no man."

His eyes were hard. "Perhaps we take?" he suggested.

"Many would die."

"*You* would die!"

"Man was born to die. It is our promise at birth." I looked at him coolly and tried to make it no threat. "Do not hasten the time."

The old man appeared to take no notice of what had been said. "We of the Cherokee hear much of He Who Tells of Tomorrow. We hear of your great medicine."

A fire blazed between us, just a small, flickering blaze.

"There is a magic on the wind, and there are spirits that wait in the shadows. They belong to no man but they sometimes favor we of the great medicine." My hand moved over the fire, opening in a smooth gesture above the flame, but the fire suddenly turned blue and green.

The Cherokees drew back, muttering, but the old man did not move. "Ah? I have heard of he who makes the fire change."

"The spirits are kind," I said, modestly. "It is nothing."

The old man was amused. "My spirits are sometimes kind," he said, "although not in the same way."

"I have no doubt," I said. "Beyond the blue mountains your name is known."

"You go beyond the Great River? It is a far way, often bloody. Some have gone from here. Some returned. Many were lost." He paused. "It was from there the white men came, the white men who wore iron shirts."

"White men in iron shirts? The Warriors of Fire?"

He shook his head. "It was later. When I was a young boy. With my own eyes I saw them.

"He came to eat in our village and he was much hungry. When he came to leave we gave him food and he went quickly away. I was a boy then, and curious. I followed."

We waited, and even the other Cherokees were curious, for the story seemed new even to them.

"He was weak, this white man. He had eaten, but still he was weak. Twice he fell down before he came to the fire where two others waited, so weak they could not stand. He gave them food."

"They wore iron shirts also?"

"They did. Two carried bows such as yours, and one carried a spear. All had long knives. They ate. They rested. They went away. I watched them as they went."

"Which way did they go?"

"Up the Great War Path. The Warrior's Path."

"You did not follow?"

"For a little way. They met with two other men, also with longbows and also with long knives, but only one had an iron shirt. This one had killed a deer. He had meat with him, and I watched them eat again. When they started on I went back to my village."

Five white men? Only the English used the longbow, and an Indian would remember the bows.

Who could they have been? The old man to whom I talked must be close to eighty, and it had been when he was a boy. Vaguely I recalled a story told by Jeremy Ring, my father's old friend, a story of some of Sir John Hawkins's men who had been left ashore in Mexico, and of how some of those men, not wishing to be imprisoned by the Spanish, had struck out to walk to the French settlements of which they had heard, not realizing how long a journey it would be. Yet three men had gotten through, walking to Nova Scotia in eleven months, from which place they were carried away to France and then to England. These could have been the men.

"You have come in peace," the old man said. "You will find peace here, and you shall leave in peace."

"With my friends the Cherokee I would have it no other way."

We were shown a lodge where we could sleep, but I knew that what had been said was spoken to me only. The Kickapoo would be left alone while in the village, but after that—

It was only then that I realized that the Cherokee who had wanted my guns had left the group before the old man had given us his permission to stay. That Cherokee would not be party to the old man's agreement. It was a thing to remember. Perhaps not intended that way, but who could be sure?

What of our canoe? Would it be safe? From the lodge to which we had been taken I judged the distance. Perhaps it would be well if we slipped away in the night, if that were possible. All we could do now was wait and see.

The village was larger than I had at first believed. There were many Indians about, and they had dogs, dozens of them, constantly moving around. Yet at night they would sleep. Or would they? Certainly they would be aware of us, and any movement at night might be considered unfriendly.

We would wait until day. We would eat, we would talk, and we would take our departure quietly, as guests should.

What happened after that was another thing, and we would be ready.

Keokotah seemed to sleep soundly, yet who could be sure? Long before daybreak I was up, my small pack prepared, my weapons ready. I expected no trouble within the village, but all did not like us here, nor had they all approved of the old man's welcome.

A voice from the door of our lodge spoke. "Sack-ett?"

"I am here."

"Come! It is time to go!"

Six warriors waited outside. We faced them, prepared for whatever would come. "We are friends." The speaker was a barrel-chested Indian of some forty years. "We have come to see you safely on your way. Sack-ett has been a friend to our people. We are friends to Sack-ett."

They formed on either side of us and walked with us to our canoe. Two men guarded it. Getting into two canoes they paddled beside us until we were well on our way. Finally, they backed water and let us go on ahead. The older Indian lifted his spear. "Go in peace!" he said, and we did.

Obviously they had feared we would be attacked and had come to see us on our way in safety.

Would our Cherokee enemies pursue? I doubted it. The warrior faction had made their position known in no uncertain terms, and it was unlikely that a few malcontents would dare oppose them.

But we were wary, as it is wise to be, trusting to nothing and prepared for anything.

My father's reputation had preceded us. He had been known as a brave and honorable man, often settling disputes among the Indians. Often they brought their sick or wounded to us for treatment that seemed beyond what their own medicine men could do. The place on Shooting Creek had become known among not only the Cherokees but other tribes as well.

We moved on through sunlight and shadow, taking our time on the river, seeing no one. Nearly every day clouds of passenger pigeons flew over us, and we also began to see flights of parakeets, adding touches of brilliant color to the bare trees.

Many trees were leafing out and much of the brush along the streams as well. Once, glancing back, I thought I caught the flash of sunlight on a paddle blade, yet I did not see it again.

We put twenty miles behind us before we made camp at a cove near a small creek, drawing our canoe well up into the willows and out of sight. Making a small fire of dry wood that offered almost no smoke, we ate some of the buffalo meat and stretched out on the grassy slope to rest.

From where we lay we could see upstream for almost a mile, and by turning our heads and looking through the willows we could see downstream for a short distance. It was a quiet, lazy time, but a time I needed to think, to plan.

If I was to find Itchakomi I must seek sign of their passing. The old man of the Cherokees might have told me something but I had forgotten to mention her to them. The Natchee had been friendly to the Cherokees, I remembered, and they might well have stopped at Hiwasee.

We had tales of Spanish men being westward, beyond the plains. I believed this to be true, but we did not know. Too little was known in England of what the Spanish were doing, and we in the colonies knew even less. From time to time the Indians brought stories of Spanish men to the westward, but far, far away.

Where would Itchakomi go? She was to seek out a new land for the Natchee, and such a land must be far enough away to provide escape from their enemies. There were fierce tribes to the north, such as the Seneca, so it was unlikely they would go far in that direction. The plains had to be where they would go, but would they stop there? What would invite them? Only that the plains were empty.

I spoke of this to Keokotah. "Where would you go?"

He had been lying on the grass and he sat up suddenly. "To the mountains," he said. "I would go where mountains are, where water is, where game can be. I would find a place hidden from eyes."

"And to get there?"

"I would follow a river, but not too close. Where water is, enemies can be. I would walk far from streams and come to them only at night, or before night."

We talked of this and of many things. Keokotah was learning more English from me, and he had a quick intelligence as well as a gift for mimicry that helped him to learn.

"You English—" he said.

"English? I do not know that I am English," I said. "My father was English, but I have never seen England. I know only America. I think I am American."

"Why you American?"

"Because I was born here. I live here. All my memories are of here."

"So it is with me, but I am Kickapoo."

"You are Kickapoo, but you are also American," I explained.

"You are American. You say I am American. What of Cherokee? What of Seneca?"

"They are Americans, too."

He shook his head. "No Seneca is American. Seneca is Seneca and my enemy."

"Far away in Boston there are people called Puritans. They are English by birth. They do not think as I do, but they are Americans, too."

"They are not your tribe?"

"No."

"Spanish men your tribe?"

"No."

"Spanish men live in Florida. That is America?"

"Of course."

"Then Spanish men are Americans?"

"Well—"

"You say Seneca are American. I say Spanish men are American."

"It would be better if we forgot who is Seneca and who is Spanish and just remembered we are all Americans."

Keokotah was silent. The idea was new to him and he was not prepared to accept it. But was I prepared to accept the Spanish, our traditional enemies, as Americans?

Keokotah spoke slyly. "Next time we meet Seneca, you tell him we all Americans. No need fight. You put down your bow. Put down your knife. You walk up to him and say, 'We all Americans.' "

"And—?"

"Your American scalp will hang in a Seneca lodge."

"What if a Seneca came to you and said, 'We no fight'?"

"I would take his scalp, cut off his hands and his genitals."

"Cut off his hands?" This, I knew, was often done as well as other mutilation. It was a custom, and a barbarous one. "Why?"

He stared at me as if my words were those of a child. "If he has no hands he cannot attack me in the time after this. If he has no genitals he cannot breed sons to hunt me down. What else is there to do?"

I started to tell him white men did not do such things and then amended it. "It is not our custom."

He shrugged. "You will have enemies waiting in the time after this, but I shall rest in peace."

"But why not have peace here? Now? Would you not like it if you could walk in the forest without danger?"

"No. Soon Keokotah lazy, fat, useless. Indians cannot live without war. Until an Indian has taken a scalp he is nothing. He cannot get a woman, he cannot speak in council."

"That, too, can change. In England most of the titled lords won their titles because of their ability at killing. A man was knighted because of his skill with weapons. Now often enough a man is given a title or knighted who would faint at the sight of blood."

"The Kickapoo are strong because of our enemies. Deny us our enemies and we would grow weak. The

Englishman taught me to pray to your Christian god," he added suddenly.

"And you do?"

"Why not? All gods are useful. Who am I to say yours is not? The Englishman prayed, and he was strong in death. The Seneca who killed him sing songs of his courage."

After a moment, Keokotah added, "If I make one last prayer I ask that your god grant me an enemy. If I have an enemy, even one enemy, I can be strong."

"It need not be an enemy," I protested, "any obstacle can do the same. Anything that makes one struggle to be stronger, to be better."

"You have obstacle. I will have enemy. You grow strong in your way, I in mine."

He was a most stubborn man, but a strong one. Yet as I protested I had to remember that England became great at sea at least in part because Spain built an armada.

6

We hid our canoe when the morning was bright on the water, and started inland. My father had put it upon me to find a new home for us and to spy out the land. For this I could not remain upon the water, but must explore. Besides, it was a strong craving in me to know what lay about me, and Keokotah felt as I did.

Rich were the grasses underfoot, and tall the trees when we came to them. There were numerous springs, yet not so many running streams, for this was limestone country, a place of many caves where the streams ran deep within them. Yet I began to see a reluctance in Keokotah, a hanging back at times, and he looked upon the hills with awe and seemed to wish to avoid the caves.

"The spirits of the dead are here," he said, when I asked him the why of it. "They are all about. And there are caves where they sleep, not dead, yet not alive."

"You have seen this?"

"I have."

"Will you take me to them?"

"I will not."

"I will make strong medicine," I said, "medicine that will protect us from evil."

That he had respect for my magic I knew, and I must

keep him respecting it, but to do that it must be used sparingly and with care.

"I have much to learn," I said, "and mayhap those who once lived here were of my people." I did not know this was true, but knew the story of Prince Madoc of Wales, and suspected a connection.

Night was coming on when we spoke of this, and we made a small camp near a spring in a nest of rocks and trees. It was a hidden place and such as we needed, for we must make fresh moccasins from skins we carried. Moccasins did not last like English boots, but we were skilled at cutting out the patterns and shaping them to our feet.

What had Keokotah meant when he had said "they lived yet did not live"?

I knew the folly of asking direct questions, on some topics at least. I said no more, but waited, wishing for him to talk but knowing he would talk of these things only when the mood was upon him.

The night was very still. We sat late beside our fire building moccasins for tomorrow and other days. Knowing we had the time we each made several pairs, and I wished to wait and hope Keokotah would decide to speak.

Finally, he did. "Cold came early that year. I saw no bears, and even the birds flew low and fluttered from bush to bush. When the snow fell it fell thick, and soon it was deep and my tracks were deep like the tracks of pasnuta."

"Pasnuta?"

He looked at me with no friendly eyes. "The big one with the long nose. The Poncas call him pasnuta."

"I did not know there was a name," I said.

"All things have names." He spoke with dignity. "Pasnuta means 'long nose.' "

After a moment he explained. "Pasnuta ver' heavy. He makes deep tracks in snow."

"It was an early snow?" I prodded him.

"I was not prepared. I had meat and a skin, but the skin was not ready. There was no time to build a lodge, and the snow was falling ver' thick. I looked along the mountain for a place where trees had fallen or great rocks. I looked for shelter from the strong wind that was coming."

"And?"

"I found a cave. Not a big cave." He held his hands not two feet apart. "A broken rock, black inside. I looked and found a big room, big as three lodges together. I went inside and it was dry, no animal, nothing.

"Outside I broke branches from a dead tree. Gathering wood for my fire. Inside there was no wind but there was a place for fire. Ver' old, this place. Ashes, but no sticks, no coals. Stones, like so." His gestures indicated rocks placed in a circle for a fireplace.

"I make a fire. The room grows warmer. Not warm . . . warmer. I think in that place it is always cool." He was silent and we worked on the moccasins. "The fire is burning. I put sticks. It burns brighter. Shadows move upon the walls. I look . . . and then I am frighten."

"Frightened? Why?"

He did not speak for some minutes, and I waited, impatient but knowing I must wait.

"Too many shadows." He looked up at me. "Shadows made by the firelight, but other shadows, too. Shadows that move not with the others, taller, thinner shadows. I am frighten, but it is cold outside, cold enough to die with no shelter from wind, no fire. And I am Keokotah, who is a Kickapoo, and not afraid."

He paused. "I say to my thoughts, 'No more sticks.' If the fire go out there can be no dancing shadows, so I let the fire die, but when there are only red coals, there are still shadows, only they dance slow.

"I build the fire again. The shadows have not hurt me and if I let the room go dark . . . who knows what can be? Maybe the fire is for the shadows. Maybe they love the fire because it makes the shadows live?

"The shadows live again. Only the tall shadows, the thin shadows, they dance slower than the others. I am frighten to sleep. All night long I feed the shadows with their firelight. I give them life and make offering of sticks. Yet I am frighten. What if my sticks are no more? I get up and the shadows seem to grow taller. Yet I show how small is the pile of sticks and I go out into the cold for more. I bring them back. I build up the fire.

"And then I think now I am slave to the shadows. When morning comes, will they let me go? I watch the fire. I watch the sticks. When morning comes I put sticks on the fire and then go out as if for more. And I run!

"Away through the snow! I run, I dodge among trees, I keep running until I can run no more. I am no longer frighten. I am free! I have escape!" He looked at me. "I will no go back. It is enough."

"And your skin? The one you took to the cave?"

He shrugged. "I think it is there. I do not want the skin. I will not go to the cave."

"You will show me?"

He shrugged. "I show you. I wait two days. If you do not come, I walk away, far away, ver' fast."

For a long time we worked in silence, and the moccasins shaped themselves in our fingers. And then I said, "You spoke of 'they live yet do not live' or some such thing. Did you mean the shadows?"

He was again silent, and when almost an hour had passed and we had put aside our moccasins he said, "There was a deeper cave. I went to it."

"Another room?"

"I do not know what is 'room.' Another cave, deeper into the mountain. I looked."

"And—?"

"Three lay sleeping. Three wrapped tight in skins. Skins hard tied about them. Only their faces showed, and their hands and feet."

"Tied?"

"Like buried. Like dead. A skin tied about each, but their faces looked old . . . so ver' old! Wrinkled—" He squeezed up the skin of his face until it wrinkled. "When I lifted the pine torch their eyes were alive! They stared at me. They were blue eyes like the Englishman, only fierce, wild, strange! I was frighten. I run back to other cave. The shadows are better than they who lie sleeping with open eyes."

The story was strange, yet I believed him. Keokotah did not lie. What he told me was what he saw, but what is it we see? Is it not often what we expect to see? Or imagine we see? He was frightened, so what part was reality and what part imagination? Sakim had taught me to be wary of evidence given by others, for in all evidence there is some interpretation. The eyes see, the mind explains. But does the mind explain correctly? The mind only has what experience and education have given it, and perhaps that is not enough. Because one has seen does not mean one knows.

I, coming from another world, would have a different supply of information than Keokotah. My explanation might be different. Moreover, I was curious. Blue eyes? Unlikely, but possible, and the three bodies wrapped in hides sounded to me like a burial, and the bodies might be mummified.

By now I believed Keokotah was my friend. To keep a friend is important and to shame him would be to lose him. Therefore I must not make light of his belief in what he had seen or believed he had seen. I must prepare for what I was to see in a way he would comprehend.

I would make medicine.

I must convince him I was making medicine to prepare myself for the ordeal that lay before me. I must make sure he knew that I was impressed by his story and that only the strongest medicine would ward off the evils I must face. I went to sleep that night thinking of what I must do and how to do it.

At the same time I was intensely curious. Seagoing men have many stories that do not reach their landlubberly friends; some are merely superstition but some are dim memories of voyages made long ago by mariners long since lost.

Many an ancient archive has been lost in fires, destroyed in sieges, or simply allowed to decay through lack of interest or awareness. Among the greatest of seamen, for example, were the Carthaginians. Descendants of the Phoenicians, who were themselves among the greatest of seafaring peoples, the Carthaginians were denied access to many sources of raw material by their rivals and enemies the Romans. Eventually the Romans destroyed Carthage, but in the meanwhile their ships were continually at sea bringing back cargoes of raw materials and much else. Hanno the Phoenician had circumnavigated Africa hundreds of years before Christ. Crossing the Atlantic would have been much less difficult.

We do not know where the Carthaginians went except in a few cases, but like their relatives the Phoenicians they were great traders and travelers. The Arabs, who were among the greatest of seafaring peoples, had access to more of the Phoenician records than had Europeans through their captures of such great trading ports as Tyre, Sidon, and Alexandria.

It was little enough I knew except from sailors' tales or from the lips of Sakim. As the Moslem religion demanded a pilgrimage to Mecca from each of its followers, many succeeded in making the long trip from wherever they lived, and in so doing brought to Mecca many accounts not only of their homelands but of other lands of which they knew or had heard.

Hence my mind was not closed to the possibilities of who the bodies might have been. Long ago, when I was a small boy, my father had walked along the outer banks where the Atlantic curls its foaming lips against the shores of America. I had not seen the sea before although there had been much talk of it at home, for my father had sailed his own craft across that ocean.

The sea, busy moving sand as always, had uncovered an ancient wreck. There was a colony in Virginia by then, but the *Mayflower* had not yet crossed the Atlantic with its Pilgrims, and the wreck we looked upon was old. Only a few gray ribs protruded from the sand. Perhaps only an abandoned ship that washed up here, perhaps some early venture. Not enough showed itself to explain its construction but my father examined it curiously. When I asked whose ship it might have been, he shrugged. "It is a construction I find strange," he said, "but I know so little of such things."

He kicked one of the timbers, as one will. "Solid," he said, "and built for the deep sea. This was no coasting craft."

Keokotah knew nothing of ships and the sea, and of all this speculation I said nothing. I knew too little myself, just enough to tantalize me and make me long to know more. Yet when I thought back to my opportunities I knew that few boys had grown up exposed to more than I.

My father's men had been soldiers, sailors, and wanderers. Sakim had been a seaman aboard a ship with my father, a prisoner taken at sea as my father had been, and several of his men had been soldiers who had fought in foreign wars.

Soldiering was an honorable trade, and many of England's men had fought on the continent or in Mediterranean lands. Each had stories to tell and we boys were avid listeners. Yet I had learned more because I was not the hunter and fisherman the others were.

After Keokotah had fallen asleep I lay long awake remembering my mother. A thought took me: she was in England . . . suppose she, too, had died and I did not know? But then I would never know now if she were alive or dead.

I thought of Brian and Noelle. I had been closer to them than the older boys had.

How different their lives would be! In the England I had never seen they would live, grow, become educated. I longed for them then, and longed for my mother, too. But my star hung over the western mountains and I knew it.

What would I find there? What, besides a Natchee princess or priestess, or whatever she was?

But I had nothing to do with her, only to find her and tell her the Great Sun was dying and she was needed. Remembering Ni'kwana, however, I began to wonder whether he really wished her to return or not. I think he feared Kapata and his ambition. But if she did not return, what life would there be for her? Where could such a one find happiness in our wild western world?

My mind was busy with that when my lids closed. How long they had been closed—it seemed but an instant—I do not know, but suddenly they were wide open, staring.

Something had moved in the forest! Some sound, some vague whispering of movement against leaves.

I put out a hand and touched Keokotah. The hand I touched held a knife.

7

Ghostlike, I slid from under my blanket and into the trees. As always, I had chosen my retreat before lying down. Often it is too late when the moment comes, and I wished to make no sound to give away my position. There was no need to worry about Keokotah. He had known nothing else since childhood and knew well what must be done.

We waited then. I knew not where Keokotah was, nor did the red coals give any light. Our blankets looked heaped as though we still slept. That, too, was an immediate reaction to attack.

There was no moon, only stars and scattered clouds above the trees. I heard no sound, but there would be none. These Indians knew what they did. The sound that had awakened me might have been a natural sound of the forest or an attacker, momentarily clumsy.

There would be no chance to use my bow in a first attack. Later—if I survived.

A wind stirred. Often Indians chose such moments in which to move, covered by the wind sounds. I waited, knife in hand. A low wind sifted through the leaves. I felt body warmth near to me, and when I looked to my right a faint gleam from a metallic armlet told me an Indian lay beside me, not two feet away!

My knife was ready, gripped in my right hand. He was lying parallel to me, and to stab he must rise up and strike with his right hand. I had known perhaps a thousand Indians and none had been left-handed. When he raised up to strike I would stab him, and it would be only an instant before he was aware of me.

He must have been a young Indian with not too many warpaths behind him, for he had eyes only for his chosen point of attack. He raised up to his knees, spear poised to throw into my heaped-up blankets. My blade cut sharply back and up, the point going in below the middle of his rib cage, driving to the hilt.

His eyes met mine in a moment of awful awareness. His spear was thrown as he took the blade. He realized death in that instant and I put my hand against his shoulder and drew back my knife. He started to cry out, but could not. His hand went back for a tomahawk at his belt but there was no strength in his fingers. He fell forward, made an effort to rise, then moved no more.

The fire blazed up from a handful of leaves and sticks thrown upon it. An Indian lay dead near the fire. Nothing else moved. Wind stirred the leaves again, and the blaze dipped in obedience to the moving air. And then there was a long silence, while the fire crackled.

A hand reached from the brush toward the fallen Indian's foot, but before I could rise to bring my bow into position an arrow drove through the air. The hand tightened convulsively into a fist and was withdrawn. And that was all.

When morning came the two dead Indians lay where they had fallen. The warrior who had taken Keokotah's arrow was gone, the arrow with him.

He looked at my Indian with approval and then gestured at the scalp. "You no want?"

"No. It is not my custom."

He did not hesitate, but took the scalp for himself as he had the other.

"What if they come again?"

"Their medicine bad. They go home now. He"—Keokotah indicated the Indian he had killed—"was chief. He dead. He medicine no good. Maybe pick another chief, maybe stay home. Two men die, medicine no good."

"How many were there, I wonder?"

He shrugged. "Maybe six, maybe eight. No more."

They were of a tribe strange to us both, but there were many such, some even now disappearing. There were Indians my father had met when first he landed in Carolina who were no more. Wars with other tribes, diseases . . . who knew what had happened to them?

Keokotah stooped and cut the string that held a medallion on the Indian's throat. He held it out to me.

It was a Roman coin. A silver coin of about the size of a nine-penny piece, dated in the third year of Antoninus Pius. The date and other inscriptions were much worn, so that I could not be sure but I figured the date to be about 137 after Christ.

This was not the first Roman coin we Sacketts had come upon, for once before an Indian had traded us another coin dated only a few years earlier than the one I now had. The dates of both were close enough that they could have been carried by one man or one group of men.

The coin did not surprise me. For every documented voyage there must have been a thousand of which no record was kept. What reason had the average ship's master or merchant for keeping records, especially when they might betray his sources of raw material or trade?

Our travel was no longer swift, for if my people were to relocate so far from known sources of material they must find new sources. They would have to make their own gunpowder, which we had done for much of the time, but they would need lead, also, or copper, from which we had occasionally made bullets.

Keokotah was sullen. He spoke little and I began to realize he did not wish to go to the cave. Moreover, when he did speak he often spoke of his own village, and I realized I might lose my companion. His own village lay not many days travel away to the north, and he had long been gone.

At night I now built a small, separate fire, and over this I muttered prayers and recited doggerel learned from my parents. To Keokotah I was making medicine, preparing for entering the cave of the shadows. All this was pure mumbo-jumbo but I liked Keokotah and did not wish him to believe I made light of his fears. "Bad," I said to him, "much bad! Bad spirits!"

The cave lay on the south side of a large river, but nearer a branch of that river which forked. He led the way, but he walked slower and slower.

One night in a camp on a shelf above the river I said to him, "Keokotah, your home is near. If you go to the Far Seeing Lands with me it will be long before you again see your village."

I had all his attention. "You could visit your village and meet me in the western lands." I took up a stick and in the clay I drew a line. "Here is the Great River, running north to south. Here"—I drew a line joining it from the west—"is another river. It is almost due west from here toward the setting sun. Perhaps a little south? You could meet me there. I will return to the canoe, and will go to the Great River and then to this river.

"It has been told me that this river"—I indicated the one flowing into the Great River from the west—"flows down from the Shining Mountains. That river I shall follow westward.

"It is also," I added, "the way Itchakomi was to go. If I am to find her I must seek signs of their passing."

"The signs will be gone."

"I do not think so. You see, Ni'kwana spoke to me alone. He told me of signs that were to be left for those to follow if Itchakomi did not return. I shall look for the signs."

He hesitated for a long time and then he asked, "You do not want Keokotah with you when you face the spirits of the Shadow Cave?"

"If he wishes," I said carefully, "but I think this is

something my medicine is strong against. It is a trial for me." An inspiration came to me. "When you won your name, your totem, did you not go out alone to fast? To dream? So it is with me. The spirits tell me this I must face alone. It is for me. It is great danger for anyone else. If I come not to the place by the Great River you will know I have failed."

Keokotah did not wish to leave me, but two things tugged at him: his desire to visit his village and his fear of the Shadow Cave.

"I will go with you even though I fear," he said. "You are my friend."

"My medicine will often protect all who are with me. In this case it will protect only me, I think. I must go into the cave alone.

"Perhaps," I suggested, "you were sent to bring me this knowledge. Perhaps those who lie in the cave are my ancestors who have words for me. I do not fear the shadow things, for they know of me. I will go to them. Do you go to your village. In two moons you will meet me at the river of which I speak. I shall leave signs for you to follow."

I held up the Roman coin. "This speaks to me across many years." I showed him the picture of the old man on one side and the young man on the other. "These were great chiefs long ago in a land far from here, but I know who they were and what deeds they did.

"Those who lie in the cave may also have words for me. We shall see."

We parted when the sun arose, and no more was said. Neither knew what lay between us and the river of which I spoke, but each knew he could find the other if he was there.

I watched him go with sadness, for I have had few friends and did not know if I would have another.

Now was my time of trial. I had said much to Keokotah because I desperately wished to see the cave where the bodies lay, but I had no faith in my charms against the shadow things. That was spoken for him, to put his fears for me at rest. I am no braver than any man, and the thought of entering the cave filled me with doubt and fear. Yet I am a curious man, and wherever I had gone I had had the feeling that I followed in the footsteps of others. This was a clue I could not, dare not, avoid. I must see, not only for myself but for that most sacred thing, the knowledge of others.

In a world of many mysteries there are a few doors left slightly ajar for us to see. He who passes one of those doors may deny man knowledge precious to us. How long might men wait before another told of the cave? How many could know of it? The knowledge had been given to me. The mission was mine.

If I could not solve the mystery of those bodies I could at least report their existence.

The opening of the cave was small, not easy to find, and such an opening as one might easily pass by, thinking it nothing at all.

That night I made camp on a branch of a fork on the river. Tomorrow I would venture into the cave. Tomorrow. . . .

And when the morning came there were no stars, but only a flat black sky, and there was a smell of rain in the air. I broiled a piece of venison and ate slowly, making coffee from chicory. The wild plants grew along old buffalo trails and elsewhere. There were no blooms this early, but within a few weeks the bright blue flowers would be visible in many a corner and meadow.

My fire burned low, a sullen flame that brought no cheer. I thought of the cave into which I was going and hesitated. Need I go? Why take the chance? I had never liked caves much, anyway. I gave myself excuses but none of them worked. The cave was there and I would see what it contained.

When the fire was low and I had drunk the last of my chicory brew I gathered my few things together, put my fire out carefully, and made up my small pack.

With my knife firmly in place and my guns ready, I

took up my bow and started up the narrow, scarcely discernible path. Now for it, I told myself.

Trees like black bars against the gray rock. Moss hanging, moss clinging. The track was slippery. If it rained I must be careful along here. Below there was a tangle of dead trees, trunks crossing trunks, all blown down by some violent gust long ago. It was a trap above which the track wound along. I could hear the water rustling by. Suddenly there was a crack in the limestone wall.

Here it probably was then. I looked all around and saw nothing. A small flock of parakeets flew from one tree to another, in pursuit of some unseen food supply.

The cave was not just as I had heard it was, but no matter. I had found it.

Black and ominous. I gathered material for a torch but then thought of the candle I forever carried in my small pack. Such a candle can keep a man from freezing in a small space. I got it out, crouched low through the opening, and lighted it. I edged forward and then stood up.

Before me was where Keokotah had built his fire. The remains of it as though it had just gone out. Some sticks lay close by to add to the fuel. The room was bare and clean, with nothing besides the fire and its ashes.

My candlelight flickered on the walls but I saw no shadows but those that should be there . . . or did I? I shook my head, angry with myself.

Imagination! Was I a child to be frightened by ghosts? Or such a savage as Keokotah, who knew no better?

Yet what did I know? Were there ghosts? Were there spirits? Who was I to say? All my life I had heard stories of such things. All my child's life I had been pleasurably frightened by such stories. We had longed for them and had begged my mother, or Lila, or Jeremy Ring to tell us such stories. Now they returned to haunt me.

I looked at the small opening into the next room. Was that where the bodies lay, with their blue eyes watching? Were they dead? Were they even there? Or were they merely waiting, lying there, waiting for me to enter?

Don't be a fool, I told myself. You're not a child. You are a man. You are not afraid of the dark or of shadows.

What was *that*? Had something moved? Or was it some sound from outside? I drew my knife.

What good was a knife against a ghost? Yet was this a ghost? What kind of creatures could they be? They were but bodies, and Keokotah had seen them.

Carefully, I looked around again. I edged back toward the entrance hole and listened.

Nothing.

Again my eyes went to the walls. The candle cast few shadows, but against the limestone walls the candle gave much light. My eyes searched for shadows, not wanting to find them but not daring to miss them.

The silent dead lay within that other room. They were the ones I had come to see.

How long ago had Keokotah seen them? Suddenly I realized I did not know. Had it been just now? A few days ago? Or had it been months? Even years?

I moved then, and something else moved. I was suddenly still, my heart pounding. *Had* something moved? Or was I dreaming? Had expectation created the sound? I took a step, and something else stepped.

It was an echo, that was all. My footstep against these walls. How carefully clean it was! As if the floor had been swept, and not long since.

My eyes went to the sticks left by Keokotah. They were neatly piled, and ready to be added to the fire, had there been a fire.

But of course there had been. He had spoken of it, and the ashes were there. This was the fire that brought the shadows to life. Should I light it again? Should I make that experiment too?

Ridiculous. I was not cold. I did not need a fire. Outside thunder rumbled. Maybe I would need a fire. It was going to rain.

Well, it was warm and dry in here. I swallowed. It seemed warm, and that made no sense. Such caves were always cool, always almost cold. Had not I heard somewhere that caves kept an even, cool temperature?

Regardless of that, this cave was warm. Almost as if there had been a fire.

The hair on the back of my neck prickled and I felt my skin crawl. For a moment I looked at the gray, dead ashes. Suddenly, impelled by what impulse I know not, I bent over and touched the ashes with my fingers.

They were *warm*!

8

I felt of them again. Soft, gray wood ashes but definitely warm.

Well, why not? Was there anything so mysterious about that? I had come to the cave seeking an answer to a puzzle, but Keokotah had come seeking shelter, so why not others after him? And before?

Again my eyes went to the entrance to the inner cave. I started forward and then stopped. There was a cobweb in the opening. Whoever had been using the cave had evidently not entered the inner cave at all.

Brushing the cobweb away I ducked into the inner cave, holding my candle before me.

The three bodies lay side by side, each wrapped in a neat cocoon of skins. They were very, very old skins and looked as if they might disintegrate at a touch. Two of the bodies were those of women, one obviously an old woman, one young. Their faces were shrunken, the skin on their hands and feet also. It was tight to the bone, but I could still tell that one had been much younger than the other. The third figure was that of a man who seemed to have been buried later than the first comers. His skin looked fresher, his face composed as though he had died in his sleep, yet his eyes were open and they seemed to be looking at me as if he were about to speak. I shuddered.

Beside the first two bodies there was a woven basket containing grain. There was a jar nearby that had no doubt contained water or some other liquid.

There were no weapons, nor was there any jewelry, yet I had a feeling that when the bodies had been left here there had been both.

Slowly, I backed away, looking about me. This cave, too, was spotlessly clean. Obviously it had been swept. In vain I looked for some clue as to who these dead might have been or where they had come from. There was nothing, and I had no wish to examine the bodies. Far better to let them lie as they had for these many years.

Years? Perhaps even centuries. The interior of the cave had a cool, almost cold temperature. It was dry. The warmth of the brief fire in the outer room did not seem to have penetrated here. I backed away, and the eyes seemed to follow me. At the opening, I paused, and something made me speak.

"I shall leave you now, as you have been. Is there anything I can do?"

No lips stirred, nor did the eyes blink. I shook my head. What was I expecting? Was I as superstitious as a child? Yet in the eyes of the young man there seemed to be a pleading, a longing, as of something unsatisfied.

"I wish I could help," I said quietly.

I crawled through the opening into the outer cave and gathered my few things. It was time to go. Yet I was slow in the gathering and felt reluctant to go.

Suddenly a voice seemed to speak. "Find them!" it said. I turned sharply, my brow furrowed. Had I actually heard a voice? Or was it in my own mind?

Find who?

Itchakomi? Or was I to find someone else? Someone akin to those buried in the inner cave? Had someone spoken? Or had it been been imagination only? No matter. It was time to go.

Slinging my pack and taking up my bow, I went out into the morning.

For a moment I stood still, listening. Every sense alert for possible danger, for it was always nearby. I heard no sound, felt nothing, saw nothing but the quiet forest and the blue sky above.

I moved out, found a trail, and began walking. As always I checked the trail to see what or who had passed. I found only the tracks of a deer and of birds and one place where a snake had crossed the path. I walked on into the morning. This was a new land for me, a land where few had been before me, and perhaps no white man after those in the cave back there.

My mind worked on two levels, as always. One was alert for danger, aware of all my surroundings, missing nothing. The other was my own inner thoughts, and this morning I was puzzled about myself.

Why had I chosen to come west? To explore new lands, I had told myself. To be the first to see, the first to experience. Yet was that all? I was uneasy with the explanation, feeling it was not enough. Was it not simply the desire to be on my own? To experience things for myself? Was I not escaping to myself?

My father and older brothers had been complete and efficient men, grown so by the demands made upon them, so when living with them I had been content to follow, to accept their judgment, and to leave the responsibility to them. I was as capable as any of them, yet lived in their shadows. To go off by myself relieved me of that tendency to go along. It left all the decisions to me and the responsibilities to them.

That might explain my actions in part, an effort to escape to myself.

Yet there was something more. There was an unheard voice that was calling me westward, something beyond my father's urge to cross the far blue mountains. I did want, however, to see what lay beyond the Great River, beyond the Far Seeing Lands, beyond the Shining Mountains. Whatever else there was might be imagination or some strange communication from someone or something. I had no explanations for that. Sakim and I had often talked of that, and my father had spoken of it.

Yance scoffed, and we were amused by his scoffing. Yance was a complete realist. He believed in things he could see, touch, taste, and feel. He had little faith in Lila's second sight or that of my father. He chided them gently or merely shrugged off their accurate predictions. He said, which was undoubtedly true, that our senses picked up vibrations of which we were unaware, warning us of changes in the weather, the approach of enemies, and other such things. He said we were aware on more than one level, of that which drew our immediate attention and of other vibrations or sensings of which our immediate attention took no notice. There was logic in what he said, and we were not inclined to argue.

The air was clear and cool. The summer sun was not yet in the sky. I moved off, carrying with me a good burden of dried and smoked meat. As I walked I chewed on a piece of this.

A squirrel chattered at me irritably. A small flock of parakeets flew up angrily, circling a crow who sat on a bare branch. The crow sat waiting, confident.

A doe started across the trace ahead of me and I froze in position. It paused, staring at me, ears wide, yet as I was not moving and the wind was from her toward me she could not make me out. She would have been an easy kill, yet I did not need meat. We watched each other until suddenly some vagrant shift of the small breeze must have brought my scent, for it bounded into the woods and was gone.

Yet the momentary halt proved a good one, for as I started to turn something flashed in my eyes, something from far away, beyond the long meadow that bordered the woods into which the deer had fled.

A spear blade? What else? Quickly I moved into the brush, careful to disturb no leaf or leave a sign of my passing. I was being followed! Or if not followed, then somebody was within too close a distance, and strangers probably were enemies.

Swiftly, weaving a careful way, I moved off through the thick woods. There was little undergrowth, but the trees, each one large, grew close together. I turned and went uphill, on the theory that someone following a trail will tend to go downhill, since that is the easiest and swiftest way.

Keokotah, I remembered, had seemed convinced we were being followed, but by whom? Kapata remained the most likely one, for who else had reason?

Luckily I came upon a small, rocky stream. There was not much water but the bed was scattered with a multitude of rocks, and I stepped from one to the other, running part of the way, moving easily from rock to rock. At midday I sat down on a rock in the shade of a huge old tree and chewed on another piece of the buffalo jerky.

The rest gave me time to study the crude map drawn for me by Ni'kwana. There had been no time to give it my full attention before this, and I was pleased to find that the western river, where Keokotah and I were to meet, was the very one up which Itchakomi must have traveled. At least, so it appeared. There were other rivers that flowed into the Great River, but this appeared to be the same.

Yet, why not? It was a large river and offered access to the western lands. It was an obvious route.

It was not our way to trust to maps, for few were to be found in the western lands or anywhere in America west of Jamestown, and those few were faulty and mostly drawn by hearsay or guesswork. The Indians we had known had a good sense of country and could often, with a few lines, explain it well.

First I must come to the valley my father had wanted me to find. Had I come straight there I should have been at the valley long since, for it was but a few days travel westward of Shooting Creek, but Keokotah and I had traveled by devious routes, as had I since, partly to reach the cave, partly to throw off pursuit.

I had found no minerals, and we needed lead or

copper as well as sulphur. For this reason I must now travel slower and study the country with greater care, for it was in the vicinity of the valley that we hoped to find what was needed. Yet if necessary we could travel many days to find lead.

Once, years before, my father had been shown a good-sized chunk of lead that had come from the westward. It was from an outcropping not many days from the river toward which I must travel. There might be other sources as well. One reason for our slow travel had been my quest for evidences of such things, although I was far from expert and knew of few indications.

Being alone I felt better. The decisions and responsibilities were mine and I need lean on no one or trust to their judgment. A man who travels with another is only half as watchful as when traveling alone, and often less than half, for a part of his attention is diverted by his companion. Several times I stopped to examine outcroppings of rock, but found nothing of which I could be sure.

Several times I paused to study my back trail but saw nothing to disturb me. I was growing tired and began looking for a place to camp, but a hidden place that would allow me to see any who might approach. The evening was far along before I found a bench back from a creek in a notch of the hills, but I avoided it because there was no back way out.

I finally settled upon a place under a couple of large old trees facing a willow thicket near a stream. Under cover of the willows I could obtain water, and the foliage of the trees would dissipate my smoke.

I went past my camping spot and then doubled back in the stream and went through the willows to the place under the trees. It offered shelter from the wind and rain, a hidden place for my fire, and access to water. Above all it was inconspicuous, a place to be passed by unseen.

My fire was small. In a dish made of bark I fixed a small stew from buffalo meat and a few herbs gathered by the way. With this I ate some cattail roots baked in the ashes of my fire. When the meal was finished and my coffee made of chicory was ready, I carefully put out my small fire.

It would soon be night. My bed was made of cattail rushes and willow leaves and I spread my oilskin on them and covered myself with my blanket. I was tired. It had been a long day. Tomorrow, with luck, I should find my valley.

According to various Indians who knew of it the valley was three or four days travel in length, which might make it anywhere from thirty-six to eighty miles, depending on the Indian and how far he liked to travel in a day.

The night was warm, for since I had left Shooting Creek spring had faded into summer. The trees, just leafing out then, had their leaves now. It seemed just a few days ago that I had left the settlement we called home, but the country changed from day to day and I was lower in altitude here and the weather was warmer.

Where was Keokotah? Had he reached his village? Or did he travel still?

And who was following me, if anybody at all?

Of these things I thought as I lay under the trees. The water rustled, the leaves brushed gently, and occasionally something splashed out in the stream. It was very quiet, very still.

And then I was asleep.

Stars were above me when my eyes opened. I knew I had not slept long, but now I was wide awake.

Something was moving out there in the night. A bear? A panther? It was some large creature.

A snort, a sound of drinking, and then of water dripping. It moved again.

A buffalo . . . no, several buffaloes. I listened, wondering if they had scented me, for they were suddenly still. I could picture them standing, their great, dark heads lifted, nostrils sensing the air, testing it for—

They moved off suddenly in a great rush. Something had frightened them.

There was another long silence and then a rustling as of movement, and I heard someone speak in a language I did not know. Another voice answered him and I caught a word which meant buffalo. There was a brief conversation in which I was sure I recognized a voice, and then they moved off.

How many? Three . . . perhaps four. I waited, listening, but heard no more.

After a while I slept, and it was full daylight when I awakened. For a time I lay still, listening to the morning sounds, placing each. There was nothing more.

Rising, I looked all around and then went down to the stream, making my way through the willows. Listening again, I scooped water in my palm and drank. On the opposite bank there were tracks where the buffalo had come into the water, although some had walked upstream. When frightened they had rushed downstream and out at some other place.

Gathering my things I took my bow and quiver and scouted around carefully. Fifty yards upstream I found tracks. At least five warriors, traveling at night. That was unusual unless they planned a surprise. Were they hunting for me?

That voice? I could not place it, yet there had been a familiar ring. Perhaps only my imagination.

Returning to camp I completed packing my things, tore off a piece of jerky to chew on, and then hesitated, thinking. The Indians seemed to have gone downstream but they might have camped nearby. I sniffed the air, but caught no smell of smoke.

Staying close to the willows I went back upstream, found a thick patch of forest, and went into it, moving quietly, scouting for tracks. I found none.

Beyond the patch of forest lay a wide meadow, and here I did find tracks. Five warriors again, no doubt the same ones. Whenever I could get a distinct print I studied it and filed it away in a corner of my mind for future reference.

The morning was bright and sunlit. From the slight elevation there was a splendid view of forest, meadow, stream, and pool. What a lovely land!

By noon I was traveling over a plateau, forested and still. Twice now I left marks on trees. I knew about what trace my relatives would follow, and now I was back in their area of travel. High on a tree I cut an A with my knife, cutting deep through the bark. The A was my mother's initial and one not likely to be associated with us.

Three miles further I cut another. In each case I cut one side of the A a bit longer to indicate direction. It was an agreed-upon code, but one any of us would have understood after a little thinking.

It might be a year, two years, or twenty before I was followed, but whenever I was followed the route could be traced by a Sackett.

Further along, I cut another A and was about to extend one side of it when looking beyond the trunk of the tree I saw a vast gulf. Stepping around the tree, I halted.

There opened before me a long valley, extending off toward the south as far as I could see. To the north it seemed to end, from where I stood, in a group of low hills. This must be Sequatchie. There were glimpses of a stream running along the bottom. Meadows, trees, it was a fair land.

An hour later I looked down into an elongated bowl, a grassy cove of what must be more than two thousand acres. A quiet, secluded, lovely place!

This was where I would return. This would be my home. I started down a steep game trail and stepped on a fallen log that broke under me. I fell. My leg caught between two deadfalls and I heard a sharp snap. I lay still, trying to catch my breath. I started to move, felt an excruciating stab of pain, and looked down.

I had broken my leg.

9

For a long moment I lay perfectly still, my brain a blank. Then I began to think.

I was alone. I could expect help from no one. If anyone came my way it would be an enemy or a potential enemy, and there were wild beasts that might flee from a man but not from a helpless one. Wolves and cougars were very quick to sense when anything was injured and helpless.

My present position, sprawled on the ground among deadfalls and brush, was impossible. Despite the pain I had to move, I had to do something.

As near as I could see, my broken bone was not far out of line. I had never set a bone, although I had once seen my father do it for an Indian. Hooking my toe under a fallen limb I pulled slightly, and the bone seemed to slip back into place. Backing off from the trap I was in I cut several strips from a green branch and made a rough splint, tying it with rawhide from a small twist I always carried for rigging snares.

Several times I had to stop and lie still, my brow beaded with sweat. Then I would force myself to continue. Every movement brought excruciating pain, but I could not remain where I was. I had no water and no shelter, and very little of the buffalo jerky was left. Yet if I ate carefully there would be enough to sustain me for several days. I tried to recall what Sakim had taught me about broken bones, but beyond what I had done I could remember nothing.

One fact was stark and clear. I would be unable to travel for several weeks. I would miss my meeting with Keokotah. Moreover, even to get where there was water I must improvise some sort of crutch, but there was nothing nearby.

Using my longbow as a staff and taking a good grip on a lower limb of a tree, I managed to pull myself erect. With great care, using the longbow, I moved from tree to tree. In my first view of the grassy cove at the head of Sequatchie I had glimpsed what seemed to be a stream. Perhaps the same one that flowed the length of the valley. It was far away, yet if I could reach it at least one part of my survival would be arranged for. I would have water.

In such a condition, what would my father have done? He would have survived. So would I survive.

The hill was steep but slowly, carefully, I edged my way to the bottom. Here the grass was shoulder high, but among some debris from fallen trees near the base of the cliff I found some sticks, one of them of proper height had a branch that grew out on a slight curve. It would make an admirable crutch until I could fashion something better. I would need it, for there were no trees to cling to in the cove's bottom unless I stayed to the edges, making my journey that much farther.

My leg was badly swollen by now and I had to slit the leg of my buckskin pants. It hurt and I cringed at each step. Twice I startled deer, but they were gone too quickly for me to bring my bow into play, even had I been able.

The sun was low in the sky before I was even halfway to where I believed I must go. Perhaps there was a curve of the stream that was closer but the tall grass prevented me seeing it. Yet fortune suddenly conferred a favor. I found a game trail.

It crossed the cove at an angle different from that I

had been pursuing, but undoubtedly would lead to water. When darkness came I simply sat down. There was no going any further and I was brutally tired. My leg had swollen enormously with the exertion, and when I sat down I simply collapsed. I lay right where I was in the grass, making no effort at a camp. I got a piece of jerky from my once-heavy pack and began chewing on it. Fortunately it was very tough and took a lot of chewing. When I had finished with the jerky I slept, and if wild beasts prowled near me I did not know and scarcely cared.

When I awakened it was broad daylight and the sun was in my face. My leg had swollen to thrice its size and I slit my pants further and rolled the buckskin high, baring my leg. Getting to my feet was a desperate struggle and twice I fell back, each time sending a stab of pain up my leg. Yet at last I reached my feet and once more began hobbling toward the stream.

The skin beneath my arm where my crude crutch rode heaviest was raw. My leg hurt and my back seemed out of kilter. Desperately I wished to sit down but doubted if I could again get to my feet, so I struggled on.

My mouth was dry and I could scarce swallow. I had upon rising licked some of the grass leaves for the dew that was upon them but it was all too little. In all this struggle I had gone but a pitifully small distance, or so it seemed, but doggedly, desperately, I struggled on. That I had a fever, I knew. That my wound might be infected was possible, for the skin had been broken although the bone had not pushed through. Then my crutch went into a gopher hole and I pitched forward to my face in the grass. The pain was almost unbearable.

I lay there, all sprawled out, and then slowly began to pull myself together. I struggled to one knee and then pushed myself erect again. Grimly, I struggled on, and then when I was about to fall from fatigue I heard the rustle of water. There was some low brush and a few scattered trees, and then a grove that seemed to climb the hill.

The creek was there, flowing out of the trees, and

when I stepped back into their shade I saw that the creek came from a cave.

Water and shelter!

There was a big old fallen tree near the entrance that made a perfect seat. Sitting down I shucked my small pack from my shoulders and carefully removed my guns and put them down behind a log with my bow and quiver. There were several broken branches about and a couple of them stout enough to make a decent crutch, but for a few minutes, with the water in sight, I just sat there, not wanting to move.

When I did move I hobbled to the water, scooped up a handful and drank and then drank again. It was only three steps back to the log, and I went there, sat down, and dozed.

The sun was warm, the afternoon well along, but I had water and I had the cave. Deep inside I had a feeling that I was going to make it. I hoped I would. So many plans, so many dreams, and all ahead of me.

And a woman I had promised to find.

Just before sundown I looked into the cave. It was large enough, and it was dry but for the place where the water ran. I crawled into a corner and slept.

When morning came I got outside to my log and took stock of my surroundings. There was very little strength in me. I needed rest, treatment, and a food supply. If I was careful I had enough of the buffalo jerky left to get me through the week. By then I might be stronger. Sitting on the log I tried to plan my next step. There might be plants about that I could eat. From where I sat I recognized two or three. There were seeds I could gather, and I must get all within the area around me.

The opening of the cave was fairly hidden from any who did not approach closely, but activity was sure to attract the attention of anyone living nearby. Yet I had seen no signs of any Indian camp, although it was a sheltered and logical spot.

Again I dozed, or perhaps I just passed out. I did not know. My head buzzed and I felt lost and vaguely too warm. I peered at the plants but lacked the energy to rise and gather them. Fumbling with my pack I got out another piece of the precious jerky. I took a bite, and then with sudden awareness I reached behind me and moved my guns to a place atop my pack to keep them from the damp ground. They were my most precious possessions, not only for what they could do but because they were given me by my father.

"Take them," he had said. "You understand them well. Someday they may save your life." He had paused, turning them in his hands to savor their beauty, their balance. "He who made these was skilled. He worked long and lovingly upon them. If what we have heard is true he staked his future upon them."

The sun was warm and pleasant. I did not wish to move. My great, swollen leg was heavy and uncomfortable. Yet if I was to survive, I must move.

Slowly, with great effort, I got to my feet and limped to the water. It was painful to get down to drink, but I succeeded. Then I noticed some watercress growing nearby. I gathered some from the water and ate it. Then I took my guns and limped back to the cave. Suddenly, fearing what might happen if I became unconscious again, I hid the guns under some dead wood in a corner of the cave.

On the following day I succeeded in setting several snares. I had seen rabbits about and squirrels. I gathered some seeds from the edge of the forest. My leg was badly swollen, so I made a bark dish in which I boiled water, and taking a bit of buckskin cut from my pant leg I used it as a cloth to bathe my leg with hot water. If it would do any good I had no idea but it felt better afterward.

That night I slept better and in the morning heated more water, not only to bathe my swollen leg but to bathe my face and hands. I changed the splints on my leg and did a better job. Now what I needed was meat. If only—

There was a barely visible track near one of my snares! A moccasin track, a foot larger than my own.

For a moment I stood very still. My bow and my quiver of arrows were in the cave. I had only my knife, for when using the crutch I could not carry water back from the stream and carry the bow as well.

Was I being watched? Leaning down I dipped my bark container into the stream and then straightened up. Using my crutch I hobbled back to the log, near which I had a small fire. With two forked sticks and a bar across them I had rigged a place to suspend my bark dish above the fire. To prevent the dish from burning I must be sure the flames did not reach above the water level.

I hesitated. Should I go into the cave for my other weapons and so betray my hiding place? For I doubted anyone had discovered the cave's existence, hidden behind trees and brush as it was.

Desperately, I wanted my weapons, but I controlled myself. Someone might be watching, but I must seem not to be aware of it.

Shaving a small corner of jerky into water I added some bits from cattails. These were pieces cut from where the sprout emerges from the root. I added some watercress and some of the inner bark of a poplar. This stew I concocted was nothing resembling what a skilled cook might have created, but it was all food, and I needed whatever I could get.

Working about the fire I contrived to get on the back side of the log, using it as a work table on which to prepare my food, but ready to drop behind it if necessary.

Every move was painful and clumsy. There was no chance of swift movement, but I tried to use what cover there was from surrounding trees and brush to make myself as difficult a target as possible. Whether I was observed or not I did not know, but must carry on as if an enemy was out there, waiting.

When my stew was ready I ate it slowly, dipping it from the bark pot with a spoon shaved from a piece of wood, and a good spoon it was. Most of those used at Shooting Creek had been made by ourselves.

As I ate I considered my position. How long it would take for my broken leg to knit, I did not know. Wounds had a way of healing much faster in this mountain country.

Very few festered or became troublesome, in part because of the fresh air, the scarcity of dirt, and the simple food. Sakim had told me that in the high mountains of Asia they rarely had trouble with festering wounds.

At least a month. I had that idea in mind, and it might be wrong, but I'd have to plan for at least that long and probably longer. Which meant I would need food. I would need meat.

The last of the buffalo meat, which Keokotah and I had carefully avoided using, as it was dried and smoked and would keep, would carry me but a few more days.

Unless I could make a kill of a fairly large animal I was faced with starvation. So far my snares had brought nothing, nor could I expect much from them. Whatever I caught would be a help, but the herbs and plants I could find within the range I could cover with my broken leg would not last long. I was under no illusions as to hunting and gathering. I had practiced it and had known Indians who did. It needed a lot of walking and searching to keep even one person alive.

I had wished to be alone, to trust to myself only, but I had not bargained for this.

Yet as I slowly ate my stew, savoring every taste and taking my time, I considered the edible plants I had glimpsed. The trouble was that with my crutch I could do little, and my range was limited. Of course, I told myself, I would come to be more adept with using the crutch. It would become easier.

The necessity for keeping my presence hidden was another factor. It was not easy to search for food and hide at the same time. The floor of the cove was covered with tall grass, grass that would move as I passed through it, betraying my presence. To work around the edges under the trees would be more difficult. Yet that was what I must do. I dare not be caught out in the middle of the cove without a place where I could fort up if need be.

Behind the log I prepared a bed for myself. I had to hope they, whoever "they" were, would not know of the cave. I listened, straining my ears for any sound, pausing to listen from moment to moment as I worked. Finally, I lay down and took a short nap. It was coming on to dusk when I awakened.

I made coffee from chicory root, speculating on how quickly the plant had gone native. Indians had told me it was unknown to their older people, but had first been seen in what the Spanishmen called Florida.

Several attempts to establish western bases in the Carolinas had been made by the Spanish, and at least one outpost had been built and occupied by Juan Pardo for a time. It was very possible he had tried plantings of vegetables and herbs, but birds, the winds, and wild animals could easily have played a part.

My fire was small, the fuel dry wood, and I had placed the fire under a tree so the smoke would dissipate in rising through the foliage. The fire itself would have filled a small cup, no more.

The chicory tasted good, and when it was ready I carefully put out my fire.

The longing for home was in me and I thought of Shooting Creek and the good food that was there. I thought of Ma, away in England, and of Kin-Ring, my eldest brother, now head of the family. He would handle it well, for he was an able man. I eased my broken leg, and tried to find a more comfortable position. If they knew the fix I was in they'd come running. That was the Sackett way, but they did not know, and could not know, and unless I used my head I would die here, in this place.

Suddenly I decided I must have my weapons, even if I betrayed the cave. I must—

He was standing over me then, a spear poised for a thrust. *Kapata!*

And three others.

It was light enough for me to see his features, and to know that he meant to kill me. I had my knife, but I could not move toward him.

Kapata raised the spear.

"No!" One of the others lifted a hand. "Ni'kwana has spoken! He is not to be harmed! Ni'kwana has said this."

"Bah! I—"

The warrior lifted a spear toward Kapata. "Take the skin, but do not kill!" That much I understood although what followed I did not. There was a moment of fierce argument, but the others joined in against him. They had followed to get the crude map Ni'kwana had given me.

One of the Indians stepped over to where my pack lay. It had been there for the food and the chicory, and the map was in the pack. Quickly, he dumped it all out, picking up the map. He shook it at Kapata and made a move to go.

Grumbling, Kapata made as if to follow, but then he stopped. He looked at me and then kicked my leg. Agonizing pain shot through me but I did not wince. I merely stared.

"Coward!" I spoke in Cherokee. "If I were on my feet—"

"I would kill you!"

Deliberately, he stooped and picked the pieces of buffalo jerky from the ground, the few, carefully hoarded bits of food to keep me from starvation.

One of the others spoke. I could make out but little of what he said but something about my leg, and leaving me to die. Then in Cherokee he said, wishing me to understand, "Let him die. Ni'kwana said no kill, so leave him. and he will die."

They walked away without a backward glance and I was alone, and alive.

I had a broken leg, and my last food was gone.

What now, Jubal Sackett? What now?

Cool was the wind. I huddled against the log as against another human and tugged my blanket around me. My leg throbbed and the night wind stirred the leaves.

10

When morning came there were no stars, only low clouds and a hint of rain. My leg felt heavy and when I struggled to sit up there was pain. I sat, half leaning against the fallen tree. My head throbbed with a dull, heavy ache and my mouth was parched.

My carefully hoarded buffalo jerky was gone. Now I must hunt, no matter the risk. Today was not good for hunting, for most animals would be lying up. Knowing there would be rain, they would stay in their beds unless starving, and there was no chance of that now. The grass was green and there were spring flowers everywhere.

All about was beauty, but the dull gray of the clouds was in my brain also. I felt heavy and tired. I had slept badly.

Slowly, I tugged myself into a better position, ever careful of my leg. I forced myself to think, to consider. First, a fire, and some chicory. A hot cup might help.

The forest was silent. The stream rustled along, making no unfamiliar sound. Hunting today would be all but useless. True, I might startle a deer from its bed, but I could never get my crutch dropped and my bow in action in time for a kill.

After the chicory I would check the snares. One thing

at a time, and I must fight despair. I must survive. After all, I was my father's son, and he had survived worse than this. Grasping a root, I pulled myself to sit on the fallen tree. Then for the first time I saw my crutch. It was broken.

Deliberately it had been placed against the log, and then stepped on and snapped. I stared at it and then looked carefully around. As always in the forest there was debris, fallen branches, slabs of bark hanging down from fallen trees, leaves and brush. I must make a new crutch, and I must make it now, or I could not move. First, a fire.

Carefully I took some shredded bark, a few broken twigs from the lower trunks of nearby trees, and some leaves from a dead branch and put together the makings of a small fire. With flint and steel I struck a spark, yet on this morning my hands were clumsy and I must have tried a dozen times before a spark landed in the leaves and shredded bark. It caught, smoked a little, and went out. Again I tried, and still again. Finally, when I was tiring from my efforts, a flame mounted and I added fuel.

Hitching myself along the tree I then rolled over and, dragging my injured leg, crawled to the stream, where I dipped up water. Inching along, I crawled back to my fire, rerigged the forked sticks and bar from which I had suspended my bark dish, and shaved chicory from the dried root into the dish.

When I had finished I was exhausted. My injury, the scarcity of food, and my exhausted condition had left me with little strength. Hitching myself into a sitting position against the fallen tree I rested, staring at my fire. From time to time I added sticks to the blaze.

The loss of the map, if such it could be called, was no great problem. From boyhood we had traveled after only a glance or two at a hastily drawn sketch in the earth or wet sand to indicate streams, paths, and mountains. Every detail of the map was in my mind and I knew where I must go and what I must do. If I got out of this.

The worst of it was that I would miss Keokotah. What would he do when I did not appear? Shrug, no doubt, and go on about his business. Traveling in wild country is never easy and many accidents can befall one. He knew that better than I.

Yet I had come to like him. We were still wary of one another, and I particularly, for the thinking of an Indian is not like that of a white man. We grow from different roots, different beliefs, and different customs. But he was a strong, courageous man and a good companion.

One is strongest when one is alone. Whenever there is a companion there is a certain reliance placed upon him, one's attention is shared, one leaves part of the alertness to him. This is a danger. Yet traveling alone is also ever dangerous, and even the most careful man can have an accident, as I had proved.

When the chicory was hot, I sipped it slowly. My stomach was hollow with hunger, but the hot drink helped, and I felt better. Adding fuel to keep some coals alive I used a tree limb to pull myself erect. First, a crutch.

Yet all the broken limbs I could see were twisted or rotted, and nothing on nearby trees was such as I needed. Using a shorter stick as a cane I hitched along to check my snares.

Nothing in the first, nor in the second. For a time then, I rested. I lay on my back on the grass staring up at the sky through the leaves. I must not get too far from shelter, for the sky looked more than ever as if there would be rain. Yet tired as I was it was not in me to lie still when there was so much to be done. I drank from the stream and then using whatever handholds I could reach on deadfalls and trees, I struggled erect. My leg was stiff because of the splints, and walking with a cane was almost impossible.

Again I studied the ground, the nearby trees, everywhere, to find a branch suitable for a crutch. Then I found one.

The branch was long and straight and still a living branch, for which I was grateful. Green wood is much easier to cut than that which is dead and seasoned. With my knife I cut a notch near the tree trunk and then cut it deeper, working to both sides. Then I broke off the branch and cut loose what remained. Then I found a bent branch that I cut from the tree to make the top of my crutch. Now I must return for the rawhide string I had used in tying the piece to the top of my former crutch.

It needed an hour for me to return the few hundred yards to my camp, and another few minutes to fashion my crutch. This was my third and by far the best. The first had been merely a branch found by chance, the second somewhat better. If I remained crippled longer I might become quite skillful. God save me!

Returning I found a bed of saxifrage lettuce, and picked as many leaves as I could find, chewing on some of them as I made my way to camp.

My coals were still warm and I nourished them back to life, ate some more of the leaves, and rested. I was exhausted and my leg hurt. The saxifrage, while it gave me something to chew and was said to be nourishing, did not satisfy.

Crawling into the cave, dragging my leg behind me, I recovered my bow and arrows, leaving the guns where they lay. If I could not stalk a deer, I could at least wait where one might come en route to water. The chance was slight, yet I must have meat and it was better than lying here where nothing would come.

Nearby was a meadow, and deer must cross it going to the stream. The grass was tall, yet there were places where it had been flattened by wind or rolling animals.

Using my new crutch I hobbled out to a large old tree and sat down to wait. I judged my distance carefully and sighted several times at openings from which deer might come. Then I settled down to wait.

The sun was still high and I dozed, waiting. I could expect no deer until after sundown, although there was always a possibility. At that time they would be feeding down toward water. They would drink, browse a little, and feed back to where they wished to bed down.

Once, lying still and resting, I thought I heard a faint whispering of leaves as of something moving among them, but when I sat up cautiously and looked around I saw nothing. Nonetheless, I was disturbed. I slipped off the thong that held my knife in place.

I was hungry. More than that, I was starving. I had eaten too little in the days before breaking my leg, and even less since.

Just before me was a faint game trail down which deer and possibly other animals had come to drink. It was upon this I placed my hope. Sitting up, I pulled myself back against the trunk of a good-sized tree, a position from which I could see anything emerging from the woods. I placed my quiver at hand and drew one arrow out for my bow. Another I placed close by in the event I missed or one was not good enough.

From the position I was in, using the longbow was difficult, but it was my only chance. I waited, dozing a little as the time was still early. Suddenly I was wide awake.

Something had moved near me!

Carefully, I looked all around. I saw nothing, heard nothing.

Something moved close by me. My eyes turned and looked directly into the yellow eyes of a giant cat.

A panther!

It was crouched, watching me. It was on my right, not thirty feet away, and there was no doubt as to its intentions. Had it been on my left loosing an arrow would have been easy, but I had to turn to my right, hitching my injured leg around, turning my whole body to face it. I wouldn't have a chance.

The cat's tail was slowly twitching. I saw the shoulder muscles bunch. I turned sharply, feeling a stab of anguish in my leg, and I loosed an arrow just as the panther leaped. Then I fell.

Turning sharply as I had I lost the support of the tree. I fell headlong to the ground, losing hold on my bow. Yet my fall was fortunate, for the panther overleaped. Spinning swiftly, it was at me with a snarl of fury.

As I fell I had drawn my knife and as the beast leaped

at me I drove sharply up with the knife. It cut into the cat's soft belly to the hilt.

Claws tore at me, jaws reached for my head. I stabbed again and then again. I knew the claws were tearing me. The teeth ripped my scalp, I felt the cat's hot breath and I swung my left fist into its ribs.

The cat sprang away, gasping. I could see blood along a shoulder where my arrow had cut the skin. The cat was bleeding, but maddened by pain and bloodlust it wanted only to kill.

Desperately, I rolled over and as the cat leaped I rolled over again and came up sitting. The cat knocked me back to the ground, its teeth going for my throat. With my left hand I grabbed the loose skin of its neck and we fought, desperately, the cat to reach my throat, I to hold him back. At the same time I swung again with my knife.

The blade sank deep, and as it did so I turned my left fist which gripped the loose skin, turned it so my knuckles pressed hard against the cat's neck. A paw came up, clawing at my hand. It ripped the buckskin of my jacket, tore the flesh on my forearm, but to let go was to die. I stabbed again and again with the knife.

It was ripping with one hindleg, but the fierce claws were digging the earth, not me. There were only short, convulsive movements from the other hind foot.

I stabbed again, and it seemed the struggles grew weaker. Again and again—suddenly I threw the cat from me.

It lay there, bloody and exhausted, staring at me with all the insane fury such a beast contained.

The grass and leaves were spattered with blood. Some of mine was mingled with it, but my knife had stabbed deep, again and again. The cat stared, tried to move, and then fell over. Once more it tried to come to itself and failed to rise. The wild eyes glared their hatred, and the beast died.

My one good leg was ripped and raw, with deep lacerations. My arm had been bitten, when I did not recall, but my forearms and shoulder had also been clawed.

My scalp was also torn by teeth, and a string hung near my eye. Yet I was conscious and aware.

Whatever had been my troubles before, they were more than doubled now. The claws and fangs of a wild beast are poisoned from the fragments of decaying meat around them. I needed to get to the stream, cleanse myself, and try to patch up this poor creature I had become.

Taking my bow and quiver, I started to crawl, and then I stopped. I had come for meat, and I was leaving meat behind me. A Catawba whom we knew had once said that panther meat was best of all, and Yance, who had eaten it on one of his forays into the deep woods, agreed. So I peeled back the hide and cut a fair-sized chunk from the panther. Then, on my feet and with my crutch and bow, I hobbled back to my camp.

Falling on the ground I crawled to the stream and lay in its shallow waters near the edge, letting the cool water run slowly over me. And when I looked up, there were stars. My fingers dug into the mud of the stream and I plastered my wounds with it.

Weak from exhaustion and loss of blood I crawled from the stream applying more mud to my wounds. Somewhere I had been told mud was useful, but I did not remember why. I cared only that it was here and that somehow the bleeding must be stopped.

Crawling to my bed I pulled the blanket over me and lay shivering. Whether I simply lost consciousness or slept I do not know, but when I opened my eyes I fumbled some sticks into the fire before passing out again.

It was daylight when my eyes opened. A few tendrils of smoke lifted from my coals and I coaxed them to flame once more, dipped water into the bark dish, and suspended it above the fire. I cut a piece of the meat and dropped it in with some other things gathered when crawling about.

After a long time I opened my eyes and the water had boiled down leaving a kind of mush of my stew. With my wooden spoon I managed a few mouthfuls before passing out again.

There was a long while then when I fought wild battles with gigantic cats, when buffalo stampeded over me and Kapata returned with his spear. It was delirium, and I knew it, and from time to time I crawled to the stream and drank. Once I made chicory coffee and then passed out still again.

Once I chewed on raw meat, and finally I slept, a deep, long sleep almost like the sleep of death.

In it I felt gentle hands—my wounds were being treated and I was home again.

Consciousness returned and my eyes opened. I was clearly awake and there was no delirium. I turned my head. An Indian sat by the fire, eating.

It was Keokotah.

11

"One leg no good," Keokotah said, and took another bite from the meat in his hands.

"I fell," I explained.

"Not you." He pointed into the brush where I had fought the panther. "Him." He chewed for a minute. "No catch deer, catch you."

"You mean that cat had a bad leg?" I struggled to sit up.

He motioned for me to be still. "You stay. You much scratch. I fix."

With gentle fingers I felt of my wounds. Where the flesh had been torn by the panther's talons my wounds were bound with some kind of poultice. It had not been a dream, then. My wounds had been treated. "I'm obliged," I said. "Are you a medicine man, too?"

He chuckled and gave me a wry look. "No medicine man. All know." He showed me the slender trunk of a young pine no thicker than two of my fingers. Then he indicated the inner bark of the plum. He had pounded them together with some wild cherry bark also, boiled the concoction, and made a poultice.

"You no come. I know something wrong. I come to

look." He pointed. "I find him. He dead. Some meat gone, so I look for you."

He had killed a deer, and he made a broth of the meat, bone marrow, and some herbs. I ate it slowly, savoring every bit. Then I was tired and I lay back, resting and willing to rest.

"Kapata was here?" said Keokotah.

When I had told my story he shrugged. "I find tracks. They go to Great River." He chewed in silence and then glanced at me again. Then he placed my bow and quiver close at hand and lay down and went to sleep.

It was night and I was tired, but no longer wished to sleep. Keokotah had come back to look for me, and a lucky thing. Could I have survived? I think so. I knew of herbs to treat wounds. I could have survived, yet he had returned. He was my friend.

Listening to the night I heard no sounds but those natural to the forest and the night—only the wind in the long grass of the cove and the chuckling sound from the stream near the cave mouth. I closed my eyes but not to sleep, only to think.

When I was up and about, we must move with speed. Kapata would seek Itchakomi and might find her before we could. He was a hard, stubborn man and not to be frustrated by any woman, yet from what Ni'kwana had said this was no ordinary woman. Still, we must hurry. I would deliver the message from Ni'kwana and protect her from Kapata if that were necessary, and then go on about my business.

It was a new land out there, and I wished to see it. I wanted to wander down the long hills, seek out the wooded canyons, follow its running streams. I wanted to live from the country, breathe the air of the high mesas, and climb where the streams were born from under the slide rock.

Now I must become well quickly. It was no time to be lying here. I finished what remained of the broth. I would need strength for the bow, strength for walking the long miles, strength for the paddle of my canoe.

Did Kapata have a canoe? Perhaps not. In that might lie an advantage.

Wind bent the tall grass, stirred among the leaves, fluttered the small flame of my fire. I closed my eyes. A morning would come.

Gently, I eased my broken leg. I could manage that leg in a canoe. I would have to sit and not kneel as I most often did, but the bone would knit as well in a canoe as lying here.

How many days had passed? I had kept no record, had only the vaguest idea. I had slept and awakened, but how long had I slept? Was I not unconscious a part of the time? No matter. It was time to move on and I would move, if only a mile a day.

How long had Keokotah been with me? Again I had no idea and when I asked he merely shrugged.

Yet for two days longer I rested, gathering strength, moving about the camp, making a better crutch, planning our move. Of one thing I was sure. Someday I would return to this place, to this grassy cove.

There was a trail that led through it, and Keokotah was convinced the stream in the cave was the same that issued far below in the Sequatchie valley. I had seen but little of the valley, yet it was a place I could come to love. It was a place where we Sacketts belonged.

On a tree near the cave I carved an A, but this time I carved an arrow beneath it, pointing down.

The first day we traveled but five miles before I tired too greatly to go on, but on the second day we reached my canoe.

The river called Tenasee flowed south, described a great curve, and turned back to the north to empty into the river the Iroquois called Ohio. There was, Keokotah warned, a great whirlpool not far south of where we were. Many canoes had been lost there and Indians drowned. Keokotah had sat on the cliffs above and watched canoes go through or into the Suck, as it was sometimes called. It was a place where Indians said "the mountains look at each other." The waters above were about a half mile wide, but where they entered the deep gorge they were compressed into a space of less than seventy yards.

"Can we go through?" I asked.

Keokotah shrugged. "It is best to hold to the south," he said. "I have seen some canoes go through."

There was a whirlpool where boats were seized and swept round and round, and some were carried into the depths, whence only bits and pieces came to the surface.

We beached our canoe above the narrow river, and on a small point of land among some willows we ate and slept. Keokotah had not known chicory before but was developing a taste for it. I shaved some of the dried and roasted root into a bark dish and made enough for each of us.

It was in my mind to collect more of the root, for I had seen less and less of it and doubted it would grow beyond the Great River, where not many white men had been.

We rested there above the gorge, and at night when all was still we could hear the muffled roar of the waters below us. It was a dangerous place for a man to go, even more so with my crippled leg. If I had to swim against a powerful current . . .

Well, one must take some chances, and to go west and not to follow the river would be hard indeed.

When evening came I paused by the water before going to sleep, and stood there facing westward toward the unknown lands.

What mystery lay waiting to be solved? What strange lands to be seen? I might well be the first white man other than the men of De Soto to see these lands. Even he had seen but little, and the Far Seeing Lands beyond . . . who knew of them?

Even the Indians had not seen most of those lands. Water was scarce and a man could not carry enough. Someday men would come with horses that could carry them far out on those wide, mysterious plains.

Were there buffalo there? Could a man break a buffalo to ride? The idea seemed ridiculous, but it stayed with me. Why not, if one was captured young and taught from birth to be friendly to a man and if the man fed and cared for it and broke it gradually to the idea?

When morning came we put the canoe into the water and shoved off, but no sooner were we in the current than we felt the difference. The river seemed to have taken on a new power. The water was dark and swift and the canoe shot forward. There was no visible turbulence, no white water, just a sense of rushing power that swept us along. Keokotah, who was in the bow, turned once to glance at me and then gave all his attention to the canoe.

Faster and faster we went until suddenly the canoe shot around a point of rocks and plunged into a rocky defile where the river hurled itself against the rock walls, against great boulders, throwing water high into the air. Keokotah was a master, and crippled though I was I had great skill at handling canoes both in rivers and on the sea. The river roared and foamed about us. Dead ahead was a mighty shelf of rock fallen from the cliff above and we were thrown at it with what seemed tremendous force, and then the water whipped us away just as we seemed about to crash. Our eyes were blinded by splashing water as spray was hurled like stones into our faces. We dipped a paddle here and there, fighting for the south edge, which had seemed safest to Keokotah watching from above.

Suddenly the great whirlpool was just before us, and we whipped around it, but riding the high side toward the south we were flung free and in a moment were sliding downstream at a faster speed than I had ever traveled in a canoe. Then we were in swift but quiet water. Drenched in cold sweat I looked at Keokotah, but his back was squarely toward me and I could not judge his fear, had there been any.

We were in a deep canyon and found no place to escape the river. Chewing jerked venison we traveled on. It was after sundown when we came upon an island. Easing behind it, we found a small beach of gravel where he could draw up our canoe.

We prepared no food, nor did we talk. Exhausted, we

rolled in our blankets and slept, and did not awaken until the sun was high.

There followed days of traveling the river. We fished, we hunted, we slept on the banks, and twice we had brief fights with strange Indians, but my longbow carried yards further than could their bows. In the first encounter, the Indians drew off after a man was wounded before they were within bow range. On the second occasion there was an ineffectual exchange of arrows, and then our lighter and faster canoe drew away from them.

We saw game everywhere—numerous deer and occasional small herds of buffalo. For mile upon mile we saw no human life or signs of any. Several times we saw bears fishing at the edges of rivers. They ignored us for the most part, one standing up to see us the better. After looking us over and deciding we were of no consequence it went back to scooping fish from the water.

The river turned north, and after a while we entered the Ohio, a much larger river. There was an Indian village near where the Tenasee entered the Ohio but we passed it at night. Dogs barked and a few Indians came from their lodges to look about. We were far out on the water and they saw us not. Some miles further we camped the night on a sandbar covered with willows, building a small fire for the smoke to keep the mosquitoes away, and at daybreak we were in the canoe once more. Ahead of us lay the Great River, which some Indians called the Mississippi.

My leg was now much better, and soon I would discard the crutch. Whenever possible I moved without it, trying to get the muscles working again.

Having no experience with broken limbs I had no idea when to get rid of the crutch.

The Mississippi, if such it was called, proved a different river. It wound and twisted through the land, carrying much debris, huge trees torn from its banks, once even a cut board, which puzzled us indeed. The other river for which we sought would be several days travel away to the south. How far I did not know.

Keokotah had been there, of course. He had waited

there for me and had come looking only when he was sure something had gone wrong.

We camped on the Great River, on a sandy island partly made up of gigantic old trees that had drifted together, moored to the bottom by their own roots and branches. These were drifted trees from somewhere far upstream. Debris and mud had gathered about them, and an island had been created of several acres. Willows had grown up and some other larger stuff had started. No doubt the island would remain until some spring flood tore it loose and scattered its bits and pieces.

Our fire was going in a sheltered place behind great roots, and fish were broiling.

I said to Keokotah, "The Englishman? How did he come to be with you?"

Direct questions rarely brought a response. He shrugged, and stripped the backbone from a fish in his hands. "He good man." He glanced at me. "Talk, all the time talk."

"To whom?"

"To me. He talk to me. He say I am his brother." Keokotah chewed a moment. "He come in canoe. Like yours. He not a big man. Smaller than you, but strong."

After a few minutes of silence he added, "He cough, much cough. I think he sick. I say so."

The fire crackled, and I added sticks. "He say he not well and he say, 'You wrong. No sick. I die soon.'

"He look much at small packet." He shaped a rectangle with his fingers. "Many leaves sewn at the back. The leaves have small signs on them. He looks at them and sometimes he smiles or speaks from them. I ask what it is and he say this is *book* and it speaks to him.

"I listen, no hear it speak."

"The signs in this book spoke to him," I said. "When you look at a trail in the morning, it speaks to you of who passed in the night. It was so with him."

"Ah? It could be so." He looked at me. "You have book?"

"At my home there were many books," I said, "and I

miss them very much." I tapped my head. "Many books up here. Like you remember old trails, I remember books. Often I think of what the books have said to me."

"What do books say?"

"Many things, in many ways. You sit by the knees of your old men and hear their tales of warpath and hunt. In our books we have made signs that tell such stories, not only of our grandfathers but of their grandfathers.

"We put upon leaves the stories of our great men, and of wars, but the best books are those that repeat the wisdom of our grandfathers."

"The Englishman's book was like that?"

"I do not know what book he had, but you said he read from the book. Do you remember what he read?"

"What he reads sings. I think he has medicine songs, but he say, 'Only in a way.' He speaks of the 'snows of yesteryear.'"

"François Villon," I said.

"What?"

"That line was written by a French poet, a long, long time ago."

"French? He say Frenchmans his enemy!"

"That was probably right," I said, "but that would not keep him from liking his poetry. Did you never sing the songs of another tribe?"

He started to say no and then shrugged. "We change them. Anyway, they were our songs once . . . I think."

"My leg is better. Tomorrow I shall walk without a crutch."

"Better you walk," Keokotah said. "I think much trouble come. I think we have to fight soon."

We slept, and once I awakened in the night. Our fire was down to coals, and above us the stars had gone. The air smelled like rain and I thought of us alone in all that vast and almost empty land.

It was a lonely, eerie feeling. Alone . . . all, all alone!

I drew my blanket around my shoulders and listened to the rustling of the river.

It was a long time before I was again asleep.

12

Now I made ready my pistols. I did not wish to use them but the need might be great. My bow was ever beside me, an arrow ever ready.

Endlessly wound the river along its timbered banks, brushing the roots of leaning trees, heavy with foliage. Dead trees, uprooted far upstream, were a danger to birchbark canoes, and at no time dared we relax. Around each bend, and the twists and turns were many, might lie enemy Indians or some obstruction to rip our bottom out.

Yet there was beauty everywhere and we were lonely on the river. The forest was dark and deep with shadows where cypress trees were festooned with veils of Spanish moss. Water oak, hickory, tupelo gum, and many other trees clustered the banks, and hummingbirds danced above the water, opalescent feathers catching the light as if they played with their own beauty.

We startled a flock of ducks, and Keokotah killed one with an arrow. We lived on and off the river, catching fish, killing wood pigeons and geese. Often we saw bears, but they seemed more curious than aggressive. Ours was an easy life.

"No mans here," Keokotah suggested.

"Sometimes it is better so."

He threw me a quick glance over his shoulder, a glance of agreement. Perhaps that was why Keokotah traveled, to be alone with all this, or almost alone. How long would it remain so? Knowing the driving, acquisitive people from whom I came, I did not give it long. We were among the first and the most fortunate. A man might travel forever here, living easily off the country, untrammeled and free.

"The Englishman? You knew him long?"

He held a hand above the water. "I am no higher when he come. I am a man when he die."

This surprised me, for I had not realized he had been with them so long. This was a mystery. Why would an educated, intelligent man choose to live his life away from all he knew? And how had he come there in the first place?

"It is good to have a friend."

He made no reply, but after a few minutes he said, "It bad. No good for me."

"No good to have a friend? But that's—"

"I ver' small. He tell stories. I like stories. No stories of coyote. No stories of owl. Stories of men in iron who fight on horseback." He paused. "What is horse?"

Of course, he had never seen a horse. "It is an animal. Larger than an elk. It has no horns. Men ride them."

"Ride?"

"Sit astride of them and travel far."

"He has long tail? Two ears . . . so?" He held up two fingers.

"That's it."

"I have seen him. Run ver' fast."

"You've seen a *horse*? But that could not be, you—!" I stopped in time. There had been that other day when he spoke of what could only be an elephant, but with long hair. I had made him angry then. "Where did you see it?"

"Many." He gestured off to the south. "I kill young one. Eat him." He looked at me to see if I believed. "Only one toe. Ver' hard."

I'd be damned. I'd be very damned. Horses here? But then, the story had it that when De Soto died his men built boats and went down the river. What did they do with their horses? If they had turned them loose they might well have gone wild. And the Spanish were inclined to ride stallions, using mares or mules for pack animals.

Horses . . . now wouldn't that be something! If we could catch and break a couple of horses—

If a man had something to ride, those plains in the Far Seeing Lands might not seem so vast.

Our canoe glided smoothly upon the waters of the Mississippi and as night came on we held closer to the western shores. Once we saw a thin smoke but kept well into the stream, for we would find no friends here. At night we camped on a muddy point and killed a water moccasin as we landed. It was a big snake.

Keokotah puzzled me. That the Kickapoo were wanderers we had learned from the Cherokees, but I sensed something else in him. Had his boyhood teacher been too good? Had the lonely Englishman taught his pupil too well? Had the Englishman's teaching created a misfit, as I was?

The thought came unbidden, unwanted, unexpected. Yet was I not a misfit, too? Had not Sakim's teaching given me ideas I might never have had?

Kin-Ring and Yance were better fitted for survival in the New World than I. Yance perhaps best of all, for he asked no questions. He accepted what he found and dealt with it in the best way he could. He lived with his world and had no thought of changing it. If a tree got in the way of his plowing he cut it down. If an Indian tried to kill him, he killed the Indian and went on about his business. Kin-Ring was much the same, although Kin was a planner, a looker-ahead.

Sakim had been a philosopher and a scientist in his own way, and like those of his time and country his interests had extended into all things. He had questions to ask and answers to seek. He had learning to do, as I had.

Keokotah had a restless mind. The Englishman had

aroused something in him that took him away from his people. I began to see that his thinking was no longer theirs.

We were strange ones, Keokotah and I, but the result was less for me than for him. The Indian peoples I had known belonged to clans, and the clans demanded that each member conform. The Indian seemed to have lived much as he had for hundreds of years, and now here and there an Englishman, a Scotsman, a Frenchman was coming among them with disturbing new weapons, new ideas. Keokotah was a victim of change. His Englishman had dropped a pebble into the pool of his thinking, and who knew where the ripples would end?

"Big village soon." Keokotah pointed ahead of us. "Quapaw." He swept a hand to include the country we were in and where we had come from. "Osage. Ver' tall mans." His hands measured a distance of a foot or more. "Taller than me."

Six and a half or seven feet tall? It was a lot. By signs he indicated they were slightly stooped and had narrow shoulders.

"No good for us. Kickapoo fight him."

The village was on the eastern shore so we hugged the western, watching for the mouth of the Arkansas River, which would soon appear. It flowed into the Mississippi from the northwest and despite its flow of water could be easily missed because of the bayous and convolutions of the Mississippi.

According to Keokotah the Quapaw were allied to or a part of the Osage people, but were inclined to be more friendly than the Osage, who were very jealous of their lands along the river.

At dusk we killed a deer.

Night came suddenly to the river. The shadows under the trees merged and became one, the day sounds ended and the night sounds began, tentatively at first. Bullfrogs spoke loudly in the night, and some large thing splashed in the water. "Alligator," Keokotah said, "a big one."

Alligators here? It could be. We often saw them in

Carolina, and Yance had seen many when he went south to trade with the Spanish for horses.

The thought of our flimsy canoe with alligators about was not a pleasant one.

He made a motion for silence and began dipping his paddle with great care. The canoe glided through the dark, glistening water. There was a smell of rotting wood and vegetation from the shore. Once, on a fallen tree lying in the water we passed only the length of a paddle from a huge bear. He was as startled as we, but we slid past in the dark water and he gave only a surprised grunt.

It was very still but for the sounds from the forest and the soft rustle of water. In the distance and across the river we heard the beat of drums and occasionally a shrill yell. Then a large island came between us and the village.

"Soon," Keokotah whispered.

Several long minutes passed. Peering into the darkness of the western shore I saw nothing but a wall of blackness where the trees were. The air was damp and still. The current was strong.

We felt the movement of water before we saw it. There was a push against the right side of the canoe, thrusting us toward the middle of the stream.

"Now," Keokotah said. "It is here!"

He turned the bow into the now strong current from our right and then he dug in, paddling with strength. No longer drifting with a current, now we were breasting one, and a strong one at that.

It was a rich and lovely country and there was beauty where the river ran. Once a canoe with four warriors tried to overtake us, but their clumsy dugout canoe was no match for our lighter craft and we drew steadily away from them until finally they gave up.

My wounds had healed well. There were scars on my skull from the teeth of the cat, and there would always be claw marks on my thighs and one hip.

Without doubt Keokotah had been correct. The panther who had attacked me had had one injured leg and could no longer capture and kill a deer except with the greatest good luck. It must have depended upon slower, less agile game. I must have seemed a perfect catch. I had been fortunate in seeing the beast before it leaped.

The wounds had healed, but the scars would be mine forever. There were none on my face. Not that it mattered. I smiled at myself. Where I was going no one would care about my looks, and my mother and Lila were far away.

The Arkansas wound about as much as had the Mississippi, and its banks were heavy with fine timber. One of the cargoes we had often sent to England for sale or trade was timber for the masts of ships. Here there were many tall, fine trees. My eye had learned to measure them, for often as a boy I had gone timber cruising with my father or Jeremy Ring.

Often we had sat long hours studying the crude charts we had and maps my father had put together from the stories of Indians and our wanderings. Somewhere to the south was a great gulf into which the Mississippi must flow. Someday men would build ships here and send their timbers, furs, and whatever else there was down the river to that gulf and to the sea.

The great civilizations had often been born of rivers or at river crossings. The Nile, the Tigris-Euphrates, the rivers of India, the Tiber, the Seine, and the Thames. One day such a civilization might grow along the Mississippi.

Always my eyes were alert for what could be found. This had been our way at Shooting Creek, for whenever we returned from a hunt our father had questioned us as to what we had seen. He wanted not only animal or Indian sign, but the kind of rocks, the timber, possible sources of minerals of which we always stood in need.

We had located deposits of sulphur, iron, and lead and of course were always alert for gems. Some had been found of real quality, and one such might buy the entire cargo of a small ship.

We had double reason for being alert now. Any Indian whom we saw was a possible enemy, and we must now watch for signs of Itchakomi and her party.

Several times we stopped at places that offered campsites, but we found nothing. How were they traveling? By canoe or over the land? The Natchee were a river people, so they must have canoes.

Our first discovery was by chance. Weary with a long day's struggle against a strong current, we had sighted a creek entering the river, and we turned our canoe into the mouth of the creek and pulled it up on the muddy bank. Keokotah had leaped ashore to scout the place and as I tugged the canoe higher and made it secure with a length of rawhide rope tied to a root I glimpsed something in the mud.

Taking hold I started to pick up what seemed like a bit of metal, and it resisted. Surprised, I dug around it and found that what I had was chain mail.

It needed time, but I dug the mud from around it and then dipped it into the stream to rinse more mud away. It was a coat of mail once worn by some Spanish soldier. One of De Soto's men? Probably not, but it was possible. De Soto had come to the Mississippi something like a hundred years ago, but other Spanish soldiers might have been around since then.

Keokotah had a fire going, and when I came up with the coat of mail he showed me the remains of another fire. He had built his own away from it so I might see. It was an Indian fire, and just back from it at the edge of the woods a shelter had been built of woven branches, some from living trees.

"Natchee," he said.

It had been a shelter for one person, and a bed of boughs and cattails had been carefully prepared. It was old. Weeks, but more likely months, had gone by. The cattails, evidently green when laid in place, were dried out and dead now.

It was a shelter for one person. Itchakomi?

There were no tracks. No other signs. Yet others had camped here; probably the wearer of the coat of mail had been one of them, in some bygone year.

Sitting by the fire that night I cleaned the mail still

more, working the rust out of it and rubbing it with sand to bring back the brightness. I explained its purpose to Keokotah.

We kept our fire small, for we had no wish to attract attention. The finding of the coat of mail on the same site as what could have been Itchakomi's camp did not surprise me. Others had stopped here for the same reason we had, and as still others would in years to come. A good campsite for one is also good for another.

Looking down at the bed where Itchakomi could have slept I wondered how she fared? Was she still alive? Had she found the place she sought?

She was a Sun, a great lady among her people, yet when she traveled it must be like any other. Among the Indians we had known there was nothing comparable, although we had heard many stories of the Natchee. She was seeking a new home for her people just as my father had done, and as I had been doing when I sought the valley of the Sequatchie. I wished her success.

As for Kapata . . . we would meet again.

I was sure of it, and when we did I would be on my feet and armed.

I hoped it would be soon.

13

There was sunlight on the water that morning, but shadows still lurked under the trees along the banks. The trees leaned over the river, brushing our heads with their leaves as we passed. We paddled on into the morning, wary of what might come, knowing that danger could await beyond every bend of the river.

Kapata was somewhere ahead of us, I believed. Our good fortune was that he did not know we followed. How long we would have such fortune we did not know.

Peace lay upon the land, the ripples caught diamonds from the sun, and a kingfisher flew up, skimmed the water ahead of us, and then veered suddenly. Keokotah shipped his paddle and took up his bow, notching an arrow. Something had startled the kingfisher, something ahead of us, just beyond the point of trees. I handled the paddle as gently as possible to provide a good shooting platform for Keokotah.

A tumble of dead trees on the point obscured what lay before us. Dipping the paddle deep I propelled the canoe past the point, ready to backwater into the protection of the driftwood.

Smoke slowly rising from burned lodges, a bloody man standing erect amidst a welter of sprawled bodies, skulls stripped of their flesh bobbing on stakes or poles, broken pots and kettles strewn about—a village destroyed, looted, its people slain. Never had I seen the like.

As we pushed our canoe ashore the standing warrior fell and we went to him. His skull was bloody, for his scalp had been ripped away when they believed him dead or did not care. A terrible gash, straight and clean, had laid open his body for all of twenty inches, and there were similar gashes in his thighs. The wounds had bled badly, but his eyes were open and aware.

He had fallen among other bodies, mutilated and dead, so we lifted him away and Keokotah brought the campfire to life and dipped water from the river into a piece of broken pot, to be heated.

We bathed his wounds clean and with sinew such as we always carried we stitched the slashes in his legs and body. He lay still, perfectly conscious, but making no sound as we worked.

No others lived. I put out a few fires, wandering about through the scene of horror. Everything of value had been carried away or destroyed. It was apparent the raid had caught them still asleep and had been totally unexpected. What weapons that had not been carried away had been thrust into the dead or dying.

I brought water from the creek, and the wounded Indian drank thirstily. When I took the cup from his lips, he spoke, looking at me.

"He say he is Quapaw," Keokotah said.

I gestured to Keokotah. "He is Kickapoo," I said.

"He knows what I am," Keokotah said. "He knows not you."

What could I say? That I was an Englishman? He would not recognize the tribe, and who was I, really? I had been born here, in this land, so I could be called an American. But what did that mean? The Quapaw was born here, too.

"I am Sackett," I said, "a son of Barnabas."

"Ah?" he whispered. "Sack-ett!"

He knew the name. Had my father's reputation traveled so far, then? It was true that he had been in America for most of thirty years, and much of that had been lived at Shooting Creek. Indians of many tribes had traded with us and we ourselves had wandered.

We moved the bodies to one side. We straightened up the camp nearest the shore and we prepared a broth for the wounded man, scarcely believing he would survive. Our treatment was whatever we each knew, Keokotah from his own people and I from mine. Sakim had spoken of the necessity of cleaning wounds, and this we had done. He had commented on the fact that wounds healed more quickly in America than anywhere he had been. Fewer people? Cleaner air? More simple food? I did not know, nor did he.

Who had attacked the village? We gathered it was a tribe from the south, the Tensas, but they were led by a man not a Tensa, and some of the warriors had been Natchee.

"They look for woman," the Quapaw said, "a beloved woman."

I knew the term from the Cherokee—a beloved woman was one who through wisdom, bravery, or both had won a revered place among her people. She was a woman whose word could stop or turn aside a war party, could overrule a chief. They occurred but rarely.

"A Natchee woman?" I asked.

"Natchee . . .gone, long time gone."

We had fumbled together a way of speaking. He knew some Cherokee, as we did, although Indians who knew the language of another tribe were rare, usually the sons or daughters of captured women or adopted sons. It was a custom among many tribes to adopt a son from among prisoners taken to replace one lost or slain.

"Big Natchee warrior want her. He lead war party. Say to Tensa he get many scalps for them. Come with him, his medicine is strong."

Kapata . . .

Yet why attack a village where he must know she would not be? To win prestige and gain followers?

Keokotah agreed when I expressed my thoughts. "He big man now. Take many scalps. His medicine strong."

Young warriors eager for renown would follow any leader who promised success. Now, after taking the Quapaw scalps, the young men of the Tensa would be eager to follow this leader. No matter that he was not of their tribe. Such things had happened before and no doubt would again.

Kapata would have no following from among the Natchee beyond the two or three who had come west with him. He would need to win followers to make up a strong party.

Who knew with what eloquence he had spoken to persuade them? But the young men of all tribes were eager to take scalps and the prestige that followed. No doubt Kapata had scouted the Quapaw village and knew that most of its young men were away and that it would be an easy victory. He would have known that Itchakomi was not there.

The passions that stir Indians are no different from those of Europeans or Asiatics. Ambition, hatred, fear, greed, and jealousy are ever-present. Kapata was the son of a Natchee man and a Karankawa woman, and the Karankawa were despised by the Natchee. Kapata must have grown to manhood fighting to overcome that stigma and striving to assert himself and his manhood. To marry a Sun would be the ultimate, to be himself regarded as a Sun. . . . He knew of no such thing happening before, but his fierce Karankawa mother had instilled in him the feeling that he could do anything. She must have told him of the Karankawa warriors, feared by all.

Sitting beside the wounded warrior, who was now either unconscious or asleep, I tried to understand he who had become my enemy.

It was not until the third day, when we had moved well upstream, that the men of the massacred village returned. We heard their wailing and I went down by canoe, approaching them warily.

Seeing me, they rushed to the shore, and I motioned

for them to follow. After a moment of hesitation, several armed and dangerous warriors did follow.

Akicheeta—for that was the name of the wounded Quapaw—was awake when they entered our camp, and he explained what had taken place. He also explained that we were seeking the Natchee woman.

I asked about the river. "Spring much water," he drew a route with his finger in the earth. Making zigzag lines to indicate mountains, he showed how the river emerged from a great cleft in the rock. Between us and where the river emerged from the canyon he showed a place where the waters would be shallow at midsummer. "No canoe," he said, making signs to indicate the water would be only a few inches deep.

"How far to the mountains?" I asked.

He shrugged, and I held up ten fingers. "More!" he replied.

"Spanishmen?"

He shook his head. "Conejeros!" He swept a wide area before the mountains and made a gesture of lifting my scalp. "You see!" he warned.

The name was strange to me, but Keokotah spoke longer with him and told me later it was the name of a very fierce tribe of Indians who lived at the edge of the mountains. They hunted buffalo and then retired in the hotter months into higher country. In the winter they hid their lodges in sheltered places where there was wood to burn.

The Quapaws treated Keokotah with respect while he ignored them, holding himself aloof for the most part.

Several commented on my scarcely healed wounds, the deep claw marks on my body, and Keokotah told them, with some embellishment I am sure, of my killing the panther with a knife when I had a broken leg. I could grasp enough of what he was saying to know that I lost no stature in the telling and that the panther had suddenly grown larger than I remembered.

Suddenly, and for the first time, Keokotah brought out a necklace of the panther's claws. Evidently he had taken them from the dead cat while I had been sleeping, and he had carefully strung them on a rawhide string. Looked at now, the claws were formidable and longer than I remembered. To tell the truth, I had been rather too busy to notice dimensions.

The Quapaw had treated me with respect before, but now my stature had grown. With a gesture, Keokotah put the necklace around my neck. He had said nothing about the cat's crippled leg, and who was I to spoil a good story, especially when it made me look so good?

All I could remember was the sudden attack, the wild, terrible scramble among trees and brush, and the hot breath of the panther, the scrape of his teeth on my skull and my stabbing and stabbing with the knife. All I had been was another animal fighting wildly, instinctively for life. The cat, in all honesty, had been a big one. I could remember its weight on me and my frantic efforts to escape it.

My broken leg had knitted well, though I still limped a little, but whether it was necessity or habit I did not know and began consciously trying to correct it.

We left the Quapaw and moved upstream slowly. The current was still strong, but there were fewer obstructions. We rarely saw drifting trees, although once we did paddle through a dozen or so dead buffalo. The stench was frightful, and we paddled vigorously to escape them.

Only rarely did we see the smoke of a village, and we passed no canoes on the river. There were trees close to the banks but we often caught glimpses of bare, grass-covered hills beyond.

Coming upon a clump of chokecherry bushes we camped to make arrows—many Indians favored the slender branches of the chokecherry over all others, although reeds and some other woods were used by some tribes, with much depending on what was available and light enough. The arrows made by Keokotah were about twenty-eight inches in length, and those I made for my longbow somewhat longer. His bow was about four feet long and he could use it with amazing speed and skill.

Every move was made with caution, as ambush was a favored tactic of the Indians, and we knew not what awaited us. Food during those weeks was no problem. There were fish, ducks, and geese, and now we found wild turkeys again and occasionally a deer. Lower down we had had to be watchful for alligators, but we saw them no longer.

On the second day after the arrow making we saw where several canoes had been drawn up at some time not long since. Edging in, we found a camp, now abandoned.

Three canoes, good-sized ones. Several warriors, maybe as many as a dozen. Keokotah found Kapata's moccasin print among them. After we had studied the ground we decided there were at least ten of the Tensa as well as Kapata and his few Natchee. They were but a few days ahead of us. Somehow, if we were to warn Itchakomi, we must overtake and pass them without their being aware.

Every day we saw buffalo, usually in small herds of two dozen or less, but many herds within a short distance of each other, so we might count fifty such within the range of our eyes.

Our supply of food was running low and so we needed to hunt, not only for food but for the warm robes of the buffalo. The cold season was coming on and the nights were already growing chill. Despite the numbers of the buffalo, we had no success in getting near them, for they had been lately frightened, no doubt by Kapata and his people.

We killed several antelopes, but their skins, while useful, would not do for the intense cold of the prairies. The water was growing more shallow, the river itself wandering from side to side in its sandy bed. Here and there in the bottom there were strips of gravel and even clumps of brush. Often the course of the stream was heavily walled by brush, and the trees along the banks grew very dense.

Long before Sakim had left us he had suggested to each that we learn as much as we could of the Indians, of their nature and customs. When we returned from hunts or visits with the Indians we had always gone to him to relate what we had learned, until the study had become a habit for each of us.

On the long days in the canoe I plied Keokotah with questions. At first he shied from direct questions, but after a while we began comparing notes on our peoples. He had never known a case of baldness and it was necessary that I describe it to him before he understood. He then recalled seeing a white man who was bald, but never an Indian. Nor had I. Nor had I seen one crippled by rheumatism, and decayed teeth were rare.

Coming upon a thick stand of willow and cottonwood we decided to abandon our canoe. The water had been growing less and we could see a strip ahead where it seemed to disappear completely. We lay the canoe bottom up among several dead logs, and scattered debris across it both to shelter it from the sun and to mask its appearance.

Our packs were small, for now our need for food had grown. For days we had found no fish, and the game shied from us. Yet that very night our fortunes changed.

We had been following the riverbed, keeping to the shelter of trees and brush when possible, and suddenly we came on a pool where a buffalo cow and a small bull calf were watering. The distance was great, so Keokotah yielded the chance to me and I brought the cow down with one arrow. The calf ran off a short distance and we moved in to skin the cow and cut out the meat.

On the shore, in a hollow we found, we built a small fire and cutting the meat into strips began the tiresome process of curing what meat we could. We gorged ourselves on fresh buffalo steaks, for I had acquired something of the Indian habit of eating enormously when there was food against the times of famine that would surely follow.

At daybreak when I went down to the thin stream of running water to bathe, I saw the buffalo calf. It stared at me, seeming unsure of whether to run or not. I spoke to it, and pitying it, I left a small mound of salt on a flat rock. As I walked back to camp I saw the calf sniffing at where I had stood. When I walked back to look again, the calf was licking the rock where I had left the salt.

14

We saw the rain from afar when we topped a ridge a quarter of a mile from the river. We saw its steel battalions marching across the plains toward us, but there was no shelter. A lone tree with arching branches offered itself but we knew better, for it is the lone trees that draw the lightning.

We moved to lower ground, skirting the trees along the riverbed. Within minutes that riverbed was no longer dry sand with a trickle of water but a rushing river, a flash flood brought by the rain.

The oilskin preserved from my father's seagoing days was quickly donned, more to shelter my guns and keep their powder dry than for myself.

The storm approached and we could see the metallic veil it drew across the country. Then it hit us and in a minute we were dripping. But we walked on, the grass slippery under our feet. Then there was mud, and we turned down the hill toward the forest along the river where we might find fuel. Glancing back I saw the buffalo calf, woebegone and lonely. "Come on!" I called. "Come with us!"

It lingered, staring after us wistfully. I called again

and it advanced a few steps and then hesitated. We dipped down a slippery bank into the trees.

All was wet and dripping, but we found a place where the tightly woven branches of several trees had kept the leaves almost dry. We stopped there and wove a few branches and slabs of bark from fallen trees into the mesh of branches above to offer more protection.

Under the canopy lay a network of fallen trees and limbs, crisscrossing each other. It reminded me too much of the place where I had broken my leg, and I walked with care. From some of the fallen trees great slabs of bark hung down, and beneath their shelter bark and leaves were still dry. We gathered some and nursed a small fire into being.

Ours was a sheltered place, deep among the trees. We laid boughs above us from one tree to the next, resting them on branches or the stubs of branches until we had made ourselves a crude but effective shelter. Large cold drops fell but they were nothing, and outside the rain poured down and winds blew.

Keokotah began working on the buffalo robe taken from the cow we had killed. He scraped away what flesh was left and staked out the hide to stretch it. All this should have been done completely before this but there had been no time. I set myself to making a pair of moccasins from the hide of a deer killed long before.

Looking around, I saw the buffalo calf not over fifty feet away, and I spoke to it. Keokotah looked and grunted something and when I looked at him again he made a derisive gesture implying the calf thought I was his mother.

"He'll leave us when we come up to some other buffalo," I said, and believed it.

From time to time we arose and added to our shelter, placing more bark to keep out especially disturbing drips. It was a makeshift camp, but pleasant enough and well hidden.

Moving about, I pushed further away from our camp and came on several elms weighted down with grapevines. A bear had been feasting here but many grapes still hung, and I gathered as many as could be carried and took them back to camp. We ate, enjoying the change from a diet of fresh meat. I carried a couple of bunches to the calf but it moved off. Still, I left the bunches I carried and later saw him nuzzling them. I suspect he ate them but did not watch, for as I returned to camp I heard the sharp crack of a breaking branch.

Crouching where I was, I wished for my bow, two dozen feet away. Instead, I drew my knife, waiting.

Our fire smoldered. Keokotah had disappeared but would be waiting somewhere near. A bow would do little good in this dense stand of trees and brush, anyway. He would have his spear.

All was still for a long moment, but then I heard something stirring not far off, and the sounds of movement such as a man might make. Then there was a sort of clicking as of sticks being piled together. Easing a step to one side, I peered through the trees.

There was a small open space nearby, and an old Indian was gathering firewood. He seemed uneasy, straightening up to look around, and I glanced around also, watching him from the corners of my eyes. He gathered more sticks, picked up his bundle, and started away, pausing to look back.

His eyes missed me, as I did not move, and finally he turned away again, walking through the trees. I had only to follow some dozen yards to see the camp, a small cluster of Indians, at least three women, several children, and a half dozen men. All but one of the men were getting on in years. That one was a boy, not yet sixteen, at a guess. At that age or older he would be out with the warriors.

Keokotah had followed. Now he whispered, "Pawnee!"

The name was unfamiliar, but there were many tribes of which I did not know.

"We speak." He spoke softly, and then he called out. The Indians turned to face him as he stepped out, lifting a hand, palm out.

Several held weapons and they waited. Then I appeared and there was a murmur of surprise from among them. Although the sun and wind had made me almost as dark as Keokotah it was obvious that I was not an Indian, or at least none such as they had ever seen.

Keokotah spoke again, some word which they understood but I did not. We walked down to their camp, and soon he was talking to them. From time to time they looked at me, and I could see he was explaining me. How, I had no idea. It developed that only one of them had ever seen a white man before. The Pawnees were a strong tribe, only moving into the area now, and where they originated I did not know. What was important was that they had seen Itchakomi.

They had also seen Kapata, but had remained hidden among the trees atop a long ridge as the Natchee and the Tensa went along the valley bottom a half mile away.

Much talk went on of which I understood nothing until Keokotah translated for me. Apparently they were fleeing back to their own people. The Conejeros—a branch of a people called Apache, of which there were many tribes—were on the warpath.

The Conejeros were destroying any other Indians they came upon, and had even killed some of the Spanishmen who had gotten too far from home. They were fierce and desperate fighting men who seemed to have conquered all between the river we followed and another great river to the south.

"What of Itchakomi?" I asked.

"They are near the mountains, but the Pawnees believe they will be killed."

"What of the Tensa?"

"They believe the Tensa are friendly to the Conejeros, but they do not know."

We talked long, and Keokotah at my prodding asked many questions about the country, the rivers, the mountains, and the game.

There were many buffalo and great herds of antelope, too. There were several kinds of deer, including a large kind that must be the wapiti or elk. There were not many

Indians apart from a few small tribes of Apaches, some of whom planted cornfields along the rivers when the season was right.

When we left them to move on, the rains had ceased, although it was still muddy along the hillsides and the river still ran with a strong current in a wide bed. More clouds hovered in the west. Soon, the Pawnees told us, we would see the mountains.

The growth along the riverbanks was less dense now, and the country away from the river was prairie country, covered with buffalo. We moved cautiously, knowing our danger and wanting no trouble.

Overhead the sky was a vast blue dome, dotted with drifting clouds. Around was a sea of grass with only occasional groves of trees along the ridges. We saw no Indians, found no tracks. Several times we sighted black bears, and once a bobcat that leaped away at our approach and then returned to where it had been feeding on a recently killed rabbit.

Twice we came upon the tracks of a gigantic bear, the tracks dwarfing those of the black bears we often saw.

When we first saw the mountains they appeared as a low blue cloud on the western horizon, and when they became clearer I thought of my father and his love of those far, blue mountains he had wished to explore. Well, he had seen them and he had gone beyond them, but what would he have thought of these?

Suddenly, Indians were there. On the open plain not more than one hundred yards off! Keokotah and I crouched in the willows from which we had been about to emerge. My heart was beating heavily, for there were at least twenty warriors in the group yonder, obviously a war party.

They had not seen us and they were following a route that took them away from us.

"Conejeros!" Keokotah whispered.

The group paused at the stream, some of them dropping down for a drink. One mounted a low hill to look around. Had we been a few steps further along we should have been seen.

That night we lighted no fire and made our beds in a thick stand of aspen. We had advanced what I believed to be about eight miles that day, leaving our tracks to mingle with the tracks of the war party ahead of us in the event anyone was following.

We had moved with great care, always studying the land before and around us before crossing any open space. The river, its waters no longer depleted by evaporation or the thirsty sand, ran with a strong current.

Where was Itchakomi now? Had Kapata found her yet? If so, we might be too late. The thought worried me and I could not sleep. I slipped out of camp and climbed a small bluff nearby. In the distance I could see the faint glow of a campfire, probably reflecting off a clay bluff. It could have been a mile off, or even further. In such clear air distances deceived.

A long time I sat in silence upon the bluff, drinking in the beauty of the night and the stars. We had traveled far in an almost empty land and now the mountains lay before us, far greater mountains than any I had seen, and the most distant seemed covered with snow.

The thought brought back the need for buffalo robes and warmer clothing. Autumn would bring cold winds and more rain and we were ill-fitted for it.

We crossed the river at a rocky ford, wading waist deep in the water. Finding no fresh tracks, we started off at a swinging trot, keeping to low ground and what cover we could find. As the war party was moving slowly we felt sure we had passed them by. Although the season was late we walked through many wildflowers, most of them of varying shades of yellow.

We were in camp among some cottonwoods when Keokotah spoke suddenly. "The Englishman, he say he live in big city"—Keokotah swept a wide gesture—"many big house. Some Kickapoo think he lie. Did he speak false?"

"He spoke the truth. I have not seen it but my father

had been there, and some of the other men who lived with us. They had seen it, and one at least was from there. It is called London."

"Yes . . . London. It is true then, the things he said?"

"That much was true. I believe all he said was true."

Keokotah was pleased. "I think he speak true. I think so."

He was silent for a time and then after a while he said, "After they say he lie he talk only to me of wonders. Not to them."

"I can understand why." Pausing, I then went on, trying to choose my words. "There are many nations. Kickapoos do not think like Natchees. But Kickapoos live much as do other Indians. It is so in Europe. The tongues they speak are often different, but the way they live is much the same."

"They hunt?"

"Only for sport. Because they wish to hunt."

"No hunt for meat?"

"There is not enough game to feed them. Many villages. Many big, big villages. No place for game. They plant corn. They raise cattle, sheep."

"Cattle?"

"Some men own many cows. Like buffalo. They keep them in big corrals and when they want meat, they kill one."

He considered that. "No hunt buffalo?"

"We have no buffalo. Cows."

"Ah? I see him. Spanishmans have cows. He talk 'city'? City is big village?"

Slowly, taking my time, I explained what was meant by a city and described the many occupations of the people who lived there, trying to keep to those occupations he would understand the best.

"Clothing is made by tailors, and there are men who make weapons—knives, guns, and armor. There are houses in which strangers can sleep, and places where they can go to eat."

This he had been told before, but his was a curious,

interested mind. Uninformed he might be, unintelligent he was not, and I could see why the Englishman had been drawn to him. Undoubtedly the man had been lonely and he had taken on the teaching of the young Indian, opening his mind to possibilities Keokotah could not have imagined.

The mountains loomed before us, and now the river was running with a strong, powerful stream, sixty or seventy yards wide. Rains had been falling in the upper mountains and there was more snow upon the peaks. We saw fewer and fewer buffalo but we pushed on. Now I was searching for tracks, for some indication of Itchakomi's direction.

We had seen occasional indications in the past, a place where they had camped long since, a place where they had crossed a stream. I had come to know her footprints, partly from their small size and delicate shape, unusual for an Indian woman, for most of them were accustomed to carrying heavy burdens.

I wished to find her, discharge my mission, such as it was, and go on about my business. If business it could be called, for I wished to wander, to explore, to learn, to see. And with winter coming on we must find shelter and kill some buffalo or gather other skins for warm clothing. I had no time to waste.

Kapata . . . he was another story. I had never wanted to kill a man. But Kapata? I might make an exception.

If we had not wanted a buffalo so desperately it might not have happened, but the buffalo was there, a big one with a fine robe. And three others trailing behind him.

They had our attention and I drew my longbow and let fly an arrow. We were directly in front of the bull and he had not seen us. His left foreleg was back at the end of its stride, just before he lifted it to bring it forward, and my shaft must have gone right to the heart.

He seemed to stagger and then stopped, evidently puzzled. Keokotah let fly with an arrow of his own at the cow that was behind the bull, and then two more before one could think. The cow staggered and fell. The bull shook his head and blood ran from his nostrils. He started forward but then slowly toppled.

From behind me there was a savage yell and they were upon us. Conejeros. Five of them. My second arrow was ready so I turned and let go. A big warrior took it right through the throat in midstride.

Then the others were upon us, with knives and spears. A sweaty body hurtled at me, my bow fell, my knife came up, and then there was blood all over my hand and I was withdrawing the knife.

15

Low and gray were the clouds above us, the earth damp from a shower that had passed. Fresh was the air with a hint of more rain to come, and I stood with a bared and bloody knife above the body of a man whom I had killed.

The attack had been sudden, unexpected, and must have seemed a certain victory for the attackers. Our attention had been upon the buffalo whose robes and flesh we needed, our only warning the grate of gravel under the moccasin of a leaping Indian, and then the yell. But the warning had been enough. Keokotah had turned like a cat, swift and sure, and another warrior had gone down before him.

The two remaining had disappeared, dropping off into an arroyo. Keokotah glanced at me. I thrust my knife into the earth to clean the blade and went over to the buffalo bull.

"They will come back," Keokotah said.

"So let them come. We need the robes."

To skin a buffalo bull weighing over a thousand pounds, and I suspected this one weighed half again that much, is not an easy thing nor one quickly done. We knew we should be off and away, but winter would soon be upon us. We worked swiftly, while keeping a sharp lookout.

Three warriors had died, and the Conejeros were fierce fighting men who would not permit them to lie unavenged.

We skinned out the bull and then the cow. We took only the tongue from the bull but from the cow we took the best cuts of meat. We shouldered our burdens and started away, but such hides are heavy and our movements were slow. We turned away from the river, heading southwest toward the mountains. It was rolling, sometimes rough country cut by a number of small creeks, some dry, some running with small streams. The bull's hide, which I carried, was a very heavy as well as awkward burden.

Several times we paused to look back. Pursuit depended on how far the Conejeros must go to reach their camp and on whether warriors were there. The mountains toward which we were headed were hours away. The place where the river ran out from its canyon was away to the north.

Shouldering our loads we started on. The robes would be lighter in weight when they had been scraped and cleaned, but there was no time for that now.

The nearest mountain was a sort of hogback, and to the north of it were several scraggy peaks. We held our course to reach the mountains between the two. When we had gone what I believed was about five miles we found ourselves following a rocky creek. We drank and then studied the terrain.

How far had the Conejeros to go for help? By now, without burdens, they should have reached their camp.

"They might have horses," I suggested.

He stared at me. "Horses?"

"They could steal from the Spanish." I waved a hand off to the south. "There are Spanish down thataway."

We had heard stories of them from the Indians. Keokotah would have heard them as well. Even before this I had been to the Great River and touched upon the plains beyond. The Cherokees told stories of Spanishmen beyond the Far Seeing Lands.

"If they have horses they could be here soon," I said. As I spoke I was thinking of how much better it would be if we had even one horse to carry the hides. I was unusually strong, but a buffalo hide was no small weight.

When we camped it was in a small cove against an overhanging cliff where an ancient river had cut away the rock into a shallow cave. Keokotah went out to cover as much as he could of our trail while I broiled meat over a small fire.

We ate, slept an hour or so, and then when the moon arose we moved out, heading toward the mountains again. By daybreak they were looming before us, though still some distance off. Keokotah moved on before me.

We plodded on, resting often, studying the terrain at every pause. Still, the Conejeros did not come. "Maybe farther than we think," Keokotah suggested. "He may go far, far out!"

It was true, of course. I had assumed their camp was not far off, but the party that had attacked us might be a war or hunting party a long distance from their camp.

We saw antelope but no buffalo. Several times we saw wolves, attracted by the still-bloody hides we carried. By the time the sun was high we had fallen upon a dim game trail that seemed to come from the mountains before us. We held to the trail.

We found our way to a small elevation, a level place with a hollow behind it where we could build a small fire of dry sticks that would give off no smoke. On the flat ground we staked out our hides and began the tedious task of scraping them clean of excess flesh. The place where we worked was backed by a brush-covered cliff, so we could not easily be seen.

Our view took in a wide sweep of country, a country seen by few white men and not by many Indians except for the few who lived in the area. There were Indians in the mountains, we had heard, but whether they were real or imagined we did not know.

"Apache!" Keokotah commented. "Many tribe! All bad!"

"All?"

He shrugged. His people were The People, and all others were mere interlopers. Some he tolerated, but for most he had no use at all. Pa had been a tolerant man and we boys had grown up feeling the same. We accepted all people as they were and trusted nobody until they had proved themselves trustworthy.

We worked hard at scraping the skins and then took some time to broil buffalo steaks and eat, while watching the plains before us. We knew what to look for. Movement is easily seen, but Indians would keep under cover until close, so we studied the places that offered cover. Many times we looked straight out over the plains, letting the corners of our eyes look for any movement.

And movement there was. A wolf, a coyote, and once a great, lumbering bear. It was at least a half mile off but we knew what it was by its movement.

We saw no Indians.

Keokotah slept then while I worked at the hides. Facing toward the plain, I could work and keep an eye on all that lay before me, careful not to let my movements fall into a pattern. Often one looks up at certain intervals, and an enemy approaching can time those intervals and remain still.

Now to find Itchakomi—somewhere out there, or perhaps even in the mountains themselves. I had given my word to Ni'kwana, and I would be faithful to the promise.

Once I had found her and made sure she was warned of Kapata and told of the illness of the Great Sun, we could be on about our business.

Off to the south there were twin peaks that towered into the sky, and to the north there were others. This was where the great Far Seeing Lands ended against the wall of the mountains. From here all streams ran to the Mississippi.

Sometimes I ceased from scraping and working on the hides and took time just to look out over the vast plains. My thoughts went back to Shooting Creek. Did it survive still? For surely the Seneca would come again, or the Tuscarora. Would our small island stand against them without Pa? And what of Brian and Noelle? They were across the sea now in England, he studying for the law and she growing wise in the ways of the city and of the people there. Ways I would never know, and a city I would never see.

But how many could see what I saw? How many would cross those plains, hunt the buffalo on its native grass, and penetrate the unknown mountains that lay behind me? This was my destiny, as I had known from the first. This land was mine.

Others would come. Oh, I knew they would come! There would be others like Pa, who could not rest for not knowing what lay about. They would seek out these lands until all was known, all was recorded.

The Indians? I shrugged. Many acres were needed to feed even one Indian, living as they did, but men would come who would grow grain where only grass grew. They would plant orchards and herd cattle and sheep, and they would provide for a still larger world, still more people. There were too many landless ones back in Europe, too many willing to risk all to better themselves, too many—

Something moved!

It was still far away. From where I sat I could see for miles, for all the while we had been moving we had been climbing, and all the land before me slanted away to the Arkansas River and from there to the Mississippi.

I saw it again, just a faint stir of movement down there that fitted no normal pattern. I longed for my father's telescope, retained from his seafaring days. I chose landmarks so that my eyes could focus upon the spot again, and I went on with my work.

After a while I looked again, bringing my eyes into focus on the chosen landmarks and seeking out from them.

I needed only a minute or two before I had them again. A small party—how many I could not tell, for they were indistinct with distance. If they continued as they were going their path would cross the one we had used.

There was a stir behind me. I turned. Keokotah shaded his eyes to look. "What do you see?"

I showed him my landmarks and he picked the movement out of the landscape at once. Quicker than I had.

He stared for several minutes, looked away, and looked again.

"How many?" I asked.

"Ten . . . I think. It is Itchakomi," he added.

"Itchakomi? How could you know that?"

He shrugged. "She has more than ten. Some are women. They travel slowly. They keep to low ground."

I stood up and looked again. It needed a moment for me to find them. They were coming toward the mountains, and as we watched, Keokotah said, "They come back. Something is wrong, I think."

"Come back? What do you mean?"

"You see? They are far out. Why, unless they have start home? And why do they come back to mountains? Something is wrong."

It was a bit more than I was willing to accept, yet it could be true. Why, at this point, would they be coming to the mountains? Unless—

"Maybe they haven't even been here yet," I suggested.

He shrugged.

The rain clouds still lowered above us, but there had been no more rain. When we looked again we could see nothing. Our travelers, whoever they were, followed a riverbed, not a wise thing in this weather unless there was something they feared more.

Had they been cut off from the river by a war party? Or . . . had Kapata found them?

Keokotah watched while I slept. We would move again at night, getting closer to the mountains. Or that had been our plan. If that was Itchakomi, it was up to us to intercept her.

When I awakened it was dusk. Keokotah had folded the hides. Gathering them and our weapons we went down off the lookout point and found the trail we had been traveling. The only tracks were those of a deer.

We stopped and I looked toward the mountains where I wished to be going. But if that was Itchakomi . . .

"The Conejeros will come looking for us," I said, "and will find them."

"It is so."

"We will wait," I said. "If they walk by night—"

"They will." He squatted on his heels. "She is much trouble, this woman. It is better to look at mountains. To find rivers. We do not need this woman."

"I gave my word."

It was many days since I had drunk chicory. I felt the want for it now, yet to build a fire was dangerous. I mentioned it and he shrugged and began putting together a fire.

When water was boiling we added the shavings from the root. I used it with care. Perhaps there was no more to be found. Perhaps it did not grow here.

Keokotah had come to like it, too, and he watched as I added it to the water and put twigs into the fire. Ours was a very small fire, hidden from sight, yet it was a risk. I could not smell the smoke but I could smell the chicory.

We often had it at home, added to our coffee to make the coffee go farther. Coffee was hard to come by at Shooting Creek, and we used a lot of it.

Pa told me that in London there were shops, where men gathered to drink coffee and tea and to talk. Much business was done there, but there were those who believed the drinking of coffee sinful. Sakim had told me there were riots in Bagdad against the drinking of coffee.

Ours tasted good. I took my time, enjoying every drop, aware that it might be long before I had more.

Yet I should have been watching out for it. Who knows where it might grow? Such seeds might be carried far by birds or blown on the wind. It was a plant that made itself at home quickly.

We heard the footsteps before we saw anyone. Keokotah faded into the darkness, an arrow ready. I drew my knife.

She stepped from the darkness, and she was tall,

almost as tall as I, and slender. She stood just for a moment and then she said, "I am Itchakomi, a Sun of the Natchee."

"I am Jubal Sackett, a son of Barnabas."

16

"What," her tone was cool, "is a 'Barnabas'?"

"Barnabas Sackett was my father, a man of Shooting Creek, and formerly of England."

She dismissed me from her attention and turned to Keokotah. "You are a Kickapoo? What do you here?"

"We look upon mountains," he said, "and he brings you word from Ni'kwana."

She turned to me again as if irritated by the necessity. "From Ni'kwana? You?"

"We were asked to seek you out and to tell you the Great Sun is failing. He grows weaker."

"He wishes me to return?"

"That was what he said, but I felt that he wished you to decide for yourself. He spoke first as Ni'kwana, second as a father."

"He is not my father!"

"I said he spoke as a father. As one who wished you well. Also," I added, "you have been followed by a man named Kapata."

"Kapata?" Her contempt was obvious.

"He intends to wed you"—I spoke cheerfully—"and become a Sun, perhaps even the Great Sun."

Her eyes were cold, imperious. "One does not 'become' a Sun. One is or is not a Sun."

"I understand that does not matter to him. He has his own ideas. He will marry you and usurp the power." I shrugged. "However, it is none of my business. I know nothing of your people or your customs."

"Obviously!"

She turned her attention to Keokotah. "You know of this?"

"We met the Ni'kwana. He spoke with us. He spoke most to him." Keokotah paused. "We have done what was asked. You may go."

"*I* may go? You dismiss *me*? I shall go where I choose, when I choose."

"Then please be seated," I said. She looked at the fire where the chicory bubbled slightly. "We do not have much, but—"

"It is *mayocup entchibil*! I smell it from far!" She was no longer imperious but like a very young girl.

"She speaks of the 'dark root,' " Keokotah said. "It is one way of speaking what you drink."

Filling a cup made of bark, I handed it to her. She accepted it, and then a woman came forward and placed a mat upon the ground near the fire. Itchakomi seated herself and sipped the drink. Slowly the others came into the camp and gathered about.

Seating myself opposite her I waited until she had drunk from the cup. "Kapata is close." I spoke carefully. "He has some of your people but more of the Tensa. They seek you."

"He is nothing,"

"He is a strong, dangerous man."

"You fear?"

"I? What have I to fear? He seeks you, not me. I shall be gone with Keokotah. You have warriors."

This I said, but I had seen her warriors. Three of them were old men, well past their prime. They had come for their wisdom, not for their strength or fighting ability. Against the Tensa they would prove a poor match. Some of the younger ones looked able enough, but they were too few. I shifted uneasily. None of this was any affair of mine. I wished only to be away, and Keokotah felt the same.

One of her Indians added fuel to the fire.

"There are also the Conejeros," I suggested. "You have seen them?"

"Their feet have left marks on the way we walk. I know them not."

"They are dangerous men. They are warriors and there are many."

"You fear?"

Irritated, I said, "We have met them. Three are dead. Two have gone for others. I suggest you find a place that is safe for the winter. Soon the snows will come. You cannot cross the plains."

"We have canoes. The water is strong."

She ignored me, speaking to Keokotah. Yet her eyes strayed to my guns in their ornate scabbards. That she was curious was obvious, but I had no intention of gratifying her curiosity.

She was, I must admit, uncommonly beautiful, and would have graced any gathering, anywhere. She had poise and intelligence and quick wit. I suspected she was not entirely of Natchee blood, judging by her appearance, but that was merely a suspicion.

We had been speaking in Spanish interspersed here and there with an English or Cherokee word, but I soon discovered that her command of English was not small. We had heard of Englishmen as well as Spanish who lived among them, and some of De Soto's men had stayed on with the Natchee, preferring the safety of the Indian villages to the long, doubtful trek that would have awaited them.

Knowing what I did of the Europeans who had lived among the Indians I was not surprised. When De Soto first landed he discovered a man named Juan Ortiz already living among the Indians, and when the French Huguenots living at Charlesfort abandoned their settlement, one young lad, Guillaum Rufin, decided not to trust himself to the frail craft they had constructed and remained with the Indians. Several of the Frenchmen in a later colonizing attempt by Jean Ribaut had escaped a Spanish attack and gone to live with the natives.

"The Tensa and Kapata look for you. The Conejeros are everywhere. To get to the river, find your canoes, and then escape will be very hard."

"So?"

"Go into the mountains, wait there for a week, then go quickly. They look for you now. If you leave no tracks, they can find none." I gestured toward the path they had followed to us. "This goes into the mountains. We will follow it."

She considered what I had said, and then Keokotah spoke. "The Ni'kwana trusted him. He thought—"

"We do not know what he thought. Only what he said." She paused. "We will do it. For three days we wait."

She arose and went to where the women had made a bed for her. She lay down and composed herself with a woman lying on each side of her, but each at least ten feet away.

Keokotah looked at me, shrugged, and rolled up in his own blankets. I withdrew the longer sticks from the fire to let it die to coals, and then lay down myself. First I checked my guns. The night was overcast. It was very still. Once a brief flame struggled against the darkness and then faded and died.

When morning came we left quickly, but not until I had gone off some distance to where there was an old campsite. Gathering some of the ancient coals I brought them back to scatter over our fire. Then I lifted handsful of dust and let it drift from my fingers over the fire, carried by the slight breeze. To casual glance our campfire would look months or even years old.

We moved out quickly, going down a slight declivity to the stream that flowed past the hogback mountain we had used for a landmark. There seemed to be an opening through which the stream flowed that would allow access to the mountains.

The stream had cut through the dark rock, and the game path along the stream was narrow. With Keokotah leading the way we climbed a steep hill and came out on top in a lovely valley. We camped where we could watch the entrance and settled down to rest, and to complete work on our buffalo hides. Keokotah and I moved our camp under several large old trees some fifty yards from the camp of the Natchee.

At daybreak I was up and scouting. The hole in which we had taken shelter must have embraced a thousand acres of fertile land, surrounded by rugged hills and cliffs covered with timber, mostly pine. Or so it seemed from where I studied them.

For several hours I scouted about. There were a number of caves, one a death trap. I tried dropping a stone into the darkness and it took some time to hit bottom. It was a place to avoid.

Here and there wildflowers still bloomed and I saw other plants I remembered—mountain parsley, wild mint, chokecherry, and a half dozen others that might be useful. Already I was planning for the coming winter. No matter what Itchakomi decided to do, this would be a good place for Keokotah and I to winter.

Game would be apt to shelter here, and if we kept our presence small the supply would be sufficient to provide us with meat. Building a shelter was not out of the question, but one of the caves might be all that was needed.

As I studied the valley and the surrounding hills I heard the song of a meadowlark, always a favorite, and several times I stumbled upon flocks of quail. The hills would give us shelter from the worst storms and there would be fuel.

Itchakomi's people were gathered about their fire when I returned. Keokotah had built our own fire. He was broiling meat, and I joined him, bringing more fuel.

"A cold time is coming," I said.

He cut a sliver from the meat with his knife and began chewing.

"There are caves. I see many deer. I see bear tracks. Quail." I cut a sliver from the meat. "It is a good place," I said.

"What they do?"

I shrugged. "She will decide. I think they will go."

"They will stay," Keokotah said. "Itchakomi has eyes for you."

"For me? No chance of that. She despises me."

Sitting beside the fire I considered their problem. If they left now and could get to the Arkansas they might float down the river to its mouth. The severe drouth that had hit the plains before we had come was gone. The river was running full and strong. To get so far as the river would call for considerable luck, and we had been fortunate so far. They must have canoes somewhere not too far off if they had not been discovered by the Conejeros.

On the other hand the Conejeros might know of this valley or might find our tracks. We had seen no signs of recent occupation or of hunting or travel, so it was possible they had not found this place. Here we might last out the winter in comparative shelter. We would need more food, of course. A little judicious hunting would take care of that. Most of all we needed a fat bear, for of all things, fat is the hardest to come by in the wilderness.

One of Itchakomi's young warriors came to our fire and squatted on his heels. "You stay?" he asked.

"We stay."

He was uneasy. "Snow?"

"Much," I said, "and much cold."

The Indian poked a stick into the fire. "Natchee not much cold," he said.

Keokotah said nothing, but I glanced around at him and said, "Living where they do on the lower Mississippi they wouldn't have much experience with cold and snow. You know better than any of us what we'll have to do."

Keokotah was silent for several minutes, and then he made a sweeping gesture. "Snow!" he said. He picked up a stick from the small pile of fuel. "No find tree for fire, all cover! No find game! Snow! Much, much snow! Stay in lodge!"

"Then we'd better hunt," I said. "We'll need meat, and we'll need a fat bear or two. We'll need to gather what seeds we can before they're all covered with snow."

They sat silent, waiting. "Keokotah? You know the problems."

The Kickapoo shook his head vigorously. "You speak! You chief!"

"The women and the older men should gather wood," I said. "We must hunt, but hunt far away from where we live. We must not drive game away from us."

There was time yet, so we went quietly about what must be done. There was much wood lying about, trees that had blown down or fallen from age or lightning, many with limbs broken off. As in all such wild areas there was no limit to the available deadwood, and we gathered it close to the cave we had chosen.

My leg was still a handicap. Undoubtedly I had begun using it, even with the crude crutches, sooner than I should have done. I limped, but also the leg tired rapidly. My other wounds had healed, although the scars on my scalp and legs would always be reminders. My strength had not returned, and I had to work in spells, resting from time to time.

"She think you weak," Keokotah said, smirking a little, "I tell her you strong. Tell her you kill big animal."

"She can think what she likes," I replied irritably. "It does not matter to me."

Yet I was angry with myself that I could do no more, for winter was coming on and we were ill prepared for the cold. We had found good shelter in the caves, and we had brought much wood close by, not touching that already close but bringing wood from afar, where it would be hard to go when winter brought snow and ice.

Keokotah and two of the younger braves from the Natchee ventured down into the plains where they killed several buffalo and brought home the meat and the hides.

At dusk on the day after the return of Keokotah I killed a large bear, killed him with three arrows and skinned him out, saving much fat meat.

Keokotah went again to the plains but returned only with an antelope.

"No good," he said. "I look. Many tracks where we kill buffalo. I think Kapata find. Now he look close by."

I did not often swear but I did then, softly and to myself. I had hoped they would not find us and would go back down the river to avoid the winter. Now we would urge them to stay on and to find us.

My leg worried me. One month, I had thought when first injured, but now the summer had gone and it was still not what it should be. Was I to be permanently crippled? I could not accept that, although I had known brave men who had been and who had achieved greatly and lived well despite it. Many hurt worse than I had gone on to lead active lives. Yet I was alone.

Keokotah was my friend but I could not impose a burden upon him, and I had no family closer than a thousand miles.

Deliberately I began going further afield. I pushed myself to hunt, to extend my movements. When I tired, I rested, but I continued to hunt, to bring wood, and to collect seeds. And then I set myself another task, to check for tracks.

Of course, along the game trail following the stream was the likely route by which an enemy might come, yet they might also come over the mountains. I tried to leave nothing to chance, but to be aware of tracks wherever I was.

Although her women dressed skins and gathered what seeds and herbs could still be found, I saw nothing of Itchakomi.

Not that I was looking. I had no business with her and no doubt she was about business of her own. Yet she was nowhere in sight, and I wondered. When Keokotah was about I never looked toward her cave. We had our own cave, our own fire. It was sufficient.

And then the snow fell.

There was a night when the skins with which we covered ourselves were not enough, there was a morning when I walked out into the crisp, cold air to find the hills about the valley white with freshly fallen snow.

That was the morning we knew winter had come. That was the morning I knew Itchakomi would not be going away downriver. It was already too late.

Icy winds would be blowing down from the north, and other Indians would be sitting warm in their lodges. Soon the rivers would freeze and no canoe would be able to travel upon them. Itchakomi had been foolish to wait so long, yet I would say nothing of that. I felt better that she . . . they . . . were staying. After all, I'd not like to think of them freezing out on those ghastly plains—ghastly in the winter, at least.

On the second morning Keokotah returned from a hunt begun before the snow, and he brought with him a prisoner, an Indian girl, an Apache.

17

The girl was young and quite pretty. Furthermore, she did not seem at all put out by her capture.

"Where'd you find her?"

"She hides."

"From you?"

"No from me. She does not see me. She is Acho Apache, and she is taken from her village in a raid. She makes runaway and hides. I see her. I tell her 'Come!' She is here."

"I see she is." She drew nearer to him. "Does she wish to return to her people?"

Even as I spoke I could see how foolish the idea was. If ever I had seen anyone who was pleased to be right where she was it was this Indian girl. "She is your problem, Keokotah," I said. "Just so she doesn't run off and bring them back on us."

"She no run," he said, and I believed him.

Limping, I walked outside. The air was cool off the snow-covered mountains. We had a few more days before the snow fell here, or so I hoped. Still, we were as ready as we were likely to be. We had buffalo robes, we had meat, and we had shelter. At the edge of the brush near the creek, something stirred. My eyes held, waiting.

It moved again. It was a buffalo calf.

I spoke to Keokotah. "The calf. Tell them not to kill it."

"They know. I speak strong to them."

Several times when I was close to the calf I spoke to it. Once I reached out to touch it, but it moved away, though not too swiftly, and I felt the poor creature was lonely. I talked to it, and sometimes when I went down by the stream it walked along not too far away, keeping pace with me. One day when Keokotah's Acho woman made fry bread I offered a piece to the buffalo calf. It smelled and then tugged it from my hand and ate it. Gradually, we became friends.

The snow came in the night, softly, silently, very white, very thick, and soon very deep. The Natchee stayed by their fires, as did we. However, later in the day I went out and after much persuading and tugging, got the calf into the cave. He would not stay, but ran outside and into the snow.

"He like snow," Keokotah said. "Animal like snow."

"Tell them not to hunt near the opening of the valley," I suggested to Keokotah. "There will be no tracks to see."

The days went by slowly, and when I could I talked to the Natchee or to Keokotah and his woman.

Her people hunted southeast from us, she told us. As to where they had come from she did not know, only that it had been a very good place. It was "over there" and now she was "here." It did not seem to matter, for they had always been somewhere. Her grandfather had lived far from here, and his father still farther.

When I could I led her to talk, and when she understood that Keokotah approved she talked willingly enough. Gradually her story became the story of many small migrating tribes, moving from place to place over the years. Often they remained for many years in one general area, and then, pushed out by others or because of drouth or the scarcity of wildlife, they moved on. Their warriors went off on raids or were raided.

I saw little of Itchakomi. She held herself aloof, although once or twice I caught her looking our way. My message had been delivered and my responsibility had ended. Yet she had spoken with Keokotah and with his Acho woman.

In all this time we saw nothing of Kapata or of the Conejeros. Faithfully, we all stayed away from the opening into the valley so as to leave no visible indication of our presence. We kept our fires to a minimum and tried not to burn them when the wind would take the smoke down through the opening along the creek. Nevertheless, I knew it was merely a matter of time.

Despite the early snow the aspen trees were a river of gold flowing along the mountain and spilling down its sides. I stood by the creek one day simply soaking up the rare beauty of the late autumn, when suddenly Itchakomi was nearby.

On this day she wore white buckskins, beaded and worked with porcupine quills. She was, without doubt, a woman of rare beauty.

Standing there with a background of the golden leaves of the aspen she was something no one could look at and remain unmoved.

"You are beautiful!" I said, the words bursting from me, without warning.

She turned her head and gave me a cool, direct look. "What is it 'beautiful'?" she asked.

The question put me at a loss for words. How to explain beauty? "The aspen are beautiful," I said. "The sunrise is beautiful."

"You think me like the aspen?"

"Yes." How did I get into this? "You are slender and lovely to look at."

She looked at me again. "You are courting me?"

The question stopped me cold. I gulped, hesitated, and then said, "Well, not exactly, I—"

"It does not matter!" She spoke sharply. "I am a Sun. You are *nothing*, a stranger."

"To you I am nothing. To me I am something."

She shrugged, but she did not walk away. "What will happen if you are not there and the Great Sun dies?" I asked.

For several minutes she did not speak, but I had an idea the question had been worrying her, also. "There will be another to take his place until I return."

"A woman can rule?"

"It has been so."

"Often?"

"No . . . once, I believe."

"The plains are wide and very cold. There are terrible storms of wind and snow, or I would take you back—"

"I do not need to be taken. When I wish to go, I shall go." She gestured. "This is a good place."

A soft wind stirred the aspens into shimmering golden beauty. A few leaves fell, dropping like a shower of golden coins onto the snow. The red leaves of the scrub oak clung stubbornly, not to be worried by any such gentle wind. The stream rustled along its banks, a thin coating of ice near its edges slowly dissolving into water again.

"Did you find the place you sought?"

She hesitated. "I did not. I found where the river comes from the mountains. It is a good place." She looked around. "This also is a good place." She glanced at me. "It is yours?"

"We found it, Keokotah and I. It is yours if you wish it."

"If it be not yours you cannot give it." Her chin lifted. "The earth belongs to the Great Sun. He lives where he wishes."

"It is a good place where you live," I said, "a pity to leave it."

She shrugged. "We shall not. I came to find a new place because the Great Sun wished it. I do not believe there is danger."

"You were visited by a trader?"

"No trader. A boat with men came. They stopped with us. They traded some things. They went away." She shrugged. "It was nothing."

We were silent for a few minutes and then I said, "There will be change. White men are coming, and they will not come only to pass on. Some will stay. They will not believe in the Great Sun. Their way of life will be different. Some of your people may wish to trade. Some of them may change."

"They will not. Our way is the best way. Our people know it."

Reluctantly I said, "There are Englishmen in what we call Virginia, and in Carolina. There are Spanishmen in Florida. The people who live near them are changing. They often make war on the English or Spanish and often it is because they want things they cannot trade for.

"The tribes who live near the white man are coming to desire the white man's things. They sometimes do not wish to live in the old way."

"The Natchee will not change."

For a long moment I hesitated and then I said, "I fear there will be no future for those who do not change. When there are no new ideas things can remain the same, but strangers are coming with different ways—"

"There are strangers in our villages. There has been no change."

"I noticed one of your men with a steel knife, a white man's knife. That is change. I saw one of your women sewing with a steel needle. That is change. Do not others want such knives and needles?"

"We do not need them."

"Need and desire have no connection," I said. "Many people desire things they do not need. Happiness can be measured by what one does not need, but often to see is to want.

"For many years"—I spoke quietly—"all was the same in the villages of the tribes. There were no new ideas. You knew all that lay about you. The weapons your warriors had were the same as those of other tribes. Now some tribes will have guns, and all will change. In the north the Dutch and the English have traded guns to the Iroquois, and the Iroquois—"

"I do not know Iroquois."

"It is said that several tribes have come together to fight as one. The Seneca are one such tribe. Now they have begun destroying the tribes that live near them.

"And what of the Creeks? Your neighbors? Some of them have guns. It is whispered they are no longer friendly."

She was silent, and I knew she was thinking of what I had said. She did not like it, but she was thinking about it. Leaves fell again from the aspen, and some fell into her hair, making there a small diadem of gold. I looked away.

This was no time for me to be thinking of a woman's beauty. I had mountains to cross.

"You live on a great river," I said, "and men have always sought the great rivers because they lead to the sea, and to trade with other peoples. They will come to your river, too, and they will come in greater numbers than all your people, and they will come with their weapons and their desires.

"They will know nothing of the Great Sun, nor will most of them care. They will have their own beliefs and their own rulers, and you will have to defend your land, by talk if possible, by war if necessary."

After a moment she said, "I cannot believe what you speak. The man you call De Soto and his Men of Fire came, and they are gone, and nothing happened. The Great Sun said they would go and be forgotten, and they were.

"Whispers have come to us of other Men of Fire wearing iron shirts who came into the Far Seeing Lands, and they, too, are gone."

"Others will come who will not go away. At first they will look for gold or pearls but then they will want land. Your people must be prepared for this."

She shook her head. "Nothing will change. Nothing ever has."

Well, what could I say? She spoke from her experience and the remembered experience of her oldest men. Year followed year, season followed season, and day followed day, and the rites of the seasons were performed and all remained the same.

There had to be a way to reach her, yet. . . . "Itchakomi, your people have not lived here forever. Have you not found old graves, old stone tools, different kinds of arrowheads?"

"So?"

"Those who passed on before you did not expect change, either, but change came. Does the leaf on the tree know winter is coming? Does the leaf know it will fall and crumble away among other leaves? If your people would survive they must be prepared.

"You are here because some among your wise men believed a new home must be found, but a new home is not the answer, for when they come they will leave no place untouched.

"See? *I* am here. Why? Because I wanted to see, to know, to understand. I wanted to go beyond the Great River. I wanted to go beyond the plains. I want even to go beyond these mountains where we now are. I think I am in this world to find beauty in lonely places. At least, that is what I wish to think.

"My father was the same. Why did he leave his home in the fens? Why did he cross the sea to this far land? Why, when he had a home at Shooting Creek, did he wish to go beyond the far blue mountains? I do not know, but I think it is something buried within us, something that makes us long for the far places.

"Nor do I believe it will stop here. When men have gone down the longest rivers, climbed the highest mountains, and crossed the greatest deserts there will still be the stars."

"The *stars*?"

"Sakim, my old teacher, told me that some wise men in India and China believed the stars were suns like ours and that somewhere out there were other worlds. Who knows if this is true or not? But do you think men will be content to wonder? Someday they will find a way to the stars and an answer to their questions."

She looked at me with wonderment. "You talk strangely. Why are you not content with this?"

"It is man's nature, Itchakomi, to wonder, and thank all the gods for it. It is through wonder that we come to know." I was silent for a moment, thinking how long their world must have remained undisturbed, their people slowly becoming content with what they had and what was near. With us in Europe it was otherwise. Our rivers and our many harbors had let strangers come with strange ideas, and our people had changed. There had been migrations from other parts of Europe and Asia, each bringing new customs, new ways. It had brought war and trouble, but it had brought change also.

We stood together in silence, I with my thoughts and she with hers, the stream rustling at our feet. Low clouds had come, and they rested in the silent valleys among the hills, and with mountains looming above. Slowly a few flakes began to fall, drawing a thin, delicate veil across the morning.

"We had better go back," I said.

She turned and looked straight at me for a moment, but said nothing. We walked back together, and then she went to her cave and I to mine.

Several days passed in which I hunted, and scouted the mountains to the west, finding another even higher valley than this where we were, and one to which we might retreat if necessary. I found a shelter and gathered wood against a time of need. It was ever my way to prepare for the possible, even if improbable. Now, in the event we had to flee from where we were, we would know where shelter was and where wood was gathered. I moved away from the place, choosing landmarks and other trail markers that could be found at night.

It was a good place, that upper valley, and I spoke of it to Keokotah, telling him of the shelter cave and the wood. "There may be a better place," I said, "but at least it is a place."

Somewhere out there was Kapata, for I did not believe he was one to quit. Somewhere were the Conejeros, but the snow was still falling and there was hope they would not discover our retreat.

That day I began for the first time to set traps for fur. If the time came when I returned to civilization I would need money, and furs were the most certain source. But we might need the furs for ourselves. I was afraid it was going to be a long winter.

Keokotah hunted each day, and each day returned with game. Often he went alone, sometimes with one of the Natchee. One night beside the fire he spoke suddenly.

"They look for us."

Startled, I looked around at him. "Who?"

He shrugged. "Conejeros. Kapata. I do not know. Somebody."

"You saw tracks? Inside the valley?"

"Outside. I am over the mountain. I am in the trees. Among the trees," he amended. "I see five mans. They look for tracks."

That sounded like Kapata. I doubted the Conejeros believed we were still about, but Kapata would be sure of it. The Conejeros did not need to find us, but Kapata did.

Of course, it came as no surprise. We had known he would be searching for us.

It was on the third day of the snow that I went to the cave mouth and looked out. All was white and still. The snow was no longer falling, but the tree branches bent under their weight of snow and wherever we looked it was a white, white world. Turning, I walked back into the cave. Keokotah was sleeping.

Suddenly I wished I had a book. It had been so long since I had read. Could a man forget how to read? The idea worried me. I checked our supply of meat. There was enough to last a long time, but we would need to hunt when we could. I found myself wishing for Keokotah's pasnuta, the creature with the long nose. Some kind of long-haired elephant would provide us with enough meat to last for a long time.

The thought amused me. The only elephants I had heard of had been from India or Africa, places that were warm most of the time. It was unlikely an elephant could survive in this country in winter, but I knew little of the beasts. In any event it was purely idle speculation.

Returning to the cave mouth I stood where I could look out over the valley. Because of falling snow I could not see the entrance to the valley.

Should we move to the upper valley now? It would be colder, and we would not have as much fuel. Our meat we could take with us.

Glancing around I saw Itchakomi. She put her hand out to catch a snowflake. It hit her palm and then vanished. She gave a little cry of amazement. "It is gone!"

"They melt quickly sometimes."

She looked at me. "You have seen snow?"

"Much of it on the mountains, and once we hunted far to the north and there was snow. We returned home."

"Will it stay?"

"For months, I think. Five or six moons," I suggested. "I do not know. Some years are colder than others."

"It is not a good place for my people," she said. "They do not understand."

"They could learn, and there is much game." I pointed toward the western hills. "They could lose themselves in the mountains. It is beautiful there."

"I shall go back," she said.

"I shall go west, I think. Or perhaps I'll stay here, at the edge of the plains." I had not thought of it until that moment but suddenly I decided. I would stay. I would find a place somewhere along the edge of the mountains, and stay.

The thought was strange to me, who thought only of wandering. A foolish thought that would go away. I was sure of that. Yet the idea lingered.

"Here?" She looked around. "But you are alone! There will be nobody!"

I shrugged. "I am often alone. It is my nature."

"But you would need a woman!"

"In time I'd find one." I smiled. "Maybe even a Conejero woman. Or an Acho, like Keokotah."

Her eyes were cool. She glanced at me and then looked away.

"Indian men need women to prepare the hides for them," I said. "After a hunt there is much work, but I can do my own, and have done them. On this trip I have made moccasins, and when necessary I can make my leggings and jacket. When I marry it will be for love."

"Love? What is love?"

It was something of which I knew nothing, yet something of which I had thought a good deal. Too much for a man who did not intend to take a woman . . . yet.

"It is something between a man and woman, something that goes beyond just being man and woman. It is a feeling between them, a sharing of interests, a walking together, it is—"

Keokotah was suddenly there. "Somebody comes!" he said.

Stepping to a place where I could look through the trees, I saw them.

Two men standing beside the creek, looking toward us.

18

We held ourselves still, knowing a movement might be seen, hoping no smoke was visible from the caves behind and above us. After several minutes of looking around they turned to go, crossing the stream and walking back toward the way they had come.

"Conejeros!" Keokotah said.

Neither of us replied. We simply watched. I know my heart was beating slowly, heavily. I thought of my guns back in the cave. It was foolish to have them and not carry them always. When their time would come I did not know, but they were something on which to rely, something that might save us all.

The Conejeros had probably fought the Spanishmen, so they would be familiar with guns, but mine were far more accurate than any other firing weapons I had ever seen. Of their kind they were masterpieces, as their maker had intended them to be. My future might depend on them, and that of Itchakomi.

Now the strangers were gone, or apparently gone. Still we did not move, for they might yet be within sight of us, might turn and look back. "Thank God," I said, "there were no tracks!"

Itchakomi turned and looked at me. "Who is God?" she asked.

For a minute I just stood there. How to answer such a question? I was no preacher or priest. I was no student of religion. I knew so very, very little!

"He is the Father. He is present in all things. He—"

"—is the Sun?"

"That would be one way in which he reveals himself. I believe he is more than just the sun."

"*Just* the Sun?" Her eyes were cool. "The Sun gives life to all things." She turned her dark eyes to me. "The Sun was our ancestor."

Religion was a topic I avoided. I felt myself inadequate to discuss it. Each man seemed to have a different idea about it. Moreover I had discovered that few things led more quickly to anger. "Perhaps you are right," I replied mildly. "Men have found many explanations and perhaps each contains some element of truth. I am not a scholar, only one who wishes he could be."

"What is it, a scholar?"

"I suppose a scholar is one who studies the origins of things, the laws of society and how men came to be what they are and where they are. I am not a scholar, and I have known but one, my teacher Sakim."

"He was an Englishman?"

"No." I squatted above the snow and with a twig I drew a rough map of Europe, Asia, and Africa. "England is here, and Sakim came from over here." I indicated a place in Central Asia not far from Samarkand, yet the map was unbelievably crude. "Long ago many scholars came from there. Now they seem to come from further west."

"Why?"

I shrugged. "I know only that civilizations seem to be like people. They are born, they grow to maturity, then they age and lose their vitality and they die, only to be born again in later years."

"And where are we?"

I moved back, indicated the breadth of the Atlantic, and then North America and a place on it. "We are about here. The Natchee lived about there." I indicated a place on a river above a gulf.

For a long time she studied it. Then the wind began to grow chill, and I shifted my feet, wiggling my toes against the cold in my moccasins.

"It is so, this?"

Keokotah had looked at it and then looked away. I do not believe he was interested. It all seemed remote to him, remote from the lands he knew, remote from these mountains.

"I do not believe this." She smudged the map suddenly with her toe. "I have heard nothing of this. Even the Ni'kwana has not spoken of it."

"You asked."

We walked back to the cave together, neither of us speaking. At the path between our two caves she stopped. "You are from this place, England?"

"My father was."

"The Warriors of Fire? They come from there?"

"From nearby. They are enemies of England, most of the time. They have many ships, many soldiers. They have conquered lands to the south. They killed many, made slaves of others. They destroyed their gods."

"They cannot destroy the Sun."

"No." I smiled. "They would not wish to. They need its warmth as we do."

She lingered. "The tracks in the snow? Could you do them for me again?"

"I shall try. Maybe on a bark, or better still a deer hide."

"I do not believe it but I should like to see what you believe. If such strange tribes had been, the Ni'kwana would have spoken of them."

"Before my father came to America he had never heard of the Natchee. The Englishmen who live near Plymouth have never heard of the Natchee. Even the Indians who live nearby do not know of the Natchee, yet the Natchee are important people. No man knows all the peoples. No man knows all the lands. So far as we know I am the first of my people to come this far, and perhaps none of my people will ever know that I came here, or that I met you."

She was silent and then her eyes lifted to mine. "Is it important that you have met me?"

"It is to me," I surprised myself by saying, "perhaps not to them."

She turned her eyes away, and then she said, "I am a Sun."

"And I am not."

She shook her head. "No, I think you must be a Sun, too. Although from another tribe, another place."

"I could be a Stinkard," I said, smiling. "I do not place much faith in names or titles."

"Do you have Suns in your country?"

"They are called royalty. We have another class as you have, called the nobility, and we also have our Respected Men."

"And you?"

"In our country we have another class, I believe. They are called 'yeomen,' and my father was one of them. It is said that there were some respected men among my ancestors, too, but my father paid little attention to that. He judged each man by himself and not by his ancestors."

We each returned to our caves, and on that day we restricted our moving about, fearful the men we had seen might come again, and we wanted to leave no more tracks in the snow. Yet already I was making plans. When another heavy snow came we would move into the higher valley, further back in the hills. We would need heavy snow to cover our tracks. Until then we would enjoy our caves.

There were many deerhides among us, some simply cured, some well tanned. One of the finest I secured from a Natchee. I would have traded, but when he discovered I wished to make a present for Itchakomi he presented me with it.

To draw a map from memory is not easy, yet Sakim had taught me well and I did the best I could, using all the space on the deerhide. Itchakomi was a girl of unusual intelligence, as I had recognized from the first, but when one is teaching one always assumes a certain degree of preknowledge or awareness, and her world was one that embraced only areas with some two or three hundred miles around, and only rumors of much of that.

She had seen the Gulf of Mexico, but knew it only as a vast body of water. Some of her people had once been to Cuba and even to Jamaica. Long ago there had been trade with Yucatan, but that was a misty tradition from a time before the Spanishmen came, which was more than one hundred years before. Ni'kwana had been one of those who had made the last voyage to Yucatan. They had found the Spanish there and had fled.

My father's last crossing of the Atlantic had taken him, if I remembered correctly, sixty-two days. It was difficult for her to imagine such a great body of water. I tried to explain about the many countries, the large cities, the riverboats.

We had food and fuel so there was no need to stir outside the caves. Nor did we wish to attract attention.

Always, there was someone on guard. Often I was the one, sometimes Keokotah or one of the Natchee. We saw no movement. A little snow fell, but only a very little. Within the cave, by firelight, I began the drawing of the map.

Long ago, when only a small boy, Sakim had each of us draw this map, and he tried to explain to us the world as he knew it, and the world we should know. Sakim was a Moslem, and Mecca was the center of the Moslem world. To it other Moslems came on pilgrimages from every part of the world bringing with them their knowledge of peoples far away and lands strange to any but themselves.

Only within the past century had Europe become aware of the many lands and beliefs that lay in the farthest corners of the world. It was required of a good Moslem that at least once during his lifetime he make a pilgrimage to Mecca, and they came by the thousands.

Pausing to replenish the dying fire I looked about to

discover that everyone slept. Several of the Natchee had begun coming to our cave to sleep, to leave more freedom to Itchakomi and her women.

The night was still, with only an occasional crackle from the fire or a hissing whisper as the flames found dampness.

Why was I doing this? Why was I drawing a map of the world she would never see for an Indian girl who probably had no wish to know of it?

Even when the map was finished how could I make her comprehend the vastness of that world out there? Moreover, was it fair to her? She had been the center of her world, but now she would find it pitifully small. Did she want that? Did I want it?

For a moment I thought to cast my map into the flames, but the task itself now engrossed me. I had a desire of my own to complete it. Supposing someday I became the father of a child? Would I not want him or her to know the world in which we lived?

Irritably, I shook my head. Such an idea was foolish. I had no plans for a family, nor plans for a wife. When spring came I was going deeper into the mountains. There was a lot of country out there I wished to see.

Yet I returned to the map, slowly tracing in the Black Sea and the Caspian. Sakim himself had come from a land near the Caspian Sea and had wandered on to Tashkent and Samarkand before going to Bagdad and Aleppo. Finally, I rolled up the map and lay down to sleep.

For a long time I lay awake, my mind alive with ideas. How to make Itchakomi understand my world?

How to make her realize her own would never be the same again? If she found a place in the mountains, it would be only a temporary refuge, and one could not hide from change. One must adapt or die.

Already among my own people I had seen it. I had seen them shed the old customs and adapt to the new. I had seen them find ways of doing things never tried before.

When I awakened I was cold, colder than I had ever

been before. Crawling from my blanket and buffalo robes I stirred the fire and added fuel, peering from the cave mouth. Nothing moved in a white world. The sky was a dull flat gray and when I looked at the stream it was a shining path of ice.

No one stirred in the cave of Itchakomi. I walked to the opening, the snow crunching under my feet, and stepping inside I stirred their fire also and brought life from the ash-buried coals. When a good blaze was taking the chill from their cave I tiptoed out and went back to my own. Beside the fire I shivered, my face burning, my back chilled. Yet slowly the cave warmed, and I got out my deerskin and began again on the map. My fingers were cold and it was hard to work, but now I was gripped by my task. Yet as I worked, I was bothered by doubts.

What would my revelations mean to her? Would she believe? I knew most Indians doubted the stories told by Europeans, and so might she.

Suppose she did believe? What would it do to her world? Her beliefs? Her personal assurance?

She was a Sun, which among her people meant she was most important. She could walk with pride among her people and the neighboring tribes, respected and looked up to. What would happen when she realized her people were unknown in the wider world and her beliefs unaccepted? I hesitated over my map and put it aside. I added fuel to the fire and stared into the flames.

It might be well to forget my map, to let her live out her days believing what she now did. But would that happen? The French, Spanish, English, and Dutch all claimed land. They would be moving in to settle, and there was no way to prevent that. Better to prepare her for what was to come. She seemed a very intelligent girl, or was I reading something into her because I wished to find it?

That stopped me. Why should I wish it? She meant nothing to me. When the weather broke we would be moving on. Further west for me, and back to her homeland for her.

Still, if she had the map and realized what had happened in other lands she might be better prepared for what would happen here.

I went to the cave's opening and looked out upon the white, empty land before me. Even the trees were lost under the heavy fall of snow. Everything before me was frozen in the icy grip of winter.

We had fuel, and knew where more could be had, and we had meat. We could last out this cold and longer. Then we must hunt again. It would be impossible to escape eastward across the plains. Yet we would have little to fear from the Conejeros now. They would be holed up in their lodges, as any sane Indian would be. Of Kapata I was not so sure.

He was a vengeful man, and he was also a man in a hurry. I did not believe the snow would stop him, or the cold. It might rob his followers of some ambition, but not Kapata himself.

As I stood at the cave's mouth, half shielded by brush and trees, which both provided concealment and helped conserve our heat, I thought of Kapata and tried to decide what his next move might be.

Our tracks had vanished beneath the snow, yet his was a shrewd mind, and he would try to decide where we had gone. Our need for shelter was the same as that of others, and a first consideration was the wind. We must have shelter from the wind. A cliffside then, or a thick grove. We could have built a shelter or found a cave. If a cave, then the mountains would be the logical place.

My thinking left me uneasy. Surely, the possible hiding places along the creeks and rivers would be few and easily found. Kapata would know of the Conejeros, and if he had not allied himself with them he would know where they had been, so one by one the possibilities would be eliminated.

It was cold out there now . . . cold!

Kapata would be seated in a shelter now, fuming at the delay, impatient to be out and doing. At any time the cold could break, and then he would come seeking.

Itchakomi's fighting men were few and not so fierce as those they must meet, for the Natchee by shrewd diplomacy had avoided wars and fighting more than most. The Conejeros were not interested in peacemaking.

Nothing moved out there. The snow stretched away white and endless. I looked again and then returned to my mapmaking.

Keokotah slept.

Few Indians moved about in the cold, knowing too well the dangers and how easily a man might die if injured. It was the Indian way, the sensible way, to lie by the fire. It was storytelling time for them.

I added fuel to the fire.

Before the day was out I would have to bring more fuel into the cave, for the flames were hungry and the dry wood burned swiftly. After a while I put down my map and broke off a piece of frozen jerky, which snapped like wood. Tucking the piece into my mouth I went again to the cave mouth.

Nothing stirred.

Going to a fallen tree I broke some of the larger branches and carried them back inside. Working steadily, I had in a few minutes gathered wood for the day and most of the night.

With a last armful of wood I was turning back to the cave when a movement caught my eye. I stopped dead still, and then slowly turned my head.

Out there, in the snow, and yet far away, something moved! Something, a man or an animal, moving toward us.

Fascinated, unbelieving, I stood, watching.

How far away? A mile? Oh, more than that! Perhaps two miles?

What was it? Who was it?

I waited, watching.

19

Keokotah was beside me. "He hurt," he said. "No walk good."

We watched the distant figure struggling through the snow, and my feelings were not Christian. Whoever it was down there could bring us nothing but grief. Whatever else he was doing he was marking a trail right to our door at a time when we could not afford to attract attention.

He seemed to be alone, which probably meant that he was fleeing from something—perhaps he had been a prisoner of Indians and was escaping.

"He know about caves," Keokotah said.

It was the only explanation. We had deliberately not moved about, so he could not know of our presence. The only reason he could have for coming this way was that he knew about the caves and was seeking shelter from the cold. He was still a long way off and was having a hard time of it. We looked beyond him but saw no pursuit in sight.

The man paused then and looked back. Was he followed? Or merely afraid of being followed? In this snow, following his tracks would offer no problem. All our efforts to remain hidden were being wasted.

Now he was coming toward us again. The snow was

deeper out there than we had believed. Once he stopped and shaded his eyes toward the cliff where the caves were. He looked right where we stood, but we knew he could not see us, for we stood among trees and brush.

Drawing back a bit further against the cliff, where there was a depression caused by runoff water, I went to the next cave. The Natchee Unstwita was on guard there. He spoke neither English nor Creek, so I made signs to indicate a man was coming. He went at once to look, and then vanished within the cave, where I heard a low mutter of voices.

Itchakomi came to the mouth of the cave, stooping to emerge. She went to look, and then turned to me. "He is a white man."

A white man? Startled, I looked again. Yes, it could be. But a white man? *Here?*

Well, I was here. And there were French far to the north and Spanishmen to the south. I drew my blanket about me to conceal my guns.

"Let them stay inside," I suggested. "Only Unstwita and Keokotah."

She agreed, and studied the man again. "Keokotah says he is hurt," I commented.

"It is so."

He must have been desperate indeed. An injured man has small chance of survival in intense cold, and the day had grown no warmer. I looked back the way he had come. There was no pursuit. Had he escaped scot-free then? Or were they taking their time, knowing he could not go far in this weather?

We waited, watching him flounder through the snow. He was quite close when he stopped suddenly, crouched as if to turn, and glanced wildly about. He had seen where we had been gathering fuel and some fragments of bark atop the snow.

"It is all right"—I spoke quietly—"you may come in."

His only visible weapon was a stout stick that he must have taken up from the ground somewhere. He stared toward us but could see nothing, for we had remained behind the brush and trees.

"Who is it?" He spoke in Spanish.

"A friend," I replied in the same language, "if you are friendly."

He came a few steps further and then halted. Now he could see me, and he could see Keokotah. "Who are you?"

"Travelers," I said, "and you?"

He did not reply, but came a few steps closer. "I am hungry," he said.

"Are they far behind you?"

"Who?" He stared at me. "Nobody is behind me." He peered at me. "I need a horse. I can pay."

"We have no horses," I replied.

"No *horses*?" He almost screamed his frustration. "I must have a horse! At *once*!"

"We have no horses," I repeated. "You are escaping from the Indians?"

He was facing me now, a squarely built, not unhandsome rascal, bearded and with what seemed a freshly broken nose. He was Spanish without a doubt, and he had recently been in a fight of some kind.

"I have seen no Indians," he replied stiffly. "Not lately, anyway. I must get back to Mexico."

"It is a long way," I replied. "You can get a horse in the Spanish settlements."

"Days!" He spoke angrily, impatiently. "Every minute is precious!"

"There is food," Itchakomi said.

He glanced at her, looked again. "My God," he said. "You're beautiful!"

I was suddenly angry. Who did he think he was, anyway? "She is a Sun"—I spoke coolly—"a Sun of the Natchee. She is a princess."

"I can believe it." He looked at her again. "Such a woman! In such a place!"

He irritated me, so I grabbed his arm and pointed the

way. He tore his arm free and reached for his belt. There was a dagger there.

He glared at me and I shrugged. "Keep on going, then. You've a long way before the settlements."

He swore. Then he said, "I am a fool! You spoke of food?"

Indicating our cave, I led the way. When I glanced back Itchakomi was watching me. I thought she was smiling, and for some reason, that made me angrier still.

He was no common soldier—that was obvious. Perhaps the leader of a wiped-out expedition? I asked him. "No," he replied to my question, "not wiped-out." He accepted the food I offered and began to eat. "We quarreled," he said then. "Diego wished to go no further. I wanted to push on. We fought."

"You lost?"

"I won." He swallowed, gulped water, and then examined the piece of meat he was eating and chose the place to bite. Then he looked over at me. "I won," he repeated, "and that dog of a Diego set the others upon me."

He ate, drank, and then paused again, gesturing with the hand that held the meat. "They tied me. They would take me back to be tried for mutiny. It would mean my death. My death, d'you hear?

"So I escaped. I shall return and tell my story first, and then we shall see! Moreover"—there was a gleam of satisfaction in his eyes—"I shall have something to offer."

"A bribe?"

"A gift. A very special gift." He smiled at me. "Thank you, my friend, for being here. I was wondering what I could do, how I could appeal to a man of his very special tastes. Now I know."

He talked no more, but he had aroused my curiosity. He recovered amazingly. With the food, the drink, and a bit of rest he was a new man.

"You might think I was a fool to challenge Diego," he commented. "He was the leader and I but a follower, yet had anything happened to him, I would have been captain. I was the only man of rank, and Diego, the fool, insisted on holding to his orders, which were to go so far and no farther and not to risk hostility from strange Indians.

"Trade! That was what was wanted! Trade be damned, as you English would say. Gold is what I wanted, and I knew where to find it! *Gold!*

"I could not make him see reason so I risked all." He glanced up at me. "A man who will not risk all is a fool! A child!"

"If it is gold you want," I suggested. "Diego evidently thought first of duty."

His contempt was obvious. "Duty? A word for slaves! For servants! A man's first duty is to himself!" He shot me an impatient glance. "Of course it is gold I want! Gold can buy whatever it is you wish. It can buy power, position, women . . . whatever." Then he smiled suddenly and said, "And women can buy all those things as well."

He threw a sly glance my way.

"You did not see any Indians when coming here?"

He shrugged. "A camp that I avoided. A dozen lodges on the bank of this river out there." He looked thoughtful. "Six or seven miles beyond the opening yonder."

His eyes were busy, estimating everything. What he had in mind I did not know, but he was making a quick judgment of all we had and what we might be doing here.

"English?" he asked.

"I am. I was born here, in America."

"You'll be thrown into prison if the Spanish find you here," he commented, "although I might intercede for you."

He sat back and looked around him again. "Diego, now, he would arrest you at once and return you to Santa Fe. Then you would be sent to Mexico, in chains."

"We hope to avoid that," I said. "We do not expect to meet your Diego."

"I could speak for you," he said, "if you will do something for me."

"When spring comes and we can travel again, we shall be leaving here."

Leaving him there with Keokotah I went outside and looked back over the route he had used. His tracks were visible for some distance. He had pointed a finger at us and if he was pursued they would certainly find us all. Moreover, any Indian who discovered his trail would follow it. I looked at the gray, overcast sky.

Itchakomi was seated by the fire when I entered her cave. The women were working, and one of the men was chipping an arrowhead. I never ceased to marvel at their skill in chipping the finest flakes, especially the bird points, small arrowheads used in killing feathered game.

She looked up as I entered, and I went and sat across the fire. We sat for several minutes in silence, and then I spoke.

"You must have a care. He has left a trail the blind could follow."

She said nothing and irritably I shifted my seat. "He is a dangerous man."

She was amused. No doubt she thought me jealous, but what had I to be jealous of? Yet he worried me.

"He has something on his mind. I could see it when he looked at you."

There was laughter in her eyes. "Most men do," she said.

My cheeks were flushing with impatience and irritation. "I did not mean that. I meant something more. I do not know what. Just be careful."

"Oh, I shall!"

A bit longer I sat, feeling uncomfortable, and then I got up and walked out. Again I looked across the fields of snow. Nothing in sight but the tracks, a furrow in the snow pointing right at us. And after all our care!

Gathering some wood from under nearby trees I made a pile near the cave mouth. It was something to keep my hands busy while my thoughts took off down another trail. Our only advantage lay in the fact that he was in a hurry to be off. From what I gathered he wished to be in Santa Fe to tell his story first, and he had implied he had something to offer.

That night, when alone in the cave for a few minutes, I donned the coat of mail I had found near the village on the Arkansas. Over it I put my fringed buckskin hunting jacket, drawing the laces tight. Feeling with my fingers I assured myself no part of it was visible. Had I a mirror . . .

I had not seen a mirror since leaving the settlement on Shooting Creek, almost a year ago.

A year! And what had I done in that year? I had broken a leg and crossed the plains to the Shining Mountains. It was little enough, but when spring came we would be over the passes and into the lands beyond.

My broken leg had mended well. True, I limped somewhat, but I could still walk and run.

Of course, I had accomplished the mission given me by the Ni'kwana. I had found Itchakomi and delivered the message entrusted to me.

Again I looked across the snow, but my mind was puzzling over the Spanishman. I could not make him out. Well, he wished to be on his way, and the sooner the better.

When I went back inside he was sleeping. He was a powerfully built man and seemed quick in his movements despite the cold that must have stiffened his muscles. He would be a dangerous antagonist.

Keokotah glanced at me but said nothing. I knew he did not like or trust the Spanishman and would be alert for mischief.

Let the Spanishman rest and eat and be off. He would have caused us trouble enough.

He thought only of his destination and what he would do there and had given no thought to hiding his trail, even had he been capable of it.

Outside I looked toward the mountains, white with snow under the cold gray sky. A low wind stirred the snow, sending faint waves of it dusting across, settling, and then stirring again. It was bitterly cold still. I carried wood into the cave, then more wood.

How lonely those icy ridges! Yet what treasures might lie there? Gold and silver, yes. Beauty intrigued me more, beauty and the glorious wonder of walking where none had walked before me. What else might await discovery? Strange plants and animals, unknown hollows in the hills, green and lovely in the summer. I could not wait to be wandering along their flanks, following nameless streams into nameless valleys. What more could man want than this? A land to discover, food for the hunting, a quiet place to rest when night falls.

When I came back into the cave the Spanishman was sitting up.

"We must talk together, you and I," he said. "We are men of the world, and we can settle this small matter between us."

"What have you in mind?"

He smiled, that quick, assured smile. "I want to buy the woman," he said. "The tall one."

For a moment I was stunned. "You want to *buy* her?"

"Why not? She is an Indian, is she not? There are many women for you, and she can be useful to me for trading purposes. With her I could buy—"

"I do not traffic in women," I said, "nor is she mine to sell. She is her own woman."

"Bah!" He waved a careless hand. "No woman is her own, least of all an Indian woman. If you will not sell her or trade, I shall simply take her."

20

The man's audacity amazed me. For a moment I just looked at him. "Tomorrow," I said, "you will be fit to travel. I would suggest you do just that."

"Of course," he said.

"You will leave here at daybreak and you will leave alone."

He smiled, showing a fine set of white, even teeth. "And if I do not choose to?"

"Bodies do not lie long upon the ground. The coyotes dispose of them."

His eyes were mocking but suddenly wary. He measured me carefully. Then his eyes shifted to Keokotah.

"Do not think of him. It is I who would kill you. Itchakomi is one of our party. I am the head of that party. If she needs protection, I shall protect her."

"You said she was not your woman?"

"She is not, yet she is under my protection."

We had not heard her enter. How long she had been standing there I did not know. We saw her at the same moment standing tall and still inside the cave mouth. A slight movement of air stirred her skirt.

"She who is not your woman thanks you, but I shall

need no protection." As she spoke the Spanishman sat up, his eyes on hers.

For the first time he realized the kind of woman she was, and certainly no queen upon a throne could have been more cool and imperious.

"My name is Gomez," he said. "You would be wise to remember it."

"*Kitch!*" She used the word contemptuously, and although he knew not its meaning he recognized the tone, and his face flushed.

Ignoring him, she spoke to me. "We talk, you and me. We talk soon, yes?"

"Of course."

She left the cave and he stared after her, his anger showing. "What does it mean, 'kitch'?" he asked.

"It is a Natchee word for dung," I said cheerfully. "In this case it was an expression of opinion, I believe."

His face flushed with anger. "I'll show that—!"

Keokotah spoke suddenly. "You think fool! She brave! She strong! She have strong medicine! You nothing to her."

Gomez swore. He got to his feet, staggering a little. I watched him, noting that he favored his side. He started to speak again but I interrupted.

"You are a guest here. Tomorrow you go. We will give you meat. Your settlements are to the south. Whatever you are, have been, or wish to be I do not know or care. You are conducting yourself as no gentleman would, and if you raise your voice or speak against anyone here, you will leave tonight."

His hand rested upon his waistband. He had a pistol there that I had glimpsed.

"I do not wish to kill you, but if you were to draw that pistol under your hand, I would."

He had not seen my guns, but I was wearing them under the buffalo coat, which I had not removed since returning to the cave.

He wanted to call my hand. It was in his mind, and I was ready.

"What could you have better than a pistol?"

My smile was cheerful. "A better pistol," I said, "or something of the sort."

Abruptly, he sat down. "All right!" He waved a dismissing hand. "Forget what I have said! I am impatient! I did not know what manner of woman she was." He looked at me. "She is truly an Indian?"

"She is. She is like no Indian you have met. Pizzaro might have met someone similar in Peru."

"She is an Inca? *Here?*"

"There may be a connection. I do not know. She is with us now, but she was the leader of her group."

"Group?"

He had seen only four of us. I smiled at him. "She has ten strong fighting men with her, and some women. She has my protection if she wishes, but she does not need it. She has ten men who would have your scalp in no time, or they might simply geld you."

"Geld *me*?" His face flushed and then paled. "What kind of talk is that?"

"It has happened," I said, "to men who thought themselves too important." I smiled again. "You are in a different land, my friend, and before you swagger too much you had best learn the customs of the country and the people."

A cold wind was blowing up outside, swirling the snow. We added fuel to the fire and then I went to my bed beyond the flames. Gomez, if that was his name, was staring into the fire, thinking.

He was a bright man, and brave enough, I suspected, but his plans had gone awry, and now he would be considering his next move. That he did not wish to arrive back among his people empty-handed was obvious, as it also was that he had contempt for anyone's feelings but his own. Yet he was no fool. He was a man of whom to be wary. In this, the smaller cave, there were but three of us.

Whatever else Gomez was, he was now desperate. Beaten and driven from Diego's expedition, he had stumbled upon us, hoping for a horse. Now he must head south through the snow to Santa Fe. I did not know the distance but it was many days travel, and I could not believe he was anxious for it.

That night I slept not well. At every move he made my eyes flared open, and Keokotah was equally on edge, yet at daybreak he shouldered the small pack of food we gave him and without so much as a thank-you he walked off into the snow, going back the way he had come.

We watched him move away, and Keokotah followed him, after he disappeared from sight, to see if he continued on his way.

When he was gone I went to Itchakomi's cave.

Two women were making moccasins, another was stitching furs together for a robe, a fourth was cooking.

We seated ourselves together near the wall. No men were in the cave. "They hunt for meat," she explained. "The winter is long, and we eat much."

"This place is good," I said. "You will bring your people here?"

She was silent for several minutes. "I do not know. My people have lived long beside the river. It is warm there and what they plant will grow. Here they must learn new ways. The planting seasons will be different. I do not believe they will wish to leave the warmth and the river. They will stay, and hope for the best."

"But you will tell them of this place?"

"People do not lightly leave what they have always known. Our old ones are buried there. The young who died are buried there also. Our memories are there, and they will turn their eyes from danger."

"And you?"

"Their place is my place also. I must be with them. I must lead and I must advise."

"If the Great Sun dies while you are gone?"

"If I do not return in time, another will take his place."

For a time we did not speak and then I said, tentatively, "It is lovely here, and in the spring—"

"When very young I went one time to the mountains.

I went with my mother, my father, and the Ni'kwana. There were others, too. We went to trade. We went to a long valley with forest all about and a small stream. There was a stockade—"

"It was my home."

She looked at me. "I do not know—"

"There was no other, except far away near the sea. We traded with the Cherokee, the Creek, and yes, the Natchee."

"We walked for many days after the river. When I saw the mountains I could not believe. Ni'kwana had spoken of mountains, but—"

"These are higher, some of them."

"I loved the mountains! Nobody understood but the Ni'kwana. I believe that was why he chose me to come here."

"It was not an easy thing for a woman to do."

"I am a Sun."

The fire was burning low, the women worked, and firelight flickered on the walls, reminding me of the cave of the dancing shadows.

"Who knows what the Ni'kwana thinks? Long ago when I was small I used to tell him of my dreams." She looked over at me. "Do you have dreams?"

"Sometimes."

"We know there is a time after this because we see those who have died in our dreams. We are in the after-world, and my mother is there and my father."

She turned to me suddenly. "What will you do when the cold is gone?"

"Go into the mountains. I want to see what is there."

"I told him of a dream. I told only the Ni'kwana. It was a dream of a boy. The boy walked on the mountains. He was alone, always alone."

"What did the boy do? Where was he going?"

She shrugged. "He was in the mountains. He walked alone. He did not do anything. Oh, yes! Once he met a bear."

"A bear?"

"A very large bear. I was afraid for the boy, but he spoke to the bear and the bear reared up on his hind legs to listen. The bear had a white streak on the side of his face, perhaps from an old wound. The bear peered at the boy who talked to him and then the bear got down on all four feet and went away."

It was very quiet in the cave. One of the women was preparing a buckskin, rubbing bone marrow into the hide to soften it and then rubbing it with a piece of sandstone. She was very quick and skillful and I watched her work. The woman wore black moccasins. I spoke of this.

"She is a Ponca who married one of our men. She was returning from the east with her father, who had been seeking the home of his ancestors."

"I have heard of them."

"They are good people, a strong people." She gestured away to the north. "Their home is there . . . far away."

At Shooting Creek my father, who wished to know all, collected what information he could gather from the Indians who came to trade. He or Jeremy Ring would talk long with the old men and women about their lives and their neighbors. Several had told us of the Ponca and of their kinfolk the Omahas, Otoes, and Osages.

"Will you go home again?" she asked suddenly.

"I do not know. I do not think so. I have dreams, too, but my dreams do not come at night when I sleep. They come by day when I am alone upon a hillside or when I lie down before I sleep. I dream of what I wish to do, what I wish to be."

"To be?"

"It is not enough to *do*, one must also *become*. I wish to be wiser, stronger, better. This—" I held out my hands. "—this thing that is me is incomplete. It is only the raw material with which I have to work. I want to make it better than I received it."

"It is a strange thought, but I like it."

We sat without talking then until I arose and left the

cave. Outside, darkness lay all about me, excepting only the dead white field of snow and the bright stars overhead. Looking about me, I shook my head. What kind of place was this? Shelter, yes, but no more than shelter. A man should have a home, a place of his own.

When I returned to the cave Keokotah was there. "He go, ver' fast. He go south."

"I wonder if he'll make it?"

"He make it. He strong." Keokotah looked up at me. "He will come back for her. Bring many mans. You see."

"She will be gone before the first grass," I said, shrugging.

He looked at me as if I were a child. "You think? Maybe you fool."

Irritated, I replied, "She's a Sun. They need her back yonder. And she wants to go back. Those are her people. That is her home."

He gathered his blankets about him and lay back on the robes.

All through the night the silent snow sifted down, covering deep the land. Our tracks, his tracks, all tracks were gone and the snow piled deep around us.

The Natchee had returned from their hunt with only an antelope. Our meat supply was dwindling and they were not accustomed to hunting in the snow. Their eyes showed their fear, for the land and the weather were strange to them. There were no gentle forests here, no hanging moss, no bayous. These rivers were frozen hard, these forests deep with snow, and the animals were bedded down, waiting out the cold.

We had hung a buffalo hide over the cave mouth to keep the cold out and the heat in.

Building the fire to last the night, edging heavier chunks together, I lay back on my own blankets and thought of tomorrow. For the moment I was the leader here. I was the responsible one.

The snow was soft and deep. I would have to make snowshoes. Turning on my side I stared into the fire.

Outside the wind moaned, the buffalo-hide curtain stirred and a sifting of snow blew in.

Shadows moved upon the walls. Had I left those other shadows behind? Or had they come with me from the cave where I had discovered them?

If they were with me I hoped they could help round up some game. I hoped they were friendly shadows. After all, I had only paid my respects to the dead; I had not disturbed them.

Suppose an enemy came in the night? So soft was the snow there would be no sound of walking, no sound of movement. When one lies awake in the night one thinks of many things, and I thought now.

Tomorrow I must go out, and I must bring back meat. We were not suffering now, but the winter before us was long and cold.

What of that huge hairy animal of which Keokotah had spoken? The pasnuta, which looked like a hairy elephant? I smiled into the darkness. Well, if there were such a thing, I needed to meet it. It might provide enough meat to last out the winter.

Where could he have gotten such an idea?

The fire crackled, and the heavy curtain stirred in the outside wind. My eyes closed and I slept, only to dream of coming face to face in the snow with a great, awesome creature, three times the size of a buffalo, a huge, hairy beast with curling tusks and red eyes, coming toward me, coming at me—

I awakened in a cold sweat. The fire had died to coals and I lay shivering, thinking of the monster of my dream, those tiny eyes, red with fury, coming at me.

I added fuel to the fire and then laid back and shivered. Just a buffalo, or a couple of red deer. I wanted nothing more than that, for I wanted to come back to—

My eyes flared open. To what? What did I have to come back to?

I wanted meat. I wanted a successful hunt. I turned

over, trying to keep the cold from seeping under my coverings. I wanted nothing more . . . nothing more.

Then I slept, fearing the hairy monster would return, but he did not. Only dawn came, cold and aware. Icy cold and still.

21

Reaching over, I laid some sticks on the coals. Then I lay back and waited for a little warmth to come into the cave. It was very cold, and it would be cold and still outside, a time for extreme care if a man would survive.

How long the cold would stay with us I could not guess, but we would need meat. We had given some to Gomez when he left, and seventeen people can eat a lot. Keokotah knew cold weather, for his experience was from a country far to the north. My only experience with cold had been a couple of brief forays into the north when I was a boy and some time spent in the high mountains.

No game would be moving in this cold. Bears would be hibernating, or at least sleeping in their dens. To find game I would simply have to stumble upon it. In the deep snow I had an advantage.

Several days before I had cut some willow wands from beside the stream and had kept them close to the fire to thaw out. Now I took one of these and bent it slowly and carefully into a rough circle and tied it. Then I tied rawhide strips across the circle and soon had shaped a couple of crude but very useful snowshoes of the bear-paw type. Later I would make better shoes, when there was time.

Taking them to the cave mouth I tied them on. Then taking my bow I started out, moving with care and where the going was easiest.

Every step needed to be taken with caution. An injured man in intense cold has small chance of survival. Rocks and fallen logs are apt to be slippery, so were best avoided. My chances of finding game were slight, but there was a patch of forest across the valley, several miles away, where we had not hunted. Deer would be bedded down in deep snow. My only chance was to startle one and make the kill before it could escape.

It was very still. The snow squeaked underfoot. I took my time, knowing that to perspire might mean to die. Perspiration can, when a man stops traveling, freeze into a thin film of ice next the skin. When I had gone about a mile I stopped in the shelter of three massive ponderosa pines, studying the terrain ahead and scanning the open area between the entrance to the valley and myself.

Soon I started on again, and when I reached the forest I stood still, looking all about me for places where deer might bed down. In good weather they preferred to be under some trees with a good view before them, but now they would have thought only of shelter from the wind.

Being alone I had no one to watch for the telltale white spots on nose or cheekbones that are the first signs of frostbite, so I covered my nose with my mittened hand. My face was stiff and raw from the cold. After a bit I moved deeper into the forest, stepping with care.

Several times I checked what experience told me were likely places for deer, but found nothing. After resting briefly, I started on. There were occasional bird tracks on the snow and once a flurry of tiny tracks and a few spots of blood. A weasel or a marten had caught some poor creature.

The morning slipped away and the afternoon began. Soon I must return if I were to make it before dark.

Swinging wide I skirted a patch of aspen, remembering how well many animals liked the aspen or the plants that grew in its shelter. The trees were bare of leaves and from a distance looked like a cloud lying upon the mountainside. The dry branches whispered in the slight wind. I turned toward an opening between aspen and scrub oak, and started forward.

The elk came off the ground almost under my feet, lunging erect, snow falling from it. It lowered its antlers at me but then thought the better of it and started away.

My bow came up, the arrow in place. I let fly. It was not the target I would have chosen but there was no time. The arrow caught it in the neck, close behind the ear, and sank deep. The elk stopped, quivered, then fell. I ran forward, feeling for my knife.

Yet as I stepped astride the elk it came up in one last lunge, came up under me so I was astride, and it sprang forward. One hand grabbed an antler, another plunged the knife. It glanced off a shoulder bone and almost stabbed my thigh, but the second thrust went home solidly. I need not have bothered, for the poor beast was dead. It fell under me and I sprang free. My bad leg folded under me and I went into the snow.

For a moment I just lay there. Then slowly I gathered myself, retrieved my bow and knife, and set about skinning the elk, getting the best cuts of meat before it froze solid.

By the time I had finished it was dark. I gathered the meat in the elk hide and then got back into my snowshoes, which I had removed for the skinning, and started back. Emerging from the woods I looked across the valley at what was now only a dark line of trees and mountains without division or feature.

For some time I had traveled in the forest, intent only on finding game, but how far west had I hunted? Before me was only a wide field of snow, and beyond was the blackness of forest and mountain. The caves were right across that field, but my burden was heavy, the snow was deep, and it was bitterly cold. If I missed my direction by but a few yards I might wander half the night finding my way. I might die out here in the cold. How cold it was I did not know, but it was far, far below freezing.

Bowed beneath the great load of meat I started across the wide stretch of snow, angling a little toward the east. I blew on my fingers. I took a step and then another, plodding slowly and carefully because of the crude snowshoes.

A wind stirred the snow. It blew a little, ceased, then started again. Snow picked up and blew in a brief flurry. I knew I would see no light unless someone happened to come outside, a slight chance at this hour.

I needed at least an hour to cross the open snow with the burden I had. Icy snow rattled against my clothing and nipped at my cheeks. I stopped, thrust my bow into the snow, and beat my hands against my legs to restore circulation.

Something black appeared on the snow just ahead of me. I stared, it moved—a wolf!

Where there was one there would be another, and another.

Without a doubt they had smelled the meat and the fresh blood. And these were wolves with little knowledge of man aside from Indians, and my smell would be different. I pushed on, walking straight at the wolf.

It wavered, hesitated, and then fled off a dozen yards further. Under the great burden of meat from the butchered elk I could move but slowly, ponderously.

Pausing at the edge of the woods I sniffed the air. I should catch a smell of woodsmoke.

Nothing.

Should I bed down right where I was? Build my own fire and prepare to defend my meat against the wolves?

But if I did not return, Keokotah or some of the others might come out to look for me. The Natchee were unfamiliar with intense cold, and some might be lost. Turning clumsily to look behind me, I saw a wolf crouched in the snow not fifty feet away!

Gesturing with my bow, I tried to warn it away, but

the lure of fresh meat was too great. The wolf ran off only a few feet and stopped.

To move at all I had to keep from under the branches, because of my towering burden. Also, I wished to avoid snagging my snowshoes on a branch or root under the snow.

Where was I? The cave might be only a few yards distant, but I had no idea where or in what direction to turn. Again I gestured at the wolf.

Wolf?

There were two of them together now, watching me. They sensed something was wrong.

The stream! If I could find the stream . . . it had to be close. I shifted the weight of meat. I was carrying enough for three men, but to leave it in the snow would be to leave it for the wolves, and how many times would I make such a kill? Hunched far over, I worked my way along the wall of the forest, seeking an opening.

The wolves kept pace with me. I shouted at them, and hoped my voice would carry to the caves.

Nothing.

Nor did the wolves pay attention. They had the smell of blood in their nostrils, and the smell was coming from me. Despite the intense cold they were hunting, which meant they were probably not just hungry but starving.

Turning about with the heavy pack was cumbersome, but I had to keep looking around. There was no guessing when one of the wolves might decide to leap.

The bow was a poor weapon against them. My guns were hard to get at, and I hated to waste a shot in the vague light. Yet it was a gun I would have to use. Pushing back my coat, I fumbled for the butt of my right-hand gun. I would have to take off the mitten, and in the cold my exposed hand would quickly freeze.

Carefully, I edged along the woods. One of the wolves moved closer, and I stepped out threateningly. It leaped back, wary again.

Something moved at the edge of the woods! Another wolf. Suddenly one of them howled, but not one of those close to me. I plodded on, avoiding projecting branches, thinking only of—

There was a break in the wall of trees, an opening! I swung a wide, sweeping blow in the direction of the wolves and then went into the wide opening.

Ice! I was walking upon ice, so I had come to the stream. The caves would be close by, for the stream swung close. I crossed the stream and mounted the far bank, trying to remember such a place.

There had been an opening upriver from the caves. I started to turn and suddenly something struck me a mighty blow from behind. I fell face downward into the snow, and my bow fell from my hand.

A wolf had sprung on me from behind, landing on the pack of meat and knocking me down. I fought to get hold of my knife. I couldn't get a gun into action.

The other wolves had leaped on me now, but they were fighting to get at the meat, wrapped in the elk hide. My knife was out. I ripped at the wolf nearest me and there was a startled yelp. Then from somewhere there was a shout and a sound of running feet. I stabbed again, missed, and felt teeth rake my exposed wrist.

With a tremendous effort I got to my knees. There were men all about me, and the wolves were gone.

Somebody had a hold on my arm and was helping me to my feet. With the weight of meat it was a struggle, but I made it. Somebody lifted the burden from my back, unfastening the rawhide with which I'd bound it to me.

Another hand shoved my bow at me, and I took it. Limping, I followed them into our cave. The Indians crowded around.

Keokotah lowered my pack of meat to the floor. "We hear wolves fighting. We come."

Exhausted and cold, I sank down by the fire. Itchakomi was there, her eyes wide and dark, looking at me.

"We needed meat," I said.

Nobody said anything. They had opened my pack and given meat to the people from Itchakomi's cave.

"We fear for you," Itchakomi said. "You gone long time."

"It was cold," I said, "cold."

There was meat enough for several days, but we could not expect a kill such as this very often. It was going to be a long and a hard winter. Of course, had the Indians been there they would have taken much more of the elk than the chunks of meat that I had saved.

"Your woman of the black moccasins," I said, "told me her people hunt west to the mountains and then down the mountains to a great peak near here. Each year they do this.

"Then they hunt back across the plains to their home, which is near the Great River. When they return you could go with them to the river and then down the river to your home."

She looked at me for a long minute and then she got up and left the cave.

I would never understand women.

And why shouldn't she go? After all, the Poncas were reported to be friendly, and she could cross the plains under their protection. She would be safer by far with a whole tribe than with her few braves.

It seemed reasonable to me. Of course—

I went to my robes and lay down, exhausted. The cold bothered my leg, but it always pained me when I did too much.

Tired though I was, sleep came slowly, and I found my thoughts wandering back to Shooting Creek Valley and my family. Pa was gone . . . I could find no words to express the emptiness that left with me.

Ma was in England, if she lived, and Brian and Noelle with her. How different their lives would be! And how far from me! Did they think of me sometimes? Did they remember the good times we'd had together?

What was England like?

Easing my leg, I tried to find a more comfortable spot in the robes. Keokotah was sleeping, and the fire burned low. Why had Itchakomi left me so abruptly? Was it that I reminded her of what awaited back there? Or because she knew she must wait until spring brought grass to the hills and water to the streams?

Dozing, I opened my eyes, raised up, and added sticks to the dying coals. Out there tonight I'd nearly tossed in my hand. I might have fought my way out of it, just might have, but the odds were all against it.

And who would have known or cared? My family would not have known. Under the robes I shifted and turned, restlessly. Why could I not sleep?

Yet after a while I did sleep, but only to dream of the great red-eyed monster with the curving tusks that had come charging upon me from the brush. I awoke in a cold sweat once more and it was long before I slept again.

In my dreams it had been shockingly clear. The monster had seen me, known me for an enemy, and charged, blasting sound as from a great trumpet. I had not fled. I had stood my ground as if frozen in place. What was wrong? Why did I not flee?

Never had I been troubled with nightmares, but this dream came again and again.

Lying awake again in the cold of breaking day I stared wide-eyed at the roof of the cave. It seemed I was gifted with second sight. . . . Was this dream a premonition of some reality to come? Was that to be my end? Was I to die impaled on one of those curving tusks, or trampled into the mud and snow under those huge feet?

Above all, why did I not even try to escape?

I sat up, put sticks upon the fire, and dressed for the cold outside.

22

A few days later Keokotah killed a deer and our snares netted a few rabbits, but with the winter only half gone we faced a starving time. To survive in wild country was never easy. Hunting had driven the wild game from the area. We had to go farther and farther afield, and the intense cold showed no sign of breaking. Even in the best of times, the gathering of nuts, roots, and herbs was a slow and painstaking business, requiring many acres to feed even one man, unless there were pecans or hazelnuts, neither of which would be available here. All such sources were now buried under deep snows.

All of us now wore snowshoes we had made ourselves. Sitting beside the fire at night, I had woven myself a pair of trail snowshoes, longer and more efficient for distance work than the bear paws I had made.

Keokotah snared some ptarmigan and I killed another deer.

Itchakomi came to my fire. I was preparing moccasins and leggings for a longer trip. "What you do now?"

"I go far," I said. "Soon there is no meat, and we starve."

"My people are learning, but all this is new to them."

"It is all right." I gestured toward the west. "There is a valley over there. There might be buffalo."

"You will need help. If there is meat it must be carried. I will go."

"You?"

"Of course. I am strong."

"It will be hard, very hard. It is a long way, and I do not know the trail."

"We will find it."

"But you will need snowshoes!" I protested.

"I have made them. I have made snowshoes like yours. I will come."

I did not want her. What lay ahead, I could guess. To find a pass without snow would not be easy and with snow upon the ground, covering the trees and rocks, it might be impossible. It would be brutally hard, and I knew only too well that one misstep might mean the end of me. It would be difficult enough alone without having another to watch out for. Alone I could attempt things I might not dare with someone else following me.

"It is no place for a woman," I said. "It is better you are here. What if the Conejeros come?"

"You wish me to be here if they come?"

"You are a Sun. Your people will need a chief."

"Keokotah is here. My people know what to do."

I was a loner and worked best alone. With Keokotah it was different. We traveled together but we did not consult. Each went his own way, each of us knowing what to do and when to do it. I did not lead him nor him me. With a woman—

She got to her feet. "It is settled then. At daybreak tomorrow?"

I started to protest, but she was already leaving the cave. I shut my mouth and swore. Behind me there was a dry chuckle, but Keokotah was not looking at me when I glanced around.

That night I did not dream. Once asleep I slept well and at daybreak was at the cave mouth. If she was late I would leave without her. I would take off so fast—

She was not late.

She had a small pack on her back when she came out. Then she stepped into her snowshoes, and without waiting for me to break trail, she started west.

There was no protest I could have made to which she might have listened. There was nothing to do but follow. Due west of us was a range of towering peaks, but we had no intention of attempting that range at this time of year. Following the small river, we bore off to the south. There was a great valley further west, but beyond our reach at this time of year.

After traveling for a short distance I moved up to break trail, and Itchakomi yielded her place. It was heavy snow, very deep in places, and fortunately, it covered many obstructions we might have had to climb over or go around. We traveled no more than eight miles that first day and found shelter under a huge old spruce tree whose branches swept the top of the snow and were themselves loaded with snow. Close to the trunk the ground was almost bare of snow, as the branches around made a natural shelter and kept out the wind. We built a small fire, and we made our beds of other spruce boughs, she on one side of the fire, I on the other.

She watched me check my guns. "What are they?" she asked.

"Weapons of fire," I explained. "Weapons of thunder. I shall use them rarely."

"They are beautiful!" she exclaimed, as they were. The Italian gunsmiths were superb artisans. It was not enough merely to make a weapon, but it must have beauty also. These were hand carved and inlaid. Yet it was my bow upon which I relied for hunting.

Our fire scarcely disturbed the cold about us, its heat lost before it reached the lowermost branches of the tree. We huddled close, enjoying the comfort of its looks more than the little heat. We chewed elk jerky and talked but little.

"Tomorrow?" she asked.

"Tomorrow we will be there, and tomorrow we will hunt. We need much meat."

She knew that as well as I. "You do not hunt for meat in England?"

"They hunt for sport."

"But they eat what they kill?"

"Oh, yes! And sometimes meat is distributed among the poor. Those who do not have enough to eat."

It was very still. Somewhere, far off, a lonely wolf complained to the night. Tomorrow we would descend into a valley no white man had seen, and probably few Indians. One thing had been obvious since leaving the Mississippi—this country was sparsely settled. The various tribes were for the most part small in numbers and widely scattered.

Long after Itchakomi lay asleep, I was awake and thinking. The last thing I wanted was to get involved with a woman. There was time for that later. For the time being I wished only to make our hunt, get what meat we could, and get back to our caves. When spring came Itchakomi would go her way and I mine.

She was a beautiful woman. That was beside the case. I had been thinking too long of wandering this country, being the first white man to see much of it, just to see it all myself for the first time. Fortunately, I told myself, Itchakomi felt the same way. We each had our private concerns. She was easy to talk to for that reason, and she had the same feeling of responsibility toward her people that I did.

At daybreak I was awake quickly. I stirred up the fire and without waiting for her to do so, prepared some food. We talked little. The fire warmed up our small space, but not enough to melt the snow around us.

The long valley that stretched away toward the southeast was scattered with meadows and cut by intervening patches of forest. The meadows were white with snow, the trees drooping under a heavy burden of it.

We went down the mountain in the cold of morning,

making no sound in the soft white snow. We did not talk. Our eyes and ears were alert for game.

Almost at once we came upon deer tracks, a lot of them. Four or five deer had moved down the mountain ahead of us. The tracks were fresh, made that morning.

West of us several peaks towered against the sky, and the valley lay open before us. Pausing beside some trees we looked down. Far away, moving in single file, we saw a line of buffalo. As we watched they scattered out, pawing into the snow to get at the grass. Nearer there were several deer.

"Wait." I spoke softly, as our voices would carry in that still, cold air. "The buffalo!"

We went on down the valley. This morning, in this valley at least, it was not so cold. We moved down, always keeping a clump of trees between us and the buffalo. When within a few hundred yards we stopped to rest. There was a shallow draw that led along behind the buffalo, and feeding close were a couple of cows.

Scanning the hills around and searching along the clumps of trees I saw no movement. There was no smoke. We seemed to be alone.

After a bit we moved out, and when I was within forty yards of the nearest buffalo I decided to chance it.

The cow was young but of good size. I waited an instant and then loosed my arrow. The cow took a step forward and then stopped, evidently puzzled. My second arrow was ready and I let go. The arrow struck home and the buffalo started forward again and then crumpled. One of the other buffalo lifted a hind hoof to scratch its jaw, looking backward as it did so. A moment later the buffalo was feeding quietly. We moved in, the buffalo moving off a little, and then we went to work, skinning out the animal we had killed.

The other buffalo moved away down the valley. Only the wolves hung about, staying off some distance but drawn by the smell of blood. They sat in the snow watching us, occasionally trotting around and coming nearer, then retreating. They were black, ominous figures against the snow and under a cold gray sky.

It was cold, very cold. We worked steadily, standing up at intervals to look all about us. We had seen no sign of Indians here, but in spring and summer this valley must be a beautiful place.

A little further south a stream emerged from a canyon, flowing down from the high mountains to the west. The stream seemed to flow eastward across the mouth of the canyon, but we were some distance off, although higher.

Itchakomi might be a Sun, but she was also an Indian woman. She worked swiftly and skillfully, wasting no time, no movements. I glanced at the meat. "It is almost too much," I said, "and we have a long way to go."

The buffalo had stopped and were feeding again not more than two hundred yards away. Just ahead of them was a stand of thick brush and trees. By following down a small watercourse I could slip into that patch and perhaps make another kill.

I took up my bow and looked around at her. "Will you stay with the meat?"

"I will stay. Have care."

As I moved toward the wolves they trotted off, and I went past them and down the shallow ravine. It was very still. I plodded steadily on until I reached the grove that began along the shallow watercourse I followed. Working up into the brush, I moved with care to make no sound. The buffalo were finding dried grass beneath the snow, and only an old bull stood guard. I was downwind of him, so he did not catch my scent. Nevertheless, he was uneasy.

Had he smelled the blood of our kill? Or was there something else about I had not seen?

Again I looked all around, my eyes searching close about me, then further out, and then further still. Each area I examined slowly, taking nothing for granted. If there was an enemy out there I wished to know it, but if he was nearby I must see him first. I found nothing.

Several buffalo fed nearby, two of them within thirty

or forty yards of the trees that were my cover. Moving through the brush, careful to make no sound, I found an open place among the trees and crossed it. Now I was closer.

The big bull was not looking at me. Something off to my left held his attention. His head was up, his nostrils flared.

My eyes turned, swept the snow fields down the valley, and then stopped.

Several men were coming up along the edge of the woods, but it was a moment before I could pick the individuals out of the background. They were following close along the edge of the trees and may have just emerged from them. Three, four, . . . five. Five men, whether Indians or not I could not say, but I was sure they were. The Spanishmen would not be out at this time of year. We needed another buffalo, and their coming would drive the animals away.

Turning, I glanced toward Itchakomi. She was making the meat into packs to be carried and her head was down. She was at least a hundred yards off, still concealed from the men below by the grove of trees that concealed me also. I hissed, but even in that still, cold air the sound was too low to carry. I waved my hand and then my bow, hoping the corner of her eye would catch the movement.

She looked up suddenly, looking at me. I pointed with the bow and she picked up the packs of meat and came toward me.

"There are five warriors," I said, "coming up the valley. If we stay hidden they may not see us."

"We leave tracks here. If they come, they will see."

Leading the way, I went into the woods and chose a place where we were well hidden yet could watch them.

"We have help soon."

"Help?"

"My people. Six men come to carry meat. I speak to them."

Well . . . that was thinking. But would they arrive in time and would they see these warriors before they were seen? We could not let them walk into an ambush. Glancing back up the valley I saw nothing. Even if they came now they would not reach us in time.

Of course, the strange warriors down the valley might turn off, but if they were themselves hunting, as seemed likely, they would be attracted by the buffalo.

They did not turn aside. They were coming on. They were Indians. My guess was they were Conejeros.

"Keep down," I advised, "and leave the fighting to me."

"I can fight."

"I do not want you hurt. Leave it to me."

"There are five."

"Soon there will be less."

We waited, hidden by the tree trunks and brush. I had a good view of them now as they trudged toward us, single file.

The big bull did not like it. He snorted and pawed snow and then began moving off. The other buffalo had stopped pawing snow from the brown grass and were starting to move, too. I glanced around again. No help in sight, yet I saw something else.

The wolves were gone.

23

"No use to let them come too close," I said. "Do you stay back. This is for me."

I stepped from the brush and stood out upon the snow. I stood alone, waiting for them.

They saw me at once and stopped.

Those following closed up, and they stood staring at me. I knew their thoughts. Who was I? Was I alone? Would I dare to step out unless others were behind me? Was it a trap?

They could see my bow, and that I held it ready, an arrow in place but pointed down. There was a fine daring within me. Why was it that I, a peaceful man, always felt exhilarated at the thought of battle? Suddenly I was challenging, poised, ready. Everything in me invited them to come.

They shouted something I did not understand, but I did not attempt a reply. I did not think they would turn and go away. It was not their way, for these were warriors, these were fighting men.

They started forward and I waved them back. They stopped again. Then one among them, arguing fiercely with the others, suddenly stepped out and started toward me. My longbow would out-range theirs by thirty yards, perhaps more. I let him take three steps and motioned again. He came on, and my bow came up. I loosed an arrow.

The arrow went where I aimed, and struck through his thigh. A dead man they could leave, but a wounded man they must care for.

The warrior staggered and then fell. He tugged at the arrow, and I waited. The others gathered around him, shouting at me.

I stood my ground, another arrow in place. They were dark against the snow, perfect targets. One of them turned toward me and shouted again. I lifted my bow and he drew back. He had taken the arrow from the fallen man and he was looking at it. My arrows were black, with black feathers to aid their flight. The arrow was strange to them, and I was strange. At the distance they could not see that I was a white man, and my garb would tell them nothing.

They would not leave their wounded brother there to die in the snow, and to attack meant someone else would die. They were brave men but not foolish. Moreover they did not know who or what I was.

So far I had made no sound and they did not know what to make of me.

Taking up their wounded companion they began to move off. One of them turned and shook a spear at me, but I did not respond. That they would be back I had no doubt. When they had disappeared down the valley I went back into the woods and we gathered our meat. The burden I shouldered was enough for four men, but we had to be off, to find shelter for the night and a way in which to escape.

"You are brave," Itchakomi said.

"If we had been taken we would have been tortured and killed. If they had come close they might have taken me from behind while others approached in front. My only chance was to stop them at a distance."

She knew. My explanation was more for me. We Englishmen, if such I was, must have reasons for our actions even when the reasons are not always good ones.

What I thought now was true. The Conejeros had a bloody reputation, but it was the way of many Indians to attack strangers unless their curiosity got the better of them.

When we had cached the meat in a small cave near a fallen tree, we built a small fire and ate of the meat. Before nightfall I killed a deer, adding its meat to that from the buffalo.

Our camp was in a good spot near the mouth of a small canyon that provided access to the mountains and the forest. It was a small cave and not deep, but it offered shelter from the wind. I gathered fuel, of which much lay about, for the fire. Night came with a cluster of stars among scattered clouds, and our fire was warm.

"They will return," I said.

She nodded. "And more of them."

"When were your people coming?"

"Tonight . . . tomorrow. Just to pick up the meat and take it back."

"You should have stayed in camp. We might have been killed today."

She was amused. "I moved about. I made them think there were more of us."

So that was why they had been staring. They had known somebody was back there but not how many. So it was not me who had frightened them off, after all.

They would come back, of course. Indians did not take defeat lightly, and one of their own had been wounded. I got up and went outside to listen. Far off, a wolf howled and another responded. There was no other sound in the night.

The smoke of our fire, small though it was, could be smelled if they were downwind of it, but tonight the fire could not be done without. Their return tonight was unlikely. They would be making medicine before they came again.

The cave was small but warm enough with the small fire. Itchakomi was seated at the back, her head leaning back against the wall. In the firelight, as in any light, she was a beautiful woman. I looked away, and sat down where I did not have to see her. I would have liked some chicory to drink, but had none with me.

"What is it like, in England? At night, I mean?"

We had been talking much and her English had gotten better. She had discarded the few French words she used and much of the Cherokee, but sometimes she still reverted to Indian talk, which I had to translate in my mind.

"People are in their homes at night. They talk, they read books, sometimes they play cards. If they are in taverns they do the same, but they drink more in taverns, I think. I only know from what I have heard."

"It is a good thing? To read?"

"We all read at home. I more than any of the others, I think. There are books about everything, and my father and mother both read, so we grew up with books about. If it were not for their books we would know nothing of the Greeks, the Romans, and many others. Nothing but some ruins. The people of England thought the Roman ruins had been built by giants, until their books were translated and brought to England."

"I would like to read!"

"I will teach you." I said it and then swore under my breath. Why was I such a fool? I wanted to get away when the grass grew green again, I wanted to walk the lonely buffalo trails and seek out the high places and lonely valleys. And here I was, promising to teach Itchakomi to read! What a double-dyed fool!

But she would forget about it. Spring was still a long time away. Or was it? I had lost count of the days. Anyway, it was probably just a notion. But I had better watch my tongue.

Crouching over our tiny fire in a cave far from anything in the world, I wondered about myself and those to come after. This was what I wanted, to come west, to seek, to find, to understand. Yet I was uneasy with my old feelings, the eerie sense that I walked in a world where others had walked, that I lived where others had lived. I did not believe in ghosts. I did not believe the dead lived beyond the grave. I did believe there was much we did not understand, but there had been a man in Virginia who had claimed he could communicate with the dead. The only messages from the dead that I'd heard had sounded as if they came from creatures that had lost their minds.

The uneasy sense of other beings having lived where I lived stayed with me. I did not know what to call the feelings I had. Second sight, some called it, but this went beyond that.

Itchakomi was watching me. "Of what you think?"

I shrugged. "I think others have been where we are. I think others have walked the trails, lived in the caves. And I do not speak of Indians."

"Your people?"

"No—not really. Just people from somewhere. I wished to come west to be the first but I am not the first."

"Does it matter?"

"No, I suppose not, only I would like to know who they were and how they got here and if they left behind any marks of their passing."

"You are not content to be. You ask who and why."

"And when."

"You are a strange one. And when you know, what then?"

"Perhaps I shall write a book. Or even a letter. Knowledge was meant to be shared. Do you not feel the same?"

"Knowledge is useful. Why share it? Use it for yourself. Why share it with others who will use it to defeat you?"

Sakim had shared his knowledge with me. So had my father's friends Jeremy Ring and Kane O'Hara. So had others. With whom would I share mine?

The night was icy cold. Several times I awakened to add fuel to our fire, and with dawn I was ready to move. If Itchakomi's people were coming to carry meat, it was meat we must have. I dragged some broken tree limbs to the cave and then took up my weapons. Itchakomi was awake, and when she started to rise I said, "Rest, if you like. I shall go where the game is."

Without saying more I started off, moving swiftly. I saw nothing on the wide expanse of snow but the tracks of yesterday. As I moved I thought of yesterday. Itchakomi had probably saved me from a fight by moving in the brush behind me. The Indians, of course, thought I was merely bait for a trap and they had backed off, not from any fear of me but of what might await them in the trees.

The buffalo were feeding further west and south near the mouth of the canyon I had seen where a stream came in from the west. I moved swiftly, keeping to low ground, and when I was within sight, I paused to select my target.

Glancing back I saw a dot upon the snow. Itchakomi was following me. I did not know whether to be irritated or pleased, and decided I was irritated.

It needed five arrows to kill two buffalo, but I recovered four of the arrows, the other was broken when the cow fell. By the time I had skinned out the first Itchakomi was working on the second. This had been the work of Indian women forever, I suspect, and certainly she was as adept as I, perhaps more so. Being a Sun she had probably done little skinning, however. I glanced over at her from time to time, but she was paying no attention to anything but the task at hand.

By midday we had both animals skinned and the cuts of meat wrapped in the hides. By that time the other buffalo had ranged out of sight. There was nothing in the wide snowfield below and around us. The meat we had was too heavy to carry, and trying to cache it with wolves about would have wasted time. They would have smelled it and dug it out before we were out of sight.

Suddenly, Itchakomi spoke. Glancing around I followed her pointing finger. Several men were walking toward us from the upper valley.

It was probably the Natchee, but I was taking no chances. We retreated into the woods and waited behind some fallen trees.

It needed an hour for them to reach us. Four warriors and two Natchee women. Within minutes they had shouldered the meat and we were walking back to our cave, where we took up the meat from the day before.

The valley below was empty when we started for home, but I looked back often and prayed for snow to cover our tracks. Itchakomi was telling her people of the meeting with the Conejeros.

The snow crunched under our snowshoes and we paused from time to time, careful not to work up a sweat. Each time we looked back the valley was empty. Would they guess where we were?

We were crossing a small stream when Itchakomi broke through the ice, going ankle deep in the icy water. Often the warmer water of a spring in the stream bed will cause the ice to be thin. Now it was necessary to move swiftly. Picking her up bodily I set her down in deep snow. Then I began rubbing snow over her moccasins. She struggled with me but I spoke sharply. "Be still! It must be done!"

She subsided and I rubbed more dry snow on her moccasins. "It will blot up the water," I said, "but always you must act quickly. Very quickly."

After a moment we started on and she was very quiet. When she spoke she said, "We do not know the cold. We have much to learn."

"It is the same with me. I know only a little, but the dry snow soaks up the water very quickly before it can soak through to your feet. My father taught me that. He learned it in New Found Land, far to the north."

We trudged on, climbing higher and higher, and then turning east into our valley. It was good to be back, but I knew how short a time our meat would last. Much had already been eaten in feeding those who had come to pack it back. In fact, the two meals eaten on the way home had seriously depleted the result of our hunt.

Had we longer to prepare we might have laid up a sufficient store of meat to last through the winter, although most Indians faced a starving time before spring came. Few had sufficient corn or meat stored to last through the season.

The wood supply was down, so I went to the forest and gathered more, and then still more. Survival was a continual struggle, with no time for loafing by the fire.

Itchakomi's Natchee went often to the hills for game. The cold was new to them, but they learned swiftly, and often they found deer, ptarmigan, or rabbits. Buffalo did not range so high in the cold months. Bears, if there were any about, were hibernating.

Suddenly in the night I awakened. For a moment I lay wide-eyed and still, listening. What I heard was dripping. Also I suddenly realized that although the fire was down I was unusually warm.

Rising, I went to the cave mouth. Outside I could see patches of bare ground where the snow had already melted away. By daybreak it would all be gone. It was one of those warm, soft winds of which I had heard, and for a time at least the weather would be clear.

If the Conejeros were going to attack it would be now, while the weather was clear.

It would be tomorrow.

24

Keokotah squatted by our fire. "Warm wind go," he said, "more snow come. You see."

Maybe. I knew nothing about the climate in this part of the country, and he knew a good deal, having grown up in the north country. Still, it looked to me like an early spring.

"No spring," he said, when I mentioned it. "This over soon, and then much snow, I think."

He stirred the fire and then turned the meat he had on a spit. "We go now," he suggested. "Go beyond big mountain."

"And leave them? What would they do without us?"

He shrugged.

The Natchee had learned quickly, and probably they could get along without us. Reluctantly, I agreed to myself that Keokotah was right, but we could not leave when trouble was coming. I said as much and he shrugged again.

Keokotah's girl went outside for fuel, and I watched her go, wondering about their relationship. Indian men often went on long hunts, and sometimes they returned, sometimes they did not. Their women found other men or lived alone, given meat by successful hunters. Was it that way with the Natchee? There was so much I did not know.

Leaning against the backrest I stretched my bad leg. Sometimes the cold made it ache. Aside from that and a slight limp it was as good as new. I could still run.

When I went outside, Itchakomi was there. She had cleaned her buckskin skirt and leggings. "You think they come?"

"Yes." I pointed toward the entrance. "Keokotah and I will be there. Your people should be in the trees along the creek and out of sight until they get close."

She looked over the ground sloping away from us. The plan was good enough and probably the only one. We could not stop them, but we might get one or two before they got through into the valley. After that it would be a fight, and there were too many of them.

"It is time to go," she said. "We must go to the upper valley."

"Wait. We may stop them this time. I do not believe there will be many this time."

Of course, I did not know, but I doubted many would come, thinking we were very few. We had little choice. A retreat to the upper valley would delay them only a little. They would find us, and where would we go then? If Keokotah was right and more snow was coming, we might be snowed in, our only retreat the high country beyond. It would be cold, and there would be danger of snowslides.

"It is a warming time," she suggested. "Does the grass come back now?"

I repeated what Keokotah had said, and she nodded. "I have heard of this. Long ago some people came to us from far up the Great River. They spoke of this. Is it so in your country?"

"In England? I do not know. My father spoke of a time when England was warmer than in his time. There had been vines growing grapes, and they made wine. Then it became colder and the vines did not grow.

"I think it was colder here," I said, "in far gone times. It was a time for the buffalo, who understand the cold.

When the wind and snow blow hard they do not walk away from it. They bunch together and turn their heads to the wind, and their heavy coats are soon matted with snow and they are warm."

She stood beside me, a tall, lovely girl, wise for her years. I moved a step to the side, putting more distance between us. Her being close disturbed me, and I felt uneasy. Anyway, I had no time to think of women. I had much land to see. And I was happier when alone. I reminded myself of this. I had always been a loner.

Even with Keokotah I was a loner, for he walked with his own thoughts and we did not intrude. We were two loners together.

Keokotah was annoyed by staying on. He felt no duty to these people and he wanted to be away. Only the snow was holding him or holding us.

"What will you do," she asked, "when the grass grows green?"

My gesture took in the western mountains. "Go out there, I suppose. I want to see what is beyond the mountains."

"And then?"

My tongue touched my lips and I shifted my feet. Well, it was a sensible question, what would I do?

"I don't know. Find a meadow somewhere with a stream running and build a cabin, I guess."

"And then?"

She was backing me into a corner and I didn't like it. I was like a buffalo calf, cut off from the herd. I was hunting a corner to duck around or a place to hide.

"It would be a place where a man could hunt," I explained, "and sort of live off the country."

"Alone?"

"I've always been alone," I said, "even when I was with folks. I don't fit in with people, somehow. Books, now. I'd like to have some books."

She didn't push me any further and I was glad. I was feeling crowded and beginning to sweat a little.

"What of your brothers?"

"They were going their own ways. Yance had found him a woman and by this time Kin prob'ly has, too. A man has to blaze his own trail, and mine was to the west."

"I would like to know your brothers."

"You'd like them. Good men. My sister, Noelle, she went back to England with Ma. By now she's probably going to balls an' such, living the life of a real lady."

"I would like to meet her. I wish—"

"What?"

"I would like to see how it is over there. I would like to see the clothes your women wear."

"Most of them are kind of silly. Seems so to me, anyhow. Hair all done up an' powdered, fancy silk skirts. Pa said they could look mighty fetching, though."

"Could I wear those clothes?"

Well, I looked at her again. She could wear anything. With that figure and the way she walked—she was more like a queen than any queen I'd heard of.

"You could," I admitted, "and you'd be beautiful in them. You would turn every head in the place."

She was pleased, so I went on and told her more about the balls and such. Ma had told us about them, told Noelle most of all, but we had listened. She told about dancing and about clothes and the ballrooms, so I repeated it to Itchakomi. "There would be nobody as beautiful as you," I finished, realizing what I said was true.

It was easier talking about such things than about my plans. Whenever she got on that tack it set me to fidgeting because I hadn't really thought it out. I'd never thought that far ahead. I'd settle down somewhere, I supposed. Maybe with some Indians, as there was not much chance of a man getting by alone.

Or I'd go back.

But I wouldn't. I had known that from the beginning. My destiny was here, where the west was. Like I'd told her, I'd find a meadow somewhere with a stream flowing through it and I'd build a log house. Maybe more than a cabin. Might be things would get better with the Spanish and I could get some books from them. I would like to be reading again. There was so much I did not know.

The sun was warming things up and I looked toward the opening of the valley. I should be over there, waiting. Those Indians would come.

Yet I lingered. A man living off the country and in a land where there's risk at every hand does not get much time to contemplate himself. He has no time to speculate on the ifs and the buts of his life, nor to ask questions of himself and his motives. Each day is a day to live and in which to keep from dying, and a man's energies are directed out from himself and his thoughts as well. Contemplation is a leisure indulgence. It is for a man in an armchair or beside a fire in his own house. It isn't for a man whose every sense is attuned to sounds outside himself.

Itchakomi had asked me questions I'd never asked myself, and I suspected she had a lot more lying in wait for their proper moments. She was a disturbing woman, in more ways than one.

Pa, being the man he was, had laid a duty on me to sort of play godfather to the Indians. They were good people, with wise men among them, and customs suited to the country, but sometimes they needed an outside opinion or in my case somebody to act for an old gentleman not up to the trip we'd made.

More than that, I liked the Ni'kwana. There was something between us, and we had sensed it when we had come together. We could have sat down and talked from the first moment like old friends.

All right, so here I was. I'd found Itchakomi and delivered his message. Why was I hanging around? Because of the cold and the snow. Would I be around if it wasn't for that? I shied from the question like a bird from a sudden move.

"There's a wind blowing in this country now," I said, "that's going to blow a lot of change. The Indian way of life will be the first to go, I think, because the white man is part of that change, and most of them can't see any way but their own.

"Pa, he was different. First off, he was raised in the fens and the life was different there, more independent and freer, and then he set up for himself and came over here.

"He didn't ask anybody for permission to come. He got no grant from any king or great lord, he just came of himself and found land where he wanted to be.

"There weren't many like him, but there were some, and the sons and daughters of those first ones were just as independent and free. The second generation moved out and set up for themselves away from the regular settlements. Their sons and daughters will be even more eager to strike out on their own. The king is just a name to them, and they will never have lived on any great lord's estate.

"Some of them will cater to Indian ways, some will resist that. They will find land they want and set up for themselves and fight off anybody who tries to take it from them, be he Indian or white.

"Pa was one of the first of a new kind of man. Maybe not a new kind, because he was probably a lot like those who crossed the Channel with William of Normandy. Most of them had nothing, so they crossed over with William and took what they wanted from the folks already in England.

"The trouble is, they'll do the same here. It's the way of the world, just like the Conejeros came in here and killed off Indians who were living here and will try to kill us.

"If we wish to live we've got to try to kill them or enough of them so they will leave us alone. I don't want it to become like it was with Pa.

"The Senecas fought him because he was a friend of their enemies, the Catawba. He whipped them so many times it became a matter of honor for every young warrior to have a try at us. I heard it was said in some villages that a warrior couldn't call himself such unless he'd had at least one go at us at Shooting Creek. They'd come down the Warrior's Path a-purpose.

"I don't want to fight all my life. I am a man of peace, and when I've come back from wandering I want that log house in the meadow somewhere. I—"

"Alone?"

Damn it! There she was again! A man couldn't— "That will be a cabin I've built myself," I said, "mighty small, as it's for one man."

"Smaller than this cave?"

"Well—not exactly. I haven't rightly figured the size of the place. It's just an idea, anyway."

"It should be larger," Itchakomi said. "You might have a visit from a friend. Or even two."

"Well . . . when it comes to that—"

My eye caught a movement from over where we had come into the valley. Keokotah was there, and he was waving something to attract my attention.

The only reason he would signal me was that the Conejeros were coming, or somebody.

"Keokotah is calling me. I'd better go."

I wasted no time. Keokotah would not call for help unless he believed it was needed, and if he needed help, more than a few were coming our way.

I started running like a coward, happy to get into a fight I thought I could win.

25

Keokotah was in the rocks and brush, where he had a good view of the trail into our valley. Much of the snow had melted, and the earth was muddy. Here and there were pools of water and patches of snow on the north slopes of hills. We could see the Conejeros coming and counted twelve.

We did not talk. Each knew what must be done and knew it would not be easy. Glancing back I could see some of the Natchee moving down to the brush along the creek, our second line of defense.

"I will take the last man," I suggested.

Keokotah made no reply. He would fight his own battle, as I would. Each of us had his own skills and his own ideas on how to expend them.

They were a hundred yards off, the last man some fifty yards further, when I selected an arrow and bent my bow, waiting just a little longer. They came on. Keokotah slipped down to a better position. The last man had to round a boulder and to do so must almost face me. He was at least fifteen feet behind the next man when I let fly.

The years of training with the bow now paid their way, for my arrow took him in the chest and he fell back, his hands grasping the arrow, struggling to withdraw it.

Keokotah's arrow went into his man's throat, and the man fell. The others vanished like a puff of smoke. An instant, and they were there—another, and they were gone.

One man I saw drop among some rocks, but knew he would not rise from the spot where he had disappeared, so I plotted in my mind his probable movements. They were trying to get into the valley, and he would use as much shelter as could be found. As I had come through that entrance myself I knew how the land lay. About thirty yards farther along from where he had dropped from sight was a gap in the cover. I knew he would make a step, perhaps two, before I could get on target, so I chose a place close to the edge of his next cover and waited.

A movement, and then he was in the open and running. My arrow caught him in midstride, just as he was about to disappear into the rocks. He missed a step, and then fell or dropped from sight.

Two down, and a casualty. I doubted the last man had been killed.

We would get no more chances here, and if we remained where we were we would be surrounded. Keeping undercover where we could, we ran, ducking and dodging, for the brush along the stream.

The Conejeros did not see us go, so they moved slowly, carefully. They had lost men. Would they believe their medicine was bad and leave? I doubted it.

At the nearest concealment I stopped and crouched to watch for them. Where Keokotah was I did not know, nor did I need to look. He was a fighting man and would be where he could be most effective.

Now came a time of waiting. The Conejeros were creeping closer, using all their wiles to come within striking distance without being seen. They could not know exactly where we were but could calculate as I had where their enemies were most apt to be.

They had the advantage of the attacker. We had a position to defend.

We knew how many they were. They could not know how many there were of us. Suddenly an Indian darted from one rock to the next, but he was gone from sight before I could turn, and he was closer.

Almost as if it were a signal, a half dozen others moved and vanished, still closer. An attacker suddenly raised up, but Keokotah was ready for him and the man dropped from sight. I did not see whether Keokotah had scored a hit or not.

Then for a long time, nothing happened. The sun climbed higher in the sky, and the air warmed. Suddenly I heard a startled cry and then a scream of pain.

It was at the other end of the line of trees, and the cry, I was sure, had come from one of ours. I worked my way undercover back toward the caves.

If they could cut us off from the caves they would have our women, as well as our extra weapons, blankets, robes, and meat. Without them, survival would be a question.

Keokotah had had the same idea. We met undercover near the caves. "I think they go," he whispered. "I think snow come."

Glancing at the sky, I could see what he meant. During the last hour the sky had clouded over to a dull, flat gray.

Snow? This might be the time to leave. Falling snow would cover whatever tracks we would leave in the mud, and when they returned they would come upon only empty caves. No doubt they had hoped to surprise us, always a favorite Indian tactic, and as surprise had failed and their medicine seemed bad, they would most likely await another time. Finally we assumed that they had been wiped out by the Komantsi.

We had lost one man. He was a young warrior of the Natchee and he had been killed and scalped.

"Conejero no like," Keokotah said. "Natchee strange Indian. There be much talk now. Who is Indian? Where he from? How many strange Indian?"

Itchakomi was waiting in her cave. Explaining took only a moment. She asked no questions, simply spoke a few quick words to the other women and then to her warriors. We had known this time was coming, so were prepared. Within minutes we were leaving the caves behind, yet not without reluctance. They had been warm shelters, and when does a man leave a place he has lived without some regret? For each time some part of him is left behind. So it was with us.

We took one last look around. If anyone was watching they would see the direction we took, but there was no help for it.

"You sad," she said to me, her eyes searching mine.

I shrugged. "It was a good place. We were warm there."

Keokotah led the way, the Natchee followed, then came Itchakomi, and I was last, a rear guard, if one was needed.

The trail we took was narrow, and the way was hard. Here and there were spots of ice and places where the bank had caved. We walked warily, and I trailed behind, pausing often to study the back trail and to see if we were followed.

It was growing cold again. Night was coming. Uneasily, I looked about. We must take shelter quickly. The air had changed. A chill finger touched my cheek, and then another.

Snow! It was beginning to snow.

Keokotah needed no word from me. He led our people into the trees and quickly they began building a shelter. There were large trees close together where interwoven tops provided some protection from the snow. With our hatchets and knives we cut notches in the trees and laid poles from one to another. While three of us did this, the others gathered branches to lay across the top and to put down upon the sides. Our house was about thirty feet long, but not straight. It followed the trees we had used, most of which were six or seven feet apart. By the time the roof was in place the snow was falling heavily.

We slanted the sides out, lean-to fashion, and thatched them with spruce branches and slabs of bark from fallen trees. With all of us working, it was little time until we had our shelter and had gathered wood for the fire. We had left a hole for the smoke and soon had a fire going and meat broiling.

The snow fell thick and fast, covering our tracks. An astute tracker, one wily enough to think of it, might still find our tracks frozen in the mud under the snow. Not all Indians were good trackers, although all could track and had spent much of their lives doing it.

When there was time to look about I saw how well Keokotah had chosen, for our shelter was well back in the trees in an unlikely place and well situated for defense. In just a short time we had made it snug, and once we were inside and had a fire going we were warm enough.

The snow continued to fall. We would not be easily found.

Itchakomi and I began talking again. She was forever curious about English women and how they behaved themselves, what clothes they wore, and what they did with themselves.

Pa had talked much of theaters. He had never cared much for bull or bear baiting, but loved the plays, and a man named Will Kempe was a great favorite. So I told her of the theaters and of the innyards used as theaters when companies were on tour. Speaking of such things kept her from asking questions of me, questions that disturbed me and left me uneasy and asking questions of myself.

Pa had talked much of the theaters, for the England in which he had grown up was much given to playgoing, and the players were well known to everyone.

"What of the women? Were there no women in the plays?"

"No, not in England. Pa said there was talk of women players in Italy, but not in England. Boys played the parts of women."

She thought that was foolish, and when I thought on it, so did I, but that was the way it was.

She plied me with questions until I told her more than I knew, things Pa had told us, forgotten until her questions dredged them up. Memory holds much more than we suspect, I found, and began to wonder what else there was I had forgotten.

Outside the snow fell, and the others fell asleep, even Keokotah, who was curious in his own mind and wishful of knowing more of England.

"And did your father know the king?"

"My father? I should say not! Kings had nothing to do with yeomen and only a little, sometimes, with knights. That's as I understand it, at least."

"The Great Sun knows his people, knows every one," she told me. "Does your king have a Ni'kwana?"

"Sort of. I guess he might be like the chancellor or an archbishop. I don't know half enough about it." I spoke irritably, for I did not like to discover that I knew less than I should.

"You speak of a king, but did you not tell me that a queen ruled in England?"

"Queen Elizabeth. My father approved of her, although it was little she would have cared for one man's approval. However, as he says it she was a good queen."

"Was?"

"We are gone from there, although my mother is there, and a brother and sister, but in any case Queen Elizabeth is gone. There is a king now." I said it with some satisfaction. "King James is on the throne."

"Will you go back?"

"I cannot go back. I have never been. Also, this is my land. I shall stay here."

"I am glad."

Here we were, getting down to personal things again. "We'd better sleep," I suggested. "Tomorrow I must hunt again."

She seemed in no way disposed to sleep, and said so, but I spread my robes close to the edge of the shelter.

Spring was going to be late this year no matter how soon it came. The cold and snow trapped a man, keeping him within the lodge and close to women. Not that I disliked women, far from it, but I was not ready to set up my own lodge or stay in one place. There was a wide land out there no man had seen, and as Pa had longed for his far blue mountains I was longing to walk these Shining Mountains to their utmost limits.

Itchakomi had said nothing lately of returning, although if she returned now she might become the Great Sun herself. I spoke of that, but she was quiet, and before she got around to speaking I was asleep, or pretending to be.

When morning came the mountains were gone, vanished under a cloak of snow, their towering black peaks lost in a whiteness that covered all. Scarcely a dark branch showed or an edge of rock. It was still, the only sound my moccasins pressing down the snow, crunching into the silence.

For a long moment I stood and looked out over the land, my breath a white cloud. Hunching my shoulders against the snow I looked carefully around. There were no enemies I could see, and no moving game, only the snow, the ice, and the cold. I broke off a heavy branch, the sound like a pistol shot, and then another, bringing them back to the hungry fire, waging its own desperate fight against the chill.

This was a land for me, these mountains, this forest, these silent streams, their voices stilled only for the time.

Keokotah came out and stood beside me. "Is good," he said, "all this."

"It is," I agreed.

"When grass comes, what you do?"

"I shall walk along the mountain where the aspen grows, and beside the lakes where the moon goes to rest. I want to find the places where the rivers begin. I want to drink where the water comes from under the slide rock. I want to walk the way of the elk, the deer, and the bear."

"You are not elk or deer or bear. You man. What you do when your knees are stiff? When the earth no longer soft for sleeping? When the cold does not leave your bones? Who will share your lodge when the last leaves fall?"

Wind breathed among the trees. Some snow fell from the stiff leaves of an oak and from the spruce.

"What of Itchakomi? Such a woman walks with the wind. Such a woman must be fought for or stolen."

"She will go home to her people. She may be the Great Sun."

"Hah! You think she go back safe? You think she pass by the Conejero? The Pawnee? The Osage? She will be taken to some warrior's lodge. You see."

"So?" The thought made me uncomfortable, but I did not like to say so, or even think of it.

"You speak, she stay. I tell you this."

"It is not possible."

He shrugged. "I think you fool. Once in a lifetime a man finds such a woman. Once! I have watched her with you. She will keep your lodge if you speak."

"She is curious about our customs, as you are. She is not interested in me."

"Hah!"

A veil of snow lifted from a peak and hung suspended against the gray sky, and then sifted softly away as though it had not been. A chill wind stirred, and frozen leaves scraped against the stiff branches. Snow drifted down from the trees and I shivered.

"You my friend. I speak as friend." For a moment he was silent. "I have no other friend."

Neither of us spoke for a long time and then I said, "And what of you?"

"I have a man to kill, if you do not."

"What?"

"He is out there. He looks for us. He looks for *her*. If we do not find him first, he will find us. It is better to hunt than be hunted."

A chaos of granite lay at the foot of the mountain, covered now with snow. Lightning-struck trees showed their stark dead stumps against the sky. My toes were cold from standing, and I half turned to go. He looked at me coolly, waiting for some word from me.

Curling my toes against the cold, I shrugged my

shoulders under the buffalo robe, seeing a dream slide away down the icy hill, and another born.

"Maybe you are right," I said. "Maybe I am a fool."

"He leave his mark. He leave his challenge."

Turning toward our lodge I looked back. "What do you mean?"

"The young Natchee who was killed. He no dead when scalp taken. He alive."

I still looked at him, waiting.

"He know who kill him. He leave a sign in the snow where he die. He leave one sign."

Everything in me waited. I knew before he said it. I knew what the sign would be and that when Keokotah spoke I must begin to seek, to hunt. And I did not want to hunt down any man.

"He left one sign: *Kapata*!"

Kapata? Well, I could make an exception.

26

I am Itchakomi Ishaia, a Daughter of the Sun, sent to find a new home for my people. This land is a good land. There is beauty here and much wild game, but there are enemies, also. The Conejeros are a fierce people, making war upon everybody. They would make war upon us.

We could defeat them, but many of our young men would die.

The Ni'kwana has sent this man to find me, to speak to me of returning. He has done so. But he says the Ni'kwana left it to me to decide, and the Ni'kwana has been my guide and teacher.

Why did he send this man to me? Why did he not say, "Come back, Itchakomi, come back to your land by the river"?

He left the decision to me. Why did he think I might not wish to return?

The Ni'kwana traveled far to meet this man, and then sent him to find me. What did the Ni'kwana know that I do not?

The Ni'kwana fears for me. He does not like or trust Kapata, and the Ni'kwana knows many things others do not.

Who is this man Jubal? What does he believe? What

am I to believe? He speaks of marvels, of customs strange to us, of peoples far away of whom I know nothing.

Why have I not known of these people? He speaks of us as *Indians*. I do not know that name. The Ni'kwana has spoken of Spanishmen who came long ago, who killed some of our people and then went away down the Great River. We heard of such Spanishmen out upon the long grass, also, and one of them who ran away lived in our lodges for a time.

I do not know this man or his people. I do not know his tribe or where his home is. Jubal speaks of great houses in some land beyond the sea, of customs strange to us, but how can I believe him?

A sea is a great water. It is not a river. It must be like the great water we saw when long ago we traveled south with the Ni'kwana.

What manner of man is he? Will he walk among us for a time and then go away to his own people? I have heard men speak of his tribe. He is a Sackett. I am Natchez.

He says he is not a Sun. His father was a yeoman, but I do not know what that is. It is a good thing to be, I think.

He is a warrior and a hunter. Keokotah says he is very brave, that he fears nothing. I think it is good to fear some things.

He speaks of things strange to me, but I like to hear him speak. I listen and try to understand, but his words are not ours. I have learned much of his tongue but not of his meanings. To know words is not always to know thoughts. He speaks from his custom, I from mine. When I use his words I cannot speak the ideas I think. I do not make myself known.

He is a wise man, I believe, a Ni'kwana among his own people.

I am a Sun. What is my duty? To return to my people or to stay with this man who does not seek to know me?

I am a beautiful woman. I know this because I have

seen myself in the Pool of the Moon's Reflection. Does he not see that I am beautiful?

Or is it that I am so different from the women of his people? Why does he avoid me? Am I not to his liking? Am I a bad taste in his mouth? A bad sound in his ears? What am I, a woman, to do?

He speaks of the Shining Mountains, and when he speaks of them his voice has a ring to it. The mountains were a far land of which he dreamed, and now he is among them, yet he has seen too little, he says. He wishes to wander down the days, through their forest and meadows and along their streams, but has it not always been so, that men prefer to wander and women to keep them close?

I could wander the far lands, too. I am not afraid.

He has terrible scars upon his head and upon his back and shoulders. I have seen his head when his hair falls a certain way, and I have seen his back when he bathed. He does not speak of the scars. He limps a little and has broken his leg. Keokotah spoke of that. He broke his leg when alone in the forest.

I am a Sun. Among my people I command men. Among my people I could choose whomever I wished, but he is not of my people and does not understand our ways, although he listens when I speak.

He does not know me. Should I return then to my own people? Should I leave him among his mountains and go back to my home beside the Great River?

I have walked beside him through the snow. I have helped to skin the buffalo he killed. Does he not see that I am a fit companion for him?

Keokotah has taken a woman. She is happy with him, but Keokotah also speaks of the far mountains. He is a Kickapoo and they are great wanderers. Are the Sacketts wanderers, too? The Natchee are not.

Kapata hunts for me. He has killed Atasha, who was a young warrior, although brave. Kapata has taken his hair, although they grew up together.

Kapata is fierce and strong, yet I do not fear him. If

he tries to take me I shall kill him. I know the ways and he does not. There are ways secret to the Suns and known to no other.

Kapata does not understand the Natchee. He does not wish to understand. He has hatred for us because we have contempt for his mother's people, who are Eaters of Men.

I will go back. When the grass grows green again and the trees have buds. I shall go to my home beside the Great River. If Jubal Sackett does not see me I will take myself from his sight.

Why did the Ni'kwana send him? The Ni'kwana who knows all and sees all?

Thus I have been thinking. I have no one to whom I can speak. I am a Sun and we speak our thoughts only among ourselves. If I spoke to the other women here they would be ashamed for me.

It has been said here that I might become the Great Sun. This is against the tradition of our people, although sometimes when a Great Sun was very young a woman has ruled. If I returned now this might be the way of it, but when I look upon Jubal I do not wish to go back, and I think the Ni'kwana knew this would be so.

Among the Stinkards at this time there are few strong young men. Many have been killed in recent fighting with the Creeks, who were once our friends. Is it that the Ni'kwana wishes for my happiness? But Jubal does not see me. He will go away when the grass turns green and let me return to my village.

I do not know how I could become a bride here. I could teach him our way. He could fasten the oak leaves in his hair and I could carry the laurel. The people who are with me would know what to do, but he does not see me and I am alone.

I am a Sun, and I have pride. I cannot be humble with this man, nor do I believe he wishes it.

I cannot go to the women and tell them my thoughts, for I am a Sun. If he does not want me, why should I want him?

I should not, but I do.

He is the man for me, and I think the Ni'kwana saw this. I think it was in his mind. It was his duty to tell me I should return, but it was in his heart that I should find happiness. How could he know this was the man? Could he have foreseen it? The Ni'kwana often sees things before they happen, but perhaps he did not see it until he spoke with Jubal beside the fire.

It is hard to be a Sun. If I were a village girl it would not matter, but I have been taught from a time when very small what it is to be a Sun, but now I find it very lonely.

Jubal is a good man. I am no foolish girl to be taken by broad shoulders and a bold way. He is a quiet man, a thoughtful man, and he has been a good leader. He has guided us well. He must come of a strong people if such a one is only a yeoman and not a great lord. He has wisdom and judgment. He plans well, and when he hunts he hunts for others, as a warrior should.

I have watched him do what is needed. He wastes no time yet is never hurried. He limps but he does not complain. He is sure that each of us eats before he takes meat for himself. He stands aside when I enter the lodge, which is what a warrior must do for a Sun, but he stands aside for other women as well.

I have tried to learn his tongue. At first we had only some words of Cherokee, a few of his tongue, and a few of French or Spanish. Each tried to make the other understand with what words we had, and we did so. Now I speak his tongue much better, as does Keokotah, who knew English from before but had not used it for some time. I speak well now, but for some things I do not have words, and for some things there seem to be no English words.

I am alone and I am bitterly unhappy. I am a Sun and cannot show how I feel. I am afraid for spring to come, for he will go far away and there will be nothing but to return to my people. I love my people and have duty to them, but I love this man also.

The Ni'kwana can lead them until there is a Great

Sun. They would need me but for a short time, and then I would be alone and have no man.

I have tried to let him see that I would be a good woman for him. I have walked with him in the snow. I have stood beside him when there was trouble. I am not a frightened woman. We Suns are taught to be strong and know no other way. We are taught not to fear what must be done and that each Sun is an example to all others of what a Sun is and must be.

When the snow began to melt I was like a frightened girl, for I thought he would go from me. So when the cold came again I was glad. Now I do not know how long the cold will last. Keokotah knows much of these things and says it soon will grow warm and leaves will bud again, and the ice will go from the streams and come into my blood, for he will go from me then and I shall be alone.

My heart is heavy with longing for what I do not have, yet I cannot show it for I am a Sun. I must be aloof, and hide my fears and my loneliness.

I will make myself more beautiful. I will make him see me.

What do the women of his people do when they are in love? How does a woman join a man in his land? Do they use the oak and the laurel as well? I do not think so.

Keokotah does not know. His Englishman never talked of that. I do not think men talk of brides and weddings and things that mean much to women. I do not think they speak of these things among themselves. I think they only speak of weapons, of hunting and war. Perhaps some talk of women, too.

He wears the claws of the cougar he killed, since Keokotah has given them to him. Only a great warrior could do what he has done, but he does not speak of it. At night beside the fire when the wind blows cold, our people tell stories of warpaths and fighting, and he listens but does not speak of what he has done.

When the Spanishman was here, the one called Gomez, he seemed suddenly jealous. I was pleased, perhaps foolishly.

Perhaps he does not know his own mind. Perhaps he does not wish to know.

I must make him see me.

Today the cold is not as great. No snow falls. The peaks are icy against the pale blue sky. He has gone to look over the other valley, but I do not think our enemies will come from there but from the valley that runs off to the south, where we killed the buffalo. That was where we were seen.

One of my warriors would have killed a young buffalo bull today, but Jubal would not allow it. He stopped the warrior, which made him angry, but then he walked out to the buffalo and went right up to it. He stood beside it and rubbed its head with his hand!

When he returned to us he said, "Never touch that one. It is a medicine bull."

The angry warrior was frightened when he knew what he might have done. The buffalo followed Jubal almost to our lodge, and then went away when he told it to. Jubal spent much time rubbing its back, talking to it.

The buffalo did not go away. I saw him again when the sun was low, standing in the snow, looking toward our lodge.

It is a good place. From a hundred feet away I could not see our lodge, and we have been careful not to make a path leading to it. We come out walking on stones and from the end of the small forest where it is. I believe we will stay here until the spring comes.

When darkness fell we were alone on the snow. I thought he might see me, but he only looked at the sky and the mountains.

"Tomorrow will be fair," he said. "We must be on watch. I think they will come."

He stood back and looked at our lodge and where it stood. "It is well hidden," he said.

Our eyes met and he looked quickly away. "You are a Sun," he said suddenly.

"I am a woman," I said.

He looked at me again and said, "Yes, you certainly are."

A little snow blew from a spruce, drifting down over us. "I must not keep you standing in the cold," he said. "Yours is a warmer country than this."

The buffalo bull stood watching us. "We killed its mother," he said. "It has no one else. Its mother disappeared and I was there."

"You are strange man," I said. I could believe he was a Ni'kwana among his own people, for he had power over animals. It truly was a medicine bull, for no buffalo ever, ever followed a man or let a man approach it.

We started back to the lodge, and then I slipped on the ice. I fell, and he caught me. For a moment he held me, his arm around my waist, and then he helped me get my feet on the snow, let go of me, and stepped back. His face was flushed. "Are you all right?" he asked.

"Oh, yes! It was the ice," I said.

I was all right. I was more all right than ever. I thanked in my thoughts the Indian girl I saw do that back on the Great River. It was a silly thing for a woman to do, especially when there was no ice.

27

Alone I sought a place among the silent peaks, following a frozen stream where snow on either side banked the trees to their icy necks. My snowshoes whispered on the snow, and blown flakes touched my cheeks with cold fingers. This was no place for men, but a place for gods to linger, a place to wait in silence for the world to end.

Pausing, I shivered, looking along the vast hollow between the peaks and across the valley beyond to even mightier mountains. It was a place of majesty and rare beauty, but there was no game here, no tracks of either animals or birds. The wind hung a veil of snow across the scene and then dropped it casually aside, as though it had not been.

My family could thrive in Grassy Cove. For myself, if someday I built a home, this valley would be the place for it. The thought came unbidden and unexpected, and I tried to keep it from my mind, but the valley lay there, a vast expanse of snow broken by trees, and a fringe of trees clung like eyelashes to the calm, still face of the mountains.

To go further now would be foolish and no doubt time wasted, yet I did push on, to get a better glimpse of the valley.

Then for a long time I stood looking and thinking

what it must be like with the snow gone and the valley all green with summer. It was a thing to think about. Then I turned, starting back.

What was I looking for? Another place like Shooting Creek? This was infinitely more vast, far more lonely, but a man could find a place here. I'd have to come back when the grass was green.

The way back was downhill most of the distance I'd come, and once far off I saw a deer floundering in the snow. The meat would be poor at this time of year and after a hard winter, but I would be glad of anything. It was growing late and I had miles to go.

In the late afternoon, the trees were black against the snow, the sky a dull gray, flat and cold to the horizon. If I had broken my leg in such a place as this I'd never have survived. So I moved with care, avoiding things that seemed to lie under the snow, whether fallen trees or rocks, one did not know.

Glancing up at the high shoulders of the mountain, its head sunk between them for protection, I knew no matter how quiet and serene it looked that there was endless war up there, a war of the winds from whatever direction, and they would be no gentle winds. As if to answer my thought, a veil of snow lifted from the mountain and blew itself away down the country. I shivered again and was glad when I came to the shelter of trees.

I did not like coming home without meat, for there would be hungry eyes looking for me and expecting more than I could give, but there was nothing. I had seen that one deer, far off, and nothing else. It was cold, too cold to be out, too cold for animals to be moving.

I took off my snowshoes and stood them near the opening and stamped the snow from my feet before I went in. There had been only a trail of smoke above the lodge, but inside it was warm and quiet.

Keokotah looked up when I entered and shrugged. He had been out, I knew, and had found nothing. Nor had the others.

No matter when spring came, it would not be soon enough.

Yet I thought of the valley. When the weather broke I would go over there. It was far away, not as close as it had seemed in all that endless white. I would find a trail where bears went, or deer. There might even be buffalo over there, although they did not favor the mountain valleys.

Itchakomi looked at me and there was something in her expression, something I could not place, but it left me uneasy. I went to my place and sat down, not asking for food. There would be little enough of that.

There was no talking in the lodge that day, and less moving about. From time to time one of us ventured into the cold to look for enemies, but they, too, must have been remaining inside.

When I ventured out just after daybreak a few stars still lingered. But the sky was clear, and when the sun arose, it was warm. By midmorning there were edges of melt around some of the rocks and on the south sides of the trees. By midday it was warm and quite pleasant. Two of the Natchee left at once to hunt down the valley, and two more went back to our former home.

It was a risk, but there might be game there, and none of us wished to starve.

Keokotah came to join me where I repaired my snowshoes. "Now they come. The young men will be eager for war. They will wish to take scalps, to count coup, to win honors. You see it."

"We must be ready."

"You go among the mountains then?"

For a moment I stopped working and looked through the trees at the far-off mountainside. Would I go? I shied from the question.

"There is a valley over there." I gestured. "I want to see it."

"Only a valley?" There was amusement in his eyes. "Or a place to build a lodge?"

I flushed. "Well, it would be a good place. I just

thought I'd have a look. After all, it's a place I haven't seen."

The days grew warmer, and the snow melted. There were slides in the higher mountains, and suddenly there were buds on the trees and a showing of green on the distant hills.

Spring was born with a trickling of water from melting snow and a dancing in the air. At home in Shooting Creek they would be opening all the doors and windows to rid themselves of bad air captured during the winter months, and hanging out the bedding, too. There were always times when doors and windows could be opened, but the circulation of air in the cabins was never good enough. We had no problem with that here, for soon the men were sleeping under the trees.

Keokotah was hunting in and around the scraggy peaks, and two of the Natchee had gone to the valley again.

One Natchee indicated my buffalo, feeding on the slope not far off. "Eat?"

"No," I said. "He's a friend, a pet."

"We hungry."

"There will be meat."

"No meat, we eat him."

For a moment I stared at him. "He has followed me because he trusts me. He eats from my hand. I will not have him killed."

Fortunately, Keokotah came back with a young bear. It was not enough for so many, but it took the edge from our hunger. The Ponca woman caught fish in the stream, now free of ice, and then Unstwita came back with meat from a big buck.

It was a clear, cloudless day, and we had eaten well. It was a good time to lie in the sun and soak up some of the heat we had missed in the winter.

Itchakomi had walked out from the lodge, going toward the river that went from us down to the lower valley where our first home had been. She was still not far and I was watching her. Suddenly she turned and started back, and then she started to run.

"*Keokotah!*" I was on my feet, reaching for an arrow.

A warrior ran at Itchakomi. Then another sprang from the brush near her. My arrow took the first one, but then they were coming from everywhere. Dropping my bow, I drew my Italian pistols. Lifting the first gun, I took careful aim and fired.

The Indian at whom I shot was nearest to me. Another had already grabbed Itchakomi, but at the thundering report of my gun, all heads turned, our own people as well as theirs. In that instant when he was off guard, Itchakomi jerked free and stabbed the man who had seized her.

The man at whom I shot dropped in his tracks. Lowering the pistol for the load to drop in place, I lifted it and fired again.

My targets were standing, stricken with astonishment. Some of them had no doubt heard the Spanish guns but had not expected anything of the kind here. One by one I fired the guns, and three men were down before they took cover, the echoes of the first shot still racketing against the hills.

Itchakomi came to me, running.

In just that first moment of attack the effect had been catastrophic for them. Four men were down, two wounded, two dead. Itchakomi's attacker, badly hurt, was crawling away. Then struggling to his feet he disappeared into the brush.

My guns had been a total surprise, but this attack was not over. They had retreated merely to take stock of the situation. I said as much to Itchakomi. "It is only the beginning. They will not be surprised next time."

Back inside the lodge I reloaded my pistols. My powder horn was still more than half full, but I'd have to find a place to make powder.

How many were out there? I glanced around at Itchakomi. "How many?"

"Many! Too many!"

An Indian that I had wounded was starting to crawl away, but I let him go. I could not make out where my bullet had struck him. I had aimed simply for his body but thought I had shot low and right. That last had been a hurried shot, and I should not permit myself such waste. Each shot must score a kill.

All was still. The sun was warm, the snow melting. Soon it would be gone. I replaced my pistols in their scabbards and took up the bow.

Keokotah came to me as I emerged from the lodge. "They wait." He paused, his black eyes sweeping the terrain before him. "I think they come soon."

We waited, our men formed around in a circle, well into the woods near the lodge, waiting for an attack that was long in coming.

"I think they come closer," Keokotah said. "This time no time. They come quick."

I agreed, and waited, and waited.

My stomach felt hollow and my mouth dry. If they were many and they attacked from close in we might all be killed. I felt for my knife, for it would come to that. They would not attack from a distance this time, but would be upon us at once. My guns, if I used them, would get off no more than one hasty shot each. I dared not take a chance on having one wrested from me.

With night it would be cold again. They would draw off then, and build fires—

They came with a rush, and from close in. But our defenses were out, and their approach could not be completely hidden. One arrow left my bow. Then I dropped it and took to the knife. A big warrior leapt at me, and my knife ripped him up. Keokotah swung a club he had been carving. One of our men went down from a thrown spear, and the Ponca woman withdrew the spear and thrust it at the Indian who bent to take his scalp. She held it low with both hands and drove hard and the Indian tried to leap away, too late. I glimpsed her pin him down, saw his eyes staring up at her as his hands grasped at the spear.

It was hand to hand. Men fell. There was a scream. I was struck from behind and driven to my knees. I came up, fell, and rolling over, kicked a man away with my feet and came up. I was face to face with a short, powerfully built Indian who was amazingly agile. He slipped away from a knife thrust and swung his knife at me. Our blades clashed and when we came close I kicked him suddenly, catching him on the knee.

His knife ripped my tunic. My upward thrust cut a thin line along his chest and nicked his chin. We circled. Then somebody leapt on me from behind and my adversary lunged to finish me off. In that moment Itchakomi thrust a spear into his back. I fell, the man atop my back was gripping my hair in one hand, his other coming up with a knife to take my scalp. His hand gripping my hair gave my neck a fearful wrench, and I struck upward with my knife, stabbing him in the side. He wrenched hard on my neck again, wanting only that scalp, and I stabbed again. I felt the cutting edge of the knife on my hair and with a frantic lunge managed to throw him half off me. I came to my knees, driving a fist into his belly.

That broke his hold and he fell back and I leapt on him. He rolled to one side but not fast enough, and I sank the knife deep.

He wrenched free of me, bleeding badly, his face contorted with fury. He leapt at me, but this time I kicked him as he came in and he staggered back. His knees buckled under him then and he fell.

All around me there had been fighting, but suddenly it was over and they were gone. Bloody, gasping, I looked around. Itchakomi was standing in a corner near the lodge, a spear in her hand, its tip bloody.

The man I had fought was crawling away and Keokotah, bloody and bleeding, thrust a spear into him.

They were gone. Why they had broken off the attack, I did not know.

Two of our men were dead, and one had been scalped. A woman had been killed. Only Itchakomi and Unstwita were unwounded.

They had carried off their dead and wounded. How many we had killed, I did not know.

Keokotah's woman, a terrible bruise on her shoulder

and a cut on her arm, was bathing the blood from his wound.

"They will come again," Keokotah said, looking at me.

"Aye, and we must be gone."

Amazingly, I was almost unhurt. There was a thin knife cut at the roots of my hair only an inch or two long and not deep and a few minor scratches. Keokotah had taken a blow on the shoulder that had left his right arm almost useless for the time.

"We will go now," I said, "in the night."

Limping and bloody, we gathered our few belongings and the little meat we had left. By the time we were ready to move it was dark. I knew only one place to go.

My valley.

28

We walked upon the mountains in the night. Limping, I led the way. Constantly we paused to listen for pursuit, but heard nothing. Often we had to pause because our lowland lungs were unaccustomed to the heights. Several times we stopped to rest.

At the first halt I went from one to the other, doing what I could to treat their wounds. It was little enough that I knew, but more than anyone there with the exception of Itchakomi. Surprisingly, she knew a good bit.

When morning came there was a dense fog, a mist lying low in the hollows of the hills. We followed a dim path, probably a game trail, and at first, for at least five miles, it was all uphill. Then the climb eased except for scrambles through boulders and the remains of avalanches that had swept down the mountain during the winter. Stiff, tired, and sore, we climbed, gasped for breath, and then pushed on.

The mist lifted away from us, revealing a world of broken granite and snow, with here and there a dwarf spruce struggling for existence against the wind and the ice. We sat down then and shared bits of jerked meat among us. There was little enough, but it was needed. A

Natchee went back a few hundred yards to watch our trail while we ate.

Their faces were gaunt and tired, their wide eyes staring emptily upon nothing. A cold wind blew off the peaks, and I shivered. This was not the way I had hoped to come to my valley.

Rising, I walked down the path, and then waited for them to rise and follow. The Natchee watching our back trail came in. "There is nothing," he said, "or nothing that can be seen. There is mist covering our valley, mist in the passes."

Halting a half mile further along, I looked back at my straggling band. How did I, Jubal Sackett, a loner, come to be in this place with these people?

A cold wind stirred the limbs of a spruce near me and whined softly through a crack in the rocks. I shrugged my shoulders against the cold of the wind and beat my hands together. Slowly, the others were catching up.

There was a creek cut across our path not far ahead, and there we would build a fire, rest, and eat what we had.

We had been coming downhill for some time now, very slightly at first, but then the descent had grown steeper. The creek was free of ice, the water chuckling along over rocks and gravel, clear and cold. We gathered broken branches and bark for a fire. Building it, we gathered close. The Ponca woman, the best fisherman among us, went to the creek away from us.

I had not eaten when the others had. There was too little food as it was, and I was strong enough to survive. When I looked up at the mountains there was black rock, perhaps wet from melting snow, and a lone golden eagle swinging on wide wings against the sky and the snow.

A thin waterfall, thin from here at least, perhaps forty feet wide where it was, fell from rocky shelf to rocky shelf, mostly melting snow. By late spring it would be only a trickle. Now the mountain was stark and beautiful, a place for no man or animal, just for the clouds and eagles.

I brought sticks for the fire and added fuel. I watched

the affectionate flames reach out and clasp the sticks in a fiery embrace, destroying what they loved.

My legs were tired. My back ached. I sat on a fallen tree and looked back the way we had come, rough, broken, and almost treeless.

The Ponca woman came to me in her black moccasins. She was a wide woman who smiled rarely but never complained. She pointed across the way at the mountains. The ones the Spanish call the Sangre de Cristos. "Caves," she said. "Big!"

"You have been here before?"

"With Ponca," she said. "My people hunt."

"Thank you," I said. "We will go to the caves."

She did not linger, but returned to her fishing, and by the time the sun was high had caught a half dozen fish. It was a help.

Keokotah killed a ptarmigan. I saw nothing, but I thought of Itchakomi. She would wish to go home now, back to her own people and the warm weather beside the Great River. Well, I was a loner, anyway. And there were always the mountains. The thought brought me no comfort.

Keokotah came to me where I sat beside the stream. "Caves no good," he said, "too much climb. Big hole inside. No good place for sleep."

The thought of climbing high among the rocky peaks did not appeal and I said so. "We'll go up the valley," I said, "find a place there."

"I see many tracks. Deer, elk, buffalo, turkey." After a moment, "Your buffalo here. He look for you."

Tired as I was I walked out on the grass beyond the creek. The buffalo was there and I went to it, standing beside it and scratching its ear. "If you're going to stay with us," I said, "I'll put you to work."

The thought had come suddenly, but the more I thought of it the better I liked it.

A few minutes before dark one of the Natchee killed an elk. We ate well that night, and for once I sat long beside the fire.

Itchakomi came and sat across from me. "My people

say they go home," she said suddenly. "Grass come soon. Much water in river. They go home quick."

If they went, she would go. She would return to their home on the Great River.

For a moment my heart seemed to stop beating. I waited a moment and then said, "It will not be easy to get past the Conejeros, and Kapata will be waiting."

She merely looked at me, saying nothing.

My mind struggled with the problem of how they could reach the Great River by way of the Arkansas without being seen. It would need a roundabout route unless . . . unless they could reach the river before it emerged from the mountains and ride it all the way down.

"I shall find a way to get you back," I said.

She arose abruptly and left the fire. I started to speak, but all I saw was her back as she retreated. I sat for a few minutes, puzzled over her abrupt departure.

Women! I'd never understand them.

When I had been sitting there for several minutes Keokotah came to me. "Look," I said, "they wish to go back. They will ride the river down."

On the clay at the river's edge I made a mark. "Here is where the river comes from the big canyon. South of there and back in here . . . that was our first camp. Now we have crossed to the west and we are in a long valley that's roughly north and south. It seems to me that if we went up the valley we could get to that river in the canyon before it reaches open country. They might slip by during the night."

He looked at the rough plan I'd drawn and put his finger at the head of the valley we were in. "What is there? We do not know."

Of course he was right. And the water through that canyon would be rough. Yet rough water was to be preferred to the Conejeros and Kapata. The more I considered the idea the more logical it seemed.

What was the matter with Itchakomi? She was their leader, and if they were going to return—

I spoke of this to Keokotah. He glanced at me out of

those cool black eyes and said, "Maybe she no wish to go. Maybe she think you try to be rid of her. Maybe she think you think she too much trouble."

That was ridiculous. She was no trouble at all! Of course, if I had not become involved with them I might now be much further west, and might have had no trouble with the Conejeros, and certainly none with Kapata. But the possibility that she might not wish to return was nonsense.

She was a Sun, a person of importance among her people. She had come west to find a place for her people, and aside from the Conejeros this was a good place. The snow had almost gone from what I thought of as my valley. It was, I guessed, more than twenty miles long and four to five miles wide. There were several streams and the runoff from the mountains, and the valley was sheltered from the worst of the winds.

When morning came we moved north, but when we camped that night on a creek near the edge of the mountains, Keokotah came to me. "Maybe no good," he said.

"It's a beautiful valley," I objected. "It is higher, and they would have to learn to plant different crops than they are used to, but I think it is a good place."

"Much trail," he said, gesturing back the way we had come. "I find Indian path, very old. Much Indian walk that path. Maybe he no like people here."

"Conejeros?"

"No Conejeros. I think maybe Ute. Very strong people. Live in mountain valleys. Very strong."

The place we had found was a good place, and the valley was fertile. As the grass began to turn it green, I could see from the variety of plant life that the soil was rich.

"We will go no further," I said. "This is where we will stop."

The location was one that was easily defended, tucked into a corner of the mountains on the east side of the valley. It was a place well supplied with water.

As soon as we went into camp several of the Natchee left to hunt.

"We must find how far it is to the river," I said. "Tomorrow, I think—"

"You stay," Keokotah said. "I go."

There was a yearning in me to see what lay to the north, but it was also necessary that a fort be built, a place we could defend in case of another attack.

A stream emerged from a canyon to flow down into the valley, and at one place the stream fell over some rocks in a small waterfall of about three feet. Nearby were some tumbled boulders at the crest of a small knoll, a flat place atop the knoll surrounded by trees at one side of the canyon but overlooking the valley.

It offered a site for a group of lodges, water from the waterfall, and protection from the boulders and trees. With two of the Natchee men I set to work to build a rough shelter to take care of us while we built a stronger cabin.

The Natchee who had gone hunting returned with two deer and several sage hens. By the time they came into camp a crude shelter for the night had been built and we had dragged several dead trees across gaps among the boulders to make a stronger wall.

Itchakomi was busy and she avoided me. Several times I started to speak, but each time she turned away and went off to some other area, avoiding me, or seeming to. Irritated, I decided if that was the way she wanted it, she mighty well could have it. So I avoided her.

Keokotah would not be back for a day or two, so that other question need not arise.

Yet I slept ill. The night through I turned and tossed, getting no decent sleep at all, and when morning came I took my weapons and went up the canyon behind our fort. It was a fairly deep canyon and led back into the mountains. There was still much snow in the shaded places, and here and there boulders in the stream were icy. When I returned it was dusk and meat was cooking. I went to the fire and chose a piece for myself and sat down near the fire.

Itchakomi was across the fire from me. After a moment, she spoke. "Keokotah has gone to find a way?"

"He will find a way to the river. The water will be rough and fast, but I believe your people might slip by your enemies, passing them at night."

"You will go with them?"

"No." I looked up at her. "My place is in the mountains, so I will stay. The river is called the Arkansas and some other names as well, but it flows into the Great River. Your people can get home without trouble. Unstwita can lead them. He is a good man."

She looked at me then, for I had not mentioned her leading them. I avoided her eyes, feeling uncomfortable. Until I had spoken I had not thought of it myself, but why had I not mentioned her? Was it not her place to lead? Would she not lead if she was going back?

"There is always danger," I said, "but Unstwita is a good man. He is both wise and brave."

"It is my place to lead."

She spoke and I was silent, chewing on a piece of meat. Then I said, "You will go with them?"

"Do you want me to go?"

There it was, right out in the open. How could I answer that?

"I would miss you." I said it reluctantly, hesitantly, yet realizing as I spoke that what I said was true. I would miss her, and I would not see her again. That gave me a pang, and I moved sharply at the thought. Then I said, "But I cannot ask that you stay. You are a Sun."

There was amusement in her eyes. "And you are not even a Stinkard." She paused. "You are a yeoman. Did a yeoman never marry a princess?"

"Never! If she did she would no longer be a princess. Or so I believe."

"Then I shall no longer be a Sun."

Our eyes met across the fire and I took another fragment of meat, slicing it with my knife.

"To me," I said, "you will always be the sun, the moon, and the stars."

The fire crackled, and a low wind stirred the flames. I added sticks to the fire. "I am strange to your ways," I said, "and you to mine, but what you wish will be done. Then we shall go south to where the Spanishmen live. There will be a priest there."

"That will be dangerous?"

"It is worth the risk. I would have it done so it is right with both your people and mine."

I went down to the stream and dipped my hands in the water, washing them. When I stood up she was beside me.

"When you wish to go to the mountains," she said, "you may go, and if you wish it, I will go with you, and when you make your camp, I will cook your meat, and when you wish to sleep, I will prepare your bed. Where you go, I will go."

29

Quickly grew the grass, and quickly came leaves to the trees. Scattered along the green hillsides the golden banner bloomed, and here and there entire hillsides turned to cascades of their yellow flowers. There were sand lilies, too, and occasional pasqueflowers.

We all walked together, for we were few, and had no knowledge of what might lie before us. Also, there was talk among the women of a wedding. I caught them looking at me, laughing among themselves, and was embarrassed. How a bridegroom was supposed to act, I did not know, nor anything else of their marriage customs.

Itchakomi had spoken of me wearing the oak and she the laurel, but what that implied I did not know. Nor could she find laurel here, so far as I knew. I had not seen it in these western mountains, although back in the Nantahalas there were often whole hillsides blushing with its pink blossoms.

Keokotah, who had found the way, led us along the eastern side of the valley to a creek that ran into a canyon. Through this canyon we must make our way, and there was danger there, a fit lurking place for enemies.

Itchakomi walked with the women, and they did not walk in silence. There was much chattering and laughter.

Once, when we had halted to rest, Unstwita came to me. "It is better I go with them," he said, reluctantly. "I have wished to stay."

"They will need you," I said. "Tell the Ni'kwana that I did as he asked. Tell him I shall do my best to make Itchakomi happy."

"I will tell him. And I shall return."

"Return?"

"I have come to the mountains in doubt. I find them . . . I find them a place for the gods to walk."

"Return, then. We shall be here, but if we leave I shall mark our way so—" I showed him the Sackett A. "You will find us."

"I will find you." He held out his hand suddenly, as he had seen me do. "You are my chief. I will follow no other."

There was a trail of sorts along the canyon. It crossed and recrossed the turbulent little creek, winding among boulders and trees below the canyon walls. We stepped carefully around stones and lifted fallen branches from across the way. We would return this way, and a little work now would make the path easier. If we did not return, it would be easier for someone else.

It had been my father's way to remove obstructions, to repair washouts in old trails, to leave each trail better than he had found it. "Tread lightly on the paths," he had told me. "Others will come when you have gone."

That was how I would remember my father. There was never a place he walked that was not the better for his having passed. For every tree he cut down he planted two.

We came at last to a place beside the river, a swift-flowing river that would become even swifter as the canyon walls narrowed. We came to an open place where aspen grew upon the slopes, and scattered cottonwoods along the river itself. We came to a place where drift logs had beached themselves on the gravelly shores. Stripped of their bark their gaunt white limbs were like skeletons among the boulders polished by the rough waters.

Here we camped, and I looked about me, for it was here that I would marry, here that I would take a wife. Watching Itchakomi, I knew my father would have approved, and my mother also.

Had we been among her people or mine the preparations would have been great. The women would have prepared a cabin for us, and there would among my people have been much sewing, cooking, planning, fussing about, all dear to a woman's heart. Here there was not the time, nor was it the place. We must make do, and perhaps make up later on for what was missed.

The Natchee people built a shelter of boughs, and the men went to the forests to find game for a feast. It was to be the wedding of a Sun, and I was not sure the people approved.

Tomorrow would be the day, so I did not go out to hunt but sat by the river and contemplated what was to be. If I was to have a wife I must have a home, and I must plan for the future. My valley was a good place, yet it was upon the path of migration for some tribes, a hunting ground for others.

We would be few, only Itchakomi, the Ponca woman, Keokotah and his woman, and myself. We would be too few to defend against an attack by the Conejeros, if they still existed, or their attackers. Yet I knew how to build a strong fortress, and would. It was something to think on. There was also the planting of crops, the gathering of seed, planning for the future. Much of this I had known from boyhood, for at Shooting Creek we had lived just that way. Only there had been more of us.

There was another defense, and it might work. Already some knew me as a medicine man. If I became a medicine man as well as a trader—

If strength could not win, one must use wit, if one has any.

Of oak leaves there was no shortage, but we had planned to use something else for the laurel until Unstwita returned from the hunt with a sprig of dwarf laurel found growing high on the mountain.

When the afternoon drew on I scouted around, making a sweep of the area, following the river down to look for tracks. But I found none. What I feared was an attack during the ceremony, and yet we had seen no recent tracks.

The morning dawned bright and clear. Unstwita had told me of the ritual and how it would proceed. When I went to the shelter they had erected for me, an old Natchee warrior waited within. He said, "Behold, you have come!"

Another old man and a woman entered then and after them, Itchakomi.

The old people asked us if we loved each other. When we had replied the old man stood beside her, representing her father. They tied oak leaves to a tuft of my hair, and Itchakomi carried a sprig of the laurel, as was the custom.

I said, "Do you want me as your husband?"

"Yes. I wish it very much and will be happy to go with you."

In my left hand I carried the bow and arrow that signified that I would not fear our enemies and that I would provide for my wife and children.

She held the laurel in her left hand, in her right a sheaf of maize. The laurel signified that she would keep her good reputation, the maize that she would prepare my meals.

Having said she would go with me she dropped the maize from her right hand, and I took it in mine and said "I am your husband," and she replied, "And I am your wife."

I took her to my bed, as the rites demanded, and said, "This is our bed. Keep it clean."

The feast was prepared and we went together to eat of it. The others gathered around, with much laughter and talk. Only Keokotah was not there. He had slipped away from the festivities, but I knew why. We knew not the land, nor who might come, and one among us must be alert.

After the feast the Natchee began to dance, a slow, shuffling dance that I knew not, though I knew many Indian dances.

While the drum beat and the Natchee danced I said to Itchakomi, "You are sure?"

"I am."

"If your people need you, we can go back. I will take you back."

"My place is with you. The Ni'kwana knew this."

"We will be much alone. There will be too few of us, but we shall build a strong fort. We will trade with the Indians."

"What of the Men of Fire?"

I shrugged. "Perhaps they will come. That we must face when they do. I have my own fire," I added, "and will use it if I must."

"When morning comes, my people will go," she said. "They will go back to Natchee, our home by the Great River, but they will always know there is a place for them if they wish to come."

"Tell them," I said suddenly, "to send a messenger to my people at Shooting Creek, to tell them I have found you and am happy."

"It shall be done."

There was a moon above the mountains, and a white glow upon the camp. The water rustled swiftly by, and the aspen leaves stirred restlessly, as always. The fire burned low and the drum ceased to beat and the Indians to dance. Beyond the leafy bower where we lay the red coals smoldered, and I knew that one of the Natchee or Keokotah would be watching.

How far were we from the fens of old England! How far from the Isle of Ely, whence my father had come, so long ago! Now I was here, where no white man was supposed to be, finding my own land in a world far from others. We would go deeper into the mountains. We would leave them all behind.

The Natchee would not have a dugout. There was not time. They would use a raft and go down the river upon it until they found my canoe, and then they would use both raft and canoe unless they were so lucky as to capture another canoe.

At dawn we helped them load their meat and the few things they possessed.

At dawn we saw them push off and watched them disappear, going down with the swiftly rushing waters. When they had gone we turned and looked around. Only five were left, in a land vast and lonely, a land where the only people of whom we knew were enemies.

We walked where the wind had blown and where the autumn leaves had fallen and rotted into soil, but there was color in the sky, and on the mountains the green lay dark where the spruce were and bright where aspen grew. We killed some sage hens and ate them, and we caught some fish from a stream. Then, on the night when we had almost reached the place we were to build, we saw a flash of light from down the long wet valley, a flash of sunlight from a blade, and then we saw them coming, six mounted men and twenty marching. Of the twenty, several were battered and bloody. Of the mounted, only two rode as if unhurt.

At dawn that day Keokotah had killed an elk, so we stood and watched them come.

At last they saw us and pulled up, looking warily. Knowing them for Spanishmen I stepped out with my right hand up, palm toward them. Slowly they came on and then drew up to look again.

I spoke then, in Spanish. They came on then and drew up, wary, wounded, weary of riding and holding themselves in the saddle.

"Get down," I said. "We'll make a fire. Have you eaten at all?"

"Not for two days," their leader said. He was a tall man, lean and with a sparse beard. He bore his own share of wounds, two that I could see.

"You are Diego?"

Surprised, he looked at me. "We met a man of yours, fleeing ahead of you and bound for the settlements."

His face shadowed. "Gomez!" he said. "Ah, that one is trouble!"

"We knew nothing of him. We fed him and he went his way, but with no liking for us, I think."

"He likes only himself," Diego said. His men had gotten down and come to the fire as to a cold spring. These were beaten men.

"You've had a fight, then? With the Conejeros?"

"With some others, strange Indians. They attacked us at once. I lost two men that first time and four since. They were hard upon us until we slipped away in the night."

We were beside a small stream with trees close by and a good defensive position.

He noticed my guns. "Handsome pistols. I would buy them from you."

"No. They were given me by my father. They are the best of their kind, made by a master in Italy."

"I was apprenticed to an armorer," he said. "I knew them at once. I knew the workmanship. You have a fine pair of pistols."

He glanced at Itchakomi, standing beside me. "Your woman?"

"My wife," I said, "by an Indian marriage, which I hold as a true one. You don't have a friar among you? Or a priest?"

"He was killed, died well, too. A game man." He glanced at me. "You wish to be married again?"

"I am a Christian," I said, "although not a Catholic. I'd like to be married again by a Christian sacrament."

"She's beautiful," he said simply, "and proud."

"Among her own people, the Natchee, she is a Sun, a princess."

"I can believe it," he said.

He walked to the fire, and the Ponca woman passed him a bowl of broth made from the elk meat. He tasted it greedily and then, shamed, looked quickly around to be sure his men were eating. They were, but I liked him for it. The Spanishmen had been our enemies, but this was a man fit to walk upon the mountains.

"Sit you," I said. "I'll care for your horses."

His hand came up sharply. "No! My men will do that. Nobody touches our horses!" Then more gently he said, "They are few and hard to come upon. We bring them up from Mexico, and the Indios have taken to stealing them. Soon they will be riding them against us."

"Indians who ride?"

"I have seen a few," Diego replied grimly, "and they ride well, too!"

He ate, and then looked at me. "English?"

"My father was. I am American."

He smiled quizzically. "American? What is that? I have not heard the name before."

"I was born in this land." Pausing, I gestured to the south. "I shall set up a trading post. You are welcome to trade."

"It will not be allowed," he said. "This is Spanish land."

"We are befriending you now, and could again. It might serve the Spanish well to have a friend out here, and not an enemy."

He shrugged. "I do not decide. There are regulations from the king."

He ate in silence until his bowl was empty. Then he cut a slice from a haunch of elk meat. "I will speak for you," he said. "I think it a good idea."

"Gomez hoped to reach the settlements before you," I said. "He has plans of his own."

"Gomez is always planning," Diego said. "I know him."

Keokotah had chosen a sleeping place for us among the rocks on a soft stretch of grass. We gathered there and left the Spanish by the fire. Most of them had fallen asleep right where they were, too tired to even think of defense.

We could even have stolen their horses.

30

Through the long day that followed, Diego and his men rested, and well they needed it. Haggard and driven, they had suffered a grievous defeat, but it was a time for learning. Here were men who had met strange Indians from the north—some of the Spanish were calling them Komantsi—and had fought them and escaped.

Diego had coffee, and he shared it with us. Over the fire we sat to talk, and Itchakomi sat with me.

"Fierce men who love to fight." Diego looked over the rim of his cup at me. "They take no prisoners, want none. They want horses," he added, "and they know how to handle them. If you stay here you will be killed."

He sipped his coffee, his eyes straying again and again to the hills. "They were not many, but their attack was sudden, without warning. They came upon us at break of day. Only a few of us were armed and ready. An arrow killed our sentry and then they charged upon us.

"I had my sword, and when I had once fired my pistol, it was only the sword. Then they were gone, as swiftly as they had come.

"They attacked us again while we marched, and then again. After that we waited until night and moved away into the mountains. I hope we do not bring them upon you."

"There will be tracks," I reminded.

"We tried to leave none," Diego said, "but with so many men and the horses . . ." He shrugged.

For a long time we were silent. Itchakomi moved away from the fire. We were making ready to go south to the place we had chosen.

She looked at me. "What we do?"

"Go back where we planned to build," I said. "It is a good place."

"You fear these Komantsi?"

"There are always enemies. These may be no worse than others." I paused and then said, "Komi, I do not wish to take you into the wilderness until we are married."

"We are not?"

"By your standards, yes. By mine, yes. But I wish a marriage that will be accepted by other Christians. My heart knows who is my wife, but other white people will not recognize our wedding. I wish it to be official, so no one will say you are just an Indian girl who shares my lodge."

"Very well. We stay. We build lodge."

Diego had fallen asleep by the fire. His men were lying about, also resting. "Sleep," I said to Keokotah. "I will watch."

There was no movement in our camp. All rested or were busy in one position. The horses had been taken into the willows near the stream where they were well hidden. I found a small knoll where I could move about among trees and rocks and yet remain unseen, and I moved rarely, only to look about, studying the hills for enemies.

It was a time for thinking. To proceed south to Santa Fe for a proper marriage would put me into the hands of those who considered themselves my enemies. I would be imprisoned and probably sent in chains to Mexico for trial. What would happen to Itchakomi one could only guess, for despite the regulations laid down by the Spanish king forbidding enslavement of the Indians, it was done.

The Spanish would not accept my venture into their territory as being anything but a spying mission. Nor would they permit the establishment of a trading post by anyone not of their own. Diego was a practical soldier, but only a soldier and with no authority except over his own command. Diego was practical enough to realize that a post where they might obtain food or other supplies was much to be desired. There was always a difference of viewpoint between the soldier in the field and the man behind the desk.

So, from the Spanish I could expect nothing but trouble, and I would certainly hear again from Gomez.

The Komantsi were another risk. It was possible I might win them over, at least to tolerating my presence.

We would build a fort, but we would arrange an escape route, scouted and planned. We would have to secure trade goods, and we could trap for fur. At first it would be very difficult. Very difficult, indeed!

When I went back into camp Diego was up and seated by the fire. I filled a cup with coffee and sat across the fire from him.

"You know the land to the west?"

He shook his head. "We do not. Some patrols have gone there, and some have gone north, much farther than this, but we know little of the country."

"The wild game?"

He shrugged. "What you know. Buffalo, elk, deer, antelope, bear—"

"Nothing larger?"

"Than a buffalo? What could be? We have seen them that weigh three thousand pounds, big bulls, very tough, very strong."

"Bears?"

"Ah! There you have it. There are silver bears, very large. We have seen them. Black bears, also, but smaller. The silver bears—ah, they are huge! Very fierce!"

We talked long, and I thought him a friendly and a lonely man, pleased to be speaking with someone on a friendly basis.

"Coronado," he said, "went far out upon the plains. He looked for golden cities. I think there are no golden cities. I think from far off someone sees the cities of mud, what is called adobe, and in the setting sun they look like gold. I think that is all."

"There is no gold in the mountains?"

He shrugged. "Of course, but the mining is hard and the Indios do not like it. They die . . . too many die! I feel sad, but who am I? I am a soldier, who does what he is told."

At dawn we arose and walked the few miles back to where we planned to build. There we said good-bye and he thanked us again for feeding his soldiers and treating their wounds. We shook hands, and to Itchakomi he bowed low.

At the last, he turned and said, "Be careful! That Gomez . . . he is a man of no morals. He wishes only for himself. He has no feelings. Yet he is a good fighter, better than me, and I fear he will have made it hard for me when I return. But do you beware. He will return. He will believe you have found gold, and only three things he wants, gold, power, and women."

He walked off down the valley after his men. Each man who had a horse led it. There would be need for their strength and speed later.

The place we finally settled upon was between two canyons that led off to the north northeast. They would lead, I thought, to the place where the big canyon opened and the river flowed down into the plains.

How fared our friends, the Natchee? If they had survived the river and the Indians at the canyon's mouth they would be well down the river by now.

For four days we worked, rolling rocks into place and settling them into the earth for a foundation, building a quick wall of defense so we might have time to build better, and further back.

Keokotah—like any other Indian—was unaccustomed to hard manual labor. Always he had been a hunter and a warrior, so I left the hunting and the scouting to him. He was willing to help, but he lacked the skills and the slights necessary. There was little in the life of an Indian that demanded labor of the kind needed. Some Indians built stockades, but these were the work of many people working together. The lodges of the Kickapoo were, I understood, though I had not seen one, domed affairs made of bark laid over a framework.

Building was not new to me. At Shooting Creek we had built largely and well, with the aid of men who knew much of such things, of notching logs and fitting them, of working with axe, saw, and adz.

Now I had planning to do as well as building, and several times I sat late by the fire drawing a rough plan on a piece of aspen bark.

The low hill where we intended to build was the source of a spring whose water trickled down to a small stream that flowed northeastward into a canyon. The top of the hill was mostly open, but I rolled the few scattered boulders to the outer edge of the hill to form part of a wall. There were trees growing and I trimmed their lower branches, constructing my house to use the trees as posts for added strength. Having no axe—only the hatchet I carried as a tomahawk—I had to choose from among the many downed trees the ones most solid and seasoned.

The top of the knoll made for good drainage, and again I used the device of cutting notches into the living trees to support my roof poles.

By nightfall I had the frame of the roof in place for a house of several rooms and considerable space. Around the perimeter of the hill I had rolled rocks to fill natural gaps in the rocks that rimmed the hill. It was a good defensive position with a view to all approaches.

During the days that followed I worked unceasingly, from dawn until dark and often long after dark, sitting by the fire to carve spoons, cups, and trenchers, the large wooden platters from which we would eat, just as they did in England.

Keokotah hunted far afield, eyes alert for enemies. He brought in a deer, an antelope, and several sage hens.

He found no tracks of men but several of the huge bears of which we had heard. "Leave them alone," I advised. "We don't need meat that bad."

West of our valley were the Sangre de Cristo Mountains, so named by the Spanish, as we had learned from Diego. They were a long, high ridge beyond which lay another, much larger valley. Keokotah had seen it from afar.

The Ponca woman, sturdy and quiet but always busy, found a granary in a natural rock shelter. An overhang had been walled in, leaving only a small window for access, and had been made into a storage place for grain. Some scattered corncobs lay about, all very small, but on the floor of the granary we found a half dozen cobs that still had grains of corn and maize.

With a sharp stick she made holes, and into each she dropped a kernel of corn. How old the corn was we had no idea, but we hoped it would grow.

Here and there we found signs of previous occupation, where some unknown people had lived for a time and passed on.

Every day I worked to build the cabin and to make our small fortress stronger. There were solid logs enough to build the cabin, and many for the stockade. Those logs in contact with the soil had usually rotted or begun to rot, but many had fallen across other logs and had only seasoned and grown stronger.

It was, I suppose, brutally hard work, but I'd been accustomed to little else, and manhandling the logs into position, sometimes rolling them, sometimes turning them end over end, simply took time. As a matter of fact, I enjoyed building. I always had.

Keokotah was ever restless, wandering the hills, scouting the possible trails, alert always as we all were. Each night when he came in we talked of what he had seen and where he had been. Occasionally, taking time off, I scouted the country myself.

Spring passed slowly into summer, and the cabin walls were up. A steeply slanted roof to shed the snow was in place. The meadows and hillsides were scattered with flowers now, Indian paintbrush, sunflower, larkspur, locoweed, and the ever-present golden banner.

Twice I ventured up the gulch, scouting my way, careful to leave no tracks, a simple thing for there were many rocks. Always, I tried to keep under cover and not to frighten any of the wildlife that might betray my presence. I found no moccasin tracks, or pony tracks, either.

We hunted far out, and often I took Paisano with me. Paisano was the name I had given the buffalo, who seemed happy to accompany me anywhere. He often carried packs for me, following me around like a puppy, a huge puppy, however, for he seemed to grow larger with every day. He would follow no one else, although he did allow Itchakomi to touch him.

We gathered roots and leaves and wild strawberries as soon as they began to appear. We smoked and dried venison, preparing for the winter to come.

It was well into the summer before I found the cave. It was well hidden, just a hole in the bottom of a small hollow behind some brush. A sage hen I had shot had dragged itself into the brush before dying and when I went to retrieve it and to recover my arrow I bent over and found myself looking into a black hole under a rocky ledge.

Taking up a small stone, I dropped it into the hole. It fell but a few feet. I tried again, with the same result. Taking my bow, I reached down and touched bottom, extending the bow and my arm, at no more than four to five feet.

I kindled a small fire and made a torch. Leaning down, I held it into the cave. I found myself looking into a room roughly oval and about ten feet wide but all of twenty to twenty-five feet deep. Several openings suggested further passages. The formation was limestone. I lowered myself into the cave, excited by my discovery. I scraped the wall with a bit of rock, bringing down a grayish-white dust.

Saltpeter!

Having nothing in which to carry it I took none with me, but crawling out I took careful sightings on nearby landmarks to find the exact spot again. Charcoal was easily had, so all that remained was sulphur.

Several times I had seen indications of ore while hunting, and at least one good outcropping that looked to be silver. And lead was often found in conjunction with silver.

Now I must conduct a serious search for sulphur, and if I could find it I could make my own gunpowder, as we had at Shooting Creek.

Excited, I started back to camp. Keokotah was awaiting me among the rocks. He stood up as I approached, Paisano following.

"I find tracks," he said.

I stared at him. "Indians?"

He spat. "Kapata!" he said. "He come, stay in rocks over there." He gestured toward the entrance to the gulch. "He watch, watch a long time."

Well, we had been expecting him. We had known he would come, yet—

"He come again. I think he come soon. He come for *her*, and he come for *you*!"

31

Itchakomi had come out from camp. "I see him," she said.

"You *saw* him?"

"He thinks he hidden, but from lodge I see him. He does not see me, as I am inside. He is not alone."

Well, I had not believed he would be. So now we must be prepared. Our season of peace was over, even though it had been a watchful peace.

As we ate, I considered the situation, and was not happy with it. Desperately, I needed more powder and more lead for bullets. My guns were loaded, and there might be enough powder to load them one more time.

Not a mile from the lodge I had discovered a ledge of silver and lead, and I was less interested in the silver than in the lead at this point. I now had niter, and there was charcoal from our fires and more to be burned. Sulphur I needed.

We had arrows, and at every available moment, seated by the fire or on lookout, we worked at making more. Our life was to be guided by the skills of our hands, and all we would have we must either find or create ourselves from materials at hand. Fortunately, I had never known any other way of life. At Shooting Creek we had had utensils from the ships, but never enough. Most of what we had we made.

Desperately, I needed a source for sulphur, but I had found no deposits, although I kept a constant watch. Each foray we made into the country around was not only for hunting, but for sources of raw materials and for the best fuel. All woods were not equally good for making fires, particularly fires that would last and leave the best coals. For these the hardwoods were best, but there were not many to be found aside from oak.

Nor did I like our situation. We were committed to defending a position, when I preferred movement. I believed in attack as a principle of war, yet our lodge and the few possessions we had committed us to defense. Keokotah was no happier with the idea than I, and spoke his mind.

"I no like," he said. "He who attacks chooses the time and the place and the how."

My feelings were the same.

"Go!" Itchakomi said. "We fight. We are three women who can use the bow and the spear."

It was tempting, yet I hesitated. The place was not easy to attack, situated as it was, and their water supply was inside the lodge. I doubted Kapata would use fire, for he did not wish to destroy Itchakomi but to capture her and return with her to Natchez. Yet we were only two, and he would have a dozen at least. Our only chance was to cut them off and kill them one by one, a thing not easily done.

It was Itchakomi who reminded me. "You are shaman. You master of mysteries. The Natchee who walk with Kapata know this."

The Indian was a believer in magic, in medicine. He was a man of many superstitions, as were we the English, only the superstitions of the English were different. Superstition could be, might be, a formidable weapon. If I could create doubt, if I could make them hesitate—

The Natchee with Kapata knew their Ni'kwana had met with me and treated me with respect. Already I was known among them as a medicine man, so if I could build upon that and use it as a mantle to protect us all, so much the better.

It would be a feeble defense, yet I had lived long enough and learned enough to know that victories are won in the mind before they are won upon the ground. Perhaps I could offer them symbols that would project the idea of magic. They need not even know what the symbols meant or were supposed to mean.

Of this I said nothing to those who were with me. Keokotah, at least, was convinced that I had strong medicine.

When evening came I went out alone. Keeping under cover I gathered the skulls of four deer we had eaten that winter, and I suspended them from a tree branch over the trail leading to our lodge.

Four deer skulls, looking up the trail.

I knew where others lay and went to find them. Soon I had skulls suspended in groups of four at various places in the trees that surrounded our lodge.

Medicine to an Indian means power, and his life is spent in seeking the right medicine. He wishes for strong medicine for himself and those he follows, and he fears it in the possession of others.

The Indian in his native land did not seek for material wealth. He hunted, gathered, and lived. What he sought was stronger medicine, greater wisdom, a power within him that could equal the power of the spirits that surrounded him and could endanger him if he could not enlist their aid.

Kapata was driven by anger, hatred, jealousy, and the desire for power among the Natchee. Those who followed him believed his medicine was strong, but what if I could cause them to lose faith in him?

It was worth the chance. It was worth anything I might do.

Within the small pack I carried I had my own medicine bag, such as every Indian had, usually wearing it about his neck. Mine possessed not the things an Indian might carry but my own small medicine makers, one of them a prism, a burning glass. Now I took it from the bag and slipped it into a small pocket in my belt. I had no idea how I would use it, but somehow, somewhere, it might be useful.

Now I must think. I must plan.

We were well supplied with meat, and the women had gathered plants from the meadows and mountainsides or along the creeks. They were stores for winter, yet if need be those stores could feed those within the fort until the issue was decided.

Kapata was out there, waiting. Nor would he wait long. He was eager and angry, and now that he had found us he would want it over quickly.

Suddenly I thought of caltrops, the devices made to throw out in the grass to impede cavalry. They were made so when thrown into the grass a point was always up, and a horse who stepped upon one was either crippled or frightened of advancing further. In the ancient days of knights and castles they had ended many a charge. Now if I could make smaller ones and scatter them in the grass about our place, leaving openings known only to us, we might slow them or stop them. At least, it would help to fend off any night attack.

A caltrop was simply a four-sided object with a point on each face, and once I hit upon the idea I began cutting pieces of wood with projecting spikes or using porcupine quills or sharp bits of bone, whatever was available.

When the women saw what I was doing they immediately went to work. It needed but a minute to make one, and by nightfall we had many. Sighting on distant trees I chose paths we would know, but elsewhere I scattered the caltrops in the grass.

Wild animals rarely approached a place where people were, at least not in wilderness areas where food was plentiful, so I had no fear of crippling an animal. Paisano would be with us for his own protection, for other Indians might kill him for meat. In any event, he preferred to be with us inside our stockade.

We worked and we talked. Itchakomi was endlessly

curious about my people and the land from which they had come. She also had come to love our songs. Not that I sang well, for I did not. However, I did sing the old ballads from England, Ireland, and Scotland sung by my father or Jeremy or O'Hara or one of the others.

On the second night after we had glimpsed Kapata, I took my bow and went outside and stood in the darkness, listening. This we had been doing at intervals, even before Kapata had appeared, and solely for the reason that sound carries better at night and we might hear our enemies.

All was very still. There were scattered clouds but many stars. Looking up at the stars I wished I could remember more of the constellations Sakim had taught us, but I remembered only a few.

There had been a brief shower earlier in the day, but now there were no more signs of rain. Tomorrow should be a clear day. Waiting, listening, I heard nothing. It was like many other nights.

Starting to go inside, I stopped suddenly. Had that been a sound? My heart seemed to slow, and my ears strained for the slightest sound. Slipping an arrow from my quiver I held it ready. It was very dark, yet from an opening in the logs, I peered out into the darkness, waiting.

There was a faint stir in the grass. An animal? My eyes could find no shape, no deeper shadow.

Then I saw them! Several shadows moved at once, coming toward us. I notched an arrow and waited. Distance was hard to estimate in the darkness, but I believed they had almost reached the edge of the area where we had scattered our miniature caltrops.

Should I call Keokotah and alert the others?

They needed sleep, and perhaps, just perhaps, they would not be needed. I lifted my bow, waiting.

They were closer now. I could make out dim shapes. Suddenly there was a startled, barely suppressed cry of pain. A figure lunged upward, and I loosed my arrow.

My target was scarcely thirty yards off, bulking black, and my arrow went true. He straightened up. I saw his hands grasping at his chest, probably at the arrow.

Others ran forward and right into our field of caltrops. In a moment they were leaping about. I tried another arrow but doubted if it reached a target. Then the night was silent except for a faint moan.

For an hour I waited, but there was no further sound, no further movement.

The arrow in my hands was returned to its quiver. I waited, paced the enclosure, and then finally went in and lay down upon my blankets. I doubted they would come back, for they had run into something unexpected and would have to decide what to do about it.

Tomorrow we would make even more caltrops. We had sown the grass with needles, and they had yielded us a minor victory.

Something moved beside me. It was Itchakomi. "What is it?" she whispered.

I told her in whispers, and after a bit we fell asleep.

Morning came, bright and clear, and we were out looking over the grass. I saw my arrow lying some distance out. The first arrow had gone straight to its target and had evidently still been in the warrior when they carried him away.

Looking out over the valley that fell away to the west of us, but ran north and south, I thought again that we had come upon one of the most beautiful spots in the mountains, and here we would stay. Kapata might try, but he would neither kill me nor drive me from this place, nor would whatever others came, Indians or Spanish. I wished no trouble with either, but here I had found my home.

How long before others of my kind came west? There was much land still in the east, but there would always be some restless one, some wanderer who would want to see what lay beyond the Great Plains.

Our corn was coming up! Our first crop and if we could keep the deer from it we would have a bountiful harvest. We had found wild strawberries and raspberries. There were several other kinds of berries whose names we did not know, and there was other wild fruit. We would make pemmican, and we could dry some of the fruit.

We found blood upon the grass, blood where the man I had hit had fallen. Had I killed him? Or was he only wounded? It made little difference to us, yet I hoped he was only wounded—not from a sense of mercy, but simply because a wounded man would be a burden to them.

For those who had attacked me when I had done them no wrong I felt no mercy.

We had won a small victory, but Kapata was a wily man and a fearless one. He would be back.

Always there was the need for fresh meat. We had supplies within our fort, but they were intended for winter and if we ate them now the winter would be a starving time.

Moreover, we had other enemies. The Komantsi were coming, sooner or later, and of course there was Gomez.

From a ridge a mile to our south I collected some silver and lead ore from an outcropping. That it was largely silver mattered little. Whatever the value of the silver might be, it was worth more to me in the shape of bullets.

Sulphur? Where was I to find sulphur? In some volcanic formation or perhaps a mineral spring.

But *where*?

Keokotah returned from his hunt with three sage hens. He had found only old tracks of deer.

Returning he had found moccasin tracks. They had come down from the east, keeping undercover until they had seen the skulls I had hung over the trail. There the tracks were confused.

"Much talk," Keokotah explained. "Many track, much moving! Nobody like skulls!"

Again I went to look for sulphur, but also to hunt. I found nothing. Too many Indians were moving about, and the game had been frightened away, had gone to the higher mountains, where I must go. Some of the peaks were volcanic, and I might find sulphur.

The next day when Keokotah started out, two arrows came at him. One cut a small gash in his shoulder, but the other missed. And they let themselves be seen. The implication was plain. They would kill us if we emerged, or we would die of starvation if we did not.

"Your medicine strong," Keokotah said. "The braves are far from home. He has not brought them victory. Soon they go."

Well, maybe. But we were eating food we had planned to eat in the coming winter. Moreover, their presence and their hunting would drive the game to the high mountains and the far meadows, game we needed to survive.

"I am going out," I said. "I am going after Kapata."

I did not wish to go. I did not want to hunt and kill, but they were there, holding us close. I did not think they would attack our fort again, because of my medicine skills and because of their experience with the caltrops, but neither could we hunt or gather food against the coming winter, and my people looked to me, their chief.

We were here because of me, and if when winter came we starved, it would be because of me.

Other enemies might come, but now there was Kapata and he was our enemy, my enemy, and the enemy of my wife.

I was going after Kapata.

32

Thunder grumbled among the peaks when I went into the night to kill Kapata.

Itchakomi stood by the door when I walked out, and she said, "Come back, Jubal."

I kissed her lightly and replied that I would, and indeed, I hoped to. Yet when a man walks out with weapons his life is suspended like dew upon a spider's web, and well I knew the men I went against. Whatever else they might be they were warriors all, men who lived to fight and who found glory only in victory.

Catching a glimpse of a tall pine against the sky I chose my way with care not to tread upon one of my own caltrops in the darkness. When beyond the area where they lay I went softly into the wet woods and walked like a ghost from tree to tree, letting my moccasins test the way before resting my weight so as to break no stick in the night and give warning that I came.

We knew not their camp, only the possible location, so I must walk softly.

There had been a brief early shower, but now real rain was coming and soon the forest would be drenched. They would be keeping to shelter on this night, and their fire if not out would be dying.

For the first few minutes sight would be limited, but by the time I had been out an hour my night vision would be excellent. I circled wide, taking my time. If I surmised correctly, they would be near the mouth of the gulch. There was an area there where during a rain several small streams came down the mountain.

Before coming out from the fort I had gone over the route in my mind and had studied the possibilities for camping. They would want to be near water, of course. They would wish to be hidden, yet in a place easy of access. As I had gone in and out of the gulch a number of times when hunting or exploring I knew what their choices would be.

The place I chose to look was a small bench from which our fort would be visible by day. There was a seep nearby and a number of big, old trees. There was an overhang of rock, a sort of wind-hollowed cave that would provide shelter from the rain.

Moving carefully along a hillside I had once crossed in stalking a deer, I crouched in the trees to look over the bench. A small fire smoldered near the overhang and I could see the bunched bodies of sleepers.

The fire had been built where others before it had been, under a waterworn crack that allowed the smoke to escape, a sort of natural chimney in the rock.

The idea came gradually as I sat studying the layout. Not twenty yards from the cave a small stream trickled down among the rocks, its nearest approach to the cave being on a level with the top of the overhang. The stream veered off to the east, but the ground near it sloped to the west. At one time the stream must have flowed that way.

Why not again?

Easing back from my vantage point I went up the slope through the trees. Crouching in the darkness beside the stream I studied it and made up my mind. Keokotah was sure the Indians who had come with Kapata were losing their enthusiasm. Kapata had failed to give them the quick victory expected, and they had not taken the scalps they wanted. Maybe we could discourage them some more.

Following the trough where the stream had flowed in the long ago I came to its banks. What I had was just an idea. The stream was no more than two feet wide and perhaps a foot deep or less. As always there were fallen trees lying about. Choosing one, I upended it and tipped it across the stream. It fell with a splash.

Lifting another, I dropped it in the water alongside the first, making a crude dam. Instantly the water was diverted and started down its old channel. It ran along swiftly, dropped through the crack from which the smoke issued, and flooded the floor of the small cave.

A startled yell, and then another. The Indians scrambled out of the cave, filling the air with angry complaints. Squatting under a tree I watched for Kapata.

A few managed to save their blankets, although they were soaked. In the darkness I could not distinguish one from the other, so content with the mischief I had created I arose and skirted their camp in the darkness and then made my way to a quiet part of the forest where I remembered that some old deadfalls had created a sort of natural shelter large enough for a man. Arriving, I crawled in and slept.

Morning came with clear skies, and taking my bowstring from a dry inner pocket I strung my bow.

A smell of smoke led me to their camp, some fifty yards from the old one, which was still overrun with water. A pot was on the fire and a man bending over it. Lifting my bow I took careful aim and then let fly, the arrow taking him through the thigh just above the knee. He cried out, dropping the pot.

The others vanished as if they had been but phantoms, and I turned and went into the woods, moving swiftly away and around. When I next approached the camp it was from the bluff above the overhang cave.

No one was in sight but the Indian I had wounded. He had extracted the arrow, which lay on the earth beside him, and he was trying to stop the flow of blood from the wound. Nothing else moved and he had troubles enough, so I retreated back up the bluff a few yards, still keeping the camp in view.

After a while they began to filter back into their camp. I counted seven, including Kapata, who towered inches above all but one of the others. There was much grumbling.

Knowing I could not fight them all, I eased back up the slope and into the trees. What I wanted was to find Kapata alone, yet I had given them trouble. No one likes to endure discomfort, and if the Tensas could be disillusioned with Kapata's leadership they might simply go home. Already they had been long from home and endured much.

When the morning sun broke through the clouds I watched a distant rainstorm far across the valley against the vast wall of the Sangre de Cristos. Above the rainstorm the morning sun had painted the peaks as those first Spanish must have seen them, when they called them the "blood of Christ," for surely they were crimson as blood.

Lying quiet in the wet brush I waited for movement from Kapata's camp.

It was he I wanted, none of the others unless they got in the way. They had come hunting me and deserved no mercy from me, yet I had no wish to kill any man who did not seek me out.

Smoke lifted in a thin, questioning column. From a pocket I took a twist of jerky and bit off a piece, worrying it with my teeth to get a proper bite.

A fawn came from the brush and with high, delicate steps went down to the meadow. Truly we needed meat, but I was after bigger game and did not wish to kill a fawn. Let it grow into bigger meat.

One of the Tensas came from their camp and went down to drink at the creek. He was too far off and I had no desire to give away my presence. He stood up, a quick, graceful movement, and wiped his mouth with the back of his hand. He looked around slowly, once seeming to look right at me, but I was well hidden.

He was a lithe, fine-looking brave, probably not yet twenty.

Another Indian came to join him and they stood talking, with much gesticulation. That they were angry about something was obvious.

Enemies they might be, but I could not escape the beauty of the situation, the green backdrop of the mountains, the forest, the small stream sparkling in the sun, and the two Indians talking. No sound came, as they were too far off, but their manner was eloquent.

A movement caught my eye, a movement from the slope behind them, but closer. The merest stirring and then nothing. Puzzled, I waited.

The two Indians squatted on their heels near the water. One wore three feathers, the other but one.

That movement again, lower down the slope. Suddenly I knew!

Keokotah!

Startled, I half came to my feet. Did he know of the hidden camp? Or was he so intent on the Indians he stalked as not to realize the nearness of the others?

Crouching, careful to move no leaf, I went down the slope toward them, to get within bow shot before anything happened. When I had Keokotah clearly in view and not over fifty yards away, I squatted down in the brush with a log before me.

The Indians were on their feet now. They would return to camp. Sunlight danced on the water, and the aspens trembled. The Indians turned, and one died, an arrow in his throat. The other Indian had started on, unaware. Yet when he had taken two more steps he turned to speak and saw his companion lying dead in the trail.

The first Indian dropped to his haunches and then dove forward into the brush. Keokotah was quick, and his arrow went through the calf of the brave's leg as he jerked it from sight.

There had been seven, but now there were six, with one wounded slightly. There was one in camp wounded, too.

Waiting in the brush, I saw no further movement and believed Keokotah had gone. Slowly, careful to move no leaf, I slipped back up the slope and circled for home. Our corn had grown tall, and circling through it I took time to pull a few weeds. It was not a large patch, but it would give us a few bushels of corn to supplement our meager diet. The earth was rich and our crop had grown well. When I looked up from the corn I saw smoke.

It was several miles away, back beyond where Kapata's warriors had camped. It was a single finger of smoke, lifting skyward. As I looked, the column broke. A single puff went up, and then another.

A signal, but for whom? Not for the Tensas, of that I was sure. It was too far away and in the wrong direction.

The Komantsi? I felt a chill. Those dreaded Indians, destroying all before them. Had they found my valley or the trail of the Tensas?

When I was near the stockade, Keokotah appeared. He had a bloody scalp at his waistband. I had seen the Tensa die, but how had Keokotah scalped him? I pointed to the smoke. He nodded his head.

"Komantsi," he said. "They come."

His tone was grim and I understood why.

Itchakomi looked up when we came in and gestured toward a pot on the fire. We ate in silence, saying nothing. She had seen the scalp and needed no explanation.

At the meal's end I bathed my hands at the stream and then went to her. "The Komantsi come," I said. "We have seen their smoke."

And I had found no sulphur.

To look for it was automatic now, for it was ever in my mind. At night now I spent some time casting bullets, killing my mold time and again. But the balls were of no use without gunpowder.

Sulphur was sometimes found in old volcanic craters, for it appeared in the last stages of volcanic activity. Sometimes pockets of the crystals could be found, often contaminated with arsenic.

When darkness was almost upon us and visibility cut

to within a few yards, I went out to move my caltrops, not wishing to mark their absence by a worn trail. It would be necessary to move them every few days if there was much going back and forth. The moccasins these Indians wore had thin buckskin soles, and the spines would penetrate them. Unless there was infection the wounds were not serious, but one was sufficient to keep an Indian inactive for several days.

Kapata was no longer mentioned. His presence and his danger were very real, but that of the Komantsi even more. We kept our fires to a minimum and were thankful that our fort was fairly hidden in the trees and brush. It could not be seen except from quite near.

On the second day after his taking of the scalp, Keokotah went again to the mountains. It was a day of low clouds and impending rain, yet he went, hoping for game. Uneasy, I remained in the fort, watching restlessly for enemies, working at making bullets, planning forays into the mountains to look for sulphur.

Often I thought of the Natchee who had returned. Had they gotten through? Had they ridden the rough waters down and slipped by the Komantsi and the Conejeros? Had they found their way back to their villages beside the Great River?

We might never know.

So far as I knew I was the first Anglo white man to come so far west. But who could actually know? Always there was some venturesome one who would not be content with the limits set by others.

When spring came we would put in our crop again, and once more we would take to the mountains and seek out the far lands. There was in me a driving wish to see, to know, to feel.

Westward loomed the mighty peaks of the Sangre de Cristos, mountains where the caves were, mountains I must explore. And beyond them? Who knew?

A great valley, we heard, a greater valley by far than this where we lived. And beyond it? The sunlight glinted sometimes on snowcapped peaks, or so the Ponca woman said, of far-off mountains, incredibly high.

Night came and the stars, but Keokotah did not come and our hearts were heavy. We did not speak of him nor of our fears, but each knew what the others thought and each knew the fear in his own heart.

Yet he came! A stirring in the night, a faint sound at the door. I drew my knife and stepped forward to meet whatever was there.

The door opened. It was Keokotah.

"Ah!" I said.

He looked at me. "They are gone . . . gone!"

"Gone? Who?"

"The Natchee, the Tensas . . . gone."

"You mean they have given up and gone home?" This I had been expecting. The Indian does not like long, drawn-out battles. He wishes to do it quickly, get it done, and go home.

"Gone . . . dead. All killed."

All? I could not believe it.

"Who?" Although I knew without asking.

"The Komantsi. They have killed them. Taken their hair."

"Kapata, too?"

"No Kapata. He is gone when they come, I think. I think he come back after. I see big tracks."

Kapata! Would we ever be rid of him?

33

They came down the canyon in a straggling line, two dozen of them at least, with three horses and a half dozen miserable dogs. Most of the men were wounded and some of the women, and all were about to fall from exhaustion. They stopped abruptly when they saw us, hesitating until I walked out to meet them.

In sign language we told them we were friendly, and they explained they had been hunting buffalo across the eastern mountains when attacked. Their warriors had been scattered and the Komantsi had killed many. They were Pawnees, seeking a place to rest and gather themselves for another fight.

The old man who came forward to meet me carried himself with pride. He was Asatiki. He had lost half an ear in some bygone battle, and his body was criss-crossed with ancient scars. The mighty muscles of his youth had turned to sagging flesh, but in his eyes the fierce pride had not dimmed.

His people were beaten but not whipped, that I saw at once. They needed to recover from their wounds and make arrows for another fight. But they were ready to fight.

My gesture included the meadow. "Stay. We are

friends. If the Komantsi come we will fight them together. Only," I added, "do not kill the young buffalo you see here. He is a medicine bull. He is Paisano."

The place they chose was several hundred yards from our fort, near a small stream and a stand of trees. They gathered sticks to build their fires and I went among them to treat their wounds.

"I am Sackett," I said, "a man of mysteries." The simple treatments I used were adequate, and I had gathered herbs against such an event. Best of all, these were a strong people and the air was fresh and clean.

In their own land they lived in earth lodges that would shelter twenty people or more, domed structures built upon a framework of timbers, but here they built of bark, for these were but temporary shelters.

Asatiki had no memories of his people that went beyond the time of his grandfather. He could tell me only stories told about the campfire in winter.

I spoke of the Tensa and Kapata. "That one is our enemy. If he comes among you, know him not. His medicine is bad. He carries the seeds of evil."

My questions were about the Komantsi. "Strange Indians," the old man said. "I do not know them. They come to steal Spanish horses, but they attack all they see. They boast of many warriors to the north, many who will come. Maybe they speak true."

He knew nothing more. There had been sporadic attacks before this, hit and run attacks by Komantsi seeking horses and stealing women.

His people, the Pawnee, had a very old tradition that the Pawnee came from the southwest and once lived in houses built of stone. Another story had it they came from the southeast. Arriving in the land where they now lived, they encountered the Skidis, with whom they fought. Later, the two tribes became friends, intermarried, and became as one people.

When we had talked much I asked about the yellow earth that both smelled and burned. There was such earth far to the southeast, he said. His Caddoan relatives used it for medicine. The old man had not been to the place where it was found, over a month of travel, but knew of it from other Indians.

Our corn was growing, and the hunting had been good. A small herd of buffalo had strayed into the lower valley. Keokotah no longer spoke of his village, and when I spoke of it he said, "My village is here."

Often I wondered about his visit to his own people at the time of my visit to the caves of the mummies. He did not speak of it, but I believed he had found himself no longer at ease among them.

The Englishman had begun it. In his loneliness he had talked long hours with the boy, until the thoughts of Keokotah had made him a stranger among his own people.

When alone Komi and I spoke of this, and she looked into my eyes and spoke of herself. "I, too, miss my people. Here we have no fire. There is no temple and no priest."

"Are you not a priestess?"

"I am."

"There can be a sacred fire."

"It would not be the same. Our sacred fire was a gift of the Sun."

"Am I not a master of mysteries?"

She looked long into my eyes, seeking the truth.

"Did not the Ni'kwana see me as such?"

"Yes, but—"

"If a sacred fire will make you happy, I shall give you such a fire. I will give you fire from the sun."

"You?"

"Soon, when the time is right, I will bring fire from the sun."

She did not believe me. "You do not worship the Sun."

"The sun gives life to all things. Without the sun this would be a dark, dead world. Perhaps," I added, "the spirit we worship is the same, and only the names are different. The message from He who rules over us all may come to each people in a different way."

Our family had had little to do with organized religion, although my father when young had gone often to a village in Lincolnshire named Willoughby. This was the same village from which Captain John Smith of the Virginia colony had come. There had been a young minister there named Wheelwright, considered a dissident, but my father had liked his ideas and enjoyed his preaching. My brother Yance, who had married a girl from the Massachusetts Bay colony, had told me Wheelwright had come over the ocean and was known there.

That night I began again the study of the stars. My father and Jeremy Ring, who both knew of navigation by the stars, had taught us much. Sakim had taught us more. How much Itchakomi knew I had no idea, but I was sure she had been instructed in such lore. To produce a sacred fire I must choose the right time and the right place.

We had much of which to talk, for Itchakomi was endlessly curious about the English way of life, and often I wished I had listened more when my parents had spoken of their lives before coming to America. It had all seemed so remote and so unimportant to our lives in the colonies.

The Pawnee were skillful hunters and often shared their kills with us. In the first days we fed them and they simply rested. One woman died of her wounds, and two of the warriors were long in recovering.

It was an opportunity to learn their language and I did so, not enough to speak it well, yet enough to exchange information and for general talk. Their villages, they said, were along another river north of the Arkansas.

We gathered nuts, roots, and berries against the winter's coming, and fuel, also. Always, at home or on the hunt, we were alert for enemies, but when they came it was not the Komantsi but the Spanish.

Keokotah saw them first, seeing the sunlight upon their armor when they were far away. We hid our women in the cave where I had found niter, a place difficult to find and easy to defend.

Old Asatiki came to me. His people were ready to fight. The Spanish had raided among them for slaves, something I knew was forbidden by their king, and the Pawnees wanted no more of it.

"Wait," I advised, "but be ready. We talk first. If talk is no good, we fight. But each choose a man, and at the first sign of trouble, kill him."

There were twelve soldiers in half armor and about twenty Indian allies of a tribe I did not know. There were two officers and a priest. One of the officers was Diego, but this time it was Gomez who was in command.

Gomez reined in his horse near me, his eyes going from me to the fort. It was an impressive building, that I knew, the stockade of upright poles and the fort itself large enough to house us all and in a dominating position.

"We went to your valley and did not find you," Gomez said.

"We have enemies," I suggested, "and you have them also. The Komantsi."

He shrugged. "They have not come against us. When they do we will grind them into the earth." He looked around. "Where is the woman?"

"Woman? Do you see women? We are warriors here."

Anger came quickly to him. He did not like being frustrated, and he was in a position of power. I was wearing my guns, but they were concealed beneath the poncho I wore. My only visible weapon was the spear in my hand.

"We have come for the woman you would not sell," he said. "All here belong to His Majesty."

I smiled. "And His Spanish Majesty has forbidden the enslavement of Indians."

His expression changed. "His Majesty does not understand conditions here. He will change that rule."

"At your behest? Since when does a minor captain instruct the king?"

His expression was not nice to see. " 'Minor' captain? We shall see." He gestured to his soldiers. "Take him. He will tell us where the woman is."

They started forward. I stepped back into the rocks where their horses could not easily follow and threw my spear. Gomez leapt his horse after me and the spear missed, striking a soldier behind him, glancing from his helm, and stunning him. Two soldiers fell, arrows in their throats, and suddenly the Pawnees raised up around them. One warrior leapt to a horse behind a soldier and wrapped an arm around his throat, wrenching him from the horse. As the soldier fell another Pawnee killed him.

As suddenly as it had begun, the attack was over. The soldiers broke and fled. Brave men they were, but their hearts were not in this fight and I suspected none of them liked Gomez, who was a petty tyrant.

Diego was the last to turn away. "This was not my doing," he said, "but he is in favor and not I. Protect your woman."

He rode away after them, and I noticed that several of the retreating soldiers gathered about him. Three soldiers and an Indian lay on the ground, and one soldier was limping away.

All but three of us had been hidden, so our attack had been a surprise. I suspect Gomez had expected resistance and welcomed it. He could have seen the lodges of the Pawnees, but they were some distance off. Their fires were smoking and they looked to be occupied. He had not expected them to be hidden in the trees and rocks.

The Pawnees stripped the coats of mail and the helmets from the soldiers. I recovered a musket and a fallen sword.

Clouds gathered over the Sangre de Cristos, and there was a feeling of rain in the air. Gomez and his men had fled down the valley, but I did not for a moment believe we had seen the last of them. They would come again, for he dared not return without the woman he had undoubtedly promised. Diego would not have been so careless or overconfident, nor would Gomez when he returned.

We had revealed our strength, and he had more men. He also had muskets, and our Pawnee friends were soon to leave. I had wished for the iron shirts for my men, but the Pawnees had taken them, although I still had my own, found so long ago upon the banks of the Arkansas, and it was a better, tighter coat of mail than these.

Keokotah came from the trees, where he had used his bow. "I go," he said. "I follow."

It was an idea that had occurred to me, also. To follow and strike them in their own camp, strike them before they could gather to come against us.

Gomez was no fool. Overconfident, yes, but he would be so no longer. He was a tough, seasoned soldier and he had good men with him. The men we had killed would have mates who would resent their death. From now on there would be no surprises, no quick victories.

On one of the dead soldiers I found a powder horn of gunpowder for the firing of his musket. It was a treasure, more to be valued than gold.

Night came and I checked the loads in my pistols. There was food in the cave and water. The women would be safe there. If I went now to see them, my going might betray their presence, so I stayed away.

The Pawnees were in their camp, and I was alone in the fort. Keokotah had gone out, scouting Gomez and his men. There was no thought of sleep, for I must be ready for an attack at any moment.

Seated by a high port that allowed me to survey the approaches, I ate some nuts and waited. My bow was beside me with a quiver of arrows. Nor did I like the waiting. I would rather be out there in the darkness with Keokotah, but if our fort was taken then all our carefully hoarded food would be lost.

Where was Paisano? He had been turned loose but would stay close.

The hours dragged. I paced the floor, went from port to port, looking into the night. Inside there were no lights, and I needed none.

There was no moon, but the stars were out. From the high ports I could see beyond the stockade. Nothing moved. Nothing—

My eyes held on an edge of brush. Had there been

movement there? Or was my vision tricking me? Or perhaps a leaf moving?

Taking up my bow, I waited.

There!

Another movement! Something or somebody was creeping closer.

A quick scurry of feet in the grass, and then another. Two, at least, and right under the stockade. Taking up an arrow I bent my bow.

A head, ever so slowly, appeared over the wall. I waited. Then suddenly the shoulders and chest appeared, and a leg was thrown over. I loosed my arrow.

It was no more than twenty paces, and the target for an instant was sharp against the night. In the stillness I heard the arrow's impact, a man's grunt, and a fall. He fell on the inside, and I could see his body lying still. But was he dead? Was he even badly wounded? Might he not be waiting to suddenly rise and rush to the gate to open it for the others?

He moved, and I let go a second arrow.

And then I heard them coming, not one, but many. And I was alone.

34

My eyes were accustomed to the darkness. Each shadow near or within the fort was known to me. I went down into the yard. I could not win this fight while seated in safety. I had my spear, my guns, and my blade.

They were coming over the wall when I reached the yard, not one but at least three. I met the first with a sharp, upward thrust of the spear. His hands were grasping the wall, and he saw the spear too late. He let go with one hand to ward it off and fell, right onto the point. The force of his fall tore the weapon from my hands just as I heard a sharp scuffing of moccasins behind me.

Swiftly I turned, striking wildly with the blade. It sliced something, and then I was facing two men, one with a spear. I had fenced long hours with my father and the others back at Shooting Creek and my blade was quick to deflect the spear's point, and thrust. He staggered back, for the thrust had gone deep, but the other man was at the gate, removing the bar.

Running toward him, I was too late. The gate burst open—a rider! I drew a pistol and fired, and then dropped the muzzle to reload.

Yet I believe it was the shock of the gunfire more than its effect that stopped them.

My first shot killed a man. It could scarcely have been otherwise, for he was within ten feet of me and my pistol had a long barrel. He fell from his horse and it clattered over the stone-flagged yard. Then it wheeled and dashed out again.

The sudden shot ended the attack. Waiting, my heart pounding, I shoved the gate back into position and dropped the bar.

They were brave men out there but they had not expected gunfire, and they had lost two men—

Two?

Three had been coming over the wall. One I had impaled on my spear, the second with the knife. Yet the third, he who had run to open the gate?

Where was he?

My pistol went back into its scabbard. I had had to let go my knife when I had drawn the pistol. Now I squatted, groping for it.

Ah, I had it! Now?

There was a man inside, I was sure. A man who waited to kill me. An Indian, I thought, one of the Indians serving with the soldiers of Gomez.

He was here, somewhere in the darkness.

Yet three men were down, including the rider of the horse whom I had shot. He lay without moving. Had my shot been good, then? But where was the other? Somewhere in the shadows there was an enemy. If they attacked again he would attack when I faced them, attack from behind me.

What were they thinking outside? They could not know that they had a man alive inside the fort, yet they must know by now they had lost three or four men. It was expensive, but Gomez was ruthless. He had a contempt for all human life but his own.

Fire?

That would be in his mind, yet he could not know that Itchakomi was not inside the fort. He dared not risk burning his prize.

Crouching, I studied the shadows. Nothing moved,

and the shadows were dark and deep. My spear was nearby, in the body of the fallen Indian. I might need it.

Where would my enemy be hiding? Each shadow was in my mind and one by one I checked them over for hiding places trying to remember each detail, each corner.

Where was he? Did he plan to open the gate when I was distracted?

The minutes plodded by on gentle feet, and my eyes searched the shadows. Had he gone around the side of the fort? Or inside? Suppose he started a fire?

There was a moment of wild panic. We would never be able to rebuild before snow fell, not if we were burned out. In the moment of anxiety I almost moved, yet somewhere my enemy was watching for me, even as I watched for him. Again it was the old story that he who moved first would die first.

How fared Itchakomi? Had their cave been discovered? Perhaps even now they were riding away with her. Listening, I heard no sound.

If we escaped this time I would begin a tunnel from the fort to that cave. In fact, a branch of that cave which we had not explored might come this way. A secret tunnel, such as my father had told me all castles had once had, a means of escape as well as a supply route if besieged.

Outside there was a stirring, a movement. What could be happening?

An attack from more than one side? Crawling up ropes thrown over the wall? Explosives under the gate? One man boosting another? Ladders?

Slowly passed the minutes. Where was Keokotah? Had he been trapped somehow? My good sense doubted it. He was a ghost in the woods, a shadow in the night. I knew no one better at moving in silence, and I also knew he would be somewhere about.

Gomez would be thinking, deciding what to do. He wanted Komi, if not for himself, then as an offering for favors, and he had undoubtedly made promises to be given command of these soldiers. He had successfully returned home through the thick of winter, no mean feat in itself, and he had undermined the standing of Diego, superseded him in command, and now was back. He would not be driven off, and he would not give up easily.

By now he would be piecing together what had been witnessed through the gate during the brief moments it was open. He would be studying what had taken place, the shots fired and the fighting.

He would guess that I was alone or almost alone.

His next thought would be about the women. He would know there were at least three. For all I knew his Indians might have been lurking about, observing us, but in any event he himself had been in our caves in the other valley. He had seen Keokotah's woman and the Ponca.

He was a shrewd, tough man, one not easily fooled.

Somebody was riding near the palisade. The rider drew up and in a quiet, conversational tone Gomez said, "I know you can hear me, Sackett, and I suggest you send the Indian girl out. If you do we will ride off and you'll be free to do as you wish.

"I might," he added, "intercede for you and try to get you a trading permit. All we want is one Indian girl." He paused and when I made no answer he said angrily, "Don't be a fool! What's one paltry Indian girl? There are dozens about, just for the taking! Surely you aren't fool enough to *die* for her?"

To have answered him, and I was not thinking of it, would have been to give away my position to the hidden Indian, wherever he was.

He waited. Then he shouted, "Don't be a fool! Waste more of my time and you'll pay for it! I'll have you staked to an anthill!"

He would not try another direct attack. He had been sure of an easy victory, not knowing of the presence of the Pawnees. Now he had lost men, losses he could not afford, and his situation was perilous. To return to Santa Fe empty-handed would be a crushing defeat. His temper and his impatience had cost him lives, but victory he must have. If he was defeated here his enemies would destroy him in Santa Fe.

Again, I wished myself outside with Keokotah where I could observe what was happening and be free to move. In the darkness I could see but shadowy stirrings, but nothing at all now, for I dared not move.

How was my concealed enemy armed? Bow and arrow? A spear? A knife? If only a knife I could chance it but if he had either a bow or a spear he could strike from the darkness, and at the short range could scarcely miss.

Gomez must have a camp now. He would have built fires and his men would wish to eat, if they had not. He must have carried supplies, and those supplies would be vulnerable. Without them he could not persist in the attack or the search for Itchakomi.

Would Keokotah think of that? Indians, who depended less upon supplies in time of war, were less inclined to think of an enemy as vulnerable in that respect. The Indian at war lived off the country as he traveled, rarely having more than enough for a day or two. The Indian thought in terms of battles. He fought a battle and he went home. There was no thought of a continuing series of battles, for the obvious reason that he had no way of supplying an army in the field.

He rarely fought for hatred or revenge. He fought for glory. He fought to take scalps and to win victories of which he could boast. In the east the tribes associated with the Seneca who were calling themselves the Iroquois were fighting wars of extermination. We had begun to hear rumors of that before I left Shooting Creek.

Yet Keokotah was beginning to think much as a white man would. He had sat too long at the knee of his Englishman, and I prayed now that he might think of their camp and their supplies.

Our women had food for but three days, scarcely more even if they ate lightly. They could endure hunger, and there were few Indians who did not know it each season before the snow began to melt, when their hoarded supplies had been eaten and hunting was difficult and gathering impossible.

My eyes grew heavy, yet I forced myself to stay

awake. Somewhere an enemy waited, and to sleep was to die.

Outside more enemies waited. Always before, wherever I might be I had known there would be a Sackett looking for me. No Sackett ever needed to feel alone, for others of the family would always come. That lesson our father had taught well, until it was second nature. But there were no Sacketts here. There was only Keokotah and the Pawnees.

I shook my head, blinking my eyes. They had almost fallen shut.

This could not be. I must move. I must hunt him down, this warrior who awaited me.

Slowly, carefully, keeping to deepest shadow, I straightened to my feet. My game leg ached from the cramped position I had held for so long. Listening, I heard no sound. The shadows were deep. Carefully, I lifted a foot, took a step, and put it down ever so gently. With infinite care, listening after every step, I began to search the shadows.

Nothing . . .

Again I moved, and suddenly, from outside and some distance away, a scream!

A long, protracted scream, a cry of sheer agony, the last cry of a dying man!

Who?

Keokotah? I did not believe it. Rather someone he had found. Keokotah could die, but if I knew him at all, he would die in silence.

Carefully I worked my way through the shadows, spear poised for use, my hand only inches from my knife. My grip on the spear was firm. I did not want it wrenched from my hands again.

Something? Something there in the darkness. I drew nearer, the spear poised for a thrust.

It was a man sitting against the building, something dark over his legs. Leaning closer I saw his head was over on one shoulder, his eyes were wide open, and he was dead.

Dead? He was the one I had sliced in the fight. He had run to open the gate and then retreated here, to die. The darkness across his legs was blood, for my blade had cut him clean across the stomach.

Angry with myself for being held immobile for so long by a dead man, I walked back across the yard to the gate. The bar was firmly in place.

From the high ports I could see their campfires, and from afar, smoke rising into the dawn from the Pawnee village. The Pawnees had drawn off and not attacked again. Why, I had no idea.

Komi and her companions would be waiting in the cave, wondering, not knowing. My fear was they would venture out and so reveal their hiding place, which was a good one, even if lacking the pleasures of home. And sorely did I miss her.

There was a stirring, a preparation in the camp of Gomez, nor could I make out what was taking place there except that they were readying themselves for something. An attack upon me?

Gomez himself was riding to the fort, but he was alone. Out of arrow range he drew up and called out, "Sackett? We are going after your friends, yonder! When we have destroyed them we will come back for you. Have the woman ready. If you surrender her now, you can go free."

Which of course was nonsense. He was a vengeful man and would kill me in an instant if he had me prisoner. Or he would do as promised and stake me on an anthill.

"You have lost men," I said calmly. "You will lose more if you attack the Pawnees. You will return to Santa Fe with your tail between your legs like a whipped dog."

"I will have her," Gomez said. "I will have the woman."

He turned his horse then rode off to join his soldiers, and I began to wonder why he had taken the trouble to inform me of his intentions. His men began to form up, and he put himself at the head of them. I wondered at the stupidity of the man. Fine soldier he might be, back in Spain, Flanders, or wherever the fighting had been, but you do not advertise your intentions when going out to fight Indians.

Several times he seemed to glance my way, and then I realized he was trying to lure me out of the fort to help my Indian friends, which could only mean that somebody waited nearby to move in the moment I moved out.

Carefully, my eyes searched the terrain, lingering on every clump of brush, every tree, ev—

There were two of them, two of his Spanish soldiers, and they were lying in wait not fifty yards from the gate.

One held a musket in his hands and was obviously waiting for me.

In a land of Indians these men would not last long, for they were but poorly hidden.

I made ready my bow.

35

The morning was clear and beautiful. The sun was still hidden behind the eastern mountains, but the valley was lovely in the dawning light. A few smokes lifted their slim columns toward the sky, but aside from Gomez and his soldiers, nothing moved.

Far down the valley some low clouds lay, and a few white puffballs of cloud lingered against the blue sky, each catching a rosy radiance from the rising sun. The soldier who thought himself hidden in the brush was eager. He edged forward, musket ready to aim, waiting for me to emerge.

His eyes were upon the gate, yet when I straightened up above the roof parapet the movement caught his attention. His head turned and he saw me, bow bent, arrow drawn back.

For a stark, shocked moment he stared, and I loosed my arrow.

There is no good time in which to die, but he must have seen my figure outlined against the morning sky, with mountains and forest behind me. Who he was I did not know, nor whether he had been born in Spain or in Mexico. No doubt he was a good enough man in his own world, and it was a pity he had to come into mine, and not by his own choice, either.

His last glimpse of this world was of the sky at dawn and my dark figure above the parapet. Could he see the bow? Could he see the arrow in flight?

He came erect suddenly, clutching at the arrow's shaft, his musket falling among the rocks. He tugged, staring at me and perhaps hearing the quick scurry of his companion's feet as he fled. My second arrow missed the companion, and I saw the soldier I had shot fall over the rocks.

Then I went down the ladder and to the gate and opened it. The sun was higher, the valley bathed in light. There seemed to be a stir of movement down near the cave where Itchakomi waited. Shading my eyes, I looked and saw nothing.

Only imagination. Suddenly and from a distance I heard a wild chorus of yells and then musket shots and a scream from a wounded man. The Pawnees had been lying in wait and had attacked before the soldiers were halfway to their village. The sides must have been almost evenly matched as to numbers, but the surprise had been complete.

Coming to a higher bit of ground, I stopped. All was confusion, dust, occasional gunshots, and then silence. The dust fell, and men had died and left their bodies on the sun-blessed hills.

Some horsemen rode away, fleeing the fight. Others scattered on foot, pursued by Pawnees.

Gomez, if he lived, had failed again.

Walking on toward the fight I came upon a scalped Indian, one of those who had come with Gomez. Then I saw two Indians holding a prisoner. It was Diego.

"He is a good man," I told them. "Let me have him."

They merely stared at me.

"This one is a friend," I assured them, but they continued to stare, clutching his arms.

Asatiki, the old warrior, came toward us, and I explained. "This one is good," I said. "He is my friend."

"He fought hard against us."

"Aye, he is a fighter. He did what he was supposed to do, and no doubt did it well, yet he did not wish to come against you and told me so. It was the other one, the one of the gray horse. He was their leader."

"He got away."

"I am sorry for that. He is bad medicine. This one is not."

"He is their prisoner."

"Are you not their chief?"

"I led the war party. I am their chief. I cannot command, only suggest. Each is his own man. He comes and goes as he wishes. They followed me because they wished, not because I demanded it. He is their prisoner."

Again I turned to them. "Will you sell him to me?"

They did not reply, just waited, looking at me. When the attack on the fort had first taken place and the gate had been briefly open a horse had been ridden through, its rider killed. That horse still stood there on the stone-flagged court. "I will trade a horse for him."

It was a horse I dearly wanted. A horse could make a difference in many ways.

"Good horse?"

"One of the best." I had no idea. The horse had looked good at the one glance I had thrown his way. I had had other things on my mind at the time and no time to waste, but what horse trader plays down his stock?

"An excellent horse," I said, "very strong, very fast."

"We see."

Together we walked back to the fort, Asatiki with us.

"Wait," I said when we neared the fort. "I shall bring him out."

One thing I had seen in that hasty glance was a powder horn on the saddle, and I wanted that. In fact, I wanted the saddle as well. Hastily, I stripped saddle and bridle from the horse and rigged a hasty hackamore with a bit of rope. Then I led the horse outside. The powder horn, by its weight, was almost full.

They looked at the horse and walked around it. I

waited. Had they seen it with its equipment they would have demanded all of it, as I would have done.

"The horse," one said, "and a musket."

Taking a firmer grip on the lead rope I turned the horse back toward the gate. "The horse is a good horse. Too good. It is an even trade, horse for prisoner. If you do not like it, take the prisoner and burn him." I kept on walking toward the gate and as I started through one of the Indians spoke up. "We take! Give us horse!"

The other Pawnee threw Diego at my feet and grabbed the lead rope and started away.

"No good," Asatiki said. "You get two, three prisoner for horse."

"Maybe," I agreed, "but I do not know the other prisoners. This man is a good man. Sometime," I advised, "you have trouble. Speak to this man. If he can, he will help."

Asatiki shrugged. "White man forget ver' quick."

My eyes met his. "Remember this, Asatiki. I did not forget this man. His people are my enemies. This man is not, and I remembered."

Lifting Diego to his feet I cut his wrists loose. "Gracias," he said, rubbing his wrists to restore circulation.

"Go inside and keep out of sight. They might change their minds."

He did so, and I walked across to the man I had killed with an arrow. His musket was there among the rocks, and on his belt there was a powder horn. It was about half full. I retrieved my arrows as well and walked back to the fort.

Glancing back over the valley I could see Indians here and there, picking up what had fallen or gathering their wounded. It was time I went for Itchakomi.

"You have food?" Diego asked. "I am very hungry."

There was jerky and I offered him some. "You stay here," I said. "In a few days you can start back for Santa Fe. It will be safer then."

"How many escaped?"

"Who knows? Several riders and some men who fled running."

"He was a fool, that Gomez, but brave enough. He has fought in many wars but not against Indians. He did not know. He thought to frighten them with a show of power."

"Indians," I said, "do not frighten easily. War is their way of life."

My eyes went to the valley. The last thing I wished to do was to betray the hiding place where Itchakomi was hidden. When night came would be soon enough, and she would understand that the fighting was over. Some of them must have heard.

"Gomez would not listen," Diego said. "He would ride boldly into battle. He would awe them with his presence and the boldness of his approach."

"He escaped, I believe."

"Of course. He is a realist, and dead soldiers win no battles. He led them into an ambush but he did not stay to die with them. Next time he will be wiser."

"Maybe."

Getting to my feet I said, "Do you lie down and rest, Diego. I shall be back soon. You are safe here."

The Pawnees who had wandered about were drifting slowly back toward their own village. A moment I watched, and then I walked out, pausing now and again.

There were bodies to be buried and plans to be made. Also, I must put all my powder together and see how much I had. Not enough, but what I had would tide me over until I could find sulphur and make my own. If I was fortunate.

And I must think about the sacred fire for Itchakomi and how to bring it to her. How important it was to her I was only now beginning to appreciate, but to give her fire without ceremony would be empty. It must have the proper trappings of magic.

My valley lay green and lovely, falling away to the south, walled by mountains on either side. Up there were the caves of which the Ponca woman had told me long ago. Beyond those mountains was a mineral spring that might contain sulphur.

This was my land, the land that I loved, the wild land, the lonely land, where men had left no scars, no beaten tracks, no signs of their passing. These few bodies that now lay about would be buried, or if left would be food for buzzards, coyotes, and ants. Whatever those men had taken from the land they would now give back, and the eternal round of birth and death would continue.

Someday I might also have a son or a daughter, and we might sit together by the fires of winter while I told them stories of Barnabas, their grandfather, and of England whence he came. Sakim, too, must be spoken of, who came from the magic lands of the Arabian Nights. My father had told me the stories before even Sakim, but from Sakim's lips they had had a special magic, for he was of their world. He had lived the life.

This was my land. Here I would sink roots. Here I would grow and help things grow. Here, I hoped, my sons and daughters would grow and be here to greet the westward travelers when they chose to come.

Another musket lay where it had fallen. Somehow the Pawnees had missed it. It lay fallen among the rocks and brush, but there was no powder horn. Further on lay a dead Spanish soldier, a handsome boy, now minus his scalp. Another one who had come seeking his fortune, accepting the chances of battle in a far country. Others might be killed, he had thought, but not him. He would survive. Now all the bright dreams were ended with his hair hanging in a Pawnee earth lodge.

Asatiki was coming toward me, walking his strange, bowlegged walk, lifting his knees toward the outside as he stepped. He paused facing me. "It is time," he said.

"Time?"

"We go. We go back to our lodges, back to our village. Our people wait and are wondering."

"I shall miss you, Asatiki." I held out my hand. "I have known a warrior."

"And I."

We stood together, looking down the long green valley. "If you come to us, you will be welcome. Our villages are north and east, along the second great river."

"One day, perhaps."

We stood a moment longer sharing the silence, and then he walked away. I watched his back as he retreated. We would miss them, and we would miss him.

Turning, I glanced toward where the cave was. They must know the fighting was over, but they had not appeared. Impatient to see Komi, I started across the grass toward where the cave was hidden.

The Pawnees were not waiting any longer, but they were going now. Pausing, I watched their thin line point itself into the mountains, watched them go, each with a burden of hides or meat. They now had seven horses, and I was still without one. Of course, I had Paisano.

As I neared the cave, I called out. There was no reply. Suddenly worried, I quickened my step and called again.

I reached the small opening and abruptly I stopped. In the dust outside the cave there was a confusion of footprints, but one stood out.

A large, clearly imprinted moccasin track. Only one man I knew made so large a track.

Frightened, I ducked into the cave, calling out.

Nothing, no sound, not so much as a whisper.

They were gone!

Somehow, during the fighting, while all had been engrossed, Kapata had slipped in and stolen my wife away, stolen her and the others.

One more futile call, and a moment of listening. My heart beating heavily I came into the open air.

Keokotah was there.

"They are gone. Kapata has taken them."

He ducked into the cave and was back in a moment. "My woman is gone," he said. "Do you get meat. I find trail."

At a trot, I returned to the fort. Scarcely thinking, I made two packs of meat and what else we had.

How long had they been gone? An hour? Two hours? Three?

They would travel fast and they would strive to leave no trail. No trail unless to an ambush.

Quickly I loaded what powder I had into two powder horns and gathered a double handful of my silver bullets.

Keokotah was waiting for me. He pointed toward the canyon where grapes grew. "They have gone that way. They go to the river, I think."

"Of course."

We walked steadily on but my heart was numb. Once, I glanced back. Paisano was following us. My brain had only one thought.

Itchakomi was gone! Itchakomi, my love . . . gone!

36

Keokotah had followed this trail to the Arkansas not long after we had begun building the fort, but I had never gone to its end.

We ran, for our enemy was time. If they had boats waiting at the river we might never overtake them, and Kapata, now that he had captured Itchakomi, would waste no minutes.

It had been a long, bitter day, but we ran smoothly and easily. A mile, another mile. We slowed our pace. It would soon be dark, and their tracks would no longer be visible. Now we had to pick our way among the rocks, weaving through trees. In the bottom of the canyon it would grow dark quickly.

Also, they might try an ambush, although I doubted that.

Kapata had taken them during the fighting, with the end of the fighting still in doubt. He would not know if I were alive or dead, and I doubted if he would think of anything but getting safely away.

At the same time, I knew he would welcome a meeting with me. Particularly as he would like to show Itchakomi he was the better man.

Here and there we stopped to listen, while trying to

make no noise ourselves. The canyon rocks carried sounds. How long had they been on the trail? At most, two hours. Hence they must be at the river or nearing it now.

They would have no campfire to help us to find them. They would offer no such invitation to the Komantsi that might still be about. My feeling was that the Komantsi had gone on to the south to steal horses in Mexico, but other enemies might be about. It was a time of change, and many tribes were on the move, displaced by others to the east who had obtained firearms.

We ran no longer, but walked, pausing often to listen. The canyon was behind us and we were moving into an area of scattered clumps of trees and occasional ridges. The general trend of the ground was sloping toward the river.

Here we were beset by a problem, for we had no idea whether they had gone directly to the river or had angled off to the east or west.

We stopped at a small stream, drank, chewed on some dried buffalo meat and listened. We heard nothing. It was completely dark and despite the stars overhead we could see nothing beyond a few feet.

Somewhere, within a mile or so, our women were prisoners. Itchakomi would be taken back to Natchez and the villages on the great river, but there was no reason to believe they would keep either the Ponca woman or Keokotah's woman alive.

"We will go now," I said at last. "You go toward the river and mountains. I will go toward the river and the plains. If you find nothing, come here at daybreak. If I am not here I have found them, and you can come to me. And if I return and you are not here, I will know you have found them.

"If either of us finds them, he will do what he can."

We parted in the night. He went westward and north, and I turned toward the east and north, angling across the country, feeling my way at first, and then weaving through the trees. My route was a zigzag, to cover as much ground as possible.

How many warriors did he have with him now? It would be a good-sized party, a dozen at least. He might have lost men. It was doubtful if he had recruited any.

The trees were thick along the slope, and I edged between them, taking each step with care and testing the earth before resting my weight. A snapping branch could be the end of me.

It was a slow, painstaking search, and I was filled with impatience. What I would do if I found them I had no idea.

On cat feet I went down over the rocks and into the trees again. Not far away was the river, and it was likely they had gone where they knew there would be water. They might not have a fire, but they would wish to drink and they would eat and rest.

There was a musty smell of rotting vegetation, the smell of pines—after a time the nose becomes sensitive to the very slightest odor. I was going steeply down a slope now, using the trees to help, gripping first one and then another.

How dark was the forest! My eyes, accustomed to the darkness, identified the trees and the shadows. A heavy odor in the air, a dampness on a tree against which I rested my hand. My fingers felt around on the bark and snagged a long hair.

A wet bear had come this way, perhaps within the last thirty minutes, a very large bear that had probably just swum the river. That stopped me. I had no desire to come upon a full-grown grizzly bear in the night.

Abruptly I changed direction, starting once more toward the river. Suddenly I stopped. What it was I had no idea, but I stopped on one foot, hesitating to lower the other.

Something, some sound in the night! I waited. A sound? Or a smell?

Something rustled, moved, and then I heard a faint mutter as of a sleeper in the night. Waiting, listening—a smell of fresh-cut wood! Of pine boughs for . . . a bed? A bed for Itchakomi?

There were some Natchee Indians with Kapata. They would prepare the bower in which Itchakomi would sleep. They had done so, and she was near, very near.

With infinite care I drew back my foot and put it down, testing the earth as it came to rest. Slowly, carefully, I backed away. When a dozen yards away, I stopped and crouched at the base of a tree to think.

Their camp was here. They would move at dawn. Had I stepped into their camp I might have been overpowered by a half dozen braves.

At daybreak they would move. At daybreak Keokotah would come to join me, so I must stop them. I must not permit them to move.

Before daybreak I would attack. Or . . . the thought came suddenly, should I challenge Kapata?

Should I challenge his courage? His leadership? Demand he fight me for Itchakomi?

If I appeared and challenged him, would he accept the challenge? Or would they all attack me at once? He was several inches taller than me, and he was heavier.

Dawn was hours away. I would rest, and when the day came, make my decision then. On a bed of moss near several trees, I lay down and slept, tuning my mind to awaken before the first hint of light in the sky, and when I slept the great beast came again, the red-eyed monster with the elephant's trunk and the long hair. It loomed through the trees and came at me. It had great tusks that curved out before it and one was red with blood. It charged, but I stood my ground. Why did I not flee? Why did I stand there, spear in hand, as it rushed upon me?

My eyes wide open in the dark I stared up at the canopy of leaves above, and then I sat up, wiping sweat from my face. Was it a warning? If so, a warning of what? Was it a pre-vision of something to come? Of my death, perhaps?

At least it was a monster that would kill me, not Kapata.

Where was Keokotah? Had something happened to him? Or was he even now lying somewhere near and waiting for the dawn, as I was?

Standing up, I moved my arms about and my shoulders, loosening the muscles. I checked my weapons. The sky was faintly gray, and easing myself down through the trees again, I could make out their camp.

The fire, Indians lying about, and among the trees, Itchakomi's bower, and wonder of wonders, three Indians lying guard before it!

The Natchee! Had they proved loyal, after all? Or would they protect her only up to a point? Kapata was half a Natchee, and a warrior respected among them. Yet, obviously, the Natchee had moved to protect her as a Sun.

Taking up my bow and spear I walked down from the trees into their camp, and it was a Natchee who saw me first. He came to his feet suddenly, facing me.

"She is my woman," I said.

"She has said this. She bears your child."

Startled, I stared at him. Was this true? Or was it a trick she had used that might protect her?

A child? Well, why not? Now there was more than ever a reason to fight.

All about me the others were rising. My eyes swept the camp. Kapata was sitting on the grass where he had slept, his eyes alive with hatred.

"I have come," I said, "to fight *him*." I glanced around again. "None of you. *Him!* He wanted my woman. Very well, let him fight for her."

They sat still, staring at me. The Tensa were fierce warriors and they wished to kill me, but I had challenged Kapata, so the fight was his.

Keokotah stood up in the trees away from the camp, overlooking all of it. "Let them fight," he said.

Itchakomi came from her bower and stood tall, looking across the fire at me. Crossing to her I took the twin guns from my waist and placed them on the ground at her feet.

"The voice that kills at a distance I shall leave with

Itchakomi," I said. Turning on Kapata I drew my knife. "Come!" I invited. "We will see if a Karankawa can bleed!"

He came off the ground like a large cat, his knife drawn, and he walked across the intervening grass to meet me. His contempt was obvious. "You fool!" he said. "I kill!"

His reach was much greater than mine, but my father had taught us all something of English boxing, so when he made a sweeping cut from right to left I used a boxer's sidestep to my left. The wicked slash of his knife cut only the air where I had been, and my backward cut scratched the skin above his hip bone and drew blood.

Furious, he wheeled and came at me. The man was fast, faster than I would have believed, but I parried his blade with mine and we circled, warily. He thrust suddenly, right at my face, coming in with a long stride, and my head shifted only just in time. I had moved to the right, which put my knife blade too far from him, so I struck him in the stomach with my left fist.

It was totally unexpected. I doubt he had ever been struck with a fist before this, and it stopped him in his tracks. He gasped, for I had hit him in the wind, and before he could adjust I swung back with my blade. In stepping back, he fell and lay on the ground almost at my feet.

I could have and should have killed him then but was averse to striking a man when he was down. So I stepped back, waving for him to come on.

He leapt to his feet and came at me and we circled and fought. Minutes passed, our blades clashed, there were lunges and parries. My boxing skills, little though they were, proved sufficient to counteract his greater reach. My refusal to accept the easy victory he had taken as a sign of contempt for him, and now he fought with unbelievable ferocity. A half dozen times I was nicked by his blade, and once I left a thin red line along his left arm.

The footing beneath us was uneven and scattered with broken branches, bits of bark, and small stones.

Suddenly a stone rolled under my foot and I fell on my back and he came at me.

Thrusting up with my leg I caught him as he rushed upon me, my toe taking him in the pit of the stomach. I shoved up and back and threw him over my head to the ground beyond.

We came up as one and I thrust quickly, missed and fell on my face. Instantly, he was upon me, astride my back, and I knew his knife was lifting for the final stabbing blow. Swinging my arm up and back I drove my knife into his side between the ribs. His knife came down but I jerked hard to one side and the blade went into the earth alongside my neck.

Off balance, he was unable to properly resist my tremendous heave to get him off me and he fell free. Our knives clashed, but mine slipped by his and sank deep. He struggled to rise, throwing me back. Stabbed twice and deep, he came at me like a wildman, cutting and slashing.

Driven back, I slipped and fell, and he sprawled over me. Instantly I was up, and he came up also, but slower. He poised, eyes alive with hatred and fury, his blade steady.

"Now," he said, "I kill!"

He did not even seem aware that he was wounded, but rushed at me. Sidestepping away, I watched him. He was bleeding badly but was as intent on killing me as ever. He lunged at me, but I was prepared and sidestepped. But this time he was also prepared and moved aside with me. My knife was held low and I brought it up hard.

It went in to the hilt and for an instant we were eyeball to eyeball.

"You could have stayed in Natchez," I said in a conversational tone. I withdrew my knife, pushing him away. He fell to his knees, struggled to rise, and then just rolled over on the ground and lay still.

Kapata was dead.

Slowly, I turned about. Their eyes were on me. "Itchakomi is my woman," I said. "I have come for her."

A Tensa spoke, but I did not know his words. Keokotah explained. "He says she is your woman. They will go home now."

We watched them as they gathered their few belongings. I glanced at the three Natchee Indians, who stood uncertainly, unsure of their course.

"Komi? Are they good men?"

"I reminded them that I was a Daughter of the Sun. They guarded me. They knew their duty."

"If you wish they can remain with us. The choice is yours and theirs."

It had been obvious to me that they hesitated to return to Natchez. They had left with Kapata, who was considered a renegade by their people, but they were young and he had been persuasive. At the end they had proved their loyalty to Itchakomi.

She spoke to them and they listened, and then assented eagerly. They would stay with us, and I was not displeased. The addition of three strong warriors and hunters could only make us more secure.

"Now we shall go home, Itchakomi Ishaia. When again we come to our place I shall do what I have promised. You shall have your sacred fire. Never again will you be without it.

"Did not your Ni'kwana recognize me as a master of mysteries? Are you not a Child of the Sun? You shall have your sacred fire."

37

We walked again along the canyon trail, but now we walked in daylight, walked where no shadows were but those beneath the trees, walked among the blooming columbine, the cinquefoil, and the fireweed. We walked in quietness, for there was no need to speak.

Once, when we stopped to rest beside a spring, Itchakomi said to me, "You can do this? Bring fire from the Sun?"

"I can."

She was silent for a long time, stirring the water with a small twig, idly, thoughtfully. "I have missed the Fire." She looked up at me, her eyes large and beautiful. "I am happy with you, but I grew up tending the Fire. It is a part of me, a part of my life."

"I know."

"Have you known many Indian women?"

"Only a few. There was one. I saw her but once. She lived close to Jamestown and was friendly with the people there. Her name was Matoaka, but she was called Pocahontas. Pocahontas was what her father called her. In their language it means playful. She spoke our language quite well, I think."

"No others?"

"No Indians lived close to us. They came to trade and sometimes we went among them for the same reason, or to hunt with them."

"You do not take scalps. We heard that long before we met any of you, but we did not believe it. If one of our men falls in battle we take his scalp rather than let an enemy have it."

"Our child will be a Sun?"

"He will. If it is a boy, only during his lifetime; if a girl, for always. With us rank descends through the woman. Is it not so with your people?"

"Rank descends through the man."

"Hah! You must trust your women very much."

"Some of us do."

We walked on, and before us our valley opened and we looked upon the fort, our cornfield lying in the sun, and the wide meadows beyond where the long grass rippled in the slight breeze.

For a moment I stopped, considering. I must plant more corn, and melons as well. It was a rich valley, and here a man could build for the future. It was a wide land, a new land, and I was among the first to see it. Others would come. Oh, I had no doubt of that, for mine were a restless people, ever moving, ever seeking, ever reaching out.

They would come, and when they arrived I would be waiting for them. Some would have goods to trade, all would be needing food, advice, and knowledge of the country.

Now I had a child to consider, as well as a home for Itchakomi. But first, her sacred fire.

We all are children of the sun. We had been given the sun to bring warmth and life to an otherwise dead world.

First, I needed to choose a place sufficiently impressive, and the rawboned mountain beyond our fort was such a place. I would clear a place of stones and debris, and then gather the fuel for a fire. And I would choose a day of bright sun, but first there was much else to do.

The Pawnees were gone. When time permitted I walked over their campsite and cleaned up what debris was left, little as it was.

Atop the mountain I cleared a spot of broken rock and debris, and then carefully constructed a cairn, or altar, using rocks that lay about, fitting them together with infinite care. The altar was four feet high and three feet to a side, with a large flat stone as the centerpiece. From trees not far away I gathered several old, long-deserted birds' nests, and about them I laid a network of twigs and small branches and then larger, heavier pieces. At the outer edge of the pile I placed a part of a bird's nest, several thin pieces of pitch pine, and shreds of bark. Unfortunately the wood of the white walnut could not be had, so I had chosen cedar instead.

Cedar was used in purification ceremonies in several tribes, and I believed it would be acceptable. We who are latecomers are forever curious as to the why of rituals, but the Indian asks no such questions. Having no written history or account of their rites, they have often forgotten the reason for certain rites, but the reason is not considered important. The ritual itself is enough. Many such ceremonies have continued for hundreds if not thousands of years. If Itchakomi would be happier with a sacred fire, she would have one, and her fire would be truly a gift of the sun.

With a wooden hoe carved by my own hands, I cultivated the corn. Often in the evenings I worked to create furniture for our house, and there was always much to do.

When the evenings were cool we walked out under the trees to look across at the Sangre de Cristos, bathed in the blood red of the setting sun, a red that lingered long after our valley was deep in shadow.

"What will your mother and sister be doing now?"

"Their home is in London now, I believe. They will be at home, or dressing to go out for the evening. I know so little of the life there.

"Brian will be with them, I expect. He will be quite

the Englishman now, I believe. I wonder if he will have gone to visit the fens which were my father's home. The fens," I added, "are a vast lowland, some of it under water, but drained by many channels and openings. There is wild game there, many eels, geese, ducks, and pigeons, as well as deer.

"My mother returned to England with several valuable gems found in Carolina. She inherited property from her father, also, I believe. They will be well off."

"Is it important to be well off?"

"It helps. Life is very hard for the poor, and for a young woman to marry well it is important that she have independent means. I believe young men think more of improving their position than of love."

"Your sister will marry there?"

"I expect, but about Noelle, one does not know. She is a girl of independent mind. She will go her own way, like the rest of us."

Deer had come from the woods and were grazing on the meadow before us. From where we stood I could see at least a dozen and several elk, bunched near some rocks some distance away.

Paisano came up from where he was feeding and stood near us, and I scratched his ear. He was huge now, a great shaggy bull that was like a puppy around us. Buffalo were considered stupid animals, but I did not find him so. I had, with some effort, convinced him to stay out of my cornfield, which I had fenced off with poles. Fences, I had learned, mean nothing to buffalo, who usually go where they wish, but Paisano had learned that the cornfield was off limits for him, and as there was no shortage of grass, he left the cornfield alone.

Winter was coming, however, and I resolved to cut some hay, enough to feed Paisano occasionally and to keep him reminded of where his home was.

There were tools we needed, but I dared not approach Santa Fe, where I would be considered an interloper and would be imprisoned and then sent down into Mexico for a trial, if I got one. Diego had implied he was interested in trade, but we had little to offer. We had some buffalo hides, as well as a few skins trapped the previous winter. This year I resolved to make a more thorough job of trapping.

Hand in hand, Komi walked with me to the fort. Keokotah was there, seated by the fire. The others were sleeping or busy with some of the many activities of our day-to-day lives.

For days now I had been watching the weather, and the days of mixed clouds and occasional rain seemed to be dwindling away for the time. When the sun was bright and the day hot I would bring the fire down for Itchakomi. Now there was something else of which I must know.

"Keokotah, long ago you spoke of the animal the Poncas call Pasnuta?"

He remembered only too well my doubts, and his features stiffened, his eyes blazing a challenge.

"I was wrong to doubt you. We who have not traveled this country as have you think such animals only appear in other, faraway places. I would have you speak of this animal."

He knew nothing of my dreams or nightmares. These dreams were not like the occasional flashes of the future that had sometimes come to me, but I was disturbed by them. Was this a foresight of my hour of death? Was I to die impaled on a tusk or trampled under the feet of such a monster?

Keokotah did not answer but turned to the Ponca woman. "Tell him of pasnuta," he said.

She came over to us and sat cross-legged on the floor. "Pasnuta beeg! Ver' beeg! We kill pasnuta. Much meat at one time."

"They surround the beast," Keokotah said. "Drive him into a swamp or over a cliff or several will challenge him, seeming to attack, and while he looks at them others come from behind with spears."

"Where do you find them?"

The Ponca woman shrugged. "Wherever. Out on long

grass. In mountains. Who knows where? We find, we kill. Much meat."

Her eyes lit with memory and remembered excitement. "Long winter, much, much cold! There is hunger in the lodges! Many long hunt, nothing! Spring no come! One day Running Bear, he find track. Beeg, beeg track! He say come, and many warrior go. They follow track. Push pasnuta in deep snow. They follow, follow, follow. Pasnuta get in deep snow, no can move good. Warrior surround.

"Pasnuta charge! He keel one. He throw one far, but that one fall in snow, not much hurt.

"They stick pasnuta with spear! Many spear! Much meat! No more hunger in the lodges."

"Do you see them often?"

"No many! One time many! Old man say so. In my life we keel three, maybe four."

All the descriptions tallied. They were hairy elephants, huge creatures, some with tusks, some without. Once there had been many, now they found them but rarely. They were fierce, but not hard to kill when there were a dozen or more warriors.

Yance, when wandering, had come upon some huge bones near a salt lick. The flesh had long been gone, but the skeleton of the beast had been intact. Yance had brought back, with the help of some Indians, two large tusks that we had sold to a trader who came into the sound with his ship.

It seemed preposterous, but who could say what did or did not exist? And I had learned to trust Indian stories. Yet what did this mean to me? Why was I dreaming of the red-eyed monster? And why when faced with such a terror did I not try to escape?

So passed the days. We hunted and then smoked and dried what we did not eat. We gathered from the forest, from the mountain slopes and the meadows. We ate what was needed and saved the rest. We gathered fuel for the winter to come, and watched for enemies who did not come.

Yet there were signs that Indians came often to this valley. From the old trails we found, these Indians came from the west. They were not the dreaded Komantsi.

One day when returning from a hunt I climbed on Paisano's back. He stood for a moment, but when I urged him on he walked off, unconcerned, carrying my weight easily. He had been handled much, had carried packs, and had been hand fed, so he had no fear of me. And he liked to be fussed over and scratched.

So I rigged a crude saddle that conformed with his body and devised a bridle that enabled me to guide him.

An evening came when the sun set in all its red glory, painting the peaks with fantastic hues. From a ridge near our fort I watched the sunset and rode Paisano down to the fort.

Our Indians had not seen me astride him, for always I had mounted Paisano when well away from camp, and now they stood back and watched, awestruck. This was big medicine, and I knew it.

Komi came outside when she heard the excitement and watched me ride in. The time was right, for tomorrow would be a clear, bright day.

"Tomorrow, Itchakomi Ishaia, tomorrow I shall bring down fire from the sun."

When morning came the sun was bright and I went early to the river and bathed. When I returned to the fort I built a fire of cedar chips and, using an eagle's wing, wafted the smoke over me. It was a cleansing rite used by Indians I had known, and I knew Itchakomi would know it for what it was.

Her religion meant much to her, and although our beliefs were not the same their roots were similar, and I would pay respect to what she believed.

When the time came to climb the mountain to the altar I had built she came forward with a crown of feathers to place on my head. The feathers were only on the forepart of the crown.

So in the hour before high noon I led the way, followed by Itchakomi, the Natchee, Keokotah, and the women to my altar, where I had laid the makings of my fire.

For a long moment I stood before the altar. Then I lifted my arms to the sun and stood for an instant, and then lowered them. In my hand I held the burning glass taken from the pocket in my belt. I brought the glass into focus and slowly moved it down until a pinpoint of intense light was on the gathered leaves.

An instant of the intense light, and then the leaves began to smoke. There was a low murmur of astonishment from behind me. The smoke lifted, and a black spot appeared on a dried leaf and began to widen. A small flame took hold and I nudged some dried moss close to the flame. It caught. The moss smoked, and then broke into flame. I slipped the burning glass back into its pocket in my belt and pushed the tinder closer.

The flame leapt up, the fire crackled, sticks caught fire. I stepped back and turned to Itchakomi. "The Sun," I said, "has given us fire."

38

We gathered our corn in the morning, breaking the thick ears from the stalks and carrying them in handwoven baskets to the fort. The ground was rich and there had been rain enough, and always there was sun. The best of the ears I put aside for spring planting, except for a couple that I hand fed to Paisano.

Along the mountainsides we gathered seeds, hunted, and watched the skies with wary eyes for the change we knew was coming. Our sacred fire had been moved from the high mountain to a cave, where it was sheltered from wind and rain. There we stored wood to keep the fire burning, stored it dry against the time of snow.

My pistols were loaded and there was powder enough taken from our enemies to load at least twice more. Working with the silver-lead ores from nearby I molded several hundred balls and stored them against the future.

Still I had found no sulphur, yet I had been told by Sakim that it occurred where there had been volcanic action, and many of the signs were near. A wandering Indian told us of a place far to the north and west, but there was no time for such a trek before snow fell.

Now darkness came before we were ready, and leaves began to fall from some trees, and fewer flowers were in bloom, only the lavender fleabane with the gold centers, fringed gentians, rabbit bush, and sulphur flower. The time of cold was coming, but the time of storytelling, too, when we would spend much time by the fire, remembering old tales from times gone by, and listening to stories the Indians told to their children. Soon Komi would be telling those stories to our child. It was a strange thought and a worrisome one. What did I know of being a father?

Of all things here I missed books the most. How I longed for something to read! The mind has no limits but those we choose to give it. The mind reaches out hungrily for learning, and mine now was finding too little upon which to feed. Each night I stirred Itchakomi to remembering, asking question after question to understand better her people, her religion, and her ideas, and I shared mine with her.

And then came an evening when the wind blew down from the Sangre de Cristos and our fire sputtered on the hearth. Venison broiled over the fire, and when Keokotah came in he walked at once to the meat and with his knife cut a thick slice. When he had eaten he said, "Now we fight!"

"What?"

"They come. All afternoon I have run to speak the message. Two come, but they come not together."

"Two men?"

"No two men. Two parties, one to make trade, one to make war."

The others gathered around. The Ponca woman put down her weaving.

"Diego comes. He has twenty pack mules. With him are six soldiers, two Indians. He comes to trade."

"You know it is Diego?"

"I speak him. The other is Gomez. He comes with soldiers and with bad Indians. He comes for war."

"How many?"

"Twenty men. He has four soldiers and many bad Indians. I think he wishes to catch Diego." Keokotah paused to chew his meat. "I speak Diego. Now he knows of Gomez. He comes this way fast."

There was silence in the room. We had enjoyed our weeks of peace, but we had known this time would come. Yet we were so few to defend against so many.

Would Diego fight beside us? I doubted it. He had come to trade, and to fight against his own people could be none of his planning, despite the fact he did not agree with them and disliked Gomez.

Diego had implied he was interested in trade, and he knew it would be good for the Spanish to have an outpost where they might resupply themselves when on forays against the Komantsi. With so many pack animals he would be bringing trade goods, but what did Gomez have in mind?

Itchakomi of course, but what else? Revenge, also, but that would not be enough. Gold? We had little gold, and of that he could know nothing. But gold was the overriding motive for all the Spanish exploration. He might assume that we had found gold.

Why else would we be staying here?

He would know the Pawnees were gone. He will believe we are alone. He will not know of our friends the Natchee who have joined us.

Yet we were few, and how were we to defend ourselves? I had but little ammunition, and the guns would no longer be a surprise.

"There are the Utes," Itchakomi said.

It was a good thought, yet danger might lie with the Utes, an even graver danger than with Gomez, for this was considered Ute land and we had moved upon it. There were indications that they came to this valley and camped here, although so far we had seen none of them.

From the beginning I had hoped to make them allies, for we had heard they were traditional enemies of the Komantsi, but I had no idea where they were nor how to find them, and they might attack without warning.

The fire crackled, and outside a wind blew cold. We did not look at one another, each huddled with his own doubts, her own fears. Our enemies were many, and we were few.

The walls of our fort were strong, but Gomez would have planned for them. He was a shrewd, dangerous fighting man, irked by his previous defeat and undoubtedly determined it should not happen again.

We could escape now. We could fly to the mountains and hide, but that would mean the destruction of our fort and our food supply. It would result in our starving in the snow, and Itchakomi was pregnant.

We could expect no help from anyone. Whatever was done must be done by us. Yet what could we do? The few defenses used on the previous attack would be known to Gomez. There would be no attacks by horse-riding men this time. They would attempt to capture the fort and us, but failing in that they would use fire.

Fire . . . ?

"I will fight outside," Keokotah said. "I no good behind wall."

"As you will, but first come with me to meet Diego."

Turning to Itchakomi, I said, "Itchakomi, you will be in command within the fort. Do you keep your Natchees to defend it with you. You they know, and you they will protect."

"And you?"

"I shall go out, but I shall return." It was in my mind to do them damage before they reached us. Yet how? What could I do?

My hand reached for Komi's and we clasped hands in the shadows, watching the fire. I was not a man who spoke much of love, although I knew such speaking was treasured by women, but it was much in my heart and I thought of her always. Now, at this moment, I feared for her, and I feared what lay before us.

What to do? They depended upon me, trusted in me. Not only was I their master of mysteries, but I was their war chief.

Now, at the beginning of our second winter, we were snug and warm. We had much dried meat and many seeds, and we had corn. We had cut wood and piled it close at hand. We were prepared for winter, for storytelling time, and now our enemies had come and my people looked to me to save them, to keep them secure.

Always, I had planned to roam, to be free, to move as I wished, when I wished, but when one has a wife and children that is no longer possible, and when one has possessions he is as often possessed by them as possessing them.

Here it was warm and quiet, here was peace and comfort, here were my few friends.

But what could I *do*?

First, to meet them outside. To hold them up in their march, to nibble away at their confidence, to lessen their numbers.

We had a good supply of arrows. We had extra spears. We knew the line of effective range for our bows. We had cut back trees and brush so any attacker must step into the open before he was within effective range of our walls. By night we had no such protection.

We had the small caltrops we had used before, and something else besides. During the summer, with something of this in mind, we had collected and dragged back to the fort many spined leaves of prickly pear and hedgehog or strawberry cactus. Knocking them loose and picking them up with forked sticks, we had piled many upon a skin and then dragged them back to the fort. Now, working in darkness and with forked sticks, we scattered them in the grass around the fort. The caltrops might stop a charge by horsemen, but these would stop men on foot wearing moccasins, which many of the Spanish soldiers now wore.

It was little enough. We had no protection against fire arrows, and they would certainly be used.

"We must rest now," I said at last. "Tomorrow Keokotah and I will go out to meet Diego. Then we shall see."

Now would my pistols be useful. There was ammunition enough to reload at least twice, and each pistol was good for twelve shots. It might be enough.

Yet even I, who am a good shot, will miss as often as I hit when shooting at moving, attacking enemies, some wearing partial armor. If I scored with even one-third of my shots I should be fortunate, fortunate indeed.

We slept, and on this night there was no red-eyed monster, and I slept soundly and well, but in the last gray light I slipped from under the robes and dressed quickly.

Bathing my hands and face, I gathered my weapons and started for the door. Komi was there, and for a moment we stood, holding hands and looking at each other. Then I took her in my arms. "Do not fear. I shall come back."

"I do not fear, and when you come, I shall be waiting."

Paisano was waiting. I put my crude saddle in place, mounted, and rode out the gate, which Itchakomi closed after me..

Trusting to Paisano's keen senses, I started south, knowing the country but letting him pick his way. Riding, I kept alert for the smell of smoke from the campfire of Diego.

Dawn was sending its first crimson arrows into the sky before I caught the smell of smoke. Then crossing a low hill I saw the glow of fire. Drawing up, I studied the small camp.

Men were up and moving about, loading packs on animals. They were less than four miles south of our fort. I recognized the tall, lean figure of Diego and rode closer, calling him by name.

"Is it you, then?" He walked toward me and then stopped abruptly. "What—!"

"It is all right," I said. "I ride a bull."

Swinging down I walked forward, the great beast following me. Paisano had grown into a huge, powerful bull, more than six feet at the hump and weighing well over two thousand pounds, perhaps closer to three thousand.

Diego swore and then spat. "What next will you do? What next?"

"I'll buy what you have to sell, if that is what you've come for. Unless you want a fight you'd better leave before Gomez comes. He's not far behind you."

"The Kickapoo told me. If he wants a fight he can have one." He paused, looking into my eyes. "I cannot join you, but if he attacks me, and you should attack him at the same time . . ."

"It could happen," I said, "but first the goods."

Gomez was nowhere in sight when we reached the fort. We drove the pack mules through the gate, but I permitted only Diego and one man inside.

With two of the Natchee watching from the high ports, Diego displayed his goods. Four axes, four shovels, a crosscut saw, several bushels of colored beads, two dozen hatchets, and various other tools and equipment, including an adz. There were also three mule-loads of brightly colored cloth.

"Tools for your own use," Diego said, "and trade goods."

In my belt I had two dozen gold coins of Spanish origin, but I wished not to use them. My father had given them to me before we had parted at Shooting Creek, and I would hold them against some greater emergency than this. Yet there were hides we had, buffalo robes, and a few ingots of silver, melted down from the purest silver I could find while making balls for my pistols.

We bargained, but not too sharply on my part, for I wished him to do well. If he did well he would come again, and without him I had no source of supply.

At the end I threw in another ingot of silver, weighing almost a pound. "Come again, Diego, in the spring. We will make good trade, you and I."

A voice called down from above, and Itchakomi said, "They come!"

When the soldier had driven the mules outside, Diego turned quickly to me. "A gift," he said, placing a packet in my hand, "and if they find out I gave you this it is a hanging matter."

In that instant he turned and ducked through the

gates and was gone. Outside I heard a clatter of feet as they drove the mules away.

The gate swung shut and I took the package and went inside.

Keokotah was outside, away in the hills that he loved, and he would fight from there as he wished.

Placing the packet on the table, I looked to my guns, and then I climbed to the high ports to look down the valley.

Diego was nowhere in sight, so they must have fled up the canyon behind us.

Gomez was outside. From the trees he called out. "Surrender now and we will let you go free! Lay down your weapons and come out!"

Long ago my father had said, "Never give up your weapons. I know of no case where weapons were surrendered that was not followed by a massacre."

The packet on the table drew my attention. Opening it I looked down . . . gunpowder! Several pounds of it.

"Thanks, Diego," I said. "Gracias!"

39

To Gomez I made no reply. Of one thing I was sure—no matter what other outcome this attack might have, one of us, Gomez or I, would die before it was ended. I wished only peace, and I felt sure that left to our own devices I could arrange a peace with the Utes. Only Gomez stood between us and the life I wished us to lead.

He shouted again, demanding our surrender.

The skies were gray now, although heavy with clouds over the western mountains. The trees stood out, stark and black against the gray. The shadows of men, or rather their dark forms that seemed like shadows, moved at the edge of the woods and on the meadows below, reminding me of those other shadows, the dancing shadows in the cave.

Unbidden there came to mind the voice that had seemed to speak from where the skin-wrapped bodies lay. An eerie feeling as of some effort at communication had come to me, and standing alone in the silence I had asked if there was anything I could do.

A foolish thing, to speak into an empty cave where lay only the mummified bodies of the long dead, but as I had turned away I had heard, or had seemed to hear, a voice saying, "Find them!"

Find who? Where? Why?

Waiting in the darkness of the fort, the air soft with impending rain, I remembered, and was sad.

What had the dead left undone? Had they spoken? Or had the voice only been in my brain? Had there been some communication, some desperate wish, some great desire that lived beyond death?

I, who might die this day, thought of that. What desire could be so driving, so compelling that it lived beyond death?

For me there could be but one. The safety of Komi and my child to be. Nothing mattered beyond that.

Was it so with them? Was this the wish of the nameless dead? But too many years, perhaps too many centuries, had passed. Their children and their grandchildren would have died long since, and yes, their great-great-grandchildren, for the bodies, I believed, had been hundreds of years old.

"Find them!"

Find who? Find what? Where?

Suddenly Komi was beside me, in her hand a cup of the coffee that had come with Diego's trade goods.

"Komi? What do you know of the Ni'kwana? Who is he?"

"He is the Ni'kwana, the master of mysteries. What else?"

I shook my head. "I do not know, only—somehow he did not seem like an Indian. There was something about him, something different."

"Ah!" She was silent, turning her own cup in her fingers. "I have heard—I do not know, but I have heard—he was not one of us. I have heard there was a people, a very few, who came to live with us long ago. He was the last of them."

"You know nothing more?"

She shrugged. "They came from the river, long, long ago. I do not know whether they came from up or down the river, but they were priests, they were teachers. I do not know where they came from or when this was, only that they came among us and taught many things. Our Ni'kwanas always came from that group. I do not know why that was, either."

She paused. "My grandmother was one of them. She was related, somehow, to the Ni'kwana."

Outside there was movement. I peered through a porthole in the palisade, but saw nothing.

"The Ni'kwana wished something more for you, I think. Why were you chosen to come west?"

She shrugged. "I was a Sun. It was I who could decide whether to go or stay. Only the Great Sun was above me, and he was unwell. It was my duty to come."

"And the direction you chose?"

"The Ni'kwana directed me. He told me he knew of a place far to the west where we would be safe. He wished me to go and see."

"It was where the river comes from the mountain?"

"No, it was beyond. It . . . it might be here, but I—"

My mind was busy, searching, examining, prying. There was something strange here, something eerie, something frightening.

The Ni'kwana was old. He was the last of his kind except for Itchakomi Ishaia, who was at least part of his blood. Did he wish to save her from something? Did he wish, and this thought came unexpectedly, her to *find something, someplace*?

Was her trip west directed back into the past of his people? Was he trying to protect her from something he knew was inevitable? To bring her back to their beginnings?

I spoke of this, speaking softly. "You must try to remember, Komi. He was your teacher, but what did he teach? Was there something only for you? Some story? Some idea?"

"Find them!"

Was there a connection between the mummified bodies in the cave and the Ni'kwana? It was absurd. Yet—I shook myself. My mind was too busy. Too much imagination. I must forget all this and tend to the business at hand. My first consideration was survival. There would be time, I hoped, after that.

Find them—find what? People? Things? Places?

Had something been lost? People left behind? Were there some lessons to be learned, and left somewhere?

The Ni'kwana had said he expected an older man. My father, perhaps? But then he knew my father was dead. But he could not have known that when he left Natchez and his people. It could not have happened by that time. My father had died later. The Ni'kwana had come expecting an older man, but when he saw me—

How much of what followed had been accident and how much direction? Had he, somehow, *wished* me to find the mummies? But that was ridiculous.

What remained was that I was here, in this far place, and I had married Itchakomi. An Indian marriage, but in its form not unlike the common law marriages that were legal in England, or had been. It was little enough I knew of such things, but there had been talk at home around the table of an evening or beside the fireplace, talk of weddings, customs, all that sort of thing. I should have listened more carefully.

But what child in his later years does not wish he had listened when his parents talked among themselves, about themselves, their families, the way they had lived? So often we do not realize how much we could have learned until it is too late and there is no going back.

It was growing light. Again the call for surrender. Impatiently, I replied, "Gomez! If you are so eager for surrender, why don't you come and fight me? You and I alone."

There was silence and then his voice cool, mocking. "As the challenged party, I choose the weapons. That is the way in civilized countries."

"Why not? Belly to belly with pistols? Knives? Whatever you wish. Let us settle this, man to man."

"Of course!" His tone was genial, yet mocking still. "I choose the weapons."

"Choose them, then. If I win, your men leave now, at once."

Gomez laughed. "And if I win? I take all!"

"And I will be the judge!" The voice was that of Diego. "Four muskets will cover your people, Gomez. If there is any attempt, during the fight, to take advantage, they will kill!"

Gomez walked down from the trees. There was a fine swagger to the man. He stood there in his coat of mail, hands on his hips, smiling.

"Pistols, then?" I suggested.

He laughed. "Not pistols, my fine friend! You shoot too well! No, we shall have swords! It will be a proper duel!"

Diego started to protest, but Gomez waved a dismissing hand. "You I shall take care of later, Diego. Sackett offered me the choice of weapons. He challenged *me*! So now we shall see how our buckskin savage does with a gentleman's weapon!"

"Cover me," I whispered, and stepped through the gate, which closed behind me.

"What would you know of a gentleman's weapons?" I asked Gomez. "You are no gentleman. You are a coward, a betrayer, a slave dealer, and a pimp, who deals in women for other men."

He started to speak and almost choked on his fury. Then he calmed down. "We shall see! Swords, my friend! Let us see how you do!"

Diego's protest was brushed aside. Yet he called out to me. "Sackett! Think what you do! The sword is *his* weapon!"

Perhaps it was, but there had been those hours and hours of fencing back at Shooting Creek when my father, Jeremy, and Sakim had all instructed me in the art. It had been nearly two years . . . still, I had been rather good, the best of them, in fact, except for my father.

Diego came down from the trees. "You may use my blade," he said. Then leaning closer he said, "Think what you do! The man is a superb swordsman! He will make a fool of you and then kill you!"

I gripped the hilt of the saber. "A fine blade, Diego. I thank you for this. I shall try not to disgrace it for you."

"Save yourself, Sackett. Run! I'll not hold it against you! Get out before he murders you!"

"Murder? It is not easily done, amigo."

"Are you ready, then?" Gomez called. "I want to kill you, and then I shall have the wench. She'll make good trade back in Santa Fe!"

Sword in hand, I walked toward him. He would be good, probably very good, and I had never fought for blood with a sword. Fenced, yes. Hour upon hour, with some of the best, but this was different. This man intended to kill me or maim me.

Contemptuous of me, he would try to make a fool of me first. He would play with me as a cat with a mouse.

The earth outside of the gate was smoothly packed. Only in the grass lurked the caltrops and the prickly pear. There was room enough, a space at least forty feet wide and half again that long of smoothly packed clay.

We moved out on the clay and I endeavored to appear awkward and unsure of myself. Yet at this moment I suddenly remembered my leg. Would it make a difference? I did not believe so. It was too late now to think of that. What I must do was to discover Gomez' rhythm, the cadence of his movements. In fencing as in boxing timing and judgment of distance were all-important, and the way an opponent moves and his reach must be quickly learned. My chance of victory would be greater if I moved at once, before he discovered I knew something of the art of the saber. Now he thought me what he had said, a buckskin-clad savage, to whom the use of the sword was completely foreign.

We circled, and I held my weapon awkwardly. Stepping in, I watched him step back and timed his movements. He was smiling now, a taunting smile. "I shall have her for myself," Gomez said, "before I use her in trade."

He was trying to anger me, to draw me in, so I did as he wished and made as if to attack, and then retreated as he attacked. His movements were wide, flamboyant and careless. My blade caught his thrust, parried, and slid along his blade. He moved even as my point touched his shoulder. He backed away, circling, looking at me with a question in his eyes. I had been too good on that one. He would be more cautious now. But he was not, he attacked again with wide-sweeping cuts and I retreated. He came on, suddenly impatient, yet I had taken his measure and caught him out of time. I thrust, quick, low, and hard.

Whether it found a break in his chain mail or drove through, I did not know, but my point went in, deep and hard. Cutting left with the edge, I withdrew sharply, and blood followed.

His face was ghastly. It had suddenly turned mottled and yellow and he staggered, trying to regain his poise. He tried an attack, but his timing was gone and I thrust again, this time at his throat. Turning the blade at the target I cut sharply left and laid open his throat. His blade dropped and he tried to speak. Then he fell over on his face.

There was a chorus of shouts and some wild yells. Looking up I beheld a circle of Indians, at least fifty of them on horseback, watching.

Keokotah came from the trees. "Utes," he said. "Speak well."

I lifted my sword to them in a salute, and then bowed with a wide, sweeping gesture.

Keokotah stepped toward them, speaking. They listened and watched as he used sign language with the words.

He who appeared to be chief listened and then spoke.

"He says you are much warrior," Keokotah said. "Offer them gifts. Tell them we are friends in their land. We wish them to come often to trade. Tell them we have come to bring the Utes presents and wish to stay in this small corner of their land and help them against their enemies, the Komantsi."

There was a brief exchange. Keokotah said, "He wishes to see your presents." Then he added, "I think you've a friend. He likes the way you fight."

Wiping my blade, I returned it to Diego, who was now talking to the men of Gomez. Picking up Gomez' sword I wiped it clean. Then I took it to the Ute chief and presented it to him with a bow.

Gravely, he accepted the sword, and I said, "I, your friend, present you with this sword to be used against your enemies. Your friends are my friends. Your enemies are my enemies."

Bowing again, I took two steps back and then turned to the gate. Now was the time to show them my medicine. Inside the gate, waiting, was Paisano.

"Food, Komi! We must feed them! We must feed our new friends!"

Paisano walked from the gate, a huge, massive beast, and I heard gasps of astonishment. Coolly, I gathered the reins and stepped into the saddle. Calmly, gravely, I walked Paisano out upon the clay to mutters of awe and astonishment. Saluting them again, I rode Paisano back into the gate as the women began to emerge with trays of food.

Much depended upon this first meeting, and well I knew it. They had seen me win a victory and they had seen me ride a buffalo, which to them was big medicine, but now to more practical things.

Showing the chief and some of the elders to seats on a log outside the gate, I warned all against walking in the grass. Then I brought out several bolts of red calico, a dozen knives, another dozen of hatchets. The Utes came to stare at what to them, at this time, was a veritable treasure.

All things are valued according to their scarcity, and a time might come when this gift would seem as nothing. What was worth little to us was worth much to them because they were things they could not get elsewhere.

Keokotah's woman and the Ponca woman brought

food to put before our guests, and they seated themselves and ate.

Suddenly, two Natchee Indians emerged from the gate, each holding a torch. For a moment they stood, until all eyes were upon them. Then slowly, with grace and poise, Itchakomi Ishaia emerged between them.

Looking neither right nor left she walked down the open space before the chiefs, and it was only then that I noticed that one of our benches, covered with a buffalo robe, had been placed opposite them.

She seated herself, and the torch bearers moved to right and left. For a long moment she said nothing, as all stared. Then she said, "I am Itchakomi Ishaia, Daughter of the Sun, Priestess of the Eternal Fire." She waited again until one might have counted to five very slowly, and then she said, "I walk with this man, who is Jubal Sackett, the Ni'kwana, master of mysteries!"

40

Never had I been so proud of my wife as at that moment. Indians dearly love ceremony, as do many of us, and there could be no doubt in the mind of anyone that she was no less than a beloved woman.

Keokotah, who knew much of the Ute language, which was similar to that of tribes he had known, spoke to them, translating her words and telling who she was.

"In the cave"—he indicated the place near our fort—"lives the fire that burns forever. She is its guardian, its priestess.

"He"—he pointed at me—"brought the fire from heaven. The fire is the gift of the Sun. I have seen it."

"And I!" said a Natchee torch bearer.

"And I!" the other repeated.

Diego moved to my side. "She is *wonderful*!" he whispered. "She has won them all!"

Awed, I looked at her. This beautiful woman, this goddess—could she be mine? Beautiful, yes, but intelligent also. She had come among them when the time had been right, and they would never forget her.

I smiled to myself. "And she didn't have to ride a buffalo to do it!"

Long after they were gone, the effect remained with

me. Surely, I would remember her always in that beaded white buckskin costume, a band about her dark hair, standing between the torches. She had beauty then, and magic, also.

One by one the Utes went to see the sacred fire, to look upon it and pass on. When they rode away with their gifts I knew we had won some friends. More than my buffalo, more than my fighting, more than my gifts, it had been Itchakomi who had done it.

"They will be friends now," Keokotah commented complacently. "We will have no trouble."

Yet as I looked down the darkening valley, I wondered. Suddenly, I shuddered. We used to say when that happened somebody had just stepped on our grave.

Perhaps—

Suddenly, just for a moment, I seemed to see a vast beast rising before me, a mighty monster with tusks like spears, lifting his great head, winding his trunk back against his brow, a red-eyed monster who looked at me and started to move, coming at me. Instinctively I reached for a spear, and there was none, and I was alone.

I shuddered again.

That, now? After all of this? Would it come now? But how could it be? There was no such beast. An elephant with long hair?

Yet that night I slept and slept well, with no nightmares, no dreams.

We had given much meat to feeding the Utes, and if we were to last the winter it must be replaced, so now was the time for hunting. Also, there was the matter of the sulphur. If we could find a workable deposit we could make our own gunpowder.

"Komi," I suggested, "let us go together to the mountains. We will visit the caves, hunt, and look for sulphur. Also, we can take a bit of food to eat as the English do on a Sunday."

"How do they eat?"

"On Sunday they do not work, so sometimes one family, sometimes several, will go together to the seashore, a lake, or a river and there in the shade of trees they will eat their food. It is a quiet time for all, a relaxing time.

"The children will run and play, the older people will laze about, talking, sleeping, sometimes singing. It is sometimes called a picnic."

"Good! We will eat a picnic. Paisano will carry the lunch and some robes to sit upon."

We were like children, and happy children at that. Sometimes back at Shooting Creek when we were very young we had gone out like this with our father and mother and others of the family or our friends. It brought good memories, and as we walked along I shared them with Komi.

"I was the quiet one. I did not run and play as much as the others, but I loved it all very much. I liked just to sit and watch, although they were always trying to get me into their games. They could never understand that I was happier just watching them be happy."

As we neared the place where the creek flowed down from the mountains there was a meadow, a deep pool in the creek, and a place where aspen came close to the water's edge. The aspen leaves whispered in the slightest movement of air and it was quiet and serenely beautiful.

"Jubal, why don't we stay right here? We will find nothing up on the mountain that is half so beautiful."

Well, why not?

We spread our robes by the pool and I started a small fire to make coffee, of which we now had a good quantity from Diego.

When the smell of coffee was in the air I took up my bow and walked out, looking for a deer or an elk. The meadows I could see were empty, yet far away something stirred in the trees. Shading my eyes, I looked toward it but could see nothing. The mountain loomed above us. The Ponca woman who had been there as a young girl had said there were lakes up there, too. Someday we would go there, Komi and I.

It was time we started back. There would be time for hunting after we had eaten.

Where was Paisano? He had followed me, but now he was nowhere about. I called and then started back, walking slowly. The sun was warm and pleasant.

Far across the valley, back along the way we had come, I saw a lone figure. Someone was coming toward us, still a long way off.

Smoke lifted from our fire. Komi was nowhere in sight.

Putting down my bow I began gathering sticks for the fire, stopping now and again to call out for her. Still no response.

Worried, I dumped my load of sticks, glancing around. In the distance the lone figure was still coming, drawing nearer but still far off. Yet he was walking not running, and if it was somebody from the fort and there was trouble, he or she would be running.

Something large and dark moved in the edge of the woods. "Paisano?"

What could he be doing that he did not come when I called? And where was Komi? Our coffee would bubble away.

She might be looking for herbs, which we gathered against times of trouble. Placing my bow beside the quiver of arrows near where our coffeepot bubbled, I started into the woods.

"Komi? Come on! The coffee's ready!"

Walking through the small patch of woods I came on an open place covered with clumps of scrub oak. And as I came in sight of it, Komi burst from the woods, running wild and frightened.

"Komi! *Here!*"

She screamed at me, waving frantically for me to leave. "*Run!*" She screamed the word, and I ran toward her.

"No! No! *Run!*"

Catching her arm, I said, "What is it? What's *wrong*?"

She started to run again, tugging at me. "*Please!* Run!"

Her panic bred panic in me, catching her arm I, too, started to run. Behind me there was a crashing in the clump of oaks, and glancing over my shoulder, I saw it.

A monstrous thing with great ears spread wide, two gleaming white tusks. Suddenly I was choking with horror. This was my dream! My nightmare! This beast, this impossible thing, this—

It saw us.

For one frightening, awful moment it stared, and then with a blast as from a great trumpet, it started for us. We turned to flee, and Komi tripped and fell flat.

It charged.

Lifting my gun, I fired, dropped the muzzle to load, and fired again. Whether the balls took effect, I could not say. I only know that as the elephant charged, I steadied my hand and fired again, aiming for the gaping mouth. I dropped the muzzle—

This was why I had not fled. Komi lay at my feet, struggling to rise. The mammoth, for such it was, was almost upon us. Then there was a bellow, and something charged across my vision.

Paisano!

Head down, he charged the mammoth and hit him just back of the foreleg, knocking the larger beast into the brush. Before it could so much as swing around, Paisano whipped his head about, ripping the monster's hide with a horn.

Struggling erect, the mammoth swung its great head around and lunged at Paisano. Amazingly, the buffalo veered away and then charged again, raking the mammoth left and right with his horns.

Grabbing Itchakomi's arm I jerked her to her feet. "Run!" I gasped. "Run and hide!"

I could not leave Paisano.

The huge buffalo had a streak of blood along his side where he had been raked by a tusk, but he charged again, smashing the mammoth back into the trees. Whether by accident or intent Paisano had attacked from the side, avoiding the tusks. Now the monster reached for a grip on a horn with its trunk, but Paisano lowered his great head and butted the mammoth again.

Steadying my hand, I held my fire, and when the monster swung his great head to bring his tusks into play, I shot him in the ear.

It was as if I had struck him with a fly whisk. He shook his great head and turned again to confront Paisano.

What could I do? The monster was three or four times the size of Paisano, but the buffalo bull was undaunted. He bellowed a challenge as the mammoth swung around and charged. Tusks low, trunk curled back out of harm's way, his little eyes red with fury, he drove at Paisano. I would have expected Paisano to meet him head on, but the buffalo bull was a wily fighter. He swung suddenly aside, avoiding the long tusks and hooking a short sharp horn at the monster's shoulder, ripping a gash.

My pistol was ready, and I waited my chance. The roaring of the bull and the trumpetlike blasts from the mammoth were deafening. Now they faced each other again, and Paisano was dwarfed by the mammoth. Moving carefully, I started to work myself around to one side to get in a shot. Paisano had come to my rescue and I could not desert him now. Suddenly Komi was beside me, gripping a spear.

"Get away from here," I said. "You'll be killed!"

"If you die I shall die with you. I can use a spear."

Blood dripped from Paisano's nostrils. He shook his huge head and began moving forward, warily, like a boxer moving in on an opponent. The great beast swung to face him, and then the mammoth seemed to see me for the first time. With a blast from his great throat, he charged. Holding steady I aimed for his eye and squeezed off my shot, using my left hand to steady the barrel.

Paisano swung his head and lunged, smashing the mammoth again in the side, where the leg joined the body. He struck with terrific impact, and the mammoth staggered and fell.

It struggled to rise, blood running from the eye socket, for a dread moment I thought the beast would rise, but it failed at last and sank down. Again it tried to rise, and mercilessly, Paisano charged, striking the monster in the head.

"Paisano! *No!*"

Many times I had yelled, but this time he seemed to hear me and he stopped, lowering his great head. Blood dripping in great, slow drops, he watched for his enemy to move. Now, no more than twenty feet from the mammoth, I could see the cause of its fury, its vicious attack.

It had been hurt. There was an arrow imbedded in its shoulder, and a great festering wound was there.

"Paisano. It is all right. Come now."

He would not move. Head lowered, he watched the mammoth, ready for it to rise.

Walking over I put a hand on his shoulder. "It is all right now, Paisano. It is finished. Come!"

Slowly, reluctantly, he turned and followed. Once he stopped and looked back, head up, peering. The mammoth lay where it had fallen, head up, but whether alive or dead I did not know.

As we sighted our camp a man was coming from it with a spear in his hand. I dropped my hand to the pistol, but he lifted a hand and called out.

It was Unstwita.

"You came back!"

"I say I come. I come."

"Alone?"

"Four other come. They come to walk behind Daughter of the Sun. To guard."

Five more, and that made eight fighting men. Five more to feed, but five more to hunt.

With water from the creek I bathed the long gash on Paisano's side. It was not deep. A nostril was torn. He had come from his fight in good shape. Rubbing his ears, I talked to him, softly. He rubbed his head against me.

Unstwita walked over to see the mammoth. The huge hairy monster had died where he had fallen, his head up, braced by his tusks.

He was huge, but old. Had he been alone, or were

there others like him close-by? I had seen no tracks. Perhaps he had been migrating, searching for others of his kind.

There was compassion in me for the great beast. How must it feel to be alone, with no others of your kind anywhere?

Perhaps there were others, but they were being hunted out of existence. Each had too much meat to offer, and the Indians had learned how to kill them. Someday I would tell the story of this monster, but who would believe me? It had coarse, shaggy hair as Keokotah had said, and which I had not believed. He was a fugitive, probably, from some much colder place.

Komi was beside the fire. She held out a cup of the coffee, which had not quite bubbled away. "Drink," she said, and I drank.

We stood together and looked up at the mountains that towered above us. Someday soon I would go up there. I had a feeling something waited for me, something I must find. There were caves up there, perhaps more than were known.

Long ago a voice in a cave had seemed to say, "Find them!" And something within me said that what I was to find was here, close-by.

My arm went about the waist of Itchakomi Ishaia. Perhaps this was what I was to find. Whether or no, I was content.

"Do you remember," I asked, "long ago when you told me of a dream you had? Of a boy who spoke to a bear? A bear with a splash of white on his face?"

"I remember."

"I was that boy."

"I know," she said.

The aspen leaves made a slow dance in the sunlight. A brief wind stirred the ashes of our fire.

"It grows late," Unstwita said. "We must go."

We stood, waiting a little, reluctant to leave. Unstwita said, "The Ponca woman has found your yellow earth. She will show you."

"Tomorrow we will come back for the tusks," I told Unstwita.

Now there were shadows in the valley, but sunlight on the mountain. My eyes followed a dim trail upward into the peaks where lay the secret lakes, the caves I must explore, and what else?

"*Find them!*" the voice had said.

Were "they" up there now, waiting?

Between Itchakomi and Paisano, I started walking back. Unstwita lingered, drinking the last of the coffee.

AUTHOR'S NOTE

There are seventeen other completed novels featuring members of the various Sackett generations. Readers interested in learning more about Jubal's mother and father, Barnabas and Abigail, and his brothers, Kin-Ring, Yance, and Brian, and sister, Noelle, can read *Sackett's Land*, *To the Far Blue Mountains*, and *The Warrior's Path*.

Succeeding Sackett generations are developed in these books, listed in more or less chronological order, starting with: *Ride the River*, which tells the story of Echo Sackett, the youngest female descendant of Kin-Ring, and *The Daybreakers* and *Sackett*, which begin the story of Tell, Orrin, and Tyrel Sackett, the brothers who follow the trails blazed by their forefathers to help settle the west. Other novels featuring the Sackett brothers and their cousins of the same generation are *Lando*, *Mojave Crossing*, *The Sackett Brand*, *The Lonely Men*, *Treasure Mountain*, *Mustang Man*, *Galloway*, *The Sky-liners*, *The Man From the Broken Hills*, *Ride the Dark Trail*, and *Lonely on the Mountain*.

In the near future, I'm planning to fill in additional portions of the Sackett family saga, including the story of the Sacketts in the Revolutionary War and Tell Sackett's early experiences in the Tennessee mountains and his service in the Sixth Cavalry during the Civil War.

Listed below are some additional points of interest about selected people and events written about in *Jubal Sackett:*

GRASSY COVE: The place where Jubal broke his leg and survived until Keokotah returned for him is a lovely spot. Jubal intended future Sacketts to locate there, only a few miles from the Crab Orchard area where Barnabas met his death.

MAMMOTH, MASTODON, etc.: According to scholars mammoths died out around 6000 B.C. Nonetheless, American Indians record hunting and killing them. One such report occurs in the Bureau of Ethnology report *The Ponca Tribe*. Returning from their "long hunt" west to the Rockies, the Poncas saw a mammoth, as well as what was probably a giant ground sloth, near what is now Niobrara, Nebraska.

David Thompson, the distinguished Hudson's Bay Co. explorer, on January 7, 1811, came upon some tracks near the Athabasca River in the northern Rockies which the Indians told him were those of a mammoth. The Indians had assured him the animal was to be found there. Many Indian tribes had accounts of seeing or hunting the mammoth.

Near Moab, at Hys Bottom close to the Colorado River, there is a petroglyph of a mastodon. And in the Four Corners area near Flora Vista a small boy found two slabs on which were carved many glyphs, including pictures of two elephants. They have been called fakes, which is the most convenient way of getting rid of something that does not fit current beliefs.

PRINCE MADOC: Prince Madoc's existence is doubted by many (not by me), and much has been written from time to time. Perhaps the best account is *Madoc, and the Discovery of America*, by Richard Deacon.

ROMAN COINS: Several Roman coins have been found in Tennessee, Ohio, and Kentucky. Comments on these are made in Judge Haywood's *Natural and Aboriginal History of Tennessee*. This history covers white settlements up to 1768 and was published in 1823. Haywood also comments on burials of bodies with blue eyes and auburn hair, wrapped in hides and left in caves.

TENNESSEE: Ramsey, in his *Annals of Tennessee*, says: "At the time of its first exploration, Tennessee was a vast and almost unoccupied wilderness—a solitude over which an Indian hunter seldom roamed, and to which no tribe put in a distinct and well-defined claim."

One hundred years before Daniel Boone, James Needham was sent into Tennessee to explore the possibilities of trade, traveling there in 1673. He had been sent by a trader, Abraham Wood, whose previous expedition in 1671 had provided too little information. With Needham was a young indentured servant, Gabriel Arthur, who was left behind to learn the Cherokee language.

A MESSAGE FROM LOUIS L'AMOUR

I hope you enjoyed reading *Jubal Sackett* as much as I enjoyed writing it. I'm flattered that so many readers of the hardcover edition of the book have been in touch with me to say how satisfied they were with it and how eager they are for the next Sackett story. As I noted a few pages back, there are a number of Sackett sagas to come that I've been doing a lot of researching for and thinking about. But I put them aside for a while because the time has come for me to tell a story with a very different main character set in a very different time and place. It's called *Last of the Breed* and writing it enabled me to fulfill my long-held desire to create a novel of contemporary adventure set in the most forbidding frontier a man could know: the Soviet Siberian wilderness—one of the coldest spots on the planet.

Perhaps the most appealing challenge of writing *Last of the Breed* was to make an American Indian the hero of one of my stories for the first time. *Last of the Breed* is the story of a captured experimental aircraft pilot, United States Air Force Major Joseph "Joe Mack" Makatozi, part Sioux and part Cheyenne, who makes a spectacular escape from a Russian prison camp. He flees into the Siberian forest, a place once and forever primeval in its arctic desolation. Relentlessly, Soviet soldiers and agents pursue Joe Mack, who is without food, shelter, clothing, weapons, or friends in the most uncharted wilderness in the largest country on earth.

But Joe Makatozi, a loyal, well-educated citizen of his country, a twentieth-century officer and gentleman, instinctively has been preparing all his life for this test of survival. For Joe, who grew up conditioned to endure long periods of hunger and exposure while hunting in the wilds of Montana, Idaho, and British Columbia, with only a bow and arrow for protection, was born out of his time. He should have ridden with Crazy Horse, or, better still, as he says, led the war parties against such Sioux enemies as the Crow and Shoshone.

The untamed Siberian wilderness liberates Joe Mack to become true to his heart, to finally become a noble savage in the spirit of his ancestors. Thus his chosen path of escape, though exceedingly dangerous, is one he seeks with pride: to follow the trail of his ancient forebears who reached America via the Bering Strait landbridge after crossing Siberia.

As a Sioux warrior, Joe Mack intends to collect on the debt of honor incurred by the Russians who shot him down: particularly Colonel Zamatev, the ruthlessly efficient officer who masterminded his capture and is orchestrating his pursuit; and Alekhin, his cruel Yakut aborigine counterpart, a Siberian Indian tracker who is his most cunning and fearsome adversary. Zamatev and Alekhin must be confronted: face to face, man to man, with their deaths or his the only possible end.

I've always had a great affinity for the American Indian, particularly those who were at war with the white man over the centuries. I like their courage, their strength, their intelligence, and above all, their will to survive. These are qualities with which Joe Mack is well-endowed.

A favorite story of mine, which I allude to briefly in the novel, has always been that of the legendary historical figure Massai, a 19th century Apache who was being deported by the government to Florida with many of his tribesmen. He escaped from the train somewhere near St. Louis and traveled all the way back to Arizona, seen by no one, managing to keep out of sight of all the men who might have been pursuing him. He did stop for at least a meal or two with one Indian family but the rest of the time he moved without being detected across the plains and desert. Massai was a great inspiration to Joe Makatozi and a great inspiration to me, of course, as well.

The idea for the story of *Last of the Breed* first came into my mind some thirty years ago during my "yondering" days as a sailor. I was briefly on the east coast of Siberia where I met a man who was the counterpart of an American Indian. He was a fine trapper and hunter who was born and raised in Siberia and knew no other life at all. He was a fascinating man whom I observed and talked to for quite a while. I became intrigued with the notion of what might happen if a man like him were pitted by circumstance against one of my Indian countrymen. My story developed gradually over the years while I researched it by going over maps and related materials, studying the country, and talking to people who had spent time in Siberia. I made a point of looking up Americans who'd had trading posts in Siberia up until 1916; there were quite a few of them, old men by then, but willing to talk to me. I also met American soldiers who occupied parts of Siberia during the time of the Russian Revolution, and their impressions and recollections were very useful.

Some of their memories formed the basis for the characters of the Siberian exiles Joe meets in the course of his odyssey. I hope you will be as intrigued as he was to be in contact with a society and culture so different from ours. Its citizens provide him with facts and share their feelings for Siberian history, lore, and customs. For instance, the aging furrier Zhikarev, whose crippled feet are a constant reminder of how he has been mistreated by the Soviet government, evolves a plan for freedom as daring as Joe's. There's the leader of the exiles, Stephan Baronas, and his daughter, Natalya, who also yearn for liberty as much as Makatozi does. So drawn is Joe to Talya that he vows one day to bring her to America. And there is Alekhin, the Yakut, who is the American's first and worst enemy, because he alone can think like an Indian and understand just how Joe Mack will try to survive. The Russian soldiers can be outwitted, and, if confronted, outfought, but Alekhin is his blood match.

But most of all, through Joe Mack's adventures, I've tried to present the awesome splendor and danger of the Siberian frontier and to convey the almost spiritual pleasure this man took in confronting the tribulations of the same untamed land his ancestors knew centuries ago. I've tried to let the reader know what it is like to be deprived of all modern-day technology and comfort and to face a vast, uncharted wilderness while perpetually cold, hungry, exhausted, with only your wits and the resources to handcraft a spear, slingshot, and bow and arrows to provide food and protection. This book gave me an opportunity to write about a subject I never tire of—how to live off the land. Making moccasins and outer garments from deerskins, setting snares, baiting traps, building a smokeless fire, tracking and removing all signs of his presence—this is how Joe Mack survives to carry forward the legacy of the "last of the breed."

Although Joseph Makatozi is very different from the heroes I write about in my other frontier stories, I think he's a character Jubal and his fellow Sacketts would understand. It's his kind of spirit and determination which, like theirs, made our country strong. And, believe me, the respect would be mutual.

Part of the fun of writing *Last of the Breed* was in making it a novel with a present-day background. It was a challenge that I was glad to meet, because once a writer is known for writing a certain type of story, as I am, it becomes too easy to settle in and do nothing else but that. I always want to be facing challenges by trying new things with my characters and stories. I hope you readers will enjoy sharing them with me.

Louis L'Amour

Louis L'Amour
Los Angeles, California

A STUNNING NOVEL OF CONTEMPORARY ADVENTURE

LAST OF THE BREED

by Louis L'Amour

Major Joe Makatozi stepped into the sunlight of a late afternoon. The first thing he must remember was the length of the days at this latitude. His eyes moved left and right.

About three hundred yards long, a hundred yards wide, three guard towers to a side, two men in each. A mounted machine gun in each tower. Each man armed with a submachine gun.

He walked behind Lieutenant Suvarov, and two armed guards followed him.

Five barracklike frame buildings, another under construction, prisoners in four of the five buildings but not all the cells occupied.

He had no illusions. He was a prisoner, and when they had extracted the information they knew he possessed, he would be killed.

A white line six feet inside the barbed wire, the limit of approach for prisoners. The fence itself was ten feet high, twenty strands of tightly drawn, electrified wire. From the barbed wire to the edge of the forest, perhaps fifty yards.

No one knew he was alive but his captors. There would be no inquiries, no diplomatic feelers. Whatever happened now must be of his own doing. He had one asset. They had no idea what manner of man they had taken prisoner.

When Colonel Zamatev looked into the eyes of his prisoner he was angered. The blue-gray eyes were oddly disconcerting in the dark, strongly boned face, yet it was the prisoner's cool arrogance that aroused his ire. He was unaccustomed to find such arrogance in prisoners brought to him for interrogation. It was not arrogance alone, but a kind of bored contempt that irritated Zamatev.

Colonel Zamatev had a dossier before him that he believed told him all he needed to know about the man before him.

A university graduate, an athlete who had competed in various international tournaments, a decathlon star of almost Olympic caliber. He had scored Expert with a dozen weapons while in the Air Force and was reputed to be skilled in the martial arts. This was straightforward enough, and there were many other officers in the Army, Navy, and Air Force whose dossiers were little different, give or take a few skills.

As much as Zamatev knew about the American flyer, there was an essential fact he did not know. Beneath the veneer of education, culture, and training lay an unreconstructed savage.

When prisoners were brought before Colonel Zamatev they were frightened or wary. They had all heard the stories of brainwashings and torture, yet there was in this man no evidence of fear or of doubt in himself. Zamatev was irritated by a faint, uneasy feeling.

"You are Major Joseph Makatozi? Is that an American name?"

"If it is not there are no American names. I am an Indian, part Sioux, part Cheyenne."

"Ah? Then you are one of those from whom your country was taken?"

"As we had taken it from others."

"But they defeated you. You were beaten."

"We won the last battle." Joe Makatozi put into his tone a studied insolence. "As we always shall."

"You would defend a country that was taken from you?"

"It was our country then; it is our country now. Our battle records, in every war the United States has fought, have been surpassed by none."

Zamatev's irritation mounted. He prided himself on an unemotional detachment, and his manner of interrogation was based upon a casual, seemingly friendly attitude that disarmed the prisoner, who, before he realized it, was trying to reciprocate. The American's arrogance was making this approach difficult.

In an effort to turn the interrogation into preferred channels, Zamatev indicated a thick-set, powerful man sitting quietly on the bench watching Makatozi through heavy-lidded eyes.

"As an American Indian you should be interested in meeting Alekhin. He is a Yakut, a Siberian counterpart of the American

Indian. The Yakuts have a reputation in the Soviet. We call them the iron men of the north. They are among our greatest hunters and trackers."

Zamatev returned his gaze to the American. "It is the pride of Alekhin that no prisoner has ever escaped him."

Joe Mack, as he had been called since his days of athletic competition, glanced at the Siberian, and the Yakut stared back at him from flat, dull eyes of black. A small blaze of white where the hair had lost color over an old scar was his most distinguishing characteristic. He exuded the power of a gorilla and had the wrinkled, seamed face of a tired monkey until one looked a second time and recognized the lines for what they were, lines of cruelty and ruthlessness. Nor, despite his weathered features, was he much older than Joe Mack himself.

With deliberate contempt Joe Makatozi replied, "I don't believe he could track a muddy dog across a dry floor!"

Alekhin came off the bench, a single swift, fluid movement, feet apart, hands ready. Joe Mack turned easily, almost contemptuously, to meet him.

For an instant Zamatev had a queer feeling that a page of history had rolled back. Suddenly, in his small, bare office, two savages faced each other, each a paragon of his kind. A thrill of excitement went through him, and for a moment he was tempted to let them fight.

Zamatev's voice was a whip. "Alekhin! Sit down!"

His eyes went to Joe Mack. "Understand your position, Major. You are our prisoner. You are believed to be dead. So far as your country is concerned, you and your plane were lost at sea. No inquiries have been made, nor are any likely to be made.

"If you are to live it will be because I wish it, and your future, if any, depends on your replies to my questions. I will accept only complete cooperation, including a complete account of your operations as a pilot of several varieties of experimental aircraft.

"You are an intelligent man, and I shall allow you twenty-four hours in which to consider your position. If you are reasonable you may find a place of honor among us. You will be permitted to retain your rank and the privileges pertaining to it. You can serve us, or you can die."

"When was a traitor honored anywhere, even among those who profit from his betrayal? You waste your time."

Colonel Zamatev said sharply, "To your country, Major, you are already dead. To us you may yet be useful. A man of your talents can do well here, and you do not appear to be a man who would willingly choose death. At home you have no ties."

"You forget the most important one, Colonel. There is my country."

Zamatev spoke to Suvarov. "Return this man to his quarters, Lieutenant. I shall speak to him again after he has had time to consider his position."

From the moment of his capture his one thought had been to escape, and to escape at the earliest possible moment.

Lying on his back on the cot in his cell, he considered the possibilities. He must expect to be fired upon. He might be hit. Once beyond the wire he could cover the distance to the woods in five or six seconds. With guns behind him to lend impetus he might do even better. If the attention of the guards could be diverted he might be under fire for no more than three seconds.

He might be killed, he might be severely wounded, but those were things he could not consider now. If either of these things happened he would be either buried or a helpless prisoner. All his attention must be devoted to escape.

All right, then. Suppose he got into the trees? He must run as he had never run before. He must put so much distance between himself and the compound that efforts to recapture him would be well behind him.

If he could run farther, faster than they expected that just might happen. So his first efforts must be for distance and then to mislead his pursuers concerning the direction he was taking.

The nearest border was with Mongolia, and beyond that, China. Of Mongolia he knew virtually nothing except that it was somehow affiliated with the Soviets. He also believed it to be a land of rolling hills, grassland, and desert, and its border with China would be patrolled with great care. It was that border, the nearest one, which he would be expected to attempt.

To the north lay the Arctic, to the east and northeast a vast stretch of taiga, tundra, and extremes of weather. Beyond it was the Bering Sea and Alaska. If the anthropologists were correct, his own people had once followed that migration route, pursuing the game that led them across the then-existing land bridge to America. If they had done it, he could do it.

At night the compound would be a glare of light, but suppose the lights could be shorted out? Undoubtedly there was a backup system. But might there not be a time lapse?

If he remained where he was they would find means to break

him and extract the information they wanted, as one would remove the meat from a cracked nut.

He was not afraid of pain. He had endured pain and could do so again.

Morning came and with it a crust of black bread and some thin gruel. He was informed there would be a fifteen-minute exercise period in which he must keep walking. If he stopped he would be shot. No prisoner was to approach to within six feet of the wire. A white line was drawn on the ground so there would be no mistake.

There were five buildings, with another beginning construction. The new building was to be of frame construction. The planks and timbers were laid out ready for work, along with slender pipes for water, kegs of nails and what looked like sacks of cement.

It was a crazy idea, yet what choice did he have? And crazy ideas had a way of succeeding, because they were unexpected.

Back on the cot again he turned it over in his mind. The situation that existed might never occur again. Somebody had not been thinking. Somebody had been careless.

The prison did not rely upon locks. Anyone seen in the compound would be shot. It was as simple as that. Only during the exercise periods or when being moved by the guards themselves was movement permitted.

The locks were simple, and Joe Mack had known what to do the minute he saw them.

One minute after his feet touched the floor his cell door was open. He took six steps to the outer door on cat feet, then waited, listening.

You haven't a chance, he told himself. *This thing is crazy! If there had only been time to plan!* Then he was outside.

Joe Mack flattened against the wall, listening, waiting, judging the time to the slender pipe he wanted. He already knew how many steps he must take and how many to the wire.

The lights went out. There were shouts from the guard towers, running feet, and he was moving. There was dampness on his face, and for the first time he realized there was a fog.

Lightly he ran to the pile of building material, grasped the pipe, lifted it, and ran. Any time now the emergency lights would come on.

A guard tower loomed through the mist. There was a questioning shout. The end of the pipe touched the ground and his body lifted. He had often vaulted over sixteen feet, but that had been with a resilient pole, and when he was dressed lightly.

His body lifted, soared. High, higher . . . he released the pole as his body shot over and down.

For one brief, awful moment he was above the wire and fear flashed through him. If he fell into it . . . !

He landed on the balls of his feet, knees slightly bent. He fell forward, his fingers touched the ground, and then he was running. As his pole hit the ground there was a burst of fire, and then the lights flashed on. The edge of the forest was just feet away.

Wet branches slapped his face, tore at his clothing. He pivoted away, saw a dip in the ground, and ran down a small declivity as bullets tore the leaves above his head. In his track days he had done the mile in four minutes and fifteen seconds. Not good enough to put him up where the winners were, but how fast could he do a mile now over strange ground and through brush and trees?

When he had covered what he believed was a half mile he slowed to a fast walk. Distance was essential, but he must conserve his energy, also. He walked a hundred fast steps, then ran again.

A road, scarcely more than a dim trail. He looked, then crossed swiftly, and ran through a small water course. His lungs sucked at the fresh, tangy air. He could smell the pines.

It would take them five minutes to discover that he had escaped. They would find the pipe, but would they guess at once that he had pole vaulted over the wire? Say another five minutes to get a search organized and moving. In the night and fog they would be handicapped in following his trail and would trust to a hurried search and patrols on all existing roads.

Through a momentary rift in the fog he glimpsed the stars. He was not far off the route he intended to follow.

Off to his right he heard the roar of a stream. He felt his way to the bottom of a small gorge where he stepped into the water and walked upstream. Several times he paused to listen, but the rush of the water drowned all other sounds.

Coming up to a stone shelf, he left the water without leaving a trace. He stepped from that rocky ledge to another, leaving no tracks. He swung from one low-hanging limb to another, then came upon a path where he ran, following it for some fifty yards. He crossed another road, dipped into the forest, and ran through the trees. Behind him he heard the roar of a motor.

A car was passing along the road he had just crossed. He stood, not moving, until it had raced away.

Before and around him was the taiga, the Siberian forest. One of the guards had mentioned Malovsky, obviously a village or town, but one of which he knew nothing. He knew the prison was in an area of the Trans-Baikal, in Siberia, and he had read enough to know that the region was changing. An almost unbroken wilderness not too many years ago, the Russians had discovered that the area was a treasure house of mineral wealth. Consequently, new roads were being built and lumbering and mining were increasing; at any time, he might come upon such operations. He must move with caution.

The prison compound had been in a basin some six or seven miles across, and except for the area around the prison, it was thickly forested. His escape had been to the west, but he had swung around to the east and was now climbing into a rocky, mountainous area scattered with pine forest. He kept under cover, for it was growing light and searchers would be sweeping the country around with binoculars. Keeping to a slope, he found his way to a small stream that ran down from the mountains toward the east.

He saw no signs of life—no wood cutting, no mining. Walking on rocks, he left few tracks, although at this stage he doubted if they would be looking for them. At first there would simply be a wide, sweeping search, and not until they failed to find him would they begin looking for tracks or a trail.

He no longer ran, but walked as steadily as the terrain would permit. The stream turned north and he followed it. From a slight elevation he glimpsed a river into which this emptied. It offered the easiest way, but one that would grow increasingly dangerous, as rivers were likely to be used or lived along. He took the chance and followed the stream down. The river ran east and west, and when he reached it he found the flow was toward the east.

The banks were heavily forested, and at one point he discovered a large drift log with many branches clinging to it that had hung up in the sand on a small point. He squatted among the branches, got onto the log, and pushed off, crouching low and hoping not to be seen.

Several times he saw deer, and once he glimpsed a brown bear. The animal looked toward him incuriously; then seeming to catch his scent it lumbered off into the trees. It was a large bear, fully as big as some grizzlies he had seen.

The sun was high and the sky cloudless. With a broken branch still retaining some foliage, he tried steering the drift log, moving in toward the shore.

He judged the drift to have been about two miles an hour, and when he finally edged the tree to shore at least eight hours had passed. He beached the tree with several of its kind and staggered ashore, his legs stiff from holding virtually a single position. He was hungry, but he had been hungry before. Working his way back into the woods he made a bed in the moss and leaves and lay down to sleep.

Hours later he awakened, drank from a nearby stream, and sat down again to study his situation.

He did not know where he was except in a very general sense. He was east or northeast of Lake Baikal, possibly in an area known as Yakutia, which was now undergoing rapid development. Hence he might come upon people at any time. These he must avoid.

He must travel with extreme care not to be seen or to leave any vestige behind that might arouse the curiosity of dwellers in the country.

He would need food, warmer clothing, a weapon, and if he could find it, a blanket. Somewhere, somehow, he must learn his location. At present what he needed was distance. Travel on the river had been slow and very risky, but also it meant no trail was left behind. Following the river was an easy way, but one that would grow ever more perilous.

Food could wait. At times he had gone several days without eating, and he could do so again.

Among the fallen timber and broken limbs he found a staff that suited his purpose. It would help in walking and would be a weapon if he needed it. And he knew how to fight with a stick.

He started walking, moving away from the river. He had gone but a few hundred yards when he came upon a trail, evidently a game trail but perhaps used by hunters as well. He walked along at a steady pace, ears alert for any sound, eyes constantly seeking, searching.

Several times he paused to listen, but heard nothing but a soft wind blowing through the trees. Occasionally he saw birds. Grouse seemed common and a kind of lark that was unfamiliar to him.

Squatting near a piece of bare earth he tried to redraw from memory the map he had studied. South was the Amur and north the Lena. He was now east of Lake Baikal and moving toward the faraway coast, toward the Bering Strait and the Sea of

Okhotsk. Between the Bering Strait and his present position lay several low ranges of mountains, much forest, swamp, and tundra lying just below or within the Arctic Circle.

Moving as he must, with great care, and traveling on foot, there was no way he could escape Siberia before winter. Nor was there any way in which he could last out the winter.

He had not the clothing, the shelter, or the supply of food necessary.

At more than fifty below, rubber tires crack and metal becomes fragile. If a car survives two to three years the owner is fortunate.

And winter was coming, with temperatures that would hover between fifty and eighty degrees below zero.

He stood up and with his boot he rubbed out his crude map. He started on, and just over the mountains the cold awaited.

Icy, bitter, deathly cold. . . .

Two days later, and some fifty miles away, not far from where the Tsipa River flowed into the Kalar, Joe Mack was huddled in a thick grove of mixed Japanese stone pine and larch watching a shack built against a cliff. Two men lived there, and one of them had just started off with an empty backpack. He had taken a path to the south, and from the way he had waved good-bye he had expected to be gone for more than a few hours. He was probably going to town.

The other man watched him go; then, taking some tools, he went into the portal of a mine tunnel.

Joe Mack waited an instant longer, and then using a carefully plotted route he went down the slope, keeping under cover until within fifty feet of the house.

He waited, trying to breathe evenly. He must make the attempt, even at the risk of discovery. An instant he poised, then he was across the open space and into the house.

A quick glance around. Warm clothing on hooks. He reached under one coat and took a thick sweatshirt. Quickly to the shelves. Rows of canned goods. He selected a dozen cans, taking them from the front row and moving others into their place so their loss would not be detected. He made a sack out of the shirt and put the cans in it.

There was much here he could use, but he wasted no time. Another quick glance around.

A hunting knife! It was under a table, lying upon some chunks of firewood.

He caught it up, took a quick look, and was out of the door and across the open space. There he paused and glanced back. No one in sight. The earth was packed hard, and he believed he had left no tracks. Carrying his sack, he climbed higher. When he had reached a point from which he could watch, he squatted on his heels and opened the first can.

Fish, of a kind he did not know. He had not eaten in two days so he ate with care. A bit, a nibble, then a bite. He drank a little of the oil in the can. Then he waited, but his stomach did not react. After a while he ate a little more, then drank from a trickle of water running from a crack in the rock. Crawling under some fallen boughs, he slept.

In the first light of morning, he finished the fish, then began to study the river. From where he sat he could see that the river he had been following flowed into a larger stream that flowed off to the northeast.

Eager to be moving on, he walked away from the river, heading east. He left the willows and poplar of the river bottom and worked his way through a larch forest, mingled with some fir and pine of an unfamiliar kind. There were thickets of chokecherry, which he remembered from boyhood days, and groves of aspen.

He took his time, speed being no longer an essential. Now he must prevent discovery and think of survival. At noon, in a tight grove of fir, he ate his second can. It was also fish.

Here and there he found a few chokecherries, but the fruit was so thin around the pits that it offered little except the tart sweetness of the taste.

He moved carefully, for at any time he might come upon a hunter or a prospecting party. Hunters he hoped to avoid, but a party of prospectors might provide what he wanted most, a map.

He was a hunted man in the largest country on earth. Most of the area where he now moved was a wilderness. His travel would be on foot, hence slow. Winter was going to overtake him, and travel in winter, in his condition, was unthinkable.

His situation had been improved by his stealing the knife and the sweatshirt, but only a little. He needed a weapon that could kill game at a distance and was silent. Well, his people had solved that question long ago with the bow and arrow.

He had often made bows and was skilled in their use. Often he had lived in the wilds of the mountains of Montana or Idaho and on up into British Columbia with no other weapon. To make a good bow needed time, so he must find a secure place in which to hide out.

He would need meat. More than that, he would need fat, always the most difficult thing for a man to obtain in the wilds. So far he had thought only of putting distance between himself and his pursuers, but by now the chase would have widened and they would be everywhere. He must move on, more slowly, seeking out a place to hide and wait, a place where he could kill some of the game he had glimpsed or whose tracks he had seen.

He must take some skins. Above all he must get some furs. He would need warm clothing.

Yet he must face reality. Acquiring a supply of food to last a winter through was virtually impossible, starting at this late date.

He considered himself. From boyhood he had at every opportunity gone back to the woods. He had lived and survived under some of the bitterest conditions. He had killed or gathered his own food; he knew how to make clothing; he had often made moccasins, something not every Indian knew how to do anymore. Joe Mack banked his small fire and bedded down in a mound of leaves with fir boughs over him. It was cold and it was drafty, but Joe Mack had lived so before this.

Suddenly his eyes opened wide.

Alekhin! Alekhin had never failed to track down an escaped prisoner. Alekhin was a Yakut, a counterpart of the American Indian. He would know the wilderness and he would know how to think about it. He would know how Joe Mack would try to survive, and he would know what he needed.

It was Alekhin, not Zamatev, who was his first and worst enemy. Zamatev might direct. He might order. He might muster all the forces in Soviet Siberia to find one man, but it was Alekhin of whom he must beware, for Alekhin would think like an Indian. He would understand survival, and sooner or later somebody would see him and report his presence.

Alekhin was a master tracker, and Joe Mack knew that no man could long deceive such as Alekhin. The Yakut would find his trail and follow him. He might even surmise where he was going and be there waiting when Joe Mack arrived.

He, Joe Mack, had no friends in Siberia. Or none that he knew of. He supposed there were dissidents. In fact, he had heard of them. There were also many people in Siberia who longed for freer and less stringent ways, but that did not mean they would be disloyal to their government. Mother Russia they had called it under the Tsars and many still thought of it so.

They might not entirely approve of their government but it was *their* government, and they had but little good news about America.

If he was seen he would be reported, captured, or shot. Although there might be people sympathetic or friendly, he knew none of them nor where to find them. He must consider every man and every woman his enemy.

Most of all he must think of Alekhin.

Read LAST OF THE BREED, Louis L'Amour's newest novel, to be published as a Bantam Hardcover. On sale Wednesday, May 28, 1986, wherever hardcover books are sold.

ABOUT THE AUTHOR

Louis L'Amour is the world's fourth best-selling living novelist with more than 140 million copies of his books in print. He is the first novelist ever to be awarded a special National Gold Medal by Congress for his life's work. In addition to *The Lonesome Gods* and *The Walking Drum*, L'Amour's best-sellers include *Hondo*, *Comstock Lode*, *Bendigo Shafter*, *The Cherokee Trail*, *Son of a Wanted Man*, *Bowdrie's Law*, and *Frontier*, a book of essays about the North American continent, with photographs by David Muench.

Look for the SUMMER IN PARADISE SWEEPSTAKES entry coupon where these bestsellers are displayed:

On May 14

JUBAL SACKETT
by Louis L'Amour
THE TWO MRS. GRENVILLES
by Dominick Dunne
SHANGHAI
by Christopher New

On June 18

IACOCCA: AN AUTOBIOGRAPHY
by Lee Iacocca and William Novak
THE CIDER HOUSE RULES
by John Irving
BEACHES
by Iris Rainer Dart

Summer in Paradise

WIN

AN ALL EXPENSE PAID TWO WEEK VACATION FOR TWO TO PARADIS ISLAND IN BANTAM'S

Summer in Paradise

SWEEPSTAKES

PRIZES WORTH OVER $250,000

RESORTS INTERNATIONAL'S
Paradise Island Resort & Casino
BRITANNIA TOWERS · PARADISE TOWERS
PARADISE ISLAND, BAHAMAS

DELTA
AIR LINES

GRAND PRIZE A deluxe two-week vacation for two a Resorts International's Paradise Island Resort & Casino in the Bahamas—First Class round-trip airfare via Delta Air Lines included.

10 FIRST PRIZES Sony Watchman™ TV

100 SECOND PRIZES Sony Walkman® Personal Stereo

250 THIRD PRIZES Bantam SUMMER IN PARADISE Beach Umbrella

1000 FOURTH PRIZES Pre-selected assortment of Bantam books every month—for half a year!

No purchase necessary. For details and applicable restrictions, see the Official Entry Form and the Official Sweepstakes Rules, availabl at participating stores.

BANTAM